MURDER
ON THE RUN

MURDER
ON THE RUN

THE ADAMS ROUND TABLE

Lawrence Block
Mary Higgins Clark
Stanley Cohen
Dorothy Salisbury Davis
Mickey Friedman
Joyce Harrington
Judith Kelman
Warren Murphy
Justin Scott
Peter Straub
Whitley Strieber

BERKLEY PRIME CRIME, NEW YORK

MURDER ON THE RUN

A Berkley Prime Crime Book
Published by The Berkley Publishing Group
200 Madison Avenue, New York, NY 10016

The Putnam Berkley World Wide Web site address is http://www.berkley.com

Copyright © 1998 by The Adams Round Table

Book design by Erin Lush

First Edition: February 1998

Library of Congress Cataloging-in-Publication Data

Murder on the run / the Adams Round Table.
      p.   cm.
    Contents: Homeless, hungry, please help / Stanley Cohen — Eunice and Wally / Joyce Harrington — The scream / Dorothy Salisbury Davis — Morphing the millennium / Judith Kelman — Amazon run / Mickey Friedman — A shooting over in Jersey / Justin Scott — Keller's choice / Lawrence Block — Another day, another dollar / Warren Murphy — Isn't it romantic? / Peter Straub — Desperate Dan / Whitley Strieber — Lady sleuth, lady sleuth, run away home! / Mary Higgins Clark.
    ISBN 0-425-16146-3
    1. Detective and mystery stories, American.   I. Adams Round Table (Group)
PS648.D4M882   1998
813'.087208—dc21   97-23375
                                                          CIP

Printed in the United States of America

10 9 8 7 6 5 4 3 2 1

CONTENTS

I SUPPOSE YOU'RE WONDERING . . .

. . . WHY I SUMMONED you all here. I was wondering myself. There is, it seems, general agreement that a collection of stories requires something in the way of introductory remarks. If the book were to begin with a rude plunge into the first story, the reader might not know what to make of it. Then, just as he (or she) had gotten his (or her) feet planted, the first story would be over and he'd (or she'd) find himself (or herself) smackdab in the middle of a second, and wholly unrelated, story.

Personally, Gentle Reader, I think you could probably handle it. But I don't call the shots around here. I've been asked to write an introduction, so that's what I propose to do. If you're confident of your own ability to cope, please feel free to skip what I've written and Get On With It.

For those of you who are still with me, what can I say? I don't propose to tell you anything about the stories gathered herein. They're quite capable of speaking for themselves, and will, once I get out of the way. Nor do I feel much inclined to rattle on about the authors of these stories. As individual writers, they're very likely already familiar to you, and in any case they can speak for themselves via their work.

So perhaps I ought to talk about them not as individuals but as a group. Specifically, The Adams Round Table. And to do that perhaps I ought to say a few words about Writing.

See, it's supposed to be glamorous.

You want to know something? I don't think *anything* is glamorous to the person who does it, not after the first twenty minutes or so. Hanging out with movie stars certainly looks glamorous, and probably feels glamorous at first, but if you do it for a while some of them turn out to be friends, and what's so glamorous about sitting around with your friends? And others turn out to be people you don't like very much, and what could be less glamorous than that?

Writing could. Writing consists of long periods of hanging out exclusively in the company of people who exist only in the writer's own imagination, of which they are, well, figments. When the most meaningful hours of your day are spent with people who do not exist outside the confines of your own mind, you're apt to be a little strange. Add in the fact that the work itself, consisting as it does of making up lies and putting words on paper, is almost always difficult and occasionally impossible. It's exhausting and depleting, and yet, infuriatingly, it doesn't burn calories.

You call that glamorous?

The Adams Round Table came into being a dozen years ago, founded by Mary Higgins Clark and the late Thomas Chastain. We meet for dinner once a month, not to be glamorous but to be gregarious, to take turns airing the problems we face in our work and our professional lives, to encourage one another (sometimes with concrete suggestions, sometimes with booster shots of self-confidence), and, perhaps most important, to enjoy one another's company. (It is, now and then, useful and instructive to hang out with someone who is *not* a figment of one's own imagination.)

Why Adams? Why Round Table?

Well, we met at a restaurant owned by a guy named Adam. And he gave us a private room, and seated us at a round table.

Then glamour struck. Over the years, we published four collections of short stories. Perhaps each of us drew energy from the group; in any event, these collections have drawn some of our best efforts, and have been quite warmly received. The group found itself in the spotlight, and our then-host decided he had a good thing going.

So he redecorated his restaurant. He removed the partition, making our private room private no more, so that other diners, drawn mothlike to the flame of our collective glamour, could flock to his establishment and bask in our glow and, well, *stare* at us.

Yeah, right.

So we got the hell out of there. The proprietor of our new restaurant is not named Adam, and the table where he seats us once a month is oblong. So what? The food's good, the company's stimulating, and we're still the Adams Round Table.

And the table's set. And you, Dear Reader, are our honored guest. *Bon appétit!*

—Lawrence Block
FOR THE ADAMS ROUND TABLE

KELLER'S CHOICE

LAWRENCE BLOCK

KELLER, BEHIND THE wheel of a rented Plymouth, kept an eye on the fat man's house. It was very grand, with *columns* for heaven's sake, and a circular driveway, and one hell of a lot of lawn. Keller, who had done his share of lawn-mowing as a teenager, wondered what a kid would get for mowing a lawn like that.

Hard to say. The thing was, he had no frame of reference. He seemed to remember getting a couple of bucks way back when, but the lawns he'd mowed were tiny, postage stamps in comparison to the fat man's rolling green envelope. Taking into consideration the disparity in lawn size, and the inexorable shrinkage of the dollar over the years, what was a lawn like this worth? Twenty dollars? Fifty dollars? More?

The non-answer, he suspected, was that people who had lawns like this one didn't hire kids to push a mower around. Instead they had gardeners who showed up regularly with vehicles appropriate to the season, mowing in the summer, raking leaves in the fall, plowing snow in the winter. And charging so much a month, a tidy sum that actually didn't cost the fat man anything to speak of, because he very likely billed it to his company, or took it off his taxes. Or, if his accountant was enterprising, both.

Keller, who lived in a one-bedroom apartment in midtown Manhattan, had no lawn to mow. There was a tree in

I

front of his building, planted and diligently maintained by the Parks Department, and its leaves fell in the fall, but no one needed to rake them. The wind was pretty good about blowing them away. Snow, when it didn't melt of its own accord, was shoveled from the sidewalk by the building's superintendent, who kept the elevator running and replaced burnt-out bulbs in the hall fixtures and dealt with minor plumbing emergencies. Keller had a low-maintenance life, really. All he had to do was pay the rent on time and everything else got taken care of by other people.

He liked it that way. Even so, when his work took him away from home he found himself wondering. His fantasies, by and large, centered on simpler and more modest lifestyles. A cute little house in a subdivision, an undemanding job. A manageable life.

The fat man's house, in a swank suburban community north of Cincinnati, was neither cute nor little. Keller wasn't too clear on what the fat man did, beyond the fact that it involved his playing host to a lot of visitors and spending a good deal of time in his car. He couldn't say if the work was demanding, although he suspected it might be. Nor could he tell if the man's life was manageable. What he did know, though, was that someone wanted to manage him right out of it.

Which, of course, was where Keller came in, and why he was sitting in an Avis car across the street from the fat man's estate. And was it right to call it that? Where did you draw the line between a house and an estate? What was the yardstick: size or value? He thought about it, and decided it was probably some sort of combination of the two. A brownstone on East Sixty-Sixth Street was just a house, not an estate, even if it was worth five or ten times as much as the fat man's spread. On the other hand, a double-wide trailer could sit on fifteen or twenty acres of land without making the cut as an estate.

He was pondering the point when his wristwatch beeped, reminding him the security patrol was due in five minutes or

so. He turned the key in the engine, took a last wistful look
at the fat man's house (or estate) across the road, and pulled
away from the curb.

In his motel room, Keller put on the television set and
worked his way around the dial without leaving his chair.
Lately, he'd noticed, most of the decent motels had remote
controls for their TV sets. For a while there you'd get the remote bolted to the top of the bedside table, but that was only
handy if you happened to be sitting up in bed watching. Otherwise it was a pain in the neck. If you had to get up and
walk over to the bed to change the channel or mute the commercial, you might as well just walk over to the set.

It was to prevent theft, of course. A free-floating remote
could float right into a guest's suitcase, never to be seen
again. Table lamps were bolted down in the same fashion,
and television sets, too. But that was pretty much okay. You
didn't mind being unable to move the lamp around, or the
TV. The remote was something else again. You might as
well bolt down the towels.

He turned off the set. It might be easy to change channels
now, but it was harder than ever to find anything he wanted to
see. He picked up a magazine, thumbed through it. This was
his fourth night at this particular motel, and he still hadn't figured out a good way to kill the fat man. There had to be a
way, there was always a way, but he hadn't found it yet.

Suppose he had a house like the fat man's. Generally he
fantasized about houses he could afford to buy, lives he
could imagine himself living. He had enough money salted
away so that he could buy an unassuming house somewhere
and pay cash for it, but he couldn't even scrape up the down
payment for a spread like the fat man's. (Could you call it
that—a spread? And what exactly *was* a spread? How did it
compare to an estate? Was the distinction geographical, with
estates in the Northeast and spreads in the South and West?)

Still, say he had the money, not just to swing the deal but
to cover the upkeep as well. Say he won the lottery, say he

could afford the gardener and a live-in maid and whatever else you had to have. Would he enjoy it, walking from room to room, admiring the paintings on the walls, luxuriating in the depth of the carpets? Would he like strolling in the garden, listening to the birds, smelling the flowers?

Nelson might like it, he thought. Romping on a lawn like that.

He sat there for a moment, shaking his head. Then he switched chairs and reached for the phone.

He called his own number in New York, got his machine. "You. Have. Six. Messages," it told him, and played them for him. The first five turned out to be wordless hangups. The sixth was a voice he knew.

"Hey there, E.T. Call home."

He made the call from a pay phone a quarter mile down the highway. Dot answered, and her voice brightened when she recognized his.

"There you are," she said. "I called and called."

"There was only the one message."

"I didn't want to leave one. I figured I'd tell what's-her-name."

"Andria."

"Right, and she'd pass the word to you when you called in. But she never picked up. She must be walking that dog of yours to the Bronx and back."

"I guess."

"So I left a message, and here we are, chatting away like old friends. I don't suppose you did what you went there to do."

"It's not as quick and easy as it might be," he said. "It's taking time."

"Other words, our friend's still got a pulse."

"Or else he's learned to walk around without one."

"Well," she said, "I'm glad to hear it. You know what I think you should do, Keller? I think you should check out of that motel and get on a plane."

"And come home?"

"Got it in one, Keller, but then you were always quick."

"The client canceled?"

"Not exactly."

"Then—"

"Fly home," she said, "and then catch a train to White Plains, and I'll pour you a nice glass of iced tea. And I'll explain all."

It wasn't iced tea, it was lemonade. He sat in a wicker chair on a wraparound porch of the big house on Taunton Place, sipping a big glass of it. Dot, wearing a blue and white housedress and a pair of white flip-flops, perched on the wooden railing.

"I just got those the day before yesterday," she said, pointing. "Wind chimes. I was watching QVC and they caught me in a weak moment."

"It could have been a Pocket Fisherman."

"It might as well be," she said, "for all the breeze we've been getting. But how do you like this for coincidence, Keller? There you are, off doing a job in Cincinnati, and we get a call, another client with a job just down your street."

"Down my street?"

"Or up your alley. I think it's a Briticism, 'down your street,' but we're in America, so the hell with it. It's up your alley."

"If you say so."

"And you'll never guess where this second caller lives."

"Cincinnati," he said.

"Give the man a cigar."

He frowned. "So there's two jobs in the same metropolitan area," he said. "That would be a reason to do them both in one trip, assuming it was possible. Save airfare, I suppose, if that matters. Save finding a room and settling in. Instead I'm back here with neither job done, which doesn't make sense. So there's more to it."

"Give the man a cigar and light it for him."

"Puff puff," Keller said. "The jobs are connected some-how, and I'd better know all about it in front or I might step on my own whatsit."

"And we wouldn't want anything to happen to your what-sit."

"Right. What's the connection? Same client for both jobs?"

She shook her head.

"Different clients. Same *target?* Did the fat man manage to piss off two different people to the point where they both called us within days of each other?"

"Be something, wouldn't it?"

"Well, pissing people off is like anything else," he said. "Certain people have a knack for it. But that's not it."

"No."

"Different targets."

"I'm afraid so."

"Different targets, different clients. Same time, same place, but everything else is different. So? Help me out on this, Dot. I'm not getting anywhere."

"Keller," she said, "you're doing fine."

"Four people, all of them different. The fat man and the guy who hired us to hit him, and target number two and client number two, and . . ."

"Is day beginning to break? Is light beginning to dawn?"

"The fat man wants to hire us," he said. "To kill our orig-inal client."

"Give the man an exploding cigar."

"A hires us to kill B, and B hires us to kill A."

"That's a little algebraic for me, but it makes the point."

"The contracts couldn't have come direct," he said. "They were brokered, right? Because the fat man's not a wise guy. He could be a little mobbed up, the way some businessmen are, but he wouldn't know to call here."

"He came through somebody," Dot agreed.

"And so did the other guy. Different brokers, of course."

"Of course."

"And they both called here." He raised his eyes significantly to the ceiling. "And what did he do, Dot? Say yes to both of them?"

"That's what he did."

"Why, for God's sake? We've already got a client, we can't take an assignment to kill him, especially from somebody we've already agreed to take out."

"The ethics of the situation bother you, Keller?"

"This is good," he said, brandishing the lemonade. "This from a mix or what?"

"Homemade. Real lemons, real sugar."

"Makes a difference," he said. "Ethics? What do I know about ethics? It's just no way to do business, that's all. What's the broker going to think?"

"Which broker?"

"The one whose client gets killed. What's he going to say?"

"What would you have done, Keller? If you were him, and you got the second call days after the first one."

He thought about it. "I'd say I haven't got anybody available at the moment, but I should have a good man in about two weeks, when he gets back from Aruba."

"Aruba?"

"Wherever. Then, after the fat man's toast and I've been back a week, say, you call back and ask if the contract's still open. And he says something like, 'No, the client changed his mind.' Even if he guesses who popped his guy, it's all straight and clean and business-like. Or don't you agree?"

"No," she said. "I agree completely."

"But that's not what he did," he said, "and I'm surprised. What was his thinking? He afraid of arousing suspicions, something like that?"

She just looked at him. He met her gaze, and read something in her face, and he got it.

"Oh, no," he said.

•   •   •

"I thought he was getting better," she said. "I'm not saying there wasn't a little denial operating, Keller. A little wishing-will-make-it-so."

"Understandable."

"He had that time when he gave you the wrong room number, but that worked out all right in the end."

"For us," Keller said. "Not for the guy who was in the room."

"There's that," she allowed. "Then he went into that funk and kept turning down everybody who called. I was think-ing maybe a doctor could get him on Prozac."

"I don't know about Prozac. In this line of work . . ."

"Yeah, I was wondering about that. Depressed is no good, but is mellow any better? It could be counterproductive."

"It could be disastrous."

"That too," she said. "And you can't get him to go to a doctor anyway, so what difference does it make? He's in a funk, maybe it's like the weather. A low-pressure front moves in, and it's all you can do to sit on the porch with an iced tea. Then it blows over, and we get some of that good Canadian air, and it's like old times again."

"Old times."

"And yesterday he was on the phone, and then he buzzed me and I took him a cup of coffee. 'Call Keller,' he told me. 'I've got some work for him in Cincinnati.' "

"Déjà vu."

"You said it, Keller. Déjà vu like never before."

Her explanation was elaborate—what the old man said, what she thought he meant, what he really meant, di dah di dah di dah. What it boiled down to was that the original client, one Barry Moncrieff, had been elated that his prob-lems with the fat man were soon to be over, and he'd con-fided as much to at least one person who couldn't keep a secret. Word reached the fat man, whose name was Arthur Strang.

While Moncrieff may have forgotten that loose lips sink ships, Strang evidently remembered that the best defense is a good offense. He made a couple of phone calls, and eventually the phone rang in the house on Taunton Place, and the old man took the call and took the contract.

When Dot pointed out the complications—namely, that their new client was already slated for execution, with the fee paid by the man who had just become their new target—it became evident that the old man had forgotten the original deal entirely.

"He didn't know you were in Cincinnati," she explained. "Didn't have a clue he'd sent you there or anywhere else. For all he knew you were out walking the dog, assuming he remembered you had a dog."

"But when you told him . . ."

"He didn't see the problem. I kept explaining it to him, until it hit me what I was doing. I was trying to blow out a light bulb."

"Puff puff," Keller said.

"You said it. He just wasn't going to get it. 'Keller's a good boy,' he said. 'You leave it to Keller. Keller will know what to do.' "

"He said that, huh?"

"His very words. You look the least bit lost, Keller. Don't tell me he was wrong."

He thought for a moment. "The fat man knows there's a contract out on him," he said. "Well, that figures. It would explain why he was so hard to get close to."

"If you'd managed," Dot pointed out, "I'd shrug and say what's done is done, and let it go at that. But, fortunately or unfortunately, you checked your machine in time."

"Fortunately or unfortunately."

"Right, and don't ask me which is which. Easiest thing, you say the word and I call both of the middlemen and tell them we're out. Our foremost operative broke his leg in a skiing accident and you'd better call somebody else. What's the matter?"

"Skiing? This time of year?"

"In Chile, Keller. Use your imagination. Anyway, we're out of it."

"Maybe that's best."

"Not from a dollars-and-cents standpoint. No money for you, and refunds for both clients, who'll either look elsewhere or be reduced to shooting each other. I hate to give money back once it's been paid."

"What did they do, pay half in front?"

"Uh-huh. Usual system."

He frowned, trying to work it out. "Go home," she said. "Pet Andria and give Nelson a kiss, or is it the other way around? Sleep on it and let me know what you decide."

He took the train to Grand Central and walked home, rode up in the elevator, used his key in the lock. The apartment was dark and quiet, just as he'd left it. Nelson's dish was in a corner of the kitchen. Keller looked at it and felt like a gold star mother keeping her son's room exactly as he had left it. He knew he ought to put the dish away or chuck it out altogether, but he didn't have the heart.

He unpacked and showered, then went around the corner for a beer and a burger. He took a walk afterward, but it wasn't much fun. He went back to the apartment and called the airlines. Then he packed again and caught a cab to JFK.

He phoned White Plains while he waited for the boarding call for his flight. "On my way," he told Dot.

"You continue to surprise me, Keller," she said. "I thought for sure you'd stay the night."

"No reason to."

There was a pause. Then she said, "Keller? Is something wrong?"

"Andria left," he said, surprising himself. He hadn't intended to say anything. Eventually, sure, but not just yet.

"That's too bad," Dot said. "I thought the two of you were happy."

"So did I."

"Oh."

"She has to find herself," Keller said.

"You know, I've heard people say that, and I never know what the hell they're talking about. How would you lose yourself in the first place? And how would you know where to look for yourself?"

"I wondered that myself."

"Of course she's awfully young, Keller."

"Right."

"Too young for you, some would say."

"Some would."

"Still, you probably miss her. Not to mention Nelson."

"I miss them both," he said.

"I mean you both must miss her," Dot said. "Wait a minute. What did you just say?"

"They just called my flight," he said, and broke the connection.

Cincinnati's airport was across the river in Kentucky. Keller had turned in his Avis car that morning, and thought it might seem strange if he went back to the same counter for another one. He went to Budget instead, and got a Honda.

"It's a Japanese car," the clerk told him, "but it's actually produced right here in the U.S. of A."

"That's a load off my mind," Keller told him.

He checked into a motel half a mile from the previous one and called in from a restaurant pay phone. He had a batch of questions, things he needed to know about Barry Moncrieff, the fellow who was at once Client #1 and Assignment #2. Dot, instead of answering, asked him a question of her own.

"What do you mean, you miss them both? Where's the dog?"

"I don't know."

"She ran off with your dog? Is that what you're saying?"

"They went off together," he said. "Nobody was running."

"Fine, she walked off with your dog. I guess she figured

she needed him to help her go look for herself. What did she do, skip town while you were in Cincinnati?"

"Earlier," he said. "And she didn't skip town. We talked about it, and she said she thought it would be best if she took Nelson with her."

"And you agreed?"

"More or less."

" 'More or less?' What does that mean?"

"I've often wondered myself. She said I don't really have time for him, and I travel a lot, and . . . I don't know."

"But he was your dog long before you even met her. You hired her to walk him when you were out of town."

"Right."

"And one thing led to another, and she wound up living there. And the next thing you know she's telling you it's best if the dog goes with her."

"Right."

"And away they go."

"Right."

"And you don't know where, and you don't know if they'll be back."

"Right."

"When did this happen, Keller?"

"About a month ago. Maybe a little longer, maybe six weeks."

"You never said anything."

"No."

"I went on about how you should pet him and kiss her, whatever I said, and you didn't say anything."

"I would have gotten around to it sooner or later."

They were both silent for a long moment. Then she asked him what he was going to do.

"About what?" he asked.

"About what? About your dog and your girlfriend."

"I thought that's what you meant," he said, "but you could have been talking about Moncrieff and Strang. But it's the same answer all around. I don't know what I'm going to do."

•   •   •

What it came down to was this. He had a choice to make. It was his decision as to which contract he would fulfill and which he would cancel.

And how did you decide something like that? Two people wanted his services, and only one could have them. If he were a painting, the answer would be obvious. You'd have an auction, and whoever was willing to make the highest bid would have something pretty to hang over the couch. But you couldn't have bids in the present instance because the price had already been fixed, and both parties independently had agreed to it. Each had paid half in advance, and when the job was done one of them would pay the additional 50 percent. The other would technically be entitled to a refund, but in no position to claim it.

So in that sense the contract was potentially more lucrative than usual, paying one and a half times the standard rate. It came out the same no matter how you did it. Kill Moncrieff, and Strang would pay the rest of the money. Kill Strang, and Moncrieff would pay it.

Which would it be?

Moncrieff, he thought, had called first. The old man had made a deal with him, and a guarantee of exclusivity was implicit in such an arrangement. When you hired somebody to kill someone, you didn't require assurance that he wouldn't hire on to kill you as well. That went without saying.

So their initial commitment was to Moncrieff, and any arrangements made with Strang ought to be null and void. Money from Strang wasn't really a retainer, it came more under the heading of windfall profits, and needn't weigh in the balance. You could even argue that taking Strang's advance payment was a perfectly legitimate tactical move, designed to lull the quarry into a feeling of false security, thus making him easier to get to.

On the other hand . . .

If Moncrieff had just kept his damned mouth shut, Strang wouldn't have been forewarned, and consequently forearmed. It was Moncrieff, running his mouth about his plans to do the fat man in, that had induced Strang to call somebody, who called somebody else, who wound up talking to the old man in White Plains.

And it was Moncrieff's blabbing that had made Strang such an elusive target. Otherwise it would have been easy to get to the fat man, and by now Keller would have long since completed the assignment. Instead of sitting all by himself in a motel on the outskirts of Cincinnati, he could be sitting all by himself in an apartment on First Avenue.

Moncrieff, loose of lip, had sunk his own ship. Moncrieff, unable to keep a secret, had sabotaged the very contract he had been so quick to arrange. Couldn't you argue that his actions, with their unfortunate results, had served to nullify the contract? In which case the old man was more than justified in retaining his deposit while accepting a counterproposal from another interested party.

Which meant that the thing to do was regard the fat man as the bona fide client and Moncrieff (fat or lean, tall or short, Keller didn't know which) as the proper quarry.

On the other hand . . .

Moncrieff had a penthouse apartment atop a high-rise not far from Riverfront Stadium. The Reds were in town for a home stand, and Keller bought a ticket and an inexpensive pair of field glasses and went to watch them. His seat was in the right-field stands just outside the foul line, remote enough that he wasn't the only one with binoculars. Near him sat a father and son, both of whom had brought gloves in the hope of catching a ball. Neither pitcher had his stuff, and both teams hit a lot of long balls, but the kid and his father only got excited when somebody hit a long foul to right.

Keller wondered about that. If what they wanted was a baseball, wouldn't they be better off buying one at a sporting goods store? If they wanted the thrill of the chase, well, they could get the clerk to throw it up in the air, and the kid could catch it when it came down.

During breaks in action, Keller trained the binoculars on a window of what he was pretty sure was Moncrieff's apartment. He found himself wondering whether Moncrieff was a baseball fan, and if he took advantage of his location and watched the ballgames from his window. You'd need a lot more magnification than Keller was carrying, but if Moncrieff could afford the penthouse he could swing a powerful telescope as well. If you got the kind of gizmo that let you count the rings of Saturn, you ought to be able to tell how well the pitcher's curveball was breaking.

Made about as much sense as taking a glove to the game, he decided. If a man like Moncrieff wanted to watch a game, he could afford a box seat behind the Reds' dugout. Of course these days he might prefer to stay home and watch the game on television rather than through a telescope, because he might figure it was safer.

And, as far as Keller could tell, Barry Moncrieff wasn't taking a lot of risks. If he hadn't guessed that the fat man might retaliate and put out a contract of his own, then he looked to be a naturally cautious man. He lived in a secure building, and he rarely left it. When he did, he never seemed to go anywhere alone.

Keller, unable to pick a target on the basis of an ethical distinction, had opted for pragmatism. His line of work, after all, was different from crapshooting. You didn't get a bonus for making your point the hard way. So if you had to take out one of two men, why not pick the man who was easier to kill?

By the time he left the ballpark, with the Reds losing to the Phillies in extra innings after having left the bases loaded in the bottom of the ninth, he'd spent three full days on the question. What he'd managed to determine was that *neither* man was *easy* to kill. They both lived in fortresses, one high up in the air, the other way out in the sticks. Neither one would be impossible to hit—nobody was impossible to hit—but neither would be easy.

He'd managed to get a look at Moncrieff, managed to be

in the lobby showing a misaddressed package to a concierge as puzzled as Keller was pretending to be, when Moncrieff entered, flanked by two young men with big shoulders and bulges under their jackets. Moncrieff was fiftyish and balding, with a downturned mouth and jowls like a basset hound.

He was fat, too. Keller might have thought of *him* as the fat man if he hadn't already assigned that label to Arthur Strang. Moncrieff wasn't fat the way Strang was fat—few people were—but that still left him a long ways from being a borderline anorexic. Keller guessed he was seventy-five to a hundred pounds lighter than Strang. Strang waddled, while Moncrieff strutted like a pigeon.

Back in his motel, Keller found himself watching a newscast and looking at highlights from the game he'd just watched. He turned off the set, picked up the binoculars, and wondered why he'd bothered to buy them and what he was going to do with them now. He caught himself thinking that Andria might enjoy using them to watch birds in Central Park. He told himself to stop that, and he went and took a shower.

Neither one would be the least bit easy to kill, he thought, but he could already see a couple of approaches to either man. The degree of difficulty, as an Olympic diver would say, was about the same. So, as far as he could tell, was the degree of risk.

A thought struck him. Maybe one of them *deserved* it.

"Arthur Strang," the woman said. "You know, he was fat when I met him. I think he was born fat. But he was nothing like he is now. He was just, you know, heavy."

Her name was Marie, and she was a tall woman with unconvincing red hair. Early thirties, Keller figured. Big lips, big eyes. Nice shape to her, too, but Keller's opinion, since she brought it up, was she could stand to lose five pounds. Not that he was going to mention it.

"When I met him he was heavy," she said, "but he wore

these well-tailored Italian suits, and he looked okay, you know? Of course, naked, forget it."

"It's forgotten."

"Huh?" She looked confused, but a sip of her drink put her at ease. "Before we were married," she said, "he actually lost weight, believe it or not. Then we jumped over the broomstick together and he started eating with both hands. That's just an expression."

"He only ate with one hand?"

"No, silly! 'Jumped over the broomstick.' We had a regular wedding in a church. Anyway, I don't think Arthur would have been too good at jumping over anything, not even if you laid the broomstick flat on the floor. I was married to him for three years, and I'll bet he put on twenty or thirty pounds a year. Then we broke up three years ago, and have you seen him lately? He's as big as a house."

As big as a double-wide, maybe, Keller thought. But nowhere near as big as an estate.

"You know, Kevin," she said, laying a hand on Keller's arm, "it's awful smoky in here. They passed a law against it but people smoke anyway, and what are you going to do, arrest them?"

"Maybe we should get some air," he suggested, and she beamed at the notion.

Back at her place, she said, "He had preferences, Kevin."

Keller nodded encouragingly, wondering if he'd ever been called Kevin before. He sort of liked the way she said it.

"As a matter of fact," she said darkly, "he was sexually aberrant."

"Really."

"He wanted me to do things," she said, rubbing his leg. "You wouldn't believe the things he wanted."

"Oh?"

She told him. "I thought it was disgusting," she said, "but he insisted, and it was part of what broke us up. But do you want to know something weird?"

"Sure."

"After the divorce," she said, "I sort of became more broad-minded on the subject. You might find this hard to believe, Kevin, but I'm pretty kinky."

"No kidding."

"In fact, what I just told you about Arthur? The really disgusting thing? Well, I have to admit it no longer disgusts me. In fact . . ."

"Yes?"

"Oh, Kevin," she said.

She was kinky, all right, and spirited, and afterward he decided he'd been wrong about the five pounds. She was fine just the way she was.

"I was wondering," he said on his way out the door. "Your ex-husband? How did he feel about dogs?"

"Oh, Kevin," she said. "And here I thought *I* was the kinky one. You're too much. Dogs?"

"I didn't mean it that way."

"I'll bet you didn't. Kevin, honey, if you don't get out of here this minute I may not let you go at all. Dogs!"

"Just as pets," he said. "Does he, you know, *like* dogs? Or hate them?"

"As far as I know," Marie said, "Arthur Strang has no opinion one way or the other about dogs. The subject never came up."

Laurel Moncrieff, the second of three women with whom Barry had jumped over the broomstick, had nothing to report on the ups and downs of her ex-husband's weight, or what he did or didn't like to do when the shades were drawn. She'd worked as Moncrieff's secretary, won him away from his first wife, and made sure he had a male secretary afterward.

"Then the son of a bitch joined a gym," she said, "and he wound up leaving me for his personal trainer. He wadded me up and threw me away like a used Kleenex."

She didn't look like the sort of person you'd blow your

nose on. She was a slender, dark-haired woman, and she had been no harder to get acquainted with than Marie Strang and about as easy to wind up in the hay with. She hadn't disclosed any interesting aberrations, her own or her ex-husband's, but Keller found himself with no cause to complain.

"Ah, Kevin," she said.

Maybe it was the name, he thought. Maybe he should use it more often, maybe it brought him luck.

"Living alone the way you do," he said. "You ever think about getting a dog?"

"I'm away too much," she said. "It'd be no good for me and no good for the dog."

"That's true for a lot of people," he said, "but they're used to having one around the house and they don't want to give it up."

"Whatever works," she said. "I never got used to it, and you know what they say. You don't miss what you never had."

"I guess your ex didn't have a dog."

"Not until I left and he married the bitch with the magic fingers."

"She had a dog?"

"She *was* a dog, honey. She had a face like a Rottweiler. But she's out of the picture now, and she hasn't been replaced. Serves her right, if you ask me."

"So you don't know how Barry Moncrieff felt about dogs."

"Of the canine variety, you mean? I don't think he cared much one way or the other. Hey, how'd we get on this silly subject, anyhow? Why don't you lie down and kiss me, Kevin, honey?"

They both gave money to local charities. Strang tended to support the arts, while Moncrieff donated to fight diseases and feed the homeless. They both had a reputation for ruthlessness in business. Both were childless and presently unmarried. Neither one had a dog, or had ever had a dog, as far as he could determine. Neither had any strong pro-dog or anti-dog feelings. It would have been helpful to discover that Strang was a heavy contributor to the ASPCA and the Anti-Vivisection League, or that Moncrieff liked to go to a basement in Kentucky and watch a couple of pit bulls fight to the death, betting substantial sums on the outcome.

But he came across nothing of the sort, and the more he thought about it the less legitimate a criterion it seemed to him. Why should a matter of life and death hinge upon how a man felt about dogs? And who was Keller to care anyway? It was not as if he were a dog owner himself. Not anymore.

"Neither one's Albert Schweitzer," he told Dot, "and neither one's Hitler. They both fall somewhere in between, so making a decision on moral grounds is impossible. I'll tell you, this is murder."

"It's not," she said. "That's the whole trouble, Keller. You're in Cincinnati and the clock's running."

"I know."

"Moral decisions. This is the wrong business for moral decisions."

"You're right," he said. "And who am I to be making that kind of decision, anyway?"

"Spare me the humility," she said. "Listen, I'm as crazy as you are. I had this idea, call both brokers, have them get in touch with their clients. Explain that due to the exigencies of this particular situation, di dah di dah di dah, we need full payment in advance."

"You think they'd go for it?"

"If one of them went for it," she said, "that'd make the decision, wouldn't it? Knock him off and the other guy's left alive to pay in full, a satisfied customer."

"That's brilliant," he said, and thought a moment. "Except . . ."

"Ah, you spotted it, didn't you? The guy who cooperates, the guy who goes the extra mile to be a really good client, he's the one who gets rewarded by getting killed. I like

ironic as much as the next person, Keller, but I decided
that's a little too much for me."

"Besides," he said, "with our luck they'd both pay."

"And we'd be back where we started. Keller?"

"What?"

"All said and done, there's only one answer. You got a
quarter?"

"Probably. Why?"

"Toss it," she said. "Heads or tails."

Heads.

Keller picked up the quarter he'd tossed, dropped it into
the slot. He dialed a number, and while it rang he wondered
at the wisdom of making such a decision on the basis of a
coin toss. It seemed awfully arbitrary to him, but then again
maybe it was the way of the world. Maybe somewhere up
above the clouds there was an old man with a beard making
life-and-death decisions in the very same way, tossing coins,
shrugging, and passing out train wrecks and heart attacks.

"Let me talk to Mr. Strang," he told the person who answered. "Just tell him it's in reference to a recent contract."

There was a long pause, and Keller dug out another quarter in case the phone needed feeding. Then Strang came on
the line. It seemed to Keller that he recognized the voice
even though he had never heard it before. The voice was
resonant, like an opera singer's, though hardly musical.

"I don't know who you are," Strang said without preamble, "and I don't discuss business over the phone with people I don't know."

Fat, Keller thought. The man sounded fat.

"Very wise," Keller told him. "Well, we've got business
to discuss, and I agree it shouldn't be over the phone. We
ought to meet, but nobody should see us together, or even
know we're having the meeting." He listened for a moment.
"You're the client," he said. "I was hoping you could suggest a time and a place." He listened some more. "Good," he
said. "I'll be there."

"But it seems irregular," Strang said, with a whine in his voice that you would never have heard from Pavarotti. "I don't see the need for this, I really don't."

"You will," Keller told him. "I can promise you that."

He broke the connection, then opened his hand and looked at the quarter he was holding. He thought for a moment—about the old man in White Plains, and then about the old man up in the sky. The one with the long white beard, the one who tossed coins of his own and ran the universe accordingly. He thought about the turns in his own life, and the way people could walk in and out of it.

He weighed the coin in his palm—it didn't weigh very much—and he gave it a toss, caught it, slapped it down on the back of his hand.

Tails.

He reached for the phone.

"This time it's iced tea," Dot said. "Last time I promised you iced tea and gave you lemonade."

"It was good lemonade."

"Well, this is good iced tea, as far as that goes. Made with real tea."

"And real ice, I'll bet."

"You put the tea bags in a jar of cold water," she said, "and set the jar in the sun, and forget about them for a few hours. Then you put the jar in the fridge."

"You don't boil the water at all?"

"No, you don't have to. For years I thought you did, but it turns out I was wrong. But I lost track of what I was getting at. Iced tea. Oh, right. This time you called and said, 'I'm on my way. Get ready to break out the lemonade.' So you were expecting lemonade this time, and here I'm giving you iced tea. Get it, Keller? Each time, you get the opposite of what you expect."

"As long as it's just a question of iced tea or lemonade," he said, "I think I can ride with it."

"Well, you've always adjusted quickly to new realities,"

she said. "It's one of your strengths." She cocked her head and looked up at the ceiling. "Speaking of which. You were upstairs, you talked to him. What do you think?"

"He seemed all right."

"His old self?"

"Hardly that. But he listened to what I had to say and told me I'd done well. I think he was covering. I think he was clueless as to where I'd been, and he was covering."

"He does that a lot lately."

"It's got a real tea flavor, you know? And you don't boil the water at all?"

"Not unless you're in a hurry. Keller?"

He looked up from his glass of tea. She was sitting on the porch railing, her legs crossed, one flip-flop dangling from her toe.

She said, "Why both of them? If you do one, we get the final payment from the other one. This way there's nobody left to sign a check."

"He takes checks?"

"Just a manner of speaking. Point is, there's nobody left to pay up. It's not just a case of doing the second one for nothing. It cost you money to do it."

"I know."

"So explain it to me, will you?"

He took his time thinking about it. At length he said, "I didn't like the process."

"The process?"

"Making a choice. There was no way to choose, and tossing a coin didn't really help. I was still choosing, because I was choosing to accept the coin's choice, if you can follow me."

"The trail is faint," she said, "but I'm on it like a bloodhound."

"I figured they should both get the same," he said. "So I tossed twice, and got heads the first time and tails the second time, and I made appointments with both of them."

"Appointments."

"They were both good at setting up secret meetings. Strang told me how to get onto his property from the rear. There was an electric fence, but there was a place you could get over it."

"So he gave the fox the keys to the henhouse."

"There wasn't any henhouse, but there was a toolshed."

"And two men went into it that fateful morning and only one came out," Dot said. "And then you ran off to meet Moncrieff?"

"At the Omni, downtown. He was having lunch at the restaurant, which according to him is pretty good. There's no men's room for the restaurant, you use the one off the hotel lobby. So we could meet there without ever having been in the same public space together."

"Clever."

"They were clever men, both of them. Anyway, it worked fine, same as with Strang. I used . . . well, you don't like to hear about that part of it."

"Not particularly, no."

He was silent for a time, sipping his iced tea, listening to the wind chimes when a breeze blew up. They had been still for a while when he said, "I was angry, Dot."

"I wondered about that."

"You know, I'm better off without that dog."

"Nelson."

"He was a good dog, and I liked him a lot, but they're a pain in the ass. Feed them, walk them."

"Sure."

"I liked her, too, but I'm a man who lived alone all my life. Living alone is what I'm good at."

"It's what you're used to."

"That's right. But even so, Dot. I'll walk along the street looking in windows and my eyes'll hit on a pair of earrings, and I'll be halfway in the door to buy them for her before I remember there's no point."

"All the earrings you bought for that girl."

"She liked getting them," he said, "and I liked buying

them, so it worked out." He took a breath. "Anyway, I started getting angry, and I kept getting angry."

"At her."

"No, she did the right thing. I've got no reason to be angry at her." He pointed upward. "I got angry at him."

"For sending you to Cincinnati in the first place."

He shook his head. "Not him upstairs. A higher authority, the old man in the sky who flips all the coins."

"Oh, *Him.*"

"Of course," he said, "by the time I did it, I wasn't angry. I was the way I always am. I just do what I'm there to do."

"You're a professional."

"I guess so."

"And you give value."

"Do I ever."

"Special summer rates," she said. "Murder on twofers."

Keller listened to the wind chimes, then to the silence. Eventually he would have to go back to his apartment and figure out what to do with the dog's dish. Eventually he and Dot would have to figure out what to do about the old man. For now, though, he just wanted to stay right where he was, sipping his glass of tea.

LADY SLEUTH, LADY SLEUTH, RUN AWAY HOME!

MARY HIGGINS CLARK

"ALVIRAH, I NEED your help."

"I'll give it if I can, Mike," Alvirah said cautiously. She was sitting on the terrace of her Central Park South apartment with Captain Michael Fitzpatrick, police chief of the 7th Precinct in Queens. She'd known Mike for thirty years, ever since he'd been a ten-year-old shouting, "Halt! Who goes there?" whenever she ran into him in the lobby of the Jackson Heights apartment building where they'd both lived. "Born to be a cop," she'd always said about Mike, and events had proven her right. She was sure he'd be police commissioner one day.

A fine-looking man, thought Alvirah approvingly. A bit pudgy as a teenager, but he'd turned out grand. Some of us never lose the pudginess, she thought with a sigh, then quickly reminded herself that Willy liked her just as she was.

It was a splendid afternoon in late September. Alvirah knew that in a few minutes, as the sun's rays slanted a bit more, it would get too cool for the terrace, but when Mike arrived at the apartment and saw the view, he'd asked if they couldn't please sit out here.

Now Mike seemed engrossed gazing over the park. He was sitting straight up on the comfortable patio chair as though afraid to slip into his familiar stance as extended

27

family member to Willy and Alvirah. His uniform jacket and trousers were smartly creased; his thin, intelligent face dominated by wise brown eyes was troubled.

Alvirah knew that today Mike was here in his role as a police captain. She also knew that she wasn't sure if she could help him. Playing "I spy" was simply not her thing to do.

Mike turned. "This view is mesmerizing," he said. "The night of my college prom, I took Fran on a carriage ride through the park and proposed. Remember how I met her the day her grandmother moved into our building?"

Alvirah nodded. "Twenty-two-fifty Eighty-first Street, Jackson Heights. I'm glad we didn't give up our apartment there, Mike. The way we figure it, we can always go back and live in it if New York State quits paying the lottery winnings and the banks fail." She shook her head in wonderment. It still seemed a dream. Until a few years ago, she'd been a cleaning woman and Willy a plumber. Then one night, as she was soaking her feet after a hard day of cleaning Mrs. O'Keefe's house, the winning ticket Willy was holding bore the number for the forty-million-dollar lottery.

"You've stayed in close touch with the old neighbors. I saw you at Trinky Callahan's funeral last month."

"It's very sad when a young person dies," Alvirah said. Now she was sure of Mike's mission.

"It's also sad if her murderer gets away with it," he said severely.

Alvirah raised her eyebrows. "Trinky fell down those old marble stairs. You know how slippery they are."

"Come on, Alvirah," Mike said. "You don't really believe that. A couple of new tenants had heard Sean shouting at Trinky that if she went barhopping one more night he'd kill her. Fifteen minutes later she was dead."

"Mike, you know many people say that sort of thing in an argument," Alvirah said dismissively.

"No," Mike said. "I don't. We can't prove it, but we're convinced that Sean pushed her down those steps hard enough to crush her skull. And I think there's a conspiracy of silence going on among the longtime tenants to protect him and his mother, and I also think that as a law-abiding citizen it's *your* job to persuade your old buddies that they have got to tell the truth about what they know."

The sliding glass door from the living room opened. "Hey, you two, come on in here and talk to me."

Alvirah smiled at Willy. In mortal fear of heights, he never came out on the terrace. But he knew that by now Mike Fitzpatrick was probably putting the heat on Alvirah about Trinky Callahan's death, and he wanted to be able to back her up. Willy was the image of Tip O'Neill, she thought admiringly. With his silver hair and blue eyes and handsome blue cardigan, Willy was a pleasure to look at.

"It *is* getting nippy," she agreed. She stood up and smoothed down the slacks of her stylish navy blue knit suit. The outfit had been purchased with the help of her friend Baroness Min von Schreiber, who on a recent visit to New York swept Alvirah into designer showrooms on Seventh Avenue. It was Min's contention that left on her own, Alvirah instinctively purchased orange-and-purple combinations.

"With your red hair, those colors are an affront to the sensibilities, dear friend," Min would sigh.

In a reflex action Alvirah snapped on the concealed microphone in her sunburst pin. The pin had been presented to her by her editor when she'd started writing articles for *The New York Globe*. And it had turned out to be a great help in solving crimes. Of course she'd never record anyone without just cause, but the word "murder" seemed to psychologically tune it up.

In the living room, Mike wasted no time in enlisting Willy's assistance. "I've known Sean Callahan since he was three years old. Heck, Willy, I've always thought of him as a kid brother. He never should have married Trinky, but that doesn't mean he had the right to kill her."

"If he did," Alvirah murmured.

Mike did not answer that remark but kept talking to Willy.

"There are a lot of hardworking new young families in Jackson Heights as well as your contemporaries. Right now I'm trying to find out who's flooding our neighborhood with drugs. Besides that, I've got a nut who's grabbing women on the streets after dark and hugging and kissing them. He's terrified six women in the last year, and it may be only a matter of time before he really hurts someone. People have to understand that any unsolved crime is a blot on the community."

"I read that the autopsy showed that Trinky had had three or four glasses of wine," Alvirah persisted. "Mike, I think you'd be better off looking for the drug dealer and the masher than trying to pin an accidental fall on a nice fellow like Sean Callahan. Suppose he was at the stairs with her and she fell and he panicked because he was afraid people would think he deliberately pushed her?"

Fitzpatrick responded swiftly. "Admit it, Alvirah. You have your doubts about what happened at the top of that staircase."

"I remember when Sean and Trinky got married, just before we came here two years ago," Willy said. "That wedding dress was practically a see-through. I thought the new pastor at St. Joan's would look for a blanket to throw over her, and the expression on Brigid Callahan's face would have stopped a clock. Sean was a dope to move into the same building as his mother." He paused, then looked at Alvirah. "Honey, I have to say, if Sean deliberately pushed Trinky down those stairs, he shouldn't get away with it."

Alvirah nodded. "I agree. On the other hand, if there's some way I can prove that it was an accident, Sean Callahan won't live under a cloud for the rest of his life."

"Then you will help?" Mike asked, looking very much the police captain as he stood up and reached for his uniform cap.

Alvirah nodded. "Guess it's time to call the painters," she told Willy.

Both men stared at her.

"The interior designer Min brought in wants me to do some redecorating. Now's as good a time as any."

"What's that got to do with Sean Callahan?" Mike demanded.

"Plenty. While this place is being gussied up, we're going to run out to Jackson Heights and move back to the old apartment. I'll have plenty of opportunity to hang around with the old girls and find out what really went on that night."

When Mike left, Willy said, "Hon, I've got to talk to you. It's been nice and peaceful lately and I can't say I've minded it. I haven't been kidnapped again, and no one's tried to shove you off the terrace or asphyxiate you. But ever since we got back from our trip, you've been aching for action. Trying to sound out the old girls shouldn't get you in trouble, but I still worry."

"Oh, Willy," Alvirah said, smiling. "This time I'm going to be like Hercule Poirot. Remember how on the cruise I read a couple of the books about him? He used his powers of deduction, his little gray cells, to solve the problem. That's the way it's going to be this time, I promise."

A week later, the arrival of Alvirah and Willy was watched with narrowed eyes from a window facing the street. The building's most famous occupants, thought the observer sarcastically. Did anyone really believe that they were moving back to this dump while their Central Park South apartment was redecorated, when with their money they could stay at a fancy hotel? Which meant of course that Mike Fitzpatrick had gone running to them for help. As Alvirah looked up and her gaze scanned the building, the observer jumped back and let the curtain fall into place. A mirthless smile accompanied the thought that a split second before her death, Trinky had been looking up too.

"Don't get too nosy, Alvirah, or you won't get to enjoy the rest of your lottery payments." The menacing whisper echoed through the room.

•   •   •

Willy locked the car and picked up the suitcases. Together he and Alvirah started toward the building. The door swung open, and a skinny boy of about twelve, with jet black hair and an impish grin, began snapping their picture.

"Millionaires Return to Their Roots," he said dramatically. "I'm Alfie Sanchez," he explained. "Reporter-photographer for the school newspaper."

"More like 'paparazzo,' " Willy grunted to Alvirah.

"He's cute," Alvirah said.

"A few more pictures, please," Alfie commanded. "And then I'd like to have a few remarks about how it feels to give up the splendor of Central Park for the less tranquil streets of Jackson Heights."

"I think that kid's a smart alec," Willy commented a few minutes later as they unpacked.

"I think he's smart as a whip," Alvirah said enthusiastically. "I told him he'll make a great reporter someday. And I do want to see his scrapbook sometime."

It didn't take them long to settle into the three-room apartment that had been their home for nearly forty years. "The rooms look so small, don't they?" said Alvirah, smiling wistfully. "I remember when we moved in here forty years ago I thought it was a palace."

"It's a good thing you didn't bring many clothes, hon," Willy observed. "No walk-in closets here. Of course, before we won the lottery, we didn't *need* walk-in closets."

"I figured that I can't go around in designer clothes and expect people to feel comfortable with me, so I decided to wear some of the things I left here," Alvirah explained. "How do I look?"

She had changed from her St. John knit suit into green polyester slacks and a T-shirt that said "NEW YORK IS BOOK COUNTRY" on it.

"Comfortable," Willy said heartily, "but I don't think you should parade that getup around Min von Schreiber. I'm gonna change too."

A few minutes later, when he went into the living room wearing his favorite old khaki pants and a Giants sweatshirt, he found Alvirah holding one of the throw pillows that had been fixtures on the overstuffed velour couch and frowning in concentration.

"Willy," she said, "somebody's been using this place. The last time I was here was in July, before we went to Italy. Remember how the night we came back we heard about Trinky and went directly to the funeral parlor and the Mass the next morning."

"That's right," Willy agreed. "We didn't stop here at all. So you're saying that sometime between July and now, somebody has been using this place."

"You bet that's what I'm saying." Alvirah pointed to a threadbare ottoman. "It's always in front of your chair, but now it's pushed against the wall." She thumped the pillow she was holding. "This was on the wing chair. It belongs on the couch." She pointed to the coffee table. "See those rings. Glasses without coasters caused them."

Before Willy could answer, the bell rang.

"News travels fast," he grunted as he walked to the door, Alvirah behind him. Then he sniffed. "Something smells good."

The formidable figure of Brigid Callahan was standing in the hallway, holding a plate of corn muffins. "Fresh from the oven," she announced. "Welcome back, the two of you."

Over a cup of tea she nervously discussed her late daughter-in-law Trinky. "Alvirah, Willy, I'm not one to talk about the dead, but you knew her. If that girl said she was going east, you could be sure she was going west. Her with her airs and practically kissing the mirror every morning. Always tossing around that mop of hair."

"She certainly did that," Alvirah agreed. With a seemingly casual gesture, she reached up and turned on the microphone of her sunburst pin.

The response encouraged Callahan. "A damn shame she set her sights on my Sean, a hardworking, good-looking young fellow who could have gone anywhere, but not with that one."

Savagely snapping the last bite of corn muffin, Brigid continued the rundown of the late Trinky's faults. "She snared him all right, and like I always told you, Alvirah, I bet she claimed she was in a family way, and honorable fellow that my Sean is, he married her. Then what happened? In two years of marriage was there any sign of a child? No. Never cooked a decent meal for that poor fellow. Kept the apartment like a pigpen. Never could hold a job. Always fired for being late. Then she starts tripping out to sit in bars with her girlfriends evenings while that poor fellow is working his head off trying to set up a law practice on his own. Girlfriends, indeed. Can't tell me those barflies weren't out to pick up men. And from bits and pieces I hear, she was carrying on with someone, God forgive her and may she rest in peace."

Brigid and I are the same age but she looks a lot older than I do, Alvirah thought. She's gone through a lot.

The widowed Brigid had moved into the building when Sean was three years old. Over the years they'd watched as she raised her son with love and firmness. Working as a waitress, she sacrificed to send him to Xavier Military Academy, Manhattan College, and St. John's Law School.

"How is Sean doing?" Alvirah asked.

Callahan's righteous wrath over the transgressions of her late daughter-in-law faded from her expression. "Quiet. Grieving, I guess. When I try to talk to him, it's 'Yes' and 'No.' That's all I get. I asked him to give me a key to his apartment so that I give it a good cleaning, but he wouldn't. And now Mike Fitzpatrick keeps sending cops over to have a little talk with Sean. What do those cops want to talk about, for God's sake?"

So that's the reason for the corn muffins, Alvirah thought. She's fishing. What's more, she's worried. "Brigid, I'm sure you could go a drop more tea."

"Half a cup, dear. Now what does it feel like to come back

to this place after Central Park South? I have to tell you that when I saw the two of you coming in with suitcases, I nearly fainted. But then Mrs. Marco said she'd spoken to you and you were redecorating your new apartment."

The network, Alvirah thought. Mike Fitzpatrick is right. If there's anything to be known about Trinky's death, someone in this building is sitting on it.

"I gotta go out for a while, Angie."

"When'll you be back, Vinny?"

"When I get here."

"Don't forget—"

"I know. I know, don't forget to change the front door lock."

The door slammed behind him, and Angie Oaker laid down the ham-and-cheese sandwich she'd been looking forward to enjoying. Her throat felt as though it had closed. She rubbed the forehead that always seemed to have a dull ache these days and closed her eyes. She'd intended to drop in on Alvirah and Willy Meehan and welcome them back, but maybe she'd wait till the headache had passed.

Angie Oaker and her husband, the late Herman Oaker, had been superintendents of 2250 Eight-first Street for twenty-five years. Herman, a born repairman, had kept steam piping through the old building and abundant hot water gushing from the faucets. Every day he'd mopped the marble floor of the shabby but still elegant entry. He'd also lovingly cleaned the twin marble staircases which led to the balcony-level apartments. It was from the left staircase that Trinky Callahan had hurtled to her death.

The building's owner kept Angie on, but it was hard work alone and none of the guys hired to assist her in the past year had been any good. So when her cousin Rosa had phoned from California to see how Angie was doing and had heard her laments, Rosa had suggested that her son, Vinny, might help out. He'd just quit a job, wanted to live in New York, and could "fix anything."

Vinny had sounded like the answer to prayer. Angie remembered him as a cute little boy. But she'd soon realized that the Vinny who moved to California seventeen years ago as an eight-year-old had not grown up to be the person she'd expected.

He was good-looking still, with his jet black hair and blue eyes, but in Angie's opinion his perpetually sullen expression would drive a saint to drink. Vinny stayed out half the night, and the rare evenings when he was in he played heavy metal music that blasted through the apartment. It was obvious that he had neither the fix-it talent his mother had claimed nor the desire to acquire it.

This morning the lock on the inside door to the vestibule had jammed again. Vinny was supposed to have replaced it. Mrs. Monahan in 4B was complaining that the sash on her bedroom window was still broken, and last week Vinny had left a bucket of sudsy water near the top of one of the balcony staircases. It was a miracle someone hadn't tripped over it, and God knows the building was still reeling from the shock of Trinky Callahan's death.

As Angie sat in her reverie, the phone rang. Another complaint, Angie thought. But it was Alvirah Meehan. Her cheerful greeting brought an involuntary smile to Angie's lips.

Alvirah and Willy wanted to pop in to say hello. A suddenly happier Angie responded, "Fifteen minutes. That would be great." As she hung up she thought that Alvirah was one of the few tenants who phoned before coming to the door. Suddenly the sandwich looked good to Angie again. A cup of tea wouldn't hurt either, she thought.

Seems to me I've been drinking tea all morning, Willy thought as he tried to ignore the remarkable discomfort of the wrought-iron chair he was sitting on in Angie Oaker's kitchen. She'd already explained with pride that she'd bought the set, a table and four chairs, at a garage sale right after Herman died, and while she knew they were considered outdoor furniture, she felt they gave a lift to the kitchen.

"Makes me feel like I'm eating in a garden," Angie had said, beaming, "and that's why I put up this flowered wallpaper."

Alvirah had admired the effect extravagantly, saying that after you lose someone it's a good idea to change things around the home a little, that somehow it makes it easier.

But now Willy could see that Alvirah was deftly introducing the subject of their own apartment.

"When I come back here I remember all the grand times Willy and I had," she said. "And I've sometimes felt selfish hanging onto the place, so I was glad when twice last year you phoned and asked if someone could stay there for a few days."

"Mrs. Casey, when the painters were doing her kitchen and her asthma kicked up, and Mrs. Rivera, when the pipe burst in her bathroom," Angela agreed. "That was very nice of both of you."

"Has anyone used it lately?" Alvirah asked.

Angie looked flabbergasted. "Oh, Alvirah, you don't think I'd just let someone come into your apartment without permission, do you?"

"Of course not," Alvirah said heartily. "What I really meant was that I certainly hoped if anyone had needed it and you couldn't reach me that you'd just feel free to let them in."

"No, I wouldn't feel free," Angie said firmly. "Not without permission."

They left a few minutes later. Just as Angie was opening the door for them, the buzzer in the foyer sounded—a long, insistent command for attention.

Angie rushed to answer it.

A shrill voice that was audible to Alvirah and Willy yelled, "The lock is broken again. How many times do I have to go through this, Angie? I swear I'm going to call the owner and tell him that this place is turning into a dump."

"Let me go," Willy offered and scurried to the stairs.

Alvirah could see that Angie Oaker was close to tears. "That was Stasia Sweeney. I can't blame her if she complains to the boss. Her key got stuck in that lock last week. It should have been fixed."

"Angie, now that Herman's gone, you need help," Alvirah said firmly.

"I'm supposed to *have* help," Angie wailed. "My cousin Rosa sent her son Vinny from Los Angeles to help me out. Help? He doesn't know the meaning of the word. He's gonna cost me my job. I better go apologize right now to Stasia."

Stasia Sweeney, whose powerful voice belied her eighty-two years, was already in the lobby with Willy and an attractive young man of about thirty who was pulling a shopping cart as well as carrying a heavy bag of groceries. Alvirah could see that Willy had already started to pour oil on troubled waters. He was complimenting Stasia on how well she looked, how glad he was to be living here for a while again because he was going to make sure everything got running smoothly. "Angie's had her hands full," he concluded, "losing Herman. Well, you know all about losing a good man, Stasia."

The feisty expression faded from frosty blue eyes magnified by oversized glasses. "Never a better one walked in shoeleather than my Martin," Sweeney agreed. Spotting Angela, she added, "Sorry if I got riled up, Angie."

"See, I told you, Aunt Stasia," a genial voice agreed. "But now if you don't mind can we possibly get these groceries separated before my arm breaks?"

"Alvirah, Willy, you don't know my grandnephew, Albert Rice," Sweeney said.

A flurry of introductions took place before Sweeney, followed by Albert, complete with grocery bags and the cart, made her slow way up the balcony steps.

"He seems like a nice young man," Alvirah said approvingly. "You can see the resemblance to Stasia. Remember how dark her hair used to be? It's nice that he's helping her. It's pretty tough to be widowed and childless. And, Willy, you notice he's wearing English Leather shaving lotion. You used to wear that."

Willy was watching Albert Rice hoisting the shopping cart. "Why all those groceries? Are they throwing an affair for the K of C?"

"Albert made Stasia get a list of what the other old girls need," Angie replied. "He said he hates to see them trying to handle heavy shopping bags, so he does some shopping for them as well. Certainly Stasia never was buying that much. Everyone knows she still has her First Communion money."

The outside door opened. Angie glared at the approaching slouched figure. "Vinny, Mrs. Sweeney was locked out again."

Alvirah saw that the newcomer's eloquent shrug had set Willy's teeth on edge.

"Angie," Willy said abruptly, "give me a list of the things that need to be taken care of. I'll make the rounds and you, Vinny, give me a hand."

Sean Callahan closed his small Forest Hills law office at three o'clock and drove five miles to Calvary Cemetery. There he parked and walked through quiet paths until he reached a small tombstone newly carved with the name KATHERINE CALLAHAN. Misery engulfed him. He knelt down and buried his face in his hands. A moment later convulsive sobs were shaking his broad shoulders. "I'm sorry, Trinky," he whispered. "It was an accident. I swear it was an accident." Tears streamed down his face as his voice rose and became audible, "I swear it was an accident, Trinky. I'm sorry."

Callahan little suspected that a concealed microphone was recording his every word.

Willy spent the afternoon doing what he loved best: fixing. Since he and Alvirah won the lottery, his plumbing skills were now exclusively commandeered by his oldest sibling, Sister Cordelia, who ministered to the sick and poor in her West Side Manhattan neighborhood. Cordelia kept Willy hopping to fix her charges' clogged heating pipes, over-flowing toilets, dripping sinks, and any other household problems her flock was encountering.

But glad as he was to help Angie out, it irked Willy to wit-ness the utter incompetence of her cousin's son, Vinny. That was why Willy, when he finally got back upstairs at four o'clock, was as close to exploding as Alvirah had ever seen him.

"*Helper!*" he snorted as he laid his toolbox on the floor of the broom closet. "That guy should be ashamed to take a dime from Angie. I don't think he ever saw a screwdriver before he came here. I tell you, hon, not only is he useless but there's something downright sneaky about him."

"Which is exactly why I think he may have been the one coming in here," Alvirah said as she opened the refrigerator, reached for a can of beer, and set it on the table in front of Willy. "You know how Angie has all the apartment keys on that board in her kitchen. He could easily have had a dupli-cate made of ours. He knows we're almost never here. I wonder what he was doing in here, and if he was meeting someone, who was it? Willy, I've got to think like Hercule Poirot and get my little gray cells working on this."

Her slightly jutting jaw firmed decisively. "I'll find out from Angie where Vinny lived in California. Maybe there's something in his past that we should know about. Think about it: why would Angie's cousin Rosa dump him on her unless maybe she wanted to get him off her hands?"

"I saw Stasia's nephew in the hall later," Willy said. "Very polite young fellow. He stopped to thank me for fixing the lobby door."

"Oh, I heard a lot about him," Alvirah said. "He's a bag-gage handler at Kennedy Airport and has been stopping by here since last spring looking after Stasia. After all she is eighty-two and getting frail. I think that's very kind of him, but naturally some of the other old girls want to know where he's been all these years."

"They would," Willy grunted.

"Let's go over it again, Sean," Mike Fitzpatrick said softly. "Why was Trinky's death an accident?"

Sean Callahan's tie was loose, the top button of his shirt open. Circles boarded his eyes. His forehead rested on his hand as though seeking relief from constant pain. A memory flitted through his mind of Mike Fitzpatrick, one of the "big kids" in the building teaching him to play stickball. But the Mike who was sitting across the table from him in the precinct house was all cop. He must know how often I go to the cemetery, Sean thought.

"Sean, I want to help you," Fitzpatrick cajoled. "Once again, you have a right to call a lawyer or to remain silent. But if you don't want to do either, let's talk. Maybe it *was* an accident. Maybe you didn't mean to push Trinky, but a jury has to decide that."

"I didn't want her to go out to that night," Sean murmured, more to himself than to Fitzpatrick.

Mike Fitzpatrick's eyes narrowed. He leaned forward. His tone was encouraging when he said, "You were right. That place is nothing more than a pickup bar these days, and Trinky bragged she had a generous boyfriend. Sean, you knew that, didn't you?"

"No, I didn't," Sean answered, his voice a monotone. "I did know that in the past year six young women in the neighborhood have been grabbed by some nut. I was worried about her going out. I knew I'd been crazy to get involved with her but I still cared and was concerned for her safety. She'd already had too much to drink that night."

"So you argued with her, then you followed her out, and at the top of the stairs you lost your temper."

Sean Callahan closed his eyes.

The door to the interrogation room opened. Fitzpatrick looked up, his expression annoyed. It was the desk sergeant.

"Captain, can you step outside? A very important phone call."

The sergeant's nod in Sean's direction was almost imperceptible.

With a sinking heart, Alvirah hung up the phone in Stasia Sweeney's apartment. Calling Mike Fitzpatrick just now was the hardest thing she'd ever done, but she knew she had no choice. An agitated Angela had phoned and asked her to come down to Stasia's apartment right away, that it was important.

Important! thought Alvirah with dismay as she watched Stasia, propped up with bed pillows on the couch, telling the team of emergency medical technicians what had happened to her.

"I guess I let myself get too excited about being locked out again. I was making Irish soda bread and I started to get chest pains. At my age, who knows what can happen? I said an Act of Contrition while I dialed nine-one-one. Then I lay down here and realized I might be going to the Lord with maybe a sin on my soul. I mean I watch a lot of police shows on TV and I know all about being an accessory after the fact."

Alvirah didn't want to hear the rest of the story again but could not blot it out. It was clear to her that Stasia's chest pains were a thing of the past. Her color was good, her eyes snapping, her body bristling with self-righteousness. Alvirah realized that the microphone in her sunburst pin was still recording, but even though she'd heard the whole story, she did not turn off the switch.

"Till now only my grandnephew Albert knew that from the balcony I'd seen Sean Callahan kneeling over Trinky at the foot of the stairs and slamming her head down when she tried to get up," Sweeney said. "Trinky stopped moving. I don't know why, but I was sure she was dead. I ran back in here and I guess I went into shock, because the next thing I remember was hearing the hullabaloo outside. I was still dazed, but I went down to the lobby. The cops were there and Sean was standing beside Trinky's body crying. Brigid Callahan had fainted dead away, and they were trying to revive her, poor thing."

Mike Fitzpatrick was right, Alvirah thought sadly. The old girls are loyal to each other. Sean did kill Trinky, and what makes it worse is that he wasn't satisfied with pushing her down the stairs but finished the job when he realized she was still alive. Which makes him a cold-blooded killer, she admitted to herself.

The EMT crew was ready to leave. "Your pulse and heart are fine now, Mrs. Sweeney," the senior attendant said briskly.

"Give me my glasses," Sweeney ordered. "You made me take them off and I'm lost without them."

"Sure, but wait a minute, let me clean them off for you. They're pretty smudged."

"The batter of the Irish soda bread," Sweeney explained. "Seems as though every time I make that bread, there's trouble."

The ringing doorbell signaled the arrival of Captain Michael Fitzpatrick accompanied by two plainclothesmen whom Alvirah was certain were detectives. For the third time she heard the damning eyewitness testimony of Stasia Sweeney.

When Fitzpatrick left, she and Willy, trailed by an anxious Angela, followed him into the hall. "Mike, are you going to take Sean into custody?" Alvirah asked bluntly.

"He already is in custody," Mike said. "Alvirah, I'm sorry I dragged you into this. It's an open-and-shut case now. He not only pushed her down the stairs but finished her off. Don't waste your sympathy on him."

Alvirah's response was preempted by an aggravated bellow from behind her.

"VINNNNNY!"

Angie's finger was shaking with rage as she pointed to the end of the corridor, where a figure was ducking out of sight.

"I've been looking for him since he left the apartment. Is he blind and deaf? Couldn't he hear the ambulance at the door? Wouldn't you think that he'd see what was going on and if he could help? Help! Ha! Watch, he's gone again."

"Maybe he didn't hear you," Fitzpatrick suggested wryly. "Isn't that your cousin's son who works for you, Angie?"

"*Supposed* to work for me."

"I don't think I've ever bumped into him." With a shrug, Fitzpatrick turned back to Alvirah and Willy. "I've got to get back."

"And I've got to find that Vinny," Angie snapped.

There was a clatter on the staircase as Alfie Sanchez appeared with his camera just as the EMT crew exited from Stasia Sweeney's apartment. He looked disappointed when he saw that the gurney was empty. "You're not rushing her to the hospital?" he asked.

"Sorry, Alfie," he was told. "No headlines this time."

"Aww." Alfie shrugged philosophically. "And I just missed the cops arresting a drunk driver yesterday. He swung a punch at them. It would have made a great shot." He grinned at Alvirah. "Remember you're gonna look at my scrapbook sometime, okay?"

"You bet," Alvirah promised.

In the stationhouse Captain Mike Fitzpatrick went directly to the room where Sean Callahan was being detained. Once again he gave him the Miranda warning and said, "Sean, you'd better call a lawyer. Stasia Sweeney saw you slamming Trinky's head on the floor."

Callahan looked stunned. "Are you crazy, Mike?" he asked.

"No, I'm not crazy. You can make one call. Who's your lawyer?"

"Forget the lawyer. I have to talk to my mother. Oh, God," he said hopelessly. "I don't know what to do."

•   •   •

Alvirah did not sleep with her usual hearty ability to enter the land of nod. Instead, vague dreams kept awakening her. Finally, at three A.M., she tiptoed out to the living room with a spiral-bound notebook and her sunburst pin. She knew she had heard something that had triggered her subconscious, something it was important to check on.

She settled on the dark gray velour couch that forty years ago had cost one hundred and fifty dollars, and she plumped a pillow behind her back. With a half smile she remembered how, when they were really broke, she and Willy used to slide their fingers down between the frame and the cushions in the hopes of coming across some money that might have slipped out of pockets.

As she entertained the thought, she moved her hand down in the old gesture and felt her index finger touch something round and solid. Trying not to push the object beyond reach, she managed to scoop it up then grasp it between her thumb and index finger. She held it to the light. It was a narrow gold bracelet, and from its weight and luster she guessed it was not just a trinket. This is worth money, she thought. How did it get here?

A name sprang into her mind. Vinny! He had access to the key to this apartment. Had he been coming here, and if so, who was his woman companion? A strange woman wouldn't have escaped scrutiny from the old girls in the building. But how could he afford an expensive bracelet?

She had her idea about who might have been Vinny's companion. Vinny was good-looking in a weak kind of way, she reasoned, and Trinky was a born flirt. Suppose . . .

She could feel her gray cells clicking. What was Vinny's life in California? Had he been in trouble? Had he maybe been involved with drugs? Her editor at the *Globe* had contacts all over the country. He could run a check on him.

That settled, she took the cassette out of her sunburst pin, placed it to her portable tapedeck, and rewound it.

The sun was coming up when she finally finished taking

notes. She leaned back on the couch, closed her eyes, and told her little gray cells to continue to concentrate.

At eight o'clock, when Willy awoke to find Alvirah's side of the bed empty, he hurried into the living room and saw her tired-but-satisfied expression. "We've got a lot to do," she said briskly. "I'm glad it's Saturday. First order of business is to call Alfie Sanchez and ask him to come and show us his scrapbook. I want to see if there's a picture of Vinny we can give to Charley at the *Globe*. I know his mother lives in West Hollywood and I already called information there. They gave me her phone number, so it's listed and it will be easy for Charley to get an address. Would you take the photo to Charley and let me know what he finds out?"

Willy rubbed the sleep from his eyes. "Okay. And then what?"

"Then I'm going to spend some time with Brigid Callahan. Willy, she was nervous as a cat when she came in here yesterday. Now that Sean's been detained and will probably be indicted for Trinky's murder, she'll be a wreck. I have to get her to confide in me. She knows something that she isn't telling."

"That's possible, hon. What else have you got up your sleeve?"

"Something that isn't clear to me yet. But the gray cells are working on it."

When Alfie Sanchez rang the doorbell of the Meehan apartment, a thick scrapbook under his arm, he was not aware that the person who'd cheerfully asked him where he was going had a profound reason for the question.

Alvirah welcomed Alfie cheerfully and brought him into the kitchen, where blueberry pancake batter was waiting to be spooned onto the pan. Willy emerged from the bedroom dressed in his Manhattan clothes, as he called them—a handsome blue linen jacket, a white turtleneck shirt, and navy slacks.

Alvirah sniffed. "English Leather. Brings back memories."

Willy shrugged. "Wore it for the first time when I went to the K of C dance where we met. How you doing, Alfie?"

"Great," Alfie replied enthusiastically. "I got a fabulous picture of Mrs. Callahan when she came back from the police station last night. She looked a hundred years old. I'm gonna caption it 'Mother of the Accused.'"

Alvirah turned the flame on under the skillet. "Alfie, you don't miss much," she said, trying to sound casual. "I wonder, did you ever take a picture of Angela's nephew, Vinny?"

"Vinny Nodder? Oh, sure," Alfie replied as he sipped the orange juice at his plate. "A great one. Here, I'll show you." He reached for his scrapbook.

The picture he pulled out caused Willy and Alvirah to look at each other over Alfie's bent head. It had obviously been taken from the balcony and showed Vinny, a mop in his hand, avidly studying the slender figure halfway down the curved stairs.

"Isn't that Trinky Callahan on the stairs?" Alvirah asked.

"Yeah, that's Trinky," Alfie said. "But what I want you to see is I tried to catch him showing how ob—. . . man, what's the word?"

"Obsessed?" Alvirah suggested.

"Right on. How *obsessed* he was," Alfie continued. "He was always looking at Trinky. Good taste, huh?"

Alvirah frowned. She should have put a new cassette in her sunburst pin. She mustn't miss anything that was being said. She realized that Alfie was a fount of information.

After breakfast, Willy headed off to Manhattan and Alvirah invited Alfie to sit next to her on the couch while she studied his scrap book. "I'll show you everything and explain it," he promised.

It turned out to be a formidable task. Alfie clearly had a nose for news. Car pileups, fires, broken shop windows—everything seemed to be grist for his mill. And Alfie had instant recall as to the circumstances surrounding all his photos.

Forty minutes later, Alvirah decided to get to the point. "Alfie," she asked, "did you by any chance take some pictures after Trinky Callahan's body was found in the lobby? I mean, it must have been exciting with so many police here."

"Oh, sure," Alfie said. "They're way back here."

He flipped through the pages until he came to one that was captioned "The Night of the Fall." It had obviously been taken from the balcony and was somber, stark photography. Trinky's body, covered by a sheet, was at the foot of the marble staircase. The lobby was swarming with police. "Poor Sean," Alvirah sighed. "He must have gone outside for a breath of air." Then her eyes widened. "Oh, my God," she breathed. "I need this picture, Alfie," she said.

On his way down the stairs to his own apartment, Alfie willingly answered the questions he was asked by the person he met on the staircase. Yes, Mrs. Meehan did take a picture from him. It was one he'd snapped when the police came after Trinky died.

She's got to be stopped, his listener observed silently but furiously. She's got to be stopped!

Brigid Callahan had paced the floor all night, not knowing which way to turn. Last evening when they finally allowed her to see Sean, the shocking thought had occurred to her that with his expression now wan and tired, his blue eyes troubled and sad, his dark hair matted and damp on his forehead, twenty-nine-year-old Sean was the image of his dying father, whose life had ended of cancer at that age. The resemblance was even more shocking when it became clear to Brigid that since Trinky died, Sean's only thought had been of trying to protect her.

Now Brigid agonized over whether the promise she had

made to Sean not to tell everything to Mike Fitzpatrick had been a mistake.

She had intended to go to his apartment as soon as she got home last night, but didn't dare to take a chance with Alfie Sanchez hanging around watching her. But now, at ten o'clock, she thought she could count on his being out of the way and started to go there. Then she met Alvirah in the hall. She tried to explain that Sean needed some personal items.

"I'm going with you, Brigid," Alvirah said decisively. "We've got to talk."

Sean and Trinky's apartment was one of the smallest in the building, with a tiny living room, bedroom, and kitchen. "Sean's cleaned it up," Brigid said dully. "He's naturally neat."

Alvirah was looking in the closet. "None of Trinky's clothes left. Did he give them all away?"

"I guess so. He hated the trashy way she dressed. Oh, Alvirah." Brigid Callahan sat on the edge of the bed and began to weep. "Everything I say is like I'm giving him a motive to hurt her. He couldn't have done what Stasia Sweeney said he did. It isn't in my Sean to hurt anyone."

Alvirah flipped on the microphone in her pin. "Brigid," she said firmly, "whatever you tell me stops right here. But you've got to be honest with me. You know something about what happened that night, and unless you tell me the truth, I can't help you."

Brigid looked at her old friend imploringly.

"I love Sean too," Alvirah said softly, "and the reason we came back here is that I wanted to help clear his name. It looks bad for him, but I still want to try."

Callahan nodded. Her voice choking with emotion, she said, "I was going out to the store that night and ran into Trinky at the landing. She was all dolled up and, Alvirah, the outfit she had on was a disgrace."

"Did you tell her that?" Alvirah asked.

"I did. And I said she should either stay home and be a wife to my son or get out." Brigid gulped. "Alvirah, the floor was a little damp. That Vinny must have just mopped. Trinky told me to go to hell and started down the first step. Her foot skidded in those crazy high heels, and I tried to grab her arm but couldn't hold her, and she yelled, "Don't push me." Then she took an awful tumble and fell and just was lying at the bottom of the stairs. I thought she was dead, but then she started to stir."

Alvirah could anticipate what was coming. "And you ran for Sean."

"Yes. He was sitting at the kitchen table. At first I couldn't even talk. I told him I thought Trinky was badly hurt. I was so scared. He rushed out. And when he came back he said that she was dead and not to say a word to anyone that some-one might believe I had pushed her." Callahan began to sob. "And now Stasia Sweeney says she saw Sean batter Trinky's head, and that's the blow that killed her. Sean didn't do that," she wailed. "No matter how upset he was, he just couldn't do that."

Alvirah patted Brigid's hand. "I believe you," she said quietly. "The trick is how we're going to prove it." She pulled the gold bracelet she'd found on the couch out of her pocket. "Did you ever see this before?"

"That's Trinky's. She said her girlfriend gave it to her for her birthday last May. Where did you find it?"

"Not important right now, but one thing you can be sure. It's expensive and no girlfriend ever gave it to Trinky for her birthday." Alvirah got up. "I've got to have a little talk with Stasia Sweeney," she said.

"Alvirah, there's something else," Brigid said, her voice faltering. "Look." She reached under the bed and pulled out a plastic garbage bag. "There's twenty-five thousand dollars in here," she whispered. "Sean found it after Trinky died and didn't know what to do with it. God only knows who gave it to her, but he said to hide it somewhere. He said that if they get a search warrant and find it, Mike Fitzpatrick will say that it's proof that Trinky was seeing another man, and that could be considered a motive for him to kill her. Will you take it, please?"

"Saints above!" Alvirah breathed as a sharp rap at the door caused Callahan to gasp.

Callahan scurried to the foyer. "Who is it?" she called.

"Police. We have a search warrant for these premises."

Oh my God, Alvirah thought. Instinctively she picked up the bag and bundled it under her arm. As Callahan turned the knob, Alvirah said in a voice that could be heard in the hallway, "Brigid, I'll get out of your way. I'll be in the laundry room if you need me."

Accessory after the fact, she thought as three minutes later she searched in her apartment for a place to hide the bag. Finally she settled for following Brigid's example and shoved it under the bed.

Then she turned on the recorder and went through everything she'd taped since she and Willy returned to Jackson Heights until she came to the segment where she'd been in Stasia Sweeney's apartment. It took three reruns until she realized what it was she'd been missing. "Ah-hah," she said triumphantly. "The little gray cells are working overtime!"

Stasia Sweeney was preparing her second batch of Irish soda bread when Alvirah dropped in to visit. "I never was a neat baker," she sighed as she wiped sticky, floury hands on her apron and adjusted her glasses.

Alvirah did not waste time on preliminaries. "Stasia," she said as she appreciatively sniffed the aroma of the baking bread. "You got me curious last night. You said that there always seemed to be trouble when you made Irish soda bread. What did you mean by that?"

Sweeney shrugged. "Oh, it's just that last night I got chest pains, and the time before when I made soda bread, Trinky Callahan was murdered. I'd call that trouble."

"I would too. But the point is you never said why you went out that evening in the midst of baking the bread. Did you hear Trinky fall down the stairs?"

"You couldn't hear that through a closed door. No, I opened my door because the apartment was hot, and then I saw the bucket near the staircase and decided to give Vinny a piece of my mind for slopping water around so late, and then I looked down and saw Sean battering her head."

"Stasia, look at this picture," Alvirah said deliberately laying it on the kitchen table.

As Sweeney looked down her glasses slipped over the bridge of her nose. She reached up and floury fingers fumbled to adjust them. Her eyes widened and impatiently she rubbed the lens smearing them even more. "Alvirah, I don't want to look at that. Just thinking of that girl's body gives me the chills."

"Who's in the doorway?" Alvirah asked quickly.

"Sean Callahan, who else?"

"It's not Sean," Alvirah said triumphantly. "It's Angie's nephew, Vinny. Look! Sean is over in the corner with Brigid. His back is to you. See what I mean, Stasia? Vinny is the same height and build as Sean, and he has the same dark hair. They're both wearing T-shirts and jeans and the lighting is poor. I bet with batter on your fingers, you smudged your glasses when you looked down, and then I bet you saw what you expected to see. Did you ever see Sean's face clearly that night?"

"I thought I did." Sweeney faltered as she peered at the picture. "Alvirah, are you saying I might have been wrong about identifying Sean? I'd like to think you're right. But why would that lazy lump Vinny want to hurt Trinky?"

"That's something I have to get my little gray cells working on," Alvirah replied, satisfied that Stasia was admitting the possibility of a mistake.

Back in her own apartment, Alvirah discovered that her newfound optimism had begun to evaporate. She had not one single smidgeon of proof; all she had were theories, and she knew exactly what Mike Fitzpatrick would do with them. On the other hand, she thought, it makes sense that

Vinny was the one who was meeting Trinky here, but where would he get the money to buy her that bracelet and maybe give her twenty-five thousand dollars?

Unless she was right and he wasn't the incompetent, lazy, good-for-nothing that he seemed to be. Everything made sense if he was the one selling drugs and fooling around with Trinky. Maybe she knew too much about him and had become a threat. Mike Fitzpatrick had said they were closing in on a drug dealer in the neighborhood. Brigid and Stasia had said that the mop and pail were by the stairs, so Vinny had to have been nearby that night.

I bet anything Willy finds out that Vinny has been in trouble in California, Alvirah thought. Now she couldn't wait for Willy to get home with his report.

As always, she chose to relieve tension by vigorously cleaning the apartment. As she vacuumed and dusted and mopped, she realized that if Vinny didn't have a record she was back to square one. There was nothing she could prove.

The long sleepless night was catching up with her. I'll just have a nice soak in the tub, she thought. That way I'll feel better, and when Willy gets back I won't be like a dead duck.

The tub began to fill quickly. Alvirah wondered if she had any of her old bath salts. As she opened the medicine cabinet a faint, familiar scent hit her, and for a moment she smiled. Then her eyes narrowed. She picked up the bottle of English Leather aftershave lotion and stared at it. This hasn't been sitting around here for two years, she thought. This bottle is almost new. She unscrewed the top and sniffed. Suddenly everything made sense, much more sense than blaming everything on that loser, Vinny.

Of *course*, thought Alvirah. What's the matter with me? Those gray cells weren't working that hard after all. Stasia's grandnephew! So helpful doing errands around the neighborhood. Dark hair, blue eyes, medium build, just like Mike and Vinny. He'd been wearing English Leather the first time she met him. And he'd try to talk Stasia out of telling what she thought she'd seen that night.

Who knew anything about Albert Rice? She'd call Mike Fitzpatrick and tell him to check on him. But first she'd better turn off the taps before the apartment got flooded. With the bottle of English Leather in her hand she turned around. Her eyes widened.

A figure was framed in the doorway, a tall figure with a medium build, dark hair, and icy blue eyes.

"I wondered how long it would be before you connected me to the aftershave, Mrs. Meehan," Albert Rice said pleasantly. "Your husband was wearing it when he left this morning. Trinky liked it. A very attractive if stupid girl. She talked too much. Very dangerous for me. Also stupid enough to remove my money from here and claim not to know what I was talking about."

He was coming toward her. Involuntarily Alvirah turned and backed up, but there was no place to go. The tub was behind her. She opened her mouth to scream, but before she could utter a sound, Albert's hands were gripping the back of her head and covering her lips.

"So many falls in this building," he whispered. "You toppled into the tub, got knocked out, and drowned. Maybe you had a dizzy spell. You really should have stayed in Central Park. You're a busybody and it will be a lot of trouble now for me to persuade Aunt Stasia that she did really see Sean smashing Trinky's head that night."

He knew I never believed Sean was a killer, Alvirah thought. But how did he get in here? Of course. He had a key. Maybe he did some shopping for Angie too and filched it from her kitchen. The little gray cells are working overtime, Alvirah thought, but it may be too late.

"Good-bye, Alvirah," Albert whispered.

She could not brace herself against the violent push that sent her toppling backward. She was falling into the tub. Her head hit the spigot sending shooting pains through her forehead and neck. Her arms flailed as she tried to push away the steely hands that were holding her down. Gurgling sounds came from her throat as the water rushed into her nostrils. She was going to die, but he wasn't going to get away with it.

Alvirah managed to raise both feet and kick them against the wall. *Thump. Thump. THUMP!* Let someone hear she prayed. She managed one more weak thump before she blacked out.

Willy jumped out of a cab as Mike Fitzpatrick was emerging from a squad car. "You're just the fellow I want to see," Willy told him.

"Later, Willy," Mike said briskly. "Stasia Sweeney is waiting for me."

"I found out something about Angie's relative, Vinny," Willy said urgently. "He's trouble."

"And from what Stasia said, he also may be a murderer," Mike replied as, accompanied by his driver, Officer Jack Hand, he bounded up the steps of the apartment building.

Alfie Sanchez was in the hallway, his ever-ready camera in one hand, an enlarged picture in the other. He had overheard Mike.

"A break in the case?" he asked excitedly.

"Get lost, Alfie," Mike snapped.

Sanchez looked injured. "Captain, I'm working for you as an unpaid detective as well as crime photographer. I'm on my way to see Mrs. Meehan. I've come across an interesting fact in the tangled web surrounding Trinky Callahan's death."

"What are you talking about?" Fitzpatrick demanded.

Alfie brandished the picture he was holding. "I showed Mrs. Meehan my scrapbook this morning. She got very excited about one of my crime-scene photos taken shortly after Trinky Callahan's body was found."

Willy didn't know why he had a sudden ominous feeling that Alvirah needed him.

"I have figured out what Mrs. Meehan picked up when observing my superb photography. She realized that from the balcony it would have been possible for Mrs. Sweeney to have mistaken Trinky's husband, Sean, for Vinny the janitor. But that fact may no longer be significant." Alfie pointed to the picture in his hand. "This was not included in my scrapbook only because it was taken after the body was removed, and therefore I considered it less newsworthy. But in examining it, you will see that even with my expert eye I mislabeled it. The man in the lobby next to Angie is not Vinny, but Mrs. Sweeney's grandnephew, Albert Rice."

"I don't know what you're talking about," Willy said, "but if Alvirah's on the track of something, she may be in trouble." He began to run up the stairs then out of the corner of his eye saw Vinny loitering in the hallway off the balcony. "Mike," he yelled, "you better collar this guy. There's a warrant for his arrest in Los Angeles. He grabs women and fondles them. That's why his mother shipped him to Angie."

On the balcony, an apartment door flew open. "There's a flood in my bathroom," Stasia Sweeney bellowed. "It may be coming from your place, Willy, right above me. And somebody's thumping on the wall. Is Alvirah into yoga or is this place is going to hell in a basket?"

"Alvirah," Willy moaned. "Alvirah."

Vinny shrank against the wall as Officer Hand rushed toward him. "I know what you think," he whimpered, "but I didn't do nothing to Trinky. She was fooling around with Albert. I seen them together a lot. He just came out of your apartment, Willy, and went down the fire stairs."

Mike Fitzpatrick grabbed Willy's arm. "Let's go."

The water was gushing into the hallway when they bounded into the apartment and rushed to the bathroom. The scent of English Leather aftershave lotion filled the air.

Alvirah was lying motionless in the tub. In a single movement, Willy dropped to his knees, bent over, and swooped her up. "Honey . . ."

"Give her to me," Mike snapped. "It can't be too late."

•   •   •

Alvirah's first impression was of breathing in the scratchy wool of the fake oriental rug that she and Willy had bought for two hundred dollars forty-two years ago. Her next thought was that she must have gotten into the tub with all her clothes on.

Then realization hit. That skunk, Albert, she thought, as she heard Willy's pleading whisper.

"Be okay, honey," said Willy. "We still have seventeen more lottery payments to go. You don't want me to spend them on a floozie."

You bet I don't, Alvirah thought, as she gulped in fresh air.

"She's coming around," Mike said. "Willy, when are you two moving back to Central Park South?"

"Well, we certainly accomplished a lot with our stay here," Alvirah said happily the next morning as she carefully folded the freshly laundered slacks and sweater that had almost been her death garments. "Isn't it nice that in twenty-four hours we proved Sean was innocent, unmasked Vinny as the stalker, and smoked out Albert Rice, a murderer and drug dealer?"

"Very nice," Willy agreed. "But Alvirah, honey, for my sake, for a while at least will you please give your little gray cells a rest?"

The bell rang. "What now?" moaned Willy as he went to answer it.

Standing in the hallway were a radiant Brigid Callahan on the arm of her son, Sean, a subdued Angie Oaker, and a sad-eyed Stasia Sweeney. They were being herded by crime investigator Alfie Sanchez and Captain Mike Fitzpatrick.

"Photo opportunity," Sanchez announced.

"We want to circulate a flyer with a group picture," Mike explained, "to show how neighborhood cooperation can make the streets and homes safe for all our citizens."

"Alvirah, how can we thank you?" Brigid asked.

"Alvirah . . ." Sean Callahan grasped her hands. "Everything worked out because of you."

Alvirah kissed him. "You've had a really tough time, Sean, and so has your mother. Take my advice. Concentrate on your law practice for a while." She looked at Brigid. "And your mother might not like to hear this, but find an apartment that isn't in this building. Be on your own for a while."

"I'm gonna make a statement that no one should think she's doing her disturbed son a favor by sending him away to prey on innocent people," Angie Oaker volunteered, tears in her eyes.

"And I'm going to say that blood relative or not, I wash my hands of anyone who could sell drugs and murder a young woman to keep her quiet," Stasia Sweeney said firmly, though Alvirah saw that her lip was quivering.

Master photographer Alfie Sanchez had clearly noted both Angie's and Stasia's distress. "I am going to suggest that kids my age volunteer to run errands for their senior citizen neighbors and help keep their apartment buildings clean," he announced grandly. "But now Captain Fitzpatrick and I have a deadline. Everyone please line up in front of the window and get ready to say cheese."

Homeless, Hungry, Please Help

Stanley Cohen

HE'D SEEN A lot of them around, but this was the first time he'd seen them as a couple, a man and a woman. Usually, it was one or the other, standing on the street divider at the light by the Sears Shopping Center. The person would be holding a sign written in large letters with a heavy marker or crayon on a battered piece of corrugated carton:

HOMELESS

HUNGRY

PLEASE HELP

Sometimes the signs read: WILL WORK FOR FOOD.

As cars pulled alongside them, waiting for the traffic light to change, some drivers would lower a window and hand them a coin, or often a bill. Although Sam was annoyed by panhandlers in general, if he got stuck right in front of one, and made the mistake of making eye contact, he sometimes found himself reaching into his pocket and holding a bill out the window.

But this time there were two of them, a white couple, man and woman. They were on the street divider in the middle of the Post Road, at the light in front of the Milford Post Shopping Center, and in the bright midday November sun, they appeared younger, cleaner, and better dressed than the usual pathetic, ragtag variety. He guessed they were in their mid-thirties, easily a good twenty or more years younger than he himself was.

The man was sitting on the concrete divider, his legs crossed in front of him, holding the typical hand-lettered sign. He had a thick but close-cropped beard and mustache to match his head of wiry dark hair, and deepset, very intense eyes. The woman stood behind him and was not unattractive, with short brownish hair and a slim figure. They were dressed alike, almost stylishly, in jeans, plaid shirts, and denim jackets. A large plastic bag, presumably holding their few belongings, was on the divider next to them.

As Sam waited for the light, studying the two of them, they looked in his direction and made strong eye contact, and the little needle of guilt pricked him. He was an obvious "have," behind the wheel of his large Mercedes, and they were "have-nots." He was in the wrong lane to hand them something out the window, but he definitely felt intrigued by their so completely atypical appearance. Then a crazy whim hit him.

He knew it was a dumb idea and a bad mistake as soon as he lowered the window, but he was curious about them, and since he was thinking about having a bite of lunch somewhere anyway, he muttered "What the hell?" to himself, and went ahead with it, something he wouldn't have done if his wife, Martha, had been with him. She was generally sympathetic to the homeless but didn't want any direct contact with them. He waved and yelled, with a friendly smile, "Whatta ya say? Wanta have lunch?"

The man jumped to his feet.

Sam pointed at the Burger King on the corner across from the shopping center and yelled, "Meet me over there."

He drove into the Burger King parking lot and got out of his car as he watched them hurry toward him. "I was just thinking about having lunch," he said when they reached him, "so I decided that inviting you to join me was something I could do to help out." And then he picked up the faint trace of an odor. Not strong. But detectable. Unbathed bodies. Homeless, like their sign says. But at that point, it was too late to do anything about it.

"You're a good man," the man said, looking him over, without smiling, and then looking at Sam's shiny Mercedes. "Maybe we can give you a hand with something to try and help you out in return. We're always ready to do a little work for a meal."

"Thanks for offering, but that's not necessary. Don't give it a thought. Glad to do it. Let's go in." Then he said, "Well, since we're going to have lunch together, my name's Sam. What're yours?"

"Hello, Sam. Name's Vince. And she's Loreen."

"Hello, Vince, Loreen."

Sam realized immediately that he didn't like or trust this man. There was an intensity, an air of threat about him. As for her, he couldn't tell much about her. Other than the fact that she wasn't bad-looking. She did justice to her jeans. But he already regretted what he'd started. It was a really stupid thing to do. But he'd get through the half hour and next time be wiser for it.

Once inside, Sam motioned at the lighted menu signs and said, "Help yourself. Whatever you'd like, it's yours. The sandwiches are good and the fries are the best around."

"Sounds like you come here often, Sam," Vince said, smirking.

"Well, once in a while, anyway. I kinda like it when I'm in a real big hurry."

Sam watched the two of them study the menu and then order. Each of them ordered two Double Whoppers, a large fries, a large Coke, and a slice of pie. Two Double Whoppers? That's a full pound of beef! And pie? That should hold them till their next meal, whenever and wherever they got it. He ordered himself a chicken sandwich and a Diet Coke, and they went to a booth and sat down. He watched them begin eating. Yes, they were definitely hungry.

"Sam Champion!"

Sam looked up, startled, and tried not to show his dismay. His friend, Harley Spence. "How's it going, Harley?"

"Sam, what the hell're you doing eating here?"

Hesitantly, "I come here once in a while when I'm in a hurry. What about you, Harley? What're *you* doing here?"

"Same thing. Want to introduce me to your friends?"

"Vince and Loreen . . . My friend, Harley."

"Why do you two look familiar?" Harley asked . . . Then he glanced at the big plastic bag and back at the two of them, and a flush of recognition crossed his face. He glanced in the direction of the street, and then back at Sam with a broad smile. "Sam, you're too much. You know that? . . . I'll leave you to your *friends*. See you at the club." He walked away and got in line to order.

"Your last name's Champion?" Vince asked.

"Name only. I was never champion of anything."

"I know I've seen that name on something, somewhere, but I don't quite remember . . ." Loreen said. "Wait. Champion Lumber?"

". . . Yes . . ."

She smiled and rolled her eyes in appreciation. "I remember seeing that big sign facing the Turnpike."

"I'm not around there much, anymore. I'm more or less retired, now."

"You live somewhere around here?" Vince asked.

"Around. Not close by."

"You married? Live alone? What?"

"My wife's in Florida at the moment. We have a place down there, and I'll be going down sometime soon." He was becoming a little annoyed by their questions. "But, wait a minute. What about yourselves? You two just don't look like homeless types. What's the story, here?"

"We both got laid off and finally had to give up our place."

"Where?"

"In Boston. We were both working in a shoe factory."

"And you couldn't find *anything* up around there?"

"Nothing." Vince said it with a little heat.

"So, what now?"

"We're gonna head South if we don't find something pretty soon," Loreen said.

"You have people down there? Family?"

"We don't have anybody anywhere," Vince said.

"No friends in Boston, or up that way?"

"Nobody in a position to help us out."

"How'd you get here?"

"We hitched," Vince said. Then, "Sam, I'll bet you could find something for us, couldn't ya'? At your lumberyard? Or your place? How about your place? We're good workers. Between the two of us, we can do just about anything. And do it well."

"Afraid I can't help you. I have nothing to do anymore with running the lumberyard. And there's nothing around the house."

"Nothing at all around your place? Come on now, Sam. There's gotta be something around there that could use some doing."

He was feeling pressure that he didn't need. "Look. There's nothing. Okay?" He said it with an air of finality, trying to get a message across to them, to put closure on the discussion. "It's been my pleasure to take you to lunch. I'm glad to do it. But once we walk out the door, we're never going to see each other again. I hope that's understood." He looked at Vince, who was scowling.

"Well, you were awfully nice to buy us lunch," Loreen said, and she smiled at him.

"As I said, glad to do it." She wasn't bad-looking at all when she smiled, but he had the feeling there was something bogus behind that smile. He'd had enough of them both. It was time to get the hell away from them, and let the whole dumb, regrettable business become history. He got to his feet. "Look. I'm finished eating, and I've got stuff to do, so I'm taking off, but you two can stay here as long as you want. Rest, use the bathrooms, even have free refills of your

Cokes if you want. See that sign? Free refills? And the best of luck to you both."

"Thanks again, Sam," Loreen said.

Sam drove his Mercedes downtown to his broker's and sat a while, discussing his portfolio, and then stayed a while longer, watching the tape. This was how he spent his days, now that he'd retired from the business. Some men went to the track. Others went fishing. Still others played golf. He liked watching the Market, while his sons ran the lumber-yard—and had been doing it very nicely for some years. He'd sent them to college so they'd be able to do exactly that.

After having enough of watching the Market, he drove home, stopped at the mailbox, and headed up the long, cir-cular drive, past stately trees and lush plantings, to the im-posing stone home completely hidden from the road. He pulled up to the doors of the three-car garage . . .

And then he saw them.

Loreen was sitting on the steps of the door leading into the house through the laundry room, and Vince was raking leaves. Sam's first reaction was to turn around, drive back down to the road, and call the cops on his car phone, but Loreen smiled and waved and stood up and came walking toward him, and Vince was industriously working, trying to make a dent in the deep blanket of leaves that covered the vast rolling lawn. Not that he needed Vince's help. His land-scape service would come with a crew and clear the leaves, using blowers and other equipment, just like they did every other year.

Without putting the car in the garage, he cut the engine.

"Hi, Sam," Loreen said, walking toward him with a pleas-ant smile. Vince walked over, carrying the rake.

"What in the hell are you guys doing here?"

"We came to see if we could do a little something to show our appreciation for the nice lunch," Vince said.

"How'd you get here?"

"We walked."

"Walked? That's got to be over five or six miles."

"It wasn't so far," Loreen said. "We're used to walking."

He tried to picture them walking the roads in his upscale town, carrying their big plastic bag. Definitely not a typical everyday sight. "How'd you know where to find me?"

"You're in the phone book," Vince said. "All we had to do was ask around for directions. Nice spread you got here, Sam."

"Thanks."

"Bet it's real nice, inside."

Sam controlled a rising sense of anger and frustration. He could thank his friend Harley for having blurted out his last name. . . What the hell business did they have coming to his home? But somehow, he felt safer playing it nice and laid back rather than getting nasty with them. He was alone with them and nobody knew they were there. He began to envision all sorts of lurid headlines. "Look. I already told you that you didn't have to feel obligated for the lunch. What's going on here with you two?"

"Sam, do you think . . ." She hesitated. "Sam, do you think we could come in and get cleaned up? We won't be any trouble."

Jesus! Now what? "What do you have in mind?"

"Could we . . . come in and take showers?"

"We'd really appreciate that, Sam," Vince added.

He repressed a strong wave of impatience. He really didn't want them in the house, but he could understand their need. . . . "There's a room above the garage with a bathroom that's got a shower. And there's towels and soap. Just bring your towels down to the laundry room when you finish."

"You're a good man, Sam," Vince said, looking like he'd just won something. "Let Loreen go up there first, and I'll keep working on these leaves."

"You don't have to. I have a service coming to do that."

"Save your money, Sam. Let me handle it."

"It's a big yard. You won't get very far doing it like that. And besides, you're about to run out of daylight."

"I can handle it."

Sam shrugged. "Well, if you insist on doing it, however far you get, you'll need a tarp to carry the leaves off into the woods down behind. I've got a tarp in the garage." Sam reached in his car door and operated the garage door remote. One of the doors rose. Another car, a Chrysler convertible, was parked inside. Sam pointed. "See that tarp? Right over there beyond my wife's car."

He watched Vince walk in, around the convertible, and over to where an array of tools and miscellany were stored, gazing around him, carefully taking in the other car and all the garage's other contents. Vince picked up the tarp and headed back to the yard.

"How do I get up to that room?" Loreen asked.

Sam pointed. "Through that door and up the stairs." He watched her as she walked to the door and started up the steps. Yes, she did fill out those jeans rather nicely. . . . But who in hell *were* these two people? Then he got into his Mercedes and drove it into the garage.

Inside the house, he went into the den and sat down at his desk to go through the mail. Most of it went directly into the wastebasket, but there were some dividend checks, which he endorsed and set aside to take to his broker's. And that done, he got into an easier chair and began reading the *Newsweek* that had also arrived. He heard a door open and approaching footsteps and was not surprised when she walked into the room, looking and smelling clean, scrubbed, and refreshed.

She gazed around as she entered, very impressed. "I just wanted to thank you again, Sam, for everything."

"It's okay." Something about her demeanor was patronizing, and he didn't like it. What was coming next? "Where's Vince?" he asked. "We need to talk about taking you two back to town."

"That's what I wanted to talk to you about. It's too dark outside for Vince to keep on the leaves, so he's cleaning up now, and . . . Sam, that room we're using up there has a double bed in it. And since it's dark, and there's not much we can do and no place we can go after dark, do you think we could stay there, tonight? I'll strip the bed in the morning and wash the sheets and make it back up, and do a little cleaning up around the house for you, and while I'm doing that, Vince can continue working on the leaves, and—"

"Hey, Loreen, hold it. All I wanted to do was buy you two lunch, and now you're moving in on me. What gives here?"

"Sam, you can't imagine how much we appreciate just being able to get cleaned up . . . and do you know how long it's been since we've slept in a nice bed? Even one night? And that room's just sitting there, not being used for anything. Sam, don't you think . . . ?"

How in hell had he managed to let them into his house? But they were there. She was being very very nice, but he didn't like or trust Vince even a little. He thought about calling the police. He knew the chief of police in the town, knew him well, in fact, but the chief wouldn't still be in his office, and if he called the number and asked for any kind of help, a car would show up with some young cop he didn't know. What would he say to him?

And if he didn't call, what was he going to do? Drive them back to the Post Road and leave them standing there in the dark?

If he let them stay, this not only let them into his house but also led to the next piece of business. Another meal, and then breakfast. Except for breakfast, he ate most of his meals out when Martha was in Florida. He ate at the club, or at one of a couple of restaurants that he liked but Martha didn't much care for. When Martha was home, they had a lady, Roberta, who came regularly and both cooked and cleaned. With Martha already in Florida, Roberta came once a week to clean, on Fridays. And Friday was four days away.

What to do for a meal? He wasn't going out to pick up something and leave them alone in his house. . . . Pizza. He'd ordered it a time or two before, when his grandsons were visiting. . . . "Okay, Loreen, you guys can use the room tonight, and I'll take you back over to town in the morning. I'll order some pizza for dinner."

"We'll never forget you for all your kindness to us."

"It's okay. Glad to help." He didn't like all the phony, bogus bullshit. All he wanted was to get through the next twelve hours and get them the hell out of there.

"I'll go tell Vince."

He ordered a couple of pizzas and then went to the kitchen and put three place settings on the table in the dining alcove: paper plates, knives and forks, a pile of paper napkins, and tall glasses, which he filled with ice. He set an unopened two-liter bottle of Coke on the table.

The pizzas arrived and they sat down around the table.

"Beautiful place you got here, Sam," Vince said.

"Thanks."

"Uh, don't you have any beer?" Vince asked.

"What's wrong with Coke?"

"Coke's okay, but I sure would like a beer or two with pizza."

"Well, sorry, you'll have to settle for Coke. We're fresh out of beer."

"No you're not. I saw some, there, in the fridge."

"When were you looking in the fridge?"

"A little while ago. I was looking for some cold water."

Were things getting a bit out of hand? Hopefully not. Besides, he liked beer with pizza himself. He looked at Loreen and forced a smile. "What kind of drunk is he? A sweet drunk, a rowdy drunk, or a nasty drunk?" He tried to say it with a light touch, just kidding around, but he was fishing for a clue. He did not like the idea of giving this man any alcohol.

"A sweet drunk," she said, almost too quickly. "In fact, he never gets drunk. . . . And, tell you the truth, we both kinda like beer with pizza."

Sam went to the fridge and got three cans of Heineken.

"The good stuff," Vince said with a nod. He got up and dumped the ice from his glass into the sink, and then did the same with the other two glasses. He sat back down and clearly enjoyed pouring the fancy imported beer into his glass. He took several swallows, groaned with pleasure, and wiped his mouth on his sleeve.

Sam watched as his dinner guests wolfed the pizzas and guzzled the beer. Vince got up without a word and took two more beers out of the fridge for himself and Loreen. This made Sam not just pissed but a little concerned. Vince seemed to be getting progressively more brusque as he drank, but nothing dramatic or overt. Nothing that spelled real danger. Sam watched Vince finally get up and help himself to the last of the six-pack in the fridge.

"You guys want some ice cream for dessert?" Sam asked. Maybe this would soak up some of the alcohol.

"Sure," Vince responded.

"Loreen, there's a half gallon of chocolate in the freezer, and you'll find bowls right up there, and spoons in that drawer." He pointed to each as he spoke.

Loreen served it in big portions, leaving the carton on the table, and it became a source of amusement to Sam to see how much food these two could consume. He'd had a total of two slices from the two large pizzas and both pies were finished. As he watched them attack the ice cream, he wondered if any of that would survive.

When they'd gotten their fill, Loreen returned the remnant of the ice cream to the freezer, cleared the table, putting everything in the sink, and then began washing the dishes. Sam showed her how to put things in the dishwasher, once they were scraped and rinsed clean.

"What are you gonna do, now?" Vince asked Sam.

Curious question. "Not much," Sam answered. "Watch a little TV for a while, and then, go to bed. See you in the morning."

"Hey, Sam, hold up. Mind if we watch with you?"

What could he say? No, you can't watch television with me? Just go to your room and stare at the walls, and be glad you've got a place to put your head down tonight? . . . What the hell? Another eight or ten hours and he'd be rid of them. . . . "Well, long as you like watching football. I watch football on Monday nights."

"That's fine. Me and Loreen love football."

They followed Sam, not missing a thing along the way as they gazed around them, until they came into his TV room, where Sam had several pieces of plush, relaxing furniture facing a giant-screen TV. Sam took his usual leather recliner, and Vince was fascinated by the deep, upholstered armchair he took that swiveled.

Loreen sat stretched out on a sofa. Yes, she wasn't a bad-looking woman. Nice lean flanks. And suddenly the presence of her full breasts inside that loose shirt became apparent. Martha's figure had surrendered to the invasion of cellulite years back. Eons, it seemed. Her limited interest in sex had disappeared, as well. And she occasionally commented on what she called "his fascination with bosoms and buns."

"Sam, where's the nearest bathroom?" Vince asked.

"What's wrong with the one you've been using?"

"I figured there was one closer."

Sam looked at him. *You couldn't use the one I'd already provided you? Too far to walk? Maybe sixty, seventy feet? Just make yourself at home, my esteemed guest . . .* Another few hours . . . "Through that door and to the right. You'll see it there, on your left. A little powder room." He wanted to try and be reasonably pleasant and sociable for the few more hours they'd be on his hands, but he wasn't finding it easy. He didn't like Vince.

The sound of Vince's exiting beer found its way back to where they were sitting. Vince hadn't bothered to close the door. The crude bastard! Jesus, couldn't he have just closed the door? Loreen tried to give the impression that she didn't hear it.

"Is there another bathroom I could use?" Loreen asked.

She couldn't wait until Vince got back and use the same one he used? Of course not. She wanted to see more of the house. "Uh, Loreen, through the door, there, and turn left. All of those bedrooms have their own baths."

She left and Sam followed her path by listening to her footsteps. She paused at every room and looked into it, then went . . . up the steps to the master bedroom? She was helping herself to an unescorted tour of the whole place. He thought briefly about Martha's jewelry but remembered that Martha always locked it up in the wall safe before leaving for Palm Beach.

They watched whatever ABC offered without much interest or conversation until time for the game, which featured America's Team, the Cowboys, against a lesser opponent, and as the intro for the game came on, Vince asked Sam if there was any more beer.

"We've had enough beer, Vince."

"A cold one goes awfully good with a football game, Sam. If you've got some more around."

Sam looked at Loreen and she smiled and nodded her assurance that it would be okay. Besides, he really liked a beer with the game himself, and Vince seemed to be behaving, so . . . A few more hours. Just a few more. Maybe it'd keep Vince sleeping better. "I think there's more in a fridge in the basement, Vince. I'll go take a look."

"Keep your seat, Sam. I'll go. Just tell me where." He was on his feet.

"The door to the basement steps is in the kitchen and the fridge is right at the bottom of the steps. You'll see it."

Vince left and returned with another six of Heineken. "You keep yourself well stocked, don't you, Sam? That thing was full." He handed one to Sam, one to Loreen, and popped the top on one for himself. He took several long swallows and then groaned his pleasured groan. They settled back to watch the game.

By the middle of the third quarter, the game had become a one-sided bore, and Sam suggested they give it up. He wanted to go to bed. They reluctantly accepted this. Sam had had one of the beers, Loreen, one, and Vince, three. Vince took the remaining one with him. Sam went up the steps to the master bedroom. . . . Just a few more hours. . . .

Sam's light sleep was disturbed by a deflection of the mattress, as if someone had just sat down on the edge of the bed, behind him. He froze in the total darkness, his heartbeat accelerating. He'd locked the bedroom door, but the lock was only a privacy lock, easy to open from the other side with a small screwdriver, or even a bobby pin. Martha'd wanted the lock to keep the grandchildren out when she napped.

Was he about to feel a blade at his throat? Whoever was there was between him and the bedside night table under which he'd hung a holster that held a fancy little handgun. Should he try to quickly shove whoever was there and go for the gun? . . .

"Sam?" A tentative whisper.

It was Loreen.

He took a deep breath and rolled over on his back. He raised himself on his elbows. "What the hell are you doing in here?"

"I just came to pay you a little visit. You know, to show my appreciation for how nice you've been to us." Her voice was different. It was quiet and throaty, not the patronizingly saccharine small talk he'd been hearing all day.

"Are you out of your head? Get the hell out of my bedroom!"

"Come on, Sam. Don't try and tell me you don't like the idea of my being here. I've seen the way you've been looking at me all day. Besides, I like you, Sam. You're a nice man." She put her hands on his chest and began running them over him, his chest, shoulders, arms . . . "Hey, Sam, are these pajamas silk? They are, aren't they?"

He flung her hands away. "Will you get outta here?"

She put her hands back on him. "Real silk. God, what class!" She put her hands back on him and moved them down toward his belly.

He grabbed her hands again and threw them aside. "Will

you get the hell out of here? What about your husband? What if he wakes up and finds you not there? I think you'd better go back to him."

She put her hands back on Sam once again and began massaging sensuously. "To begin with, he's not my husband. And second, he doesn't own me. And third, he ain't gonna wake up. He's dead to the world. All that beer he had? . . . Sam, when was the last time you had yourself a great time in the rack? I'm talking a really great time. Come on. Be honest. I've seen the picture of your wife, downstairs."

"Martha's a lovely lady."

"I'm sure she is, Sam. And she's really hot, too. Right?"

He couldn't think of a snappy reply to that. "Listen, I appreciate your wanting to be so nice to me, but you get the hell out of here and back where you belong. Go on."

"Like you really want me to. Right?"

"Right. You've got no business in here."

She slid her hands inside his pajamas and leaned over and nibbled his earlobe. "Come on, Sam," she whispered. "I can see you don't mean it. And don't worry. I even brought a condom so you wouldn't have to worry about anything. And you wouldn't have, anyway, because I know how to take care of myself. Now, relax, Sam, and have a night to remember. What've you got to lose? Vince is out of it, and your wife's not here. . . . God. Silk. Pure silk. . . . Here, lemme help you out of those. . . . Easy. . . . Let's don't rip the buttons off." Her breath in his ear affected him despite himself as she began fumbling with the drawstring on his bottoms.

"Uh-oh, Sam, I think it got knotted."

"Don't worry about it." He yanked them off without untying it. "What are *you* wearing?" he asked.

"Nothing but a tee shirt, and I'm gonna be out of that in about two seconds."

He held his breath and felt his pulse accelerate as he listened to the wispy sound of the cotton tee being peeled off her body in the darkness.

"Come on, Sam. Move over a little. . . . That's it, sugar."
Her feet were a bit chilly, but the rest of her . . .

He smelled coffee when he came downstairs. He walked
into the kitchen and they were there. He looked at Vince to
see what he could read in his face, but couldn't tell anything
for sure.

Loreen, all sweetness and light again, said, "I found some
eggs and some cheese, so I'm making eggs and cheese.
Sound good?"

He seldom ate eggs. It was usually orange juice and instant oatmeal, and maybe a cup of instant coffee. "Don't
make me much of that." He got himself a glass of juice.
She'd set the table and he saw toast sticking out of the
toaster.

They sat down and he managed a few bites of the eggs but
wasn't impressed with her cooking. And that was a major
understatement. He had some of the toast and coffee. . . .
Just a little while longer. . . . "Okay, now that we've had
breakfast, where in town do you two want me to drop you
this morning? Back over there where I found you?"

"That's not what we had in mind, Sam," Vince said
quietly.

"What's that supposed to mean?"

"I think we'll be staying here a while."

"You'll what?"

"I think we'll be staying here."

"You don't have that option, Vince. Hear what I'm saying? Now, look. I've provided you two with three meals, a
night's lodging, drinks, and entertainment, and that's it.
Let's get you back out there where you can be on your way.
I told you yesterday after lunch that I never expected to see
you again. And you showed up here. What the hell's going
on here, Vince?"

"Sam, you're gonna *like* what we have in mind. We're
gonna stay here and help you out. Make your life easier.
We'll work around the place, inside and out, and between

us, handle most anything. Cooking, housekeeping, outside work. You're gonna be pleased as punch."

"Forget it, Vince. C'mon, get your stuff together and I'll be pleased as punch to take you back to town, wherever you like, and that's it." He was firm but kept his voice quiet; he didn't want a dangerous situation to develop, and he was becoming a little unnerved.

"Sam, why don't I talk it over with Martha?"

What? "What are you talking about?"

"I already had a little chat with her this morning. But I didn't tell her about anything much. Like some of your *late night* activities. Or where I was calling from. At least not yet."

Sam felt sick. Like he'd taken a boot in the solar plexus. "You called Martha? Where'd you get the number?"

"Off your little bulletin board here in the kitchen. And just so I wouldn't lose it, I wrote it in permanent ink across my belly. But don't worry about it, Sam. I'm sure we'll work something out, and maybe I won't have to call her again."

He looked at Loreen and she was smiling. A winner's smile. . . . So that was the way it was. This would take some thought, but no precipitous action, at least for the moment. He got up and walked out of the room, his fists clenched.

He couldn't leave the house. Not even to shop for groceries. He didn't want to leave them alone in it. And he certainly wouldn't give either of them a car and money to go off shopping. He'd just order everything from "Tiffany's," the small supermarket known by that nickname for very good quality stuff and even better prices. Tiffany's delivered.

Since he was less than impressed with Loreen's culinary skills, he ordered simple foods, deli for lunches, and steaks and chops, which he'd grill, and potatoes, which even she could bake. And desserts. Pies and ice cream. And beer by the case.

He spent time watching the Market on cable and talking to his broker by phone, reading the *Times,* and sitting around, watching other stuff on television. The days dragged. He was a prisoner in his own house. He didn't want to get the cops involved, even though he knew the chief. Most everything that happened in town requiring police involvement found its way into the town's weekly, and often into the New Haven *Register.* He didn't want that. . . . And there was always the fact that Palm Beach could be reached by phone.

The beautiful weather held and Vince would go out and disappear, always taking a few beers with him. Loreen lolled around, doing little, often disappearing into some room where there was a TV. She seemed to love running the laundry. Apparently, washing towels made her feel like she was taking care of the house. . . . He had to think about what to do with them. . . . And, do it soon!

"Sam, here's your mail."

"Vince, just do *your* stuff and let me get the mail. Okay?"

"I thought I'd do you a favor and save you the walk down to the mailbox."

"Don't do me that favor. I happen to *like* the walk down to the mailbox."

He didn't want Vince to be seen at the road. And what if Vince knew how to recognize the window envelopes that contained checks. "Wanta do me a favor, Vince? Just get the leaves done."

"I've got that under control. It'll get done."

"It's got to." He wanted to call his landscape service and have them come and do it, but what would he have left to keep Vince occupied?

"Vince, I've got another job for you. Know how to split logs into firewood with a wedge and maul?"

"Sure, I can do that. Like I told you, I can do anything."

"There's a big oak down near the edge of the lawn in back. It's been cut into logs, but they need splitting. Think you can handle that? You'll find the wedge and maul in the garage."

"I'll take care of it."

"You're still a long way from finishing the leaves."

"It'll all get done. Don't worry about it."

Always that cocky assurance, and the man didn't do squat.

"Sam, me and Loreen're gonna move from that little room over the garage into one of the bedrooms here in the house."

"Is that so?"

"Yeah. That bed's too small for the two of us. We got used to a king-size when we had our own place. And this one's also not too comfortable. And besides, sleeping over the garage makes us feel like outsiders. You don't want that, do you? One of the bedrooms off the hall, here, has got a king-size bed, and a TV. And a *nice* bathroom. And nobody else is using it. So we're moving, today."

"Is that so?" He had to think of something! He had to get them out of his house!

"Don't make yourself too comfortable," he said in a quiet voice, after Vince had left him.

"What *are* these, Sam?" Loreen asked.

"They're veal chops. Rib veal chops."

"They must be two inches thick. I never saw any kinda chops anything like this. And you really cooked 'em good."

"And you did a nice job baking the potatoes, Loreen."

Vince got up from the table and got himself another Heineken.

"How're you coming with the work outside, Vince? The leaves aren't up, yet. What gives?"

"Everything's coming along nicely."

"And the log splitting?"

"Don't bust a gut, Sam. I'm dividing my time between that and the leaves. It'll all get done in due time."

He hadn't done much of anything with the leaves. What

did he do out there besides drink beer? Sam clenched a fist so tightly beneath the table that his hand ached. He had to get rid of them!

"Sam, I've been thinking. We've been here a few days now, and working very hard, and I feel like we should be paid for all the stuff we're doing. A person needs a little money in their jeans or they don't feel like a person. You know that. Right?"

Now they want to be paid for accepting free room and board. What next? "That's interesting, Vince. Tell me what you have in mind."

"I was thinking two hundred a week apiece, for now. That'd be about right. Maybe later on, when we get a better handle on what needs to be done around here, I might want to negotiate a little better deal for us. How's that sound?"

Like rape. He had to get them out of there! He took out his wallet and removed four one-hundred-dollar bills. He handed two to each of them. "That'll hold you for a week."

"And, Sam," Vince said, stuffing the two bills into his shirt pocket, "when do you plan to head south to be with Martha?"

"Don't know, just yet. Why?" What was he up to, now?"

"Because I decided that what we're gonna do is stay here while you're gone and take care of the place for you over the winter. That way you won't have to worry about a thing. I'm sure you'll like that, and I know Martha'd agree. And we can even run the other car every once in a while. You know, it's not good to leave a car standing around without ever running it. 'Specially in the winter. You can just mail us our money."

Now they planned to spend the winter playing house in his house with a fancy new convertible to drive around and four hundred a week to spend on food and drink. They'd probably even move into the master bedroom. "I don't think that'll be necessary, Vince. We've been leaving the house in the winter for years with no problems."

"I think you need to take advantage of my offer, Sam. Maybe I'll call Martha and discuss it with her."

"I don't want you calling my wife, again, Vince. Ever. Okay?"

"Well, then you better think seriously about my offer, Sam."

He had been thinking seriously about the situation. And he had to come up with something. Soon! "I'm going to do that, Vince. I'm going to think about it."

They hadn't called Martha and identified themselves. At least, not yet. He called her at night, every couple of days, and she never mentioned them. But he believed they'd called the number to check it out, and were holding the threat over his head. He didn't want them carrying out that threat.

He lay in bed, wide-eyed, unable to sleep, staring into the darkness, his face hot, radiating the heat of total frustration over what to do about getting rid of his boarders . . . his house staff.

His thoughts skittered back to the time he'd spent in Vietnam, and he recalled his first time he was positive he'd been solely responsible for a kill. It had been a strange sensation. The next time it happened, and each time after that, it became a little less strange. He came home from there with a profoundly changed sense of appreciation for weapons and what they could do.

After returning home, he married Martha and got into the family business, the lumberyard, and took up hunting for recreation. Killing a deer got to be practically kid stuff. Bringing down that moose—now that had been excitement! And he thoroughly enjoyed stopping off in Tennessee, on his annual drive to Florida, to shoot ducks with old army friends. What great fun! Just aim and squeeze and watch 'em flutter to the ground. . . .

He sat up in bed, turned on the TV, and flipped from channel to channel for a couple of hours, watching one thing and another, until his brain finally cooled down a little. Then he put his head back down and managed to get some sleep.

He *had* to make a run into town. His broker had some important papers for him to sign, right away, in front of a notary. He had his usual juice, toast, and coffee, and left the two of them packing away messy-looking bacon and eggs. He drove toward New Haven, and some ten minutes along the way, realized that in his haste, he'd forgotten some dividend checks and other papers he'd meant to take with him. He headed back home. He wasn't worried about the checks; he felt sure that if Vince got into them, he had the brains to see that they were already endorsed for deposit at his broker's.

When he reached the house, Loreen wasn't anywhere downstairs. She was usually doing laundry or wandering around, looking like she wanted to think the place was hers. "Playing house." He went into the hall and heard their voices. They were upstairs in the master bedroom, laughing and talking loudly because no one else was there.

He walked quietly up the carpeted steps and into the master bedroom, taking them totally by surprise. Vince was stretched out across Martha's favorite satin bedspread, his filthy shoes on the bed, the beer in his hand also resting on the bed. Loreen was going through drawers.

"Sam!" Loreen gasped. She looked at Vince, who quickly sat up and dropped his feet over the side of the bed.

"Looking for anything in particular?"

"Oh God, Sam, I'm so embarrassed, but you know I'd never bother anything. Just looking. Everything's so beautiful."

"Let me make you two an offer. I'll give you a thousand dollars apiece to leave here and never come back." He watched Loreen look at Vince to see how he was going to respond.

"Thanks, Sam, for the offer," Vince began, over the shock of Sam's sudden appearance, "but I think we'll stay here. I really like the idea of being able to stay around and take care of things for you and Martha over the winter."

"Let me sweeten the offer. I'll make it two thousand apiece."

"I think we'll still settle for the two hundred a week and the chance to be of help to you, Sam."

"Here's my final offer. Three thousand apiece. You think about that one. That's a lot of money between the two of you."

"That is a good offer, Sam, but I still say we'd rather stay here, being of service, for just our little money every week." Then, Vince winked at him.

"You're missing out on a very good deal, Vince. I hope you know that."

Vince shrugged and didn't bother to comment or remove the half smile from his face.

"Well, I've still got to make the quick trip into New Haven. See you later. And incidentally, Loreen, if you find something up here you really want, check with me later and maybe I'll let you keep it." Sam smiled, watching this line take them by surprise.

Sam left for town. It was time to do something before *they* did something. Get them before they got him. He was ready to go to Florida, and it was duck-hunting season in Tennessee. And he wasn't about to leave them in his house all winter, and pay them money to stay there and enjoy themselves.

Sam was hungry when he returned from town. He went into the kitchen and fixed himself a good sandwich, something he'd found that Loreen couldn't do. As he thought about it, neither of them could do much of anything, and neither seemed to have a trace of a work ethic. He'd worked his own ass off during his years running the lumberyard.

He wasn't surprised they'd been fired from some factory in Boston. Assuming their story was true. If they worked for him he'd fire them in a minute. . . . They'd been good, though, at setting up a little scam for taking him. They'd done that beautifully. Whoever heard of panhandlers turning down six thousand dollars?

After eating the sandwich with a beer, he decided to take a walk around the property and see what Vince was doing. He went outside, into the brilliant sunlight. October and November, so far, had been perfect, the fall colors spectacular. He often wondered why Martha rushed to Florida so early. She was missing the best part of the year. And he missed her.

The leaves needed doing. Vince had hardly started. If they weren't up by the first snowfall, the lawn would be wrecked. He walked down toward the back of the grounds and, as he approached the oak logs to be split, got a good look at just what Vince's work ethic was. Vince was sleeping in the sun, his head resting on one of the logs, his arms folded on his chest. The maul was beside him, its handle also resting on the log. Three empty beer cans lay nearby.

Suddenly Sam's pulse began to pick up speed. The time had come. A complete plan popped into his head. This was it!

He looked in all directions. He could not be seen from anywhere. Not even from the house. And no one knew the two of them were there. *This was it!* He walked right up to Vince and Vince didn't so much as blink. He reached down and picked up the maul, not trying to do it quietly, and still Vince didn't stir. He felt the heft of the maul. It was heavy, but he could still handle it. His heart was pounding. *This was it!* Could he do it?

He walked around behind Vince and set his feet. He was in the batter's box . . . Or on the first tee. . . He brought the maul all the way back and then, with all his strength, swung it down, feeling bone give way under the mass of dark curly hair on Vince's head; the experience was a sensation suggestive of hitting a pumpkin. Vince's limbs jerked violently with the blow and then shuddered a few times before falling still. His eyes and mouth came open. . . . .

A good clean kill. No real mess. A little blood in Vince's

mouth. Now that he was started, he wanted to move quickly. And think clearly. Not overlook anything. He reached into Vince's shirt pocket and took back his two hundred dollars. Vince wouldn't be needing it. He pulled out his own shirttail and polished the maul, head and handle, and the wedge. He picked up the beer cans. He had a large bag of those to take to the supermarkets and feed to the recycling crushers.

And now for Loreen. His .22 target pistol came to mind. After all the TV he'd watched and the detective novels he'd read about nice clean gang killings, it sounded like just the ticket. He went into the garage, left the wedge and maul, and pulled the three beer cans out of his pockets, dropping them into the big garbage bag of returns.

He moved down the back steps into the basement recreation room where his hunting arsenal was stored. He got the gun out, dropped the clip, inserted a few rounds, and shoved the clip back into place. He noticed a small first aid kit among the hunting stuff and picked out the largest Band-Aid he could find. He dropped this into his pocket.

Loreen was in the laundry, pulling a load of towels out of the dryer, and as he walked toward her, his right hand behind his back, she looked at him curiously, as if she couldn't quite make any sense of the expression on his face.

"Sam?"

He walked right up to her, and with his hand shaking, abruptly jammed the gun under her chin, aimed upward, and fired two quick shots. She crumpled to the floor. He looked her over. Good job. The bullets had not come out. He fumbled in his pocket for the Band-Aid, managed to get it unwrapped and stripped, and stretched it over the entry hole. He wanted no blood anywhere. He worked his hand into her tight jeans pocket and found *her* two hundreds.

He went into the garage, got a couple of heavy sections of the *Times* out of the recycle basket, and lined the trunk of his Mercedes. Then, back to Loreen.

The phone!

He walked uneasily into the kitchen to answer it. "Hello?" He could see Loreen from where he was standing.

"Sam, how's my friend, that benefactor of the down-trodden?"

It was Harley Spence. Sam took a couple of deep breaths. "I'm fine, Harley. What can I do for ya'?"

"You sound out of breath. I catch you at a bad time?"

He took another deep breath. "No, I'm fine. What's up?"

"Haven't seen you around much, lately. What'cha been up to?"

"My usual. Watching the Market. Getting ready to head south."

"What'd you do with those street people after you fed them?"

"I sent them on their way."

"You're too much, Sam. You know that? Listen, we haven't seen you in a while, and I know you're alone, with Martha in Palm Beach, so I called to invite you to have dinner with Letitia and me at the club, tonight. Whatta ya say?"

That would fit quite nicely into things. And he could use a good meal, for a change. "I'd be delighted, Harley. What time?"

"Drinks at seven?"

"See you then."

He returned to Loreen, dragged her into the garage, hoisted her torso over the rim of the trunk of the Mercedes, then her legs, and closed the trunk. He backed the car out of the garage and headed across the grounds toward the woods behind, thankful the place was as big as it was. How would he explain to someone passing why he was driving his Mercedes around the yard? He reached Vince and struggled with Vince's limp body. He now had just about a full trunk of dead blackmailing panhandlers. He pulled a scrap of newspaper from under them, wadded it up, and stuffed it in Vince's mouth. No bloodstains in the trunk, please.

He drove back to the garage, went into the house, and sat down to make a list. He had a bunch of stuff to get done in one afternoon if he was to be on his way south that night: pack a few things, stop by the post office and leave his change-of-address card, take all the beer cans to a supermarket and crush them, call the landscape service to get them on the leaves, clean all perishables out of the fridge, run the dishwasher, cut off the water to the outside faucets, put the thermostats on the winter settings, go over the house for all of *their* stuff and throw it into a Salvation Army Dumpster somewhere, wash the linens they'd been using and make the room back up, notify the alarm company and the town's police that he'd be leaving so they'd know to keep an eye on things for him, and what else? . . . Call his friends in Tennessee and check on the duck hunting. . . .

He declined valet parking when he got to his country club. He didn't think he'd leave his keys with them. But he gave the boys a couple of bucks tip anyway, since he knew them all so well.

The evening just hit the spot. A few good Scotches with hors d'oevres, followed by a perfect steak dinner and a fine red wine. His first good meal in a while. He could hardly believe how relaxed he was, considering the contents of his trunk, and Harley's jabbering to Letitia about how he'd taken a couple of homeless types to lunch.

He left the club after ten, drove to the Wilbur Cross Parkway, headed south to I-287 westbound, and onto the Tappan Zee Bridge. Bridge traffic was light at that hour, as he'd expected, and when he reached the middle of the structured section, he slowed down almost to a stop, lowered a window, and heaved the target pistol, into the middle of the great wide Hudson, just past the truss superstructure. Let them find it there.

After the bridge, he drove until he came to the exit for the Palisades Parkway, southbound. He was headed for a perfect spot he remembered, one of the parkway's secluded, off-the-road, high-bluff overlooks, facing the river. It was nearly midnight when he made the U-turn and pulled into the unlit area.

And almost before he could decide which way to position the car, a Highway Patrol car roared up to him, seemingly from out of nowhere.

The trooper got out of his car and came walking over. He shined a flashlight into the car and into Sam's face.

Sam lowered his window.

"What are you doing in here at this hour?" the cop asked. "These are for daytime use."

"Uh, officer, I was driving down the parkway and getting a little sleepy and decided I needed to take a snooze before I fell asleep at the wheel. I was afraid to stop on the road, out there."

The trooper looked around the back seat with his flashlight. "Is that a weapon in back, there, in that leather case?"

"Yes, it is, officer. A shotgun. I'm on my way down to Tennessee to go duck hunting with friends."

"May I see your license and registration? And step out of the car, please."

Sam got the registration out of the glove compartment and climbed out of the car. He was beginning to get a little shaky.

The trooper examined them. "Champion. Champion. Sounds familiar. . . . That wouldn't be that big lumberyard by any chance? I used to live up that way."

"My sons run it now."

The trooper's tone changed. "Small world. I used to buy a lot of stuff there. Mr. Champion, I wouldn't recommend staying here very long at this hour."

Sam managed a smile. "Matter of fact, I think I'm awake enough now that I can make it onto the Jersey Turnpike and rest at one of the rest stops there."

"Good idea, Mr. Champion." Then, with a chuckle, "*You* wouldn't have anything in your trunk you wouldn't want me to know about. Right?"

Sam felt faint. "Just more luggage and stuff."

"Have a good time duck hunting, Mr. Champion." He walked back to his car and roared out of the area, onto the parkway.

Sam was trembling when he got back into his car. *Did he dare still unload there? . . . Did he? . . . He didn't know of anyplace else!*

He started the car and maneuvered around until it was parallel to the large rocks near the edge of the cliff. He cut the engine. And then his pulse really began to flood. He just sat for a few minutes. What if someone else showed up? . . . Not at that hour. And the trooper had left. He wouldn't come right back. Sam pulled the trunk release.

Shaking like a leaf, he managed to get Loreen's body over the rim of the trunk, onto the ground. He dragged it to the edge of the cliff and pushed it over, into free fall in the darkness. Judging from the sound, it dropped a long way before hitting anything. Hopefully, it would disappear into the brush and not be noticed; too bad the leaves were disappearing from the trees. He went back for Vince and, struggling harder because he was heavier, sent him after Loreen.

He drove out of the area and to the New Jersey Turnpike. He pulled off at the first rest stop and cleaned the newspapers out of the trunk, throwing them into a trash receptacle. Then he went inside and had coffee. He'd get the car cleaned and vacuumed when he got to Florida.

He returned to the turnpike and drove for a while longer. Spotting a motel sign, he got off and took a room for the night.

The duck-hunting season proved to be one of the best ever. From there it was on to Palm Beach and their condominium at the Biltmore, where Martha immediately dragged him kicking and screaming into her usual social whirl. She seemed to know everyone there, just as she did in their circle back in Connecticut.

Vince and Loreen had almost completely disappeared from his thoughts when, a few days before Christmas, a local plainclothes cop came to call, escorting a detective from New Jersey.

"Mr. Champion, we're investigating a couple of homicides involving two people who were found . . ."

Sam found it hard to listen. He absolutely didn't want to hear it. He hoped it didn't show on his face. That or the fact that he was trembling.

". . . and the reason we wanted to talk to you is that the male of the two had an envelope in his pocket containing a rather large check made out to you. A dividend check, I understand. We contacted your chief of police, who helped us find you down here."

Think! Keep your wits about you! "You know," Sam said, "the two you describe sound like a couple of homeless I befriended and bought lunch for at a Burger King"—*Harley saw me there*—"back one day in Milford. Afterward, they showed up at the house, looking for work, and he must have taken the check out of my mailbox. I'd been wondering about whether I wasn't supposed to be receiving that check, now that you mention it.

"Since it was late that day, I fed them pizza"—*Domino's may have a record of the order for two large pizzas*—"and let them stay overnight in our servants' quarters, and sent them on their way the next day. And now, I find out, I did all this after he'd taken a check out of my mailbox. What do you think of that?"

The New Jersey detectives seemed impressed that Sam had been so kind to a couple of homeless, but he caught a glimpse of Martha raising an eyebrow and shaking her head when she heard this. She apparently couldn't believe her husband had done anything like that. The detective asked more questions, but not in a manner suggesting he might consider Sam a suspect, and the two cops finally left.

Sam felt a little ill. Vince and Loreen weren't out of his life just yet. *If the case came to the attention of that highway trooper, and it probably would, he could place Sam on that overlook, late at night!* Were there any other details he'd forgotten? He'd found no blood or other traces of any kind in the trunk after getting to Florida. What about the excessive quantities of food and beer he'd ordered from Tiffany's over the days preceding the scene on the overlook? Not typical of any past shopping pattern. And his total absence from the club, and his broker's, over that same stretch of days. . . . *And, oh, God! Had Vince really written the Palm Beach phone number on his belly? And was it still legible when they found him? . . .* Maybe Vince had been bluffing. Wouldn't the cops have mentioned that? Had they missed it? . . . Or were the cops playing cat and mouse? . . . He wasn't going to be sleeping too well for a while. . . .

If he became a suspect, and all of this stuff came out, and possibly more stuff he hadn't yet thought of, could he beat the rap? Maybe. With a very good lawyer. Or team of lawyers. Everything was circumstantial and coincidental. Yes, maybe he'd beat it. But not without a great deal of notoriety and expense, neither of which was among his favorite things. . . .

And all because he'd taken a couple of homeless to lunch.

THE SCREAM

DOROTHY SALISBURY DAVIS

SALLY HAD CALLED him a "mother's boy" when he wanted to leave the party at eleven. It hurt and angered him, but what angered him most was that he hadn't left right then. He stayed on as though that was going to change her feelings toward him. She'd turned her attention to guys he didn't even know and didn't think she did. She said she'd hitch a ride in one of the other cars. Now he was really late. He drove up the ravine trail furiously, scattering stones and gravel, ripping through the bramble. Midnight wasn't late for that gang, even on a school night, even though they'd lost the beer to the cops who had intercepted them on the way down. He had an old-fashioned mother who pretended she wasn't a single parent. Sometimes she told people her husband was away on business. But sometimes, when she and David were alone, she would call him the man of the house and say how much she depended on him.

As soon as he cleared the park drive he opened up the Chevy. He'd got in the habit of worrying about his mother when he didn't get home on time. This angered him, too. What he worried about was her worrying about him, and it made him feel tied up. Or down. He kept flooring the accelerator until he turned off the highway onto a two-way short-cut via the old County Road.

He thought of Sally and the guy who'd been trying to

make out with her when David took off. He was a wimp. David hated him. Sally seemed to like wimps. She had an overload of energy and breasts like ice cream cones. He hit top speed again. Nobody used the County Road except the locals. With not a car in sight, he reached into his breast pocket and fished out the orange packet. He rolled down the window thinking, One more for the road: his joke on himself. He had yet to use one of the damn things in a real situation, yet to suggest to Sally or any other woman that he had one in his pocket. He threw it out against the wind and felt immediately that it might have blown back into the car. He glanced around. In less than a breath of time he turned back to the road. A car, dead ahead, no lights, had stopped half on the pavement, half on the shoulder. He swerved across the middle line, then starting to careen, he let the wheel take control. The Chevy swung back and he saw the woman coming around in front of the parked car. He saw her scream. Didn't hear it. Her face, the mouth wide, seemed to zoom at him. He pulled the car away from her and fought to control it by acceleration. The woman flung herself against her car, sandwiched between it and the Chevy when he passed. He got command, his hands frozen around the steering wheel. He was faint with fear, but he hadn't hit her. He was sure of it. He would have heard something, a thump, a noise, something, if he had. He was sure of it. He did not stop.

"Davie, is that you? Are you just getting in?"

"I've been downstairs for a while," he lied. He squeezed the words through a dry, tight throat.

"Then you should have finished your studies before you went out."

"I know." At her bedroom door he said, "Good night, mother."

"I need a kiss," she said, and when he brushed her forehead with his lips, "Now I'll be able to sleep."

He drew the door almost closed. The cat wriggled through

and followed him down the hall. It wove itself between his legs in the bathroom and then rubbed against him when he sat on the edge of his bed to take off his sneakers. As soon as he removed one, the cat jumped it and worried its head into the toe.

"Allie, it stinks!" He buried his face in the crook of his arm. "Like me."

He woke up before he finished the Our Father. In the next second the spiraling plane would have hit the ground. He lay, abruptly wide awake, knowing what he had dreamt, and wondered why he had not been scared. He'd felt calm and oblivious to the other passengers, who were also about to die. "Forgive us our trespasses . . ." Suddenly he remembered the face he'd kept seeing while he lay in bed last night, unable to fall asleep, the scream he couldn't hear. If he looked at the wall now he would see it again. If he closed his eyes he would see it. He wrenched himself out of bed. Every bone in his body ached. Every muscle was taut.

His mother called to him from downstairs wanting to know if he was up. She had called him before and he had fallen back into sleep, into the dream. He leaned over the banister and shouted down that he'd be ready in ten minutes. In the shower he told himself that he must go back to where it happened. What good would it do now? He couldn't have hurt her. She'd have been scared, fainted maybe. But how could he *not* have hurt her? With him going at that speed, the wind could have pulled her to him. But he'd have known it, felt it. And if he had, wouldn't he have stopped? He had not stopped. That was why he had to go back.

David resembled his mother. He was slight, with straight, tawny hair, very blue eyes. The sharp, delicate features made him feel that he looked like a choir boy. He'd got in the habit of pulling down the corners of his mouth. Tough guy, his mother said of it once, which was exactly what he wanted. The one thing he didn't want now was his mother getting a good look at his bloodshot eyes. "I had an awful dream before I woke up," he said. It might explain or distract.

She sat, her chin in her hand, and watched him pour milk shakily into his cornflakes, not seeming to notice anything different in him from other mornings. She was dressed for work, waiting for her ride to arrive any minute. "Want to sort it out?" she said.

"I was going down in a plane crash. There were lots of people screaming, but I wasn't scared." He'd made up the screaming part. He couldn't remember them screaming.

"What else do you remember? Little things," she coaxed. She liked to interpret his dreams for him. She had done it since he was a little kid, a game he kind of liked.

Now he wished he hadn't mentioned this one. "I woke up before we crashed."

"If you weren't scared, what were your feelings?"

He shrugged. "Like philosophical. I said the Our Father." He pushed away from the table. "Mom, I got to go. Professor Joseph always calls first on the kids who come in at the last minute. We call him Sneaky Joe."

"You miss your father. That's what your dream's about."

"Yeah." He got up. The cornflakes barely touched, he put the dish on the floor for the cat.

"Why don't you write and tell him that, Davie?"

Again he shrugged.

"I know you could tell him things you don't tell me," his mother said.

"Okay, Mom, I'll do that." He was desperate to get away from her. He couldn't even manage the usual peck on the cheek.

"Are you going to be all right to drive?" she called after him.

"Why not?" Each day he drove the twenty miles to St. Mary's College, picking up two classmates on the way.

"You're jittery. You're working too hard. You ought not to work late at night. Your sleep's important, Davie. You're still growing."

"Yes, Mother. Yes!" If only her ride would come. He wanted to call his passengers and tell them they had to get to school on their own that morning. It would commit him to going back there.

She called after him: "I have pot roast in the Crock-Pot if you'd like to bring someone home to dinner."

He was shocked at the scratches on the fender and the door when he first saw the car in daylight. It must have happened going down or coming up from the water's edge. Going down he'd been concentrating on Sally's hand getting nearer and nearer his thigh. And then the Sheriff's Patrol had stopped the three cars and confiscated the beer. The cops had made them get out of the cars, and they asked each one if they had any joints or other dope. They hadn't searched anybody. Sally said afterward that if the deputy had laid a finger on her, her father would have had his badge by morning. Some of the other boys went to St. Mary's too, which had turned coeducational recently. Like him they were day students, but they were upperclassmen. One of the deputies had flashed his torch in David's face and then asked to see his driver's license. He couldn't believe David was a college student. Sally tittered. She didn't say it then, but later— mother's boy. He took a chamois to the scratches and turned up the local station on the radio. The only traffic incident reported was a three-car crash on the interstate. He'd bet no one ran away from that one.

The macadam was still silvery from the overnight frost when he turned onto County Road. Tire tracks crisscrossed and then disappeared where the sun's first rays skimmed the surface. The temptation to turn back was getting to him. He made himself go on, one road sign to the next. He reached the underpass beneath the suburban railway. Then he lost his nerve. He turned around beneath the arch and headed for school.

It was too late to go to his first class. In the library he asked at the desk if he could see the *County Sentinel,* not yet on the shelf. The librarian wanted to know if he had a hot number. The lottery. "Look, you never know," David said.

He went through the paper column by column. "Crime Watch": "The Sheriff's Patrol reported no arrests, significant crimes or serious accidents." He was disappointed. Crazy, but that was how he felt. He returned the paper and headed for his second class. It struck him then: the accident on the interstate had not been reported either. It was too soon. But not for it to have been on the radio. Could that mean that nothing very serious had happened on County Road? But something had happened. Suppose he never found out. He didn't think he'd forget it. But say that woman wasn't supposed to be where she was, it was a stolen car maybe, and say that by a miracle she wasn't hurt, or suppose there was someone in the car she wasn't supposed to be with, say someone dragged her into the car afterward. Maybe she *was* hurt. Or dead. If she had banged her head, say, on her own car, he wouldn't have heard that, would he? Just because he hadn't heard anything didn't mean nothing happened. All morning he kept turning over in his mind different possibilities, knowing that only one of them, or maybe none, was so. His imagination would not let go. He was such a good liar, why couldn't he lie to himself? He ought to keep track of the lies he told. A priest once said to him about confession, "Don't simply pick a number as though it's a lottery." Which was exactly what he used to do.

Lying was his big problem from when he was a little kid. It always surprised him that people, his mother for example, took for granted he was telling the truth. Or did they pretend, too? Pretend they believed him. During his first session with the St. Mary's student advisor they'd had a long talk on why people lied, even professional liars like spies, and what it did to a man's character to lie habitually. Women did it for fun, the advisor said, and then added quickly that he was making a joke. David wasn't sure. But he wound up taking as his elective the Christian Ethics course the advisor recommended. His mother was pleased. Someone told her Father Moran would be supportive. Of a student with a father absent from home David supposed, though nobody said it to him.

He kept making up excuses to himself to skip ethics class that afternoon. He didn't want to blurt out something he couldn't explain. The kids taking the class were hound dogs on the scent for heresy. Some of them had flunked out of seminary and were going through a kind of rehab. Father Moran paid them special attention. The Church needed more priests and nuns to make up for the dropouts. Father Moran was one of the few religious on the faculty and probably wouldn't have lasted at St. Mary's till now if there wasn't the shortage.

David kept returning to his car all morning to catch the local news on the radio. He was nauseous, and in the mirror he looked as pale as a boiled potato. In the mirror, behind his own face, was the image of a man approaching, looking, David thought, at the license numbers of the cars as he worked his way through the parking lot. David felt in his bones the man was looking for him. He switched off the radio.

The stranger wore an out-of-date polo coat that was too big for him and a slouch hat that made his face look small, his features pinched, mean. He stooped to look in at David and took a quick survey of the inside of the car at the same time. He pushed his hat back and gestured that he wanted David to roll his window down. Reluctantly David obliged.

The man couldn't smile. The attempt was like a nervous tic. "You're David Crowley, right? I'm Dennis McGraw." He handed David his business card:

DENNIS HENRY MCGRAW
ATTORNEY-AT-LAW

"I'm an associate of Deputy Sheriff Addy Muller's. Deputy Muller was on the welcoming committee when you and your friends went down to the beach last night." He gave the tic of a smile. "He could have hauled you in—you know, a public beach. Do you mind if I get in the car with you? It's cold out here."

"I have a class in twenty minutes, Mr. McGraw."

But the man was already lurching around to the passenger side. He took notice of the scratches and pursed his lips to show his awareness. He eased into the seat alongside David. His coat overflowed it. "They say it's going to rain. Feels more like snow. It's a funny time of year for a beach party. Coming up Halloween, I suppose. And privacy's no problem on the beach in October, is it?" Again, the smirk. "Relax, David. We'll get you to your class on time. Addy said it was a long shot, but he remembered you lived in Oak Forest and could have been driving on the County Road last night. . . ."

Once again the lie seemed safer to David. He shook his head.

"The interstate?"

"That's right," David said.

"Well, Addy said it was a long shot. I don't know why anyone would take the County Road unless the interstate was shut down . . . or they had some mischief in mind. About what time was it when you got home?"

David took alarm. He ought not to have lied. He pumped himself up and said, "It's none of your business, mister, and if you don't get out of this car, I'm going to turn you over to the security police."

McGraw spread his hands. "What did I say?"

"I want to know why you're asking me these questions."

"You aren't giving me a chance to tell you."

If David could have stopped his ears, he would have, rather than hear the very thing he wanted to know.

"But there's no point to it if you didn't take the County Road," McGraw went on. "The reason I asked about the time: there was an accident that shut down the interstate for a couple of hours after midnight. Nobody got through going your direction."

David was about to say that he must have got through just ahead, but he bit his tongue. He might be able to back out now before he got in deeper. "Could I see your identification, Mr. McGraw? Anybody could pick up that business card you showed me."

"Smart boy. I'm like Abe Lincoln, David. I have an office but mostly I carry my business in my hat. All you got to do is call up the Sheriff's Office and speak to Deputy Addy Muller. He'll tell you who I am."

David drew a deep breath, and tried to lie himself out of the lie. "I didn't want to get involved in anything. I mean you're a lawyer and that generally means trouble."

"I can't argue with you on that, David. I'm the first person my clients call when they get in trouble."

"I did go home by the County Road, but I don't know what time it was. I was supposed to be in by midnight."

"Driving alone, were you?"

"I didn't know many kids at the party. My girlfriend invited me."

"Didn't you take the young lady home?"

"She got a ride from one of the other guys. I don't know what you want from me, but I've got to go now and I want to lock the car."

"Five minutes more?" McGraw said.

"No, sir. I don't know you and I don't see why I should talk to you."

"Then I'll tell you what you should do, David. First chance, drive over to the Sheriff's Office. You now where that is. Ask for Deputy Muller. He's investigating an incident on the County Road last night. He's looking for witnesses."

And there it was: something *had* happened. He'd run away from something real. "Okay, I'll do that," David muttered, his voice shaky. Then, realizing what hadn't been said: "Witness to what?"

"If you don't know, you better ask Deputy Muller." McGraw stuck out his hand as though expecting David to shake it. He withdrew it before David had a chance to take or refuse it. "Unless you'd like me to represent you? I'm well thought of in the County Building. It's never a mistake to have legal counsel, David, always a mistake to go it on your own. You told me you went home on the interstate. Why did you tell that little lie? Addy's going to want to know."

David turned the key in the ignition. He wasn't sure what to do—one security guard for the whole campus. He had to get rid of this guy. He was a crook, an ambulance chaser. But he knew something.

"No hard feelings," McGraw said. He opened the car door and slipped out, pulling his coat after him. It clung to the seat and he had to yank it free. David wanted to laugh. And cry. McGraw stood wriggling, trying to straighten himself inside the oversize garment. David revved the motor and circled fast. There was a terrible familiarity to the whirr of the tires. He did not look back.

The whole class jumped on him when he said he thought Judas Iscariot wasn't as bad as the Christians made him out to be. Maybe he thought of himself as a whistle-blower, that Jesus wasn't good for the Jewish people—"Too much for-giveness—you know, like the woman who committed adul-tery."

"Money, money, money," students in the back of the room chanted. "He did it for money." It was their way of breaking into David's tirade.

"But he didn't want the money. Look what he did with it!" David didn't know what was happening to him to be shoot-ing off like this. He didn't even know how long he'd been on his feet. Father Moran had settled his backside on the edge of the desk and folded his arms like a fat Buddha. He was enjoying himself. He loved it when his boys got their adrenaline flowing. Always his boys—he hadn't yet got used to the presence of girls in the class. "I don't think Jesus himself was fair to him," David went on. "He knew Judas was in trouble. He was the one who said the disciples should pray 'Lead us not into temptation.' Man, did Judas ever get led into temptation. What I'm saying is, Jesus knew. He knew what was going to happen to Judas. Look what he said to Saint Peter: 'Before the cock crows, you'll deny me three times.' And Peter did. And he cried. So did Judas. He went out and wept bitterly." David lost his train of thought. Actually, it was Peter who went out and wept bitterly.

Father Moran took over. "Well, Crowley. You certainly got our adrenaline flowing. Watch out the devil doesn't catch up with you. He's always on the lookout for a good advocate." The priest shifted his weight, one buttock to the other. "Tell me, what do you understand to be Iscariot's greater sin—that he betrayed the Lord or that he despaired of being forgiven?"

"Despair is the greatest sin." It was an answer out of his childhood catechism.

"Why?"

"I don't know, Father." He did not want to be quizzed like a ten-year-old. His moment of self-assurance was going down the drain.

The priest nodded to one of the volunteers. The back row all had their hands up.

Then David caught hold of another idea. "But despair is a sin against yourself, isn't it? Being your own judge. Betraying somebody is worse, it seems to me. You're hurting somebody else."

"Mitchell, you're on," the priest said to the volunteer, ignoring David's attempted postscript, except to say, "Thank you, Crowley."

David tried to listen to Mitchell's definition of despair as a sin against hope, and his denunciation of Judas because he had given up hope. It went on and on. David could have put it in one sentence. Somebody had done that, he realized, which was how it came into his mind: Abandon hope, all ye who enter here. Meaning hell.

It looked like the class wasn't going to get back on track until everybody had their say on why Judas was so despicable—the kiss, the pieces of silver; somebody said he was jealous of John, the disciple whom Jesus loved. "I know! He was gay!" one of the girls put in. She covered her mouth and giggled. The giggle was infectious and those around her laughed. David pretended to be amused, but he wasn't. He felt he'd been on to something important and had been cut off before he got to the heart of it. He'd had a question he wanted to ask that he felt would shake up even Father Moran. Now he couldn't remember it.

Between Christian Ethics and his last class, he copied a friend's notes for Twentieth Century French Literature, the class he had missed that morning, but his mind kept going back to Dennis McGraw and what he called "the incident" the sheriff's deputy was investigating. You wouldn't call anything serious an incident, would you? Suppose he found out tomorrow that the screaming person had not been hurt, not the least bit hurt, that the scream was an act, would that mean he was not guilty of anything? Look now: was guilt a matter of luck? Getting caught was, maybe. Wasn't that why he was in ethics, to learn why getting caught was not part of the moral issue? And wasn't getting caught what he was really afraid of? He didn't care about that woman at all. Not for her own sake. The person he cared about was David Crowley.

He tried to focus on the Valéry poem in which he was supposed to trace the symbolist influence, but he couldn't concentrate. It was hopeless, and he was supposed to be good in French. David felt as though something inside him was writhing, a stomachful of snakes. The school day was almost over, but terrible as it had been he dreaded for it to end. He didn't want to go home. He had to talk to someone. For just a minute he wondered if he should have been such a smart-ass with Dennis McGraw. McGraw wanted to talk to him. McGraw knew something. He didn't.

On his way home he thought about his father and what his mother had said at breakfast, how he could tell his father things he couldn't tell her. He was pretty sure she was talking about sex, but if his father was around would he be able to tell him what he'd done, how he'd run away when he might have hurt somebody? He could see his father going out to the car and saying, "Get in, David." He'd order David's mother back into the house and he'd drive straight to the Sheriff's Office and say, "My son has a statement to make." Even so, David thought, he could tell him sooner than he could tell his mother. What he wanted most was not to have to tell anybody, to wake up and find out it was a dream.

He drove around the block twice before turning into the driveway in case McGraw or someone from the Sheriff's Office was waiting for him. He saw no one, and when he parked in front of the garage door, the nearest neighbor was coming out of her house. She waved to him, got into her car, and drove off. Perfectly normal. In the house he got the same feeling of normalcy. It made him uneasy, as if he might step where there was nothing for his foot to land on. There were no messages for him on the answering machine. Even the cat ignored him. He looked up Dennis McGraw in the yellow pages. He'd thought he might not be there, but he was, the address the County Building. Something was real, anyway, Dennis McGraw, attorney-at-law. He had an enemy, David thought. For the first time in his life he had a real enemy. That was crazy. All McGraw wanted was to make a buck out of him. *Unless you'd like me to represent you. . . .* But David hadn't admitted anything, except going home on the County Road. McGraw had looked for him because Deputy Muller had a hunch. Oughtn't car license numbers to be available to the police only? Everybody knew the Sheriff's Office was corrupt. The patrol shouldn't have just taken the beer away last night, they ought to have chased the kids out of the park or arrested them for bringing beer there in the first place. He wondered if any of the other guys had been approached by McGraw. Whoever took Sally home would have had to use the interstate or the County Road; he hadn't thought of that before. They almost certainly had to go that way, and if they had, it would have been after David's trip home.

He hated to call Sally. He was shaky, and if there was any-one he wanted less than his mother to know what he'd done, it was Sally. He kept putting off calling her until it was al-most time for his mother to come home, and then he went out and used the nearest public phone.

"I wanted to be sure you got home all right last night," he explained.

"You'd have known by now if I didn't. It was real mean of you, David, to go and leave me with that pack of wolves."

"I didn't leave you! You said . . . whatever you said. It doesn't matter. What happened?"

"What almost happened on the way home was worse. We had to go the County Road—the interstate was closed. . . ."

"I know," David said. "What happened to *you,* I mean?"

"The guys were fooling around. They're sex fiends, and all of a sudden we almost hit a car parked halfway on the highway. No lights, nobody around, like it died and some-body just left it there."

David saw the whole thing in his mind's eye. "Did you stop?"

"Why should we have? We didn't hit it or anything. But it cooled off Micky's sex urge. When we got to Oak Forest, he dropped me at our driveway and took off."

If the car was still there later, what did it mean? What had happened to the woman?

"If I didn't see it," David said, the words of denial slip-ping out, "you must have come home a lot later than me."

"Not much. I kind of agitated to get us on the road. I'm sorry I said what I did, David. You shouldn't be so sensitive. Women can be frustrated too, you know. You're not crude like those other guys, and I admire that. I admire a lot about you."

"Thanks," he murmured.

"What do I have to do to make up for what I said? Ask you for another date? I was the one asked you last night, you know."

"I'll call you real soon, Sally."

"I go back to school on Sunday." She was on midterm break.

"I'll call you," he said again.

"Okay, David. Thanks for calling." The phone clicked off.

Now he had hurt her, but he couldn't help it. He stood in the booth after hanging up, and tried to find the words with which he could tell Sally what had happened to him. It went fine until he had to say, I didn't stop. They hadn't stopped either, but they'd not seen the screaming woman.

A man waiting to use the phone pushed open the door. "Do you always go into a phone booth when you want to talk to yourself?"

After an early dinner at the kitchen table David attacked his class assignments. He surprised himself with what sounded to him like a great exposition of the Valéry poem. It felt good, as though he'd made some kind of reparation in getting it done. He took it in to where his mother was writing letters and read it to her. He'd been pretty quiet at dinner and she hadn't fussed or probed. He was making up.

She listened thoughtfully. Then, out of a clear sky, she said, "Would you like a year of study in France if it could be managed?"

David was stunned. It was as though she had said she no longer needed him. He'd been thinking all along that he was tied to her for life, and now it turned out she felt she was tied down by him. Maybe she had a man he didn't even know about, somebody at the bank. . . . A tumult of alarms possessed him.

"Well?" she prompted.

"Yeah, sure. I mean that's a third-year alternative and I'm only a freshman."

"Only a freshman," she repeated. "You put yourself down, Davie. You shouldn't do that. The essay is very good."

"It isn't long enough to call it an essay."

"Nevertheless, would you like to read me the poem itself?"

He was on his way to get the book when the phone rang.

His mother called out to let the machine take it for now. He pretended not to hear her. All evening, except for when he lost himself in the poem, he had anticipated something heavy about to happen. Nevertheless, when he heard Mc-Graw's voice, his heart gave a sickening thump.

"David, I hope I'm not interrupting your dinner. We need to make a date, you and I. Tonight is convenient for me, or first thing in the morning."

"No," David said. "It's not convenient for me."

"Then you must make it convenient. It's not a matter of choice, young man. Are you with someone now so that you can't talk?"

"My mother's home," David muttered.

"Well now, sooner or later, you will want to involve her. Maybe not. That's not my business. Let's meet somewhere in the morning. I would say my office, but it's being decorated. Unavailable really. And I don't want to meet in your car again. We're not conspiring thieves, are we?"

"David?" his mother called inquiringly from the study.

"I'll be in in a minute, Mother." To McGraw, he said, "You can come here in the morning, but not before eight-thirty." It was his mother's turn to drive. She'd leave by eight o'clock.

McGraw repeated the time and checked David's address. He had it right.

Returning, book in hand, to where his mother was waiting, David explained, "I got some scratches on my car going down to the beach last night. A guy's going to paint them for me."

"Have it done by a professional, David. I'll help you pay for it."

"Great," he said.

"Not everything is great," she said. Then, "Shall we put off the poem until another time?"

McGraw arrived not long after the hall clock struck the half hour. David had again cut loose his riders. He took the lawyer to the kitchen. McGraw was wearing the same top-coat. He took it off and put it on the back of a chair and perched the hat on top of it. "It's a good thing I make house calls, isn't it? Any coffee left in the pot?"

David poured half a mugful and heated it in the microwave. McGraw was taking inventory of every convenience in the kitchen—like he was pricing it for a yard sale.

He took the coffee black. "Why don't we start with your side of the story first, David—what really happened to you on the way home?"

"I'm not going to tell you anything," David said.

"In that case, hear this," McGraw said. "A farmer whose address is rural box seventeen on the County Road heard a woman scream out in front of his place after midnight last night. It woke him from a sound sleep. He looked out, thought he saw a car stalled on the road, and decided to call the Sheriff's Patrol. The call was clocked at twelve-twenty. But on account of the accident on the interstate, the patrol didn't pick up on it till daylight. I went out there myself with Addy Muller, drove him in fact. He was dead on his feet after a double shift. But the farmer was pissed at how long it took the sheriff's men to show up. I'm telling it to you straight, David. . . ."

David didn't say anything. McGraw took a noisy sip of his coffee. "Addy remembered you kids on the beach and figured you might've been heading home about then. He remembered you lived in Oak Forest. He asked me if I'd like to look you up while he made the rounds of the hospitals. You were the one he remembered by name and school. He thought you were too young to be running with that crowd.

"You didn't want to talk to me, David, you didn't show much respect for the truth either. In other words, you were scared. I can see why.

"It turns out the woman was on her way home from work, tired, late, and she had to relieve herself. No traffic that she could see. She pulled halfway off the road, turned off the

lights, and went in front of the car. Now wouldn't you like
to take it from there?"

David was silent.

"David, there was a witness. You were driving at high
speed, came out of nowhere just as she came around from in
front of the car. You could have made sausage meat of her,
and you didn't even stop."

"I didn't hit her. I know that."

"How do you know?"

"I just do."

"So what do you think happened to her?"

David shook his head.

"But you didn't care as long as you could get away."

"I did care, but I knew I hadn't hit her."

"You *knew?*" McGraw waited, breathing noisily, a snort.

"What happened to her, mister?" David could feel that
terrible tightness in his throat.

"I'm not a doctor," McGraw said.

"Is she all right?"

"I wouldn't say that. Oh, no. But *she* is alive."

David caught the emphasis on "she." "You said there was
a witness. Were they in the car with her?"

McGraw gave him the sad smirk of a smile. "No, David,
you are the witness."

He wondered how that could be and then realized he had
in effect confessed to McGraw. He'd been trapped. He had
trapped himself. And he was all he cared about. Not the
woman. She wasn't a real person to him. She was a scream,
like a face he'd brought up on the computer screen.

"I want to see her," he said. What he wanted was to *feel*
her, to flesh-and-blood feel her.

"You could have seen her at the scene. Now it's up to her
whether or when she will see you."

"What am I supposed to do, mister?"

"Exactly what I advised you to do yesterday: go over to
the Sheriff's Office this morning and give Deputy Muller
your statement."

"And if I don't?"

"They'll come and get you, David. I can promise you that. The woman will swear out the warrant for your arrest."

And the arrest would be reported in the *County Sentinel*'s "Crime Watch." But the woman was alive: why couldn't he say thank God and mean it? He hated himself for what came into his mind and for saying it, but he did: "What if I asked you to represent me?"

"It's too late for that," McGraw said, sounding regretful.

"You're representing her, aren't you?"

"Such a smart young man, David, would you believe me if I told you I don't wish to represent either of you in a court of law? You will agree surely that you owe the unfortunate woman something simply on the strength of the information we have exchanged here this morning?"

"Isn't this some kind of blackmail, mister?"

"What a dirty word. No, David. I am offering you an honorable solution to something that could be very nasty. It could mess up your life, your career, people knowing you'd run away like that. What I haven't told you till now—the woman was pregnant, David. She miscarried after the accident."

David felt the message like a blow to the stomach. He had trouble getting his breath.

"I think we can call it an accident," McGraw went on, "but in her mind it was murder."

"I'm sorry for her," David said finally, and it wasn't associated with McGraw's mention of murder. It was for something lost.

"Sorrow's too cheap, David. Think about it and after you've seen Deputy Muller, let's talk again. She's a poor, hardworking woman. A settlement would not impoverish your family."

David watched McGraw down the driveway, the coat as he struggled into it swished out like Batman's cape. He tucked it around him as he got behind the wheel of a car marked SHERIFF'S OFFICE.

The woman was human, David thought, a human being, and the sorrow he felt was for her, not for himself. It was going to be McGraw's word against his, no matter what happened, he reasoned. Not that he was thinking of the lie he could tell to get out of his admission, but he wanted time to think about what he was going to do. He didn't think McGraw would make any move until he had turned himself in, until he signed something saying he had left the scene where someone might have been hurt due to his reckless speed. He was trying to tell himself the truth, the way it was now. In a way, he had hit the woman and he wanted to go back and pick her up. He couldn't do that, but if he could find her, he could ask her to listen to him, and he could tell her he was sorry. Murder, he felt sure, was McGraw's word. It was meant to scare him. The funny thing was it didn't, but McGraw still did.

David knew he needed help. Maybe he did need a lawyer, but he just didn't think so. What he needed first was a private detective, something as remote from his experience as a TV melodrama. What he needed was his father. Not available. He'd recommend a lawyer anyway, and in spite of what his mother had said about David's being able to talk to him, he didn't think his father would be able to listen.

He drove to school and got to see Father Moran in his office. The priest shook hands with him, not the usual start of a student interview. He knew a troubled young person when he saw one. He told David to move his chair so the light wouldn't shine in his face.

"I got to thinking after yesterday's brouhaha," the priest said, "one of those what-if questions. What if, after hiding out overnight, Iscariot had showed up at the foot of the cross and said, 'Lord, forgive me.'"

David grinned. There was nothing to say and yet there was a lot.

"What can I do for you, Crowley?"

"I did a bad thing, Father." David told his story, even to having thrown the condom into the wind.

The priest lifted an eyebrow. "Standard equipment," he growled. It was the only comment he made until David was finished. Then, after a few seconds of thought: "And when you find her?"

"I don't know," David said. "I just want her to know I'm sorry for what happened to her."

"Even a decent lawyer would advise you against self-incrimination."

"I don't care!" David all but shouted.

"By the grace of God, I'm not a lawyer," the priest said. He took the phone book from the bottom drawer of his desk. "Let's start with the nearest hospital to where this misfortune occurred."

Within the half hour he had the name and address for Alice Moss. When she hemorrhaged with the miscarriage, she had taken herself back to St. Vincent's Hospital. It was where she worked on the custodial staff.

"If you didn't hear me scream," the woman said after she'd thought about it, "how were you going to hear if something else happened to me?"

"I don't think I wanted to hear anything," David said.

Mrs. Moss scraped a bit of congealed egg from the table with her thumbnail. They sat in the hospital employees' cafeteria, where midafternoon traffic was light. She did not in any way resemble the face behind the scream. Her salt-and-pepper hair hung in a clamp at the back of her head. Her eyes were tired. She seemed confused, slow, but her question was on the mark. She twisted uncomfortably on the metal chair. "I don't like you coming to me like this," she said. "I'd just as soon never know you."

"I'm sorry," David said.

"You said that already and I believe you're telling the truth. But I think you're sorry over something I'm not real sure I feel the same way about. That lawyer got me all confused, telling me how I feel when I don't feel that way at all." She concentrated on ST. MARY'S COLLEGE, the lettering on the breast of his sweater. "David—Mr. Crowley . . ."

"David's fine," he said.

"I'm not saying what I want to say, and maybe I should keep it to myself." She drew a deep breath and looked at him directly. "I didn't want to have a baby at all, but I'm a church person and I felt I had to go through with it. Mind, I could have been killed myself last night, I know that . . ."

"I do too," David said.

"And maybe that would have been murder, but I still couldn't call the other thing murder. I was thinking when I came back to work this noon: wasn't I lucky on both counts?"

Before the next Christian Ethics class David told Father Moran about his meeting in the hospital cafeteria.

"Did she forgive you?"

"I think so."

"You're lucky, my lad," the priest said. They reached the classroom door. "I have a word of advice for you, Crowley. One word. . . ." He waited.

"Yes, Father?"

"Abstinence."

Amazon Run

Mickey Friedman

Tropical Hotel: Outside Manaus, Brazil

Charles Buckland Devore was nursing a *caipirinha* in the Igapó Bar when the woman came in, sat down on a stool, and rested her face in her hands. From his own stool not far away he heard her mutter, "Oh, God."

Until then, it had been a somnolent day. Sweaty and sun-dazzled after a languid lunch by the wave pool, Buck had showered and taken refuge from the heat. In this quiet up-stairs hideaway, he was sampling the mixture of cane liquor and lime juice that was the drink of the region. Not a bad way to spend a February afternoon when the northeastern U.S. was locked down under Arctic air masses.

Outside, just beyond the manicured grounds, the Rio Negro, an almost impossibly wide tributary of the Amazon, gleamed like molten metal. Not far away it met the Rio Solimões, the other major tributary, to form the mighty Amazon. Stretched in his deck chair, Buck had read about the "meeting of the waters" in a brochure he'd picked up at the front desk. If he was here another few days, he might even take a boat tour to see it. His instructions were to stay at the hotel until contacted, but nobody was in a hurry to contact him.

Right now, he had a newly arrived damsel in distress for distraction. She continued to sit in an attitude of misery. She was wearing a uniform-like outfit of navy skirt and white blouse. On her small bosom was pinned a plastic tag imprinted with—Buck leaned forward and squinted—imprinted with the name "Wendy."

Wendy lifted her face from her hands long enough to order a fizzy mineral water. With her uniform, multitude of freckles, and short brown hair, she brought to mind a nurse or a nanny. Buck had nothing against either job category, and damsels in distress were one of his specialities. He waited until she was sipping her mineral water and sniffling only slightly before he said, "Bad day?"

She focused on Buck for the first time. He was looking, as he well knew, like a character out of Graham Greene, minus the spiritual torment. His artistically rumpled white linen suit set off his tan and blended nicely with his steel-gray hair. His collarless blue shirt echoed his eyes. Completing the picture of tropical chic was the wide-brimmed Panama hat reposing on the bar. Buck was on the far side of sixty and didn't look a day younger, but it didn't matter. In some cases it had even proved to be an advantage.

After giving him a long, wet-eyed stare, Wendy said, "Do you believe in love at first sight?"

All right, Wendy! But before Buck could compose a modest reply she continued, in a tone of distress, "That's what they say it was. Can you believe it? All because they happened to sit next to one another in the departure lounge in Miami. They got seats together on the flight. Now they won't even *talk* to me."

This basic scenario was not unfamiliar to Buck. As Wendy glugged down the rest of her mineral water he winged it. "My advice is to forgive. These things happen, Wendy. It's a fact of—"

Wendy put her glass down with a thump. She said, "I don't care about Mrs. Bartram. She won't get her money back. Let her sue. But I can't believe he would do this to me. How could he? He knows how much I need him." Her eyes reddened once more.

Buck motioned to the bartender to bring her another mineral water. He knew when his ministrations were required. He moved over the several stools that separated them and offered her a pressed and pristine handkerchief. He said, "Wendy, I know this is difficult for you now, but it will work out."

She opened the hanky and blew her nose. "It will not," she declared. "We sail tomorrow. A nuclear device wouldn't blow them out of that room by then."

Now that Buck was closer, he saw that Wendy's name badge was marked, in small letters, "Constellation Cruise Lines." He said, "Wendy, are you telling me your boyfriend stood you up for another woman on the eve of a cruise? What a scoundrel!"

Wendy recoiled with a look of astonishment. "My *boyfriend!*" she exclaimed. "He isn't my boyfriend. My God, he's fifty-five years old!"

She honked into the handkerchief again and returned it to Buck. As he tried, in a gingerly way, to maneuver it back into his pocket, he thought perhaps he'd had his fill of Little Miss Wendy.

She, on the other hand, was studying him intently. She said, "Tell me, Mr. . . . ."

"Devore. Buck Devore."

"Mr. Devore, do you know how to dance?"

Buck had now taken her measure, and knew this was not an invitation to while away the evening at the hotel night-club. "Of course I know how to dance."

"I mean, better than just the box step most men do."

Who did she think she was dealing with? "Wendy darling," Buck said with forbearance, "I can foxtrot, waltz, cha-cha, samba, tango. I can do the funky chicken—"

"And do you have a dinner jacket?"

"I have a tuxedo *and* a white dinner jacket. Both with me." He would sooner have left home without his tooth-brush. You never knew where you might be invited.

She took a deep breath. "Are you married?"

"Divorced." This was an exaggeration. He wasn't sure whether Cyndee had actually filed yet.

Hope had dawned on Wendy's plain, freckled face. "Mr. Devore," she said, "how would you like to cruise down the Amazon and around the coast to Rio? For free?"

Buck still hadn't forgiven her for *He's fifty-five years old!* "I can't do it, Wendy. I'm here on business."

"Oh, Mr. Devore! Are you sure? Can't you at least think it over?"

At last, in a breathless rush, Wendy explained herself. She was the social director of the *Andromeda,* a luxury cruise liner currently docked at Manaus. The *Andromeda* was due to sail tomorrow. She needed a dance host, and she needed him now.

"A dance host?" Buck's career had been checkered, but he had never heard of a dance host.

"We always have at least two extra men to dance with the women who don't have partners. You have to be of good character, and of a certain age, and of course not married, and a good dancer"—

Buck raised his eyebrows. Certainly he met at least some of these criteria.

—"and in exchange for circulating and dancing with the unattached women, you get a free passage."

One of Wendy's dance hosts and a passenger had become enamored in the Miami airport, and their romance had blossomed on the flight to Manaus. Instead of boarding the *Andromeda,* the lovebirds had taken a room in the Tropical Hotel, the better to explore their relationship in private.

Poor Wendy was left in a terrible spot. Who was going to dance with all those ladies? "Mr. Devore, I'm begging you—"

"I wish I could. Really. But—" Buck Devore as a dance host. It was like asking a fox to guard the chicken coop. But why should he exert himself doing the samba with merry widows when he could luxuriate right here, sunning by the pool, eating open-pit barbecue every night, and enjoying life as a spy? He took the card Wendy scribbled with explicit instructions for reaching her, bid her farewell, and ordered another *caipirinha*.

The Igapó was quiet once again. Brass ceiling fans revolved overhead. At the end of the bar a phone gave a subdued burr, and the bartender strolled down to answer it.

Buck wasn't really a spy, although he liked the sound of it. He was more of a courier. The job was the easiest money under the most comfortable circumstances he'd seen in a long time. It was as if fate had said, "Hey, Buck! Cyndee driving you nuts? Weather getting you down? I've got a deal for *you!*"

All Buck had to do was hand over an envelope. Somebody would contact him and set up a meeting. It had been three days. No rush, as far as he was concerned.

Eager as Buck had been to do this job, he'd tried to be cautious. "No drugs," he'd said to Duncan Crowley. "I don't want to spend the rest of my life in a Brazilian jail."

They were in the library of Duncan's club, having brandy and cigars after dinner. Duncan was one of Buck's many acquaintances. Buck couldn't even remember where they'd met. When a man lived by his wits, doing a little of this and a little of that, he needed lots of acquaintances.

"For heaven's sake, Buck," Duncan protested, swirling the liquid in his snifter. "Do I look like a drug dealer?"

The answer, of course, was no. Duncan looked like an overweight, ruddy-faced businessman.

Buck wanted to go on the trip, couldn't wait to get home and pack, but he said, "I have to be sure I'm not going to get in trouble, Duncan."

Duncan shifted his bulk in the leather chair, his face glowing with brandy and the fire in the fireplace. "I'll say two words to you," he said. "*Microwave ovens.* Is that tame enough? Pretty trivial to you and me, Buck, but there's a plant down there that has paid well to get an edge on the competition."

Microwave ovens. Not even something as exciting as a

computer chip, but so what? If microwave ovens would get him out of range of Cyndee, he'd be delighted.

"The Brazilian economy is booming. Manaus is a free-trade zone, a lot of manufacturing going on there for the South American and Caribbean market. It's a major city right in the middle of the Amazon jungle," Duncan droned. Tuning him out, Buck stared into the fire and thought about Cyndee.

The scrumptious Cyndee Doolittle Devore, strawberry blond and curvy, had been a miscalculation. None of Buck's three previous wives had created anything like this kind of hell when the inevitable happened and Buck continued to act like Buck. Buck had been blinded by Cyndee's beauty—she'd once been a runner-up for a slot with the Dallas Cowboy cheerleaders—and the fact that her father was the fabulously wealthy CEO of a conglomerate called Metropolitan Industries.

But Dad Doolittle, an intense, shaggy-eyebrowed number cruncher a few years Buck's junior, hated Buck's guts. He was only too happy to pay for the detectives who confirmed his darling daughter's suspicions. He had spoiled Cyndee rotten. Buck shuddered. Hysterical phone calls at all hours. Communiqués from a battery of lawyers. And the worst: Buck had received in the mail a voodoo doll with a number of pins bristling from the groin area.

No wonder he had consented to take an envelope of microwave-oven schematics to Brazil.

In the Igapó Bar, the bartender turned from the phone and looked at Buck. He said, "You are Mr. Devore? This is for you."

It was the call.

The last traces of a spectacular sunset were fading over the Rio Negro when Buck made his way, as instructed, down to the hotel dock with a palm-thatched roof where the river excursions originated. A hot wind swirled as he stopped for a moment on the esplanade. Far, far away, a thin black line on the horizon, was the opposite bank of the river. Buck pulled on the brim of his Panama. He was tense, although why he should be he couldn't imagine. Microwave ovens, for heaven's sake!

He had the envelope with him, a plain nine-by-twelve manila, sealed with filament tape. He hadn't tried to look in it. Had no desire to. His instructions were to go to the dock and give it to the person he'd meet there. He started down the stone steps to the riverbank. Nobody else around, but wasn't there someone sitting in a chair in the gloom of the dock? Buck gave a tentative wave and the person stood up, a black outline against the glimmering water.

It was really quite dark under the thatched roof. Water sloshed against the rubber tires mounted around the dock's edges. Buck could smell the river, hear insects whirring. He couldn't make out the face of the man who stood only a few feet before him. Buck cleared his throat and said, "Hi." That brought no response, so he held out the envelope. At the same instant, the wind picked up again, a strong warm gust plucking Buck's Panama from his head and carrying it out over the surface of the Rio Negro.

The damned hat wasn't even paid for! Buck lunged to one side, reaching after it as it sailed beyond his reach. He hardly heard the quiet *thock!* behind him.

As the hat landed, floating on its brim like a toy sailboat, Buck heard a gargled gasp. He realized his companion had crumpled, ever so quietly, and was falling off the end of the dock.

Simultaneous with the splash he made—not a large splash—Buck heard running feet. By this time, he didn't know when he'd done it, Buck had hit the deck and flattened himself against the damp planks. Turning his head to one side, he saw a huge dark figure lumbering away along the rocky strip of sand between the esplanade wall and the river's edge. He could make out no details of the person's appearance beyond the fact that he—it was a man, Buck was sure—had an unruly shock of very light hair.

Buck was vibrating. He was still clutching the envelope with the microwave information in it. That had been a shot. *A shot.* And the other guy—

Buck shifted to look out over the Rio Negro. No sign of the other guy. No bubbles, no thrashing, no groans. Just the placid expanse of the huge river and, drifting ever farther away, Buck's new Panama.

The platinum-blond gunman was gone, too. Ever so slowly, Buck lifted himself from the floor of the dock and brushed himself off. He hadn't imagined these people would take the microwave business so seriously. A guy had been shot and killed. Buck would have to . . . he'd have to . . .

Buck would have to call the Brazilian police. He would have to tell them that while he, Charles Buckland Devore, was in the act of handing over industrial secrets to an unknown contact, a taffy-haired gunman had shot and killed said contact. He imagined a roomful of beefy carabinieri smirking and fingering their holsters. Or maybe carabinieri were Italian. Anyway . . .

Buck sprinted off the dock, scrambled up the steps, and jogged through the gloaming to the hotel, all the while fingering in his pocket the business card given him in the Igapó Bar by darling, darling Wendy. With the phone jammed between ear and shoulder as he loaded tux, dinner jacket, microwave envelope, shaving kit into his suitcase, he listened to six or eight rings before, Oh God, somebody answered, but it wasn't Wendy. Wendy was seeing off a group of passengers on their way to the Brazilian folklore show at the opera house. Could Buck phone back in maybe half an hour?

No. No. Buck had to talk to Wendy. He had to. Buck could not wait one minute, much less half an hour. He hoped this person understood that he could not wait. *He had to talk to Wendy.*

Not long afterward, Wendy was on the line. Buck tried not to babble. He instructed himself to imagine how Cary

Grant would act. He said, "Wendy? Wendy, it's Buck. Buck Devore, your new dance host."

The next day, as the *Andromeda* prepared to sail, Buck surveyed the port of Manaus from the deck of the imposing white ocean liner. He was feeling considerably more like himself. He had managed to make a quiet exit from the hotel and had met with no further untoward incidents. He had even—and he took this as an excellent omen—found another Panama for a pretty good price at a nearby shop. His accommodations, a cabin down on Pisces Deck in the bowels of the ship, were not up to the luxurious standard of the Tropical Hotel, but he'd adjust.

Buck felt bad about the microwave guy who'd been shot. He believed in capitalism, but he couldn't approve of competition as ferocious as that. Still, in all honesty, it was their battle and not his.

The ship's horn gave a long blast, and the loudspeaker began to play "Anchors Aweigh." All around him, lined up at the rail, were Buck's fellow Amazon cruisers, draped with cameras and glistening with sun block. The air was full of their excited chatter. Bye-bye, Manaus. The *Andromeda* began a stately withdrawal from her berth, pulling away from the clutter of riverboats and smaller vessels, from the parking lot with its souvenir stalls, from the teeming dark-haired crowd below on the concrete quay.

As Buck studied that teeming dark-haired crowd, he noticed they weren't all dark-haired. In fact, one unusually tall man down there was also unusually blond, with an unruly head of hair the color of taffy. Taffy-head seemed to be looking up in Buck's direction.

Buck turned to the woman on his right, a redhead in bermuda shorts who was holding a pair of binoculars to her eyes. He said, "Excuse me. May I borrow those for a second?"

"Of course," the woman purred as she handed them over. Automatically, Buck noted that her hair was skillfully dyed, her eyes bright green, her figure not at all bad for her age.

He put the binoculars to his eyes and focused on Taffy. The blond man's face zoomed toward him. On it was an expression of hatred. And Buck would swear he was looking right at Buck.

It had to be the gunman from the night before. How had he tracked Buck down? The bartender had surely overheard Buck's conversation with Wendy. Had Taffy talked with the bartender?

A chill invaded Buck's solar plexus. The guy must really want that envelope. For the hundredth time, Buck cursed himself for not leaving the damned thing on the dock. At least Buck was getting out of Manaus. When Manaus was behind him, this malevolent-looking hulk would be behind him as well. Buck vowed not to set foot off the ship until they reached Rio.

"Are they focused all right?"

It was the second time she'd asked, Buck realized. He'd forgotten the owner of the binoculars, standing at his elbow. He lowered the glasses with shaking hands. "Yeah. Thanks," he said, giving them back to her.

"My name is Rita Randall." She was smiling brightly. On one of her hands she wore a major ring—aquamarine, Buck guessed, which was surrounded by diamonds—and on the opposite wrist she wore a diamond tennis bracelet. Buck saw her glancing at his own bare ring finger.

Some other time, Rita. He excused himself and pushed through the excited passengers, away from the railing and the blond man's menacing face.

BOCA DA VALERIA

Buck's vow to remain on board the ship was kept approximately as long as most vows he'd ever made. The next morning, Wendy informed him he was expected to ride herd on the passengers during a shore excursion to Boca da Valeria. He was to help people in and out of the tenders, lend an arm to anyone who had trouble walking, and make sure nobody was left behind in the "authentic caboclo village" when the interlude was over.

Wendy was turning out to be something of a martinet. Clearly, Buck would more than earn his "free" passage. At the Bon Voyage party the previous evening, she had given him trenchant instructions about not concentrating his attentions on the younger and spryer women, and she'd been very disgruntled to find him sitting out and playing the slot machines in the casino while he caught his breath between exertions on the dance floor.

Buck's feet hurt, and one of his toes was the worse from somebody's spike heel. His limbs felt like dishrags. He wanted only to sit in a deck chair, sip iced tea, and watch the muddy brown water and the tangled green riverbank slide past. He was not up for an encounter with "real Amazonian culture."

"The tenders are launched, Buck," Wendy said. "Better get below, with the others."

So Buck joined the throngs waiting to be loaded into the orange and white shuttle boats and hauled to shore to experience native life for a couple of hours. His appearance caused some nudges and a bit of a buzz among the ladies, a reaction he was accustomed to. He had already been given a box of candy by an old dear who had spent their interminable rumba describing to him, in harrowing detail, her husband's last illness five years ago.

A voice said, "Isn't this exciting, Mr. Devore?"

It was Rita Randall, the redhead with the binoculars. She was looking sleek in a white sun visor and shades, her hair pulled back in a curly little ponytail. Had he danced with her last night? He thought possibly so, on one of the ladies'-choice numbers. "Certainly is, Ms. Randall," he said with all the heartiness he could muster. She was wearing the tennis bracelet again, but no rings today. They continued to chat, and got in a tender together. It was close quarters. During the short ride across the water to the village, Rita Randall's tanned and shapely leg pressed firmly against Buck's. He could feel the warmth through his white duck trousers.

Boca da Valeria, a cluster of thatched huts on a patch of bare pink earth between the jungle and the river, had not exactly escaped the curse of civilization. Small children dressed in feathered costumes, their faces painted, clutched wads of dollar bills exacted from tourist photographers. The tariff was the same to photograph one of the mournful sloths tethered to poles along the village path. There were blowguns and painted wooden parrots for sale in thatched sheds. Moping amid the buzz of commerce, Buck looked longingly at the *Andromeda,* floating serenely out of reach beyond an expanse of marsh grass.

The weather got hotter as the afternoon wore on. Someone started selling lemonade at a stand near the dock. River craft glided past through the narrow channels. Buck was going for a glass of lemonade when he was summoned. "Mr. Devore! Come with us! They say there's another village over this hill!"

Obediently, Buck followed the indefatigable Rita Randall and a group of others up a narrow red-clay path through the jungle. Red-combed chickens skittered out of the way in front of them. Vines caught at his pants legs. The sun was broiling, and the mosquitoes were ferocious. Buck fell behind the chattering group. His stamina wasn't what it used to be when it came to tropical treks. He pushed up the brim of his hat and mopped his forehead. To hell with the other village. He'd go back to the dock, have his lemonade, and wait for the tenders to leave.

When he turned around, standing on the path not far behind him was a very large man with a shock of taffy-colored hair.

Galvanized, Buck followed his first and only impulse, which was to run. He charged a few steps up the path, but the evil microwave lunatic would surely catch him that way, so he veered off into the vegetation, flailing through pliant branches, stumbling over rotten logs, disturbing birds, insects, and unnameable other creatures.

He could hear Taffy barging through behind him. The air was suffocating. Buck's sneakers were slipping on mud, or something of that consistency. A thorny branch whipped across his arm, leaving a thin trail of blood. A loud whirring sound came from the leafy thicket in front of him. Buck halted. This was insane. There were snakes here. Snakes, and who knew what else. He couldn't barge through the Amazon rainforest outwitting not only this big blond killer but the boa constrictors and whatever. He had to try something else.

Taffy stepped through the trees into Buck's view. He had leaves in his hair, a scrape on his cheekbone. He was a rawboned fellow with cool blue eyes, Scandinavian-looking. He was holding a gun in his pale hand, and the gun was pointed at Buck.

Buck raised his hands. He now deeply regretted the madness that had sent him careening through the undergrowth. He said, "I don't have a gun." Taffy blinked without a sign of comprehension. Did he speak English? Buck didn't know any Scandinavian. Trying to edge his way back toward the path, Buck said, "I don't have the envelope, either. I left it on the ship. If I'd known you'd be here, I'd have brought it with me."

Still no response. Taffy took a step closer, as if to get a better bead on the region around Buck's racing heart.

Buck tried again. "I don't want it, and I'll be happy for you to have it," he said. "I'll give it to you. Comprendo? Look, if you've got some paper, just write down an address. I'll send it immediately, OK? I swear. If you'll just tell me where . . ."

It wasn't going to work. Sweat was pouring into Buck's eyes. He looked at the gun, at the big thick finger on the trigger.

"Mr. Devore? Mr. Devore, what happened to you? The tenders are about to leave, Mr. Devore!"

The voice was very close by. If Buck got out of this, and could ever afford it, he'd buy the blessed woman another diamond bracelet. He saw Taffy's eyes cloud in confusion. He bellowed, "I'm right here, Ms. Randall!" Before Taffy could decide to go for broke, Buck crashed back toward the path where Rita Randall stood, craning her neck in search of him.

"My goodness, you vanished into thin air," she cooed. Then, taking in his appearance, "What on earth happened?"

"I decided to do some exploring on my own," Buck said as they hurried toward the village. He could see passengers clustered at the dock, waiting to board the tenders.

She laughed musically. "You're quite an adventurer, Mr. Devore."

"Call me Buck," Buck said.

ALTER DO CHÃO

Buck took the envelope with him to Alter do Chão the next day. He knew he'd be seeing Taffy again. He'd never be rid of Taffy until Taffy had the microwave schematics. If Taffy had followed the *Andromeda* to Boca da Valeria—by riverboat, canoe, motorboat, the possibilities were endless—he could follow it to Alter do Chão. Hell, he could follow it to Rio. Buck had to put an end to this.

Buck had had no time to recoup from his trauma at Boca da Valeria. Almost immediately on his return to the ship, he'd been required to appear—dressed in tux and dancing pumps—at the Captain's Welcome cocktail party. He had danced himself to exhaustion, gone down to his cabin during the floor show and doused himself with ice water, and returned to repeat the performance, staying on the floor until the orchestra sounded the last notes of "Good Night, Irene." He had turned down several invitations to partake of the midnight buffet, one of them from Rita Randall, a sight for sore eyes in her slinky silver lamé formal, a several-carat emerald pendant nestled in the hollow of her throat. When he pleaded fatigue, she smiled an understanding smile, leaned close, and whispered, "See you tomorrow, Buck," her lips grazing his ear.

Rita was intriguing, but Buck couldn't concentrate on her. He had to get rid of the microwave schematics and get the big Swede, or whatever he was, off his trail. Then, and only then, could he weigh his options with Rita Randall.

Alter do Chão was billed as a beach party, and a party atmosphere prevailed. A band—trombone, steel drums, cornet, saxophone—played on the dock as the tenders arrived, and *Andromeda* cruisers clad in bathing suits fanned out quickly over the strip of white sand. Palms swayed, the Amazon waters were brilliant, the T-shirt salesmen were on red alert. Buck could have loved it, but he plodded joylessly along the baking strand. In the canvas carry-all slung over his shoulder was a pair of shorts, a towel, and the most important item, the envelope. He looked up and down the beach. No Taffy. No Taffy among the souvenir vendors in the shady town square. He walked the couple of blocks through town to the Center for the Preservation of Indigenous Art. Taffy was not there. At a loss, he returned to the beach, to swim and picnic with Rita and some of her friends.

Even a dip in the warm Amazon didn't revive him. Dripping, he stared moodily out over the water. "You're not happy, Buck," said Rita softly. "What would it take to make you happy?"

Buck sighed. He surveyed the tranquil scene, as if looking for the secret of happiness in the sand, the river, the luxuriant trees, the T-shirt vendors. He said, "Rita, it's something I can't—"

Dammit, there was Taffy. There the son of a bitch was, skulking at the edge of a stand of coconut palms. Buck jumped to his feet, grabbed his canvas bag, and pelted toward the blond man, not worried about kicking sand all over Rita, because he'd forgotten she existed.

The big man watched him approach. Buck saw that he'd put mercurochrome on the scratch on his cheek. Buck pulled the envelope out of the bag and waved it. "I brought this for you!" he cried. "Take it! Take it and leave me alone!" He stood in front of Taffy, panting and disheveled. He held out the envelope, which vibrated as if in a stiff breeze.

Taffy took the envelope. He glowered at Buck. He dropped the envelope in the sand and leaned over it. Buck saw his massive, unshaven jaws work briefly. He expectorated a huge gob of spit on the envelope. Then he stepped toward Buck and poked Buck in the chest. His fetid breath was hot on Buck's face. He said, in a guttural tone, "Watch you back. I kill you, sure." He loped off through the trees.

Buck's knees gave way, and he found himself squatting in the sand beside the defiled envelope. *I kill you, sure?* What the hell was that about? Why hadn't Taffy taken the microwave plans?

The gob of saliva lay soaking into the envelope. Buck picked up the envelope by one corner. Avoiding the wet place, he turned it over, tore it open, and extracted the document inside.

It was not a schematic diagram, but a colorful instruction book entitled *How to Use Your New MetroCook Microwave.* Crouched there, Buck leafed through it. Power levels. How to pop popcorn. Inserting the rotating tray. He didn't see any top secrets here. This pamphlet, surely was given to anybody who bought a MetroCook microwave. Was there a code embedded here somewhere? He looked through again, but he didn't think there was a code. He didn't think there were any microwave secrets. He kept hearing Taffy's guttural words: *I kill you, sure.*

Buck turned the instruction book over and looked at the back. The MetroCook microwave was made by MetroCuisine, Inc., in Akron, Ohio. MetroCuisine had plants worldwide, and they were listed in small print. One of them was MetroCuisine da Amazonia S. A. in Manaus, Brazil. And guess what? The tiniest print at the bottom of the page told it all: "A Division of Metropolitan Industries, Inc."

Damn. Dad Doolittle, the infuriated Cyndee's father, was the CEO of Metropolitan Industries. With abrupt and painful clarity, Buck saw that none of this was about microwaves. It was about getting rid of Buck Devore to please Cyndee, daddy's little girl.

Buck started to remember where he had met Duncan Crowley, who had lured him into this cockamamie scheme. He had met Duncan at one of Dad Doolittle's cocktail parties.

Buck's head swam. Talk about hell having no fury! He now realized that he, certainly, was the intended victim at the dock at the Tropical Hotel. Buck had moved out of the way at the last minute, reaching for his hat, and Taffy had shot his own confederate by mistake. Taffy was so inept. Buck almost felt hurt that after spending all the money to get Buck down here Dad wouldn't have sprung for a more efficient hit man. Except the story wasn't over yet. What he lacked in finesse, Taffy obviously made up for in persistence. Buck had to make sure Taffy's persistence didn't pay off.

Watch you back. I kill you, sure. Thoughtfully, Buck returned to Rita Randall, who was waiting on the sand. Spurning her efforts at conversation, he tried to concentrate. Where would Taffy strike? Soon, the beach party would end and the *Andromeda* would sail for Santarém, the last Amazon stop, a couple of hours away. After Santarém, it was out the mouth of the Amazon and on to Rio.

Maybe Taffy would lie in wait in Santarém. If he did, he was out of luck. Wendy had informed Buck this morning that he would not be required to leave the ship at Santarém. The port there was deep enough for the *Andromeda* to dock at a quay, and the passengers would be able to walk on and off the ship at will. That was excellent. Buck could stay tucked away on the *Andromeda,* and tomorrow they'd sail away, leaving the Amazon and Taffy.

Buck relaxed, momentarily. Then he reconsidered the phrase "walk on and off the ship at will."

Taffy, Buck did not doubt, would get on the ship somehow. He would come after Buck on the *Andromeda,* where

Buck thought he was safe and had his guard down. Buck groaned, and felt Rita patting his back in a consoling way. Taffy, the son of a bitch, would never let up until he could report to Dad Doolittle that Buck Devore was dead. Buck gave himself up to despair as Rita continued to pat his back.

Maybe it was the relaxing rhythm of the patting, maybe it was coincidence, but after a few minutes Buck got an idea. He let it ripen for a while, admiring it from every angle. When it was fully formed, he turned to Rita. He said, "Rita, there's something I want to tell you. I hope you'll hear me out, and not judge anything until I'm through. Will you do that?"

Rita looked as if her birthday and Christmas had arrived unexpectedly on the same day. "Of course! You can tell me anything!"

Buck told Rita the entire story. Not the story about Cyndee and Dad Doolittle, and being gulled and lured to Brazil to be shot. He told the story about being a sort of unofficial James Bond, a top secret operative for the government. He told how his cover had been blown by an inept cohort, and now his life was in danger because an evil Scandinavian master spy was on his trail.

Rita listened with rapt attention. At the end, she shook her head in amazement. She said, "I had no idea our relations with Scandinavia had deteriorated so badly."

Buck nodded, his face somber. "There's a lot I can't talk about. I've said too much already."

"What can I do to help, Buck? Please tell me if there's anything I can do."

Buck thought there was something she could do. He told her what it was.

ABOARD THE ANDROMEDA

As the *Andromeda* made way for Santarém, Buck Devore came in runner-up in the limbo contest. He taught a group of carousers the Macarena. He cha-chaed to "Tea for Two," waltzed to "The Tennessee Waltz," tangoed to "Adios Muchachos." He fended off three dirty propositions, none of them from Rita Randall.

In fact, he barely saw Rita until the midnight buffet on the Polaris Deck, where they just happened to stand next to each other in line. Rita looked fetching in her white silk toreador pants. Buck allowed himself a quick peek into the plunging décolletage of her red silk blouse, and he liked what he saw. They moved slowly past the tubs of trifle, the mountainous chocolate cakes, the flans, the platters of pastry. In the middle of the long table was a centerpiece of piled-up fruit. When they reached it, Rita pointed out a large cantaloupe. "How about that one?"

"Perfect." Buck reached over and extracted it from the pile. He dropped it in Rita's large straw handbag.

They had dessert on deck. The *Andromeda* had docked at Santarém, and the lights of the town glittered through the sultry evening. Buck could eat only a couple of spoonfuls of trifle. What if he'd figured the situation all wrong?

But if Buck had been given to dwelling on things he might have done wrong, he'd have had no time for anything else. It was, therefore, with his trademark panache that he winked at Rita and said, "I'd better get down to my cabin."

"Good night, Mr. Devore," she said demurely.

Ten minutes later, he heard her tap on his cabin door. She bustled in, clutching her straw bag. She looked nervous. "Do you think this will work?" she said, biting her lip.

"Absolutely. No problem. It's a tried-and-true technique." He felt compelled, as a gentleman, to add, "If you'd rather not be part of it, Rita—"

She squeezed his hand. "Don't be silly. I'm in."

What a woman! Buck hoped to God Taffy wouldn't shoot her.

In silence, they unmade Buck's narrow bunk and shoved the extra blanket between the sheets. In silence, they placed the cantaloupe on the pillow and snuggled the covers up around it. Then they turned off the lights.

Some illumination from the quay came through the thin curtains, but not much. The effect was real enough to give Buck a queasy feeling. He checked to make sure the cabin door was unlocked—he didn't want to give Taffy any undue difficulties—and then he joined Rita in the bathroom.

The bathroom was small, and completely dark. Buck gallantly allowed Rita to sit on the closed toilet seat, while he took up a post by the shower stall. The luminous dial of his watch told him it was going on two A.M. Now, they could only wait.

They conversed sporadically, in low voices. Rita told him something about herself. She was the head of her own software company, had passed on marriage in favor of her career. Recently, though, she'd found herself having second thoughts. "I've made a fortune, Buck, but I've missed out on a lot, too. Now it's time to stop and smell the roses."

"That sounds like a wonderful idea," Buck whispered enthusiastically.

At four A.M., it finally happened. They heard the click of the cabin door opening, heavy footfalls in the room. Buck felt, rather than heard, Rita shift into position. He had to trust her, now. He was gritting his teeth, waiting for the next sound.

There it was—the soft, hateful, *thock!*

Rita, right on schedule, did her part. She pushed the handle, and the toilet flushed noisily. She called out, actually managing to sound a little sleepy, "Buck? What's going on out there, darling?"

Buck wasn't breathing. Now was the moment. Either Taffy opened the bathroom door and sprayed them both with bullets, or he . . .

Taffy did his part, too. A hurried scuffling across the floor, and the cabin door clicked. Galumphing footfalls receded outside. Taffy had gotten out of there before he'd had time to inspect the "corpse."

Buck leaned against the bathroom wall. He said, "Rita, you're wonderful."

She stayed to help him clean up the mess made by the shattered cantaloupe. There was nothing they could do about the bullet embedded in the thick burlap wall covering. Buck would think of something. Hang a picture over it. Something. It would be all right. Everything would be all right. Buck Devore was dead and well.

By the next evening, the *Andromeda* had left the Amazon and was proceeding south through Atlantic swells. The lights in the lounge were dusky gold, and the orchestra was playing "The Look of Love." Buck led Rita to the dance floor and rested his hand against her back. They began to move to the music. He was looking forward to Rio.

EUNICE AND WALLY

JOYCE HARRINGTON

NEVER THOUGHT I'D live to see this day. And that's the truth. Thought I'd be long gone. But now it's Wally that's gone and I'm just a tad sorry about that. Not much, but I kind of miss him. He was reliable, you know. Could always be counted on to get himself into a window-smashing, bottle-throwing hissy fit every month or so. Talk about women having their monthlies.

My Great-aunt Augusta, she's the one that's pushing one hundred years young and just can't wait to get her letter from the President, always said I'd never see thirty, the way I lived and all. Now I admit, I was a bit wild when I was a girl—a tomboy, like. But I did settle down some when I married Wally, and if she thinks I'm the one to notify the Prez of her coming birthday, she's dead wrong. That'd be a fine thing, wouldn't it? The President of the United States of America getting a letter from a jailbird. Bet he'd just as soon get a letter from a space alien. Anyway, here I am, Eunice Eulalia Eustis Waddell, thirty-six come Christmas Eve, and it looks like I've got a full, rich, interesting life ahead of me. Ha-ha!

How I came to be named Eunice. My daddy told me, once I'd growed enough to start being bratty, that it was really pronounced "you nice" and it meant "you better be nice or

I'll whip your butt till it looks like the star-spangled banner, red and white and blue all over."

And he did that. Lots. At least until I got a tad taller than him and knocked him into the pig trough one time. Guess I was a handful. I don't know where the Eulalia came from. Nobody ever told me and there's no such name on either side of the family.

Well, miss, I don't guess you want to hear all the gory details of the Eustis family history. Oh, you do? Hum. Thought you wanted to know about me and Wally. Oh, that, too. Well, okay. If you're sure. I can't imagine how come a nice woman like you, looking so pert and trim in your pink suit and ruffly blouse, wants to know all that garbage. I'd purely like to have some earrings like yours, if I'd ever got around to getting my ears pierced.

No, I never saw that show. A TV talk show, you say? Like *Oprah* and *Geraldo*? Never paid much mind to them things, but a lot of the ladies here get into fights over which ones to watch. And they might want me to be on it if the warden gives permission? Don't guess he would, so it looks like you're just wasting your time here.

What! He chose me for you to talk to out of all the others in this dump? Now that's just plain foolish. Why would he go and do that? Most all the others is better-looking. And we all know who his pets are. Oh, yeah. Special privileges and letting them wear their own clothes on Sundays. They get to see their babies three, four times a year, them that has kids. I ain't seen my kids in six years or so. But I wouldn't let that fat slob get his paws all over me just to visit with them crumbsnatchers. Not that he's ever tried to. I bet he's just setting me up for a big letdown.

Or else you paid him. How much you paid him, miss?

No, of course you can't talk about that. That's okay. It's enough that I know. Will you buy me a new outfit to go on TV? And get my ears pierced? And a manicure? I won't do it without. Might not do it at all. Why should I spew out my guts for the whole world to snicker at? I could hear 'em now.

"What else could you expect from a great ugly cow like that?" Wally used to call me that when he was in a good mood. Ugly cow. Hate to tell you what he called me when he was pissed off.

Yeah, yeah, tell me about it. How this is gonna help a whole lot of other women who killed their rat bastard husbands. Point is, how will it help *me*? Tell me that, please.

A parole? Don't be silly. Lots of people around home was screaming for me to get the death sentence. Bet they was mighty disappointed when I got off with life. Of course, they was mostly good old boys, friends of Wally. Drinking buddies. Their wives had to go along with it or else take their lumps. I know that for a fact. One of them, a true friend if I ever had one, wrote me a letter about it. Of course, she couldn't come right out and say it 'cause they read the mail here and they'd just black out all that stuff they didn't want me to know about, but I knew what she was driving at. Wish she'd write more often. Don't hardly hear from her no more.

Nobody, not a single soul from that town, would stand up in court and say what everybody knew—that Wally was famous far and wide for bragging about how he knew how to keep his woman in her place. Honestly, he went and told his drinkin' buddies each and every black eye and broken bone he ever dealt me.

Them that did get up swore to Jesus that Wally was a righteous and God-fearing gent, a family man and loving husband, and wasn't it a crying shame that his evil and ungrateful wife turned on him like that and swatted him not once but four times with a stray machete just happened to be laying around the house. See, I'd been using it that day to chop down some of the underbrush that was taking over my vegetable garden.

Anyway, I'm not properly remorseful about it according to the judge, so they'll never let me out. If I went on TV, I'd probably tell the world I'd be happy to do it all over again, only next time I'd make sure I wouldn't get caught. So I don't guess anybody's gonna go to bat for me, even if I did go on TV and tell the truth about what really happened. Which never came out at the trial, of course.

But I'll tell you what you could do. I like to grow things. Corn and string beans and tomatoes. Things like that. Flowers, too. Used to make hollyhock princesses for my girls. Guess it comes from growing up on a farm. Wish they'd let me have a garden here. It's truly the only thing I really do miss. Do you think you could get them to give me a little bit of ground for a garden, and a few seeds? Wouldn't have to be much. And it would sure improve the diet around here.

Well, never mind. I already asked and they said the only open ground was the softball field and I couldn't have that.

What do you mean, what about my kids? What about them?

Oh, well. Their grandma's taking care of them. At least she was the last I heard. Of course, she didn't do so good in raising up Wally, did she? Just as mean and nasty as a scorpion, he was. But he could be sweeter than sugar when he wanted something, if you know what I mean.

How many? Five or six, I don't know. Can't keep their names straight anymore. I ain't even got a picture of them. I wrote once and asked their grandma, but she never wrote back. She never did like me none. Always said her Wally deserved something better than one of them no-account Eustises, and the ugliest one to boot. I'm real surprised she took over the kids after she spread it all over town about them probably not being Wally's.

Fact is them kids all belonged to Wallace Otis Waddell and if he ever said otherwise, he was lying. But he never did, as far as I know. No, he fairly doted on them, couldn't wait to see me swell up and drop another one. All girls, you know. Let's see now, the oldest one, that'd be Angel Dora, she'd be about nineteen by now. That's where the trouble started, you know. With Angel Dora.

Not that there wasn't trouble before, but I mean real, rotten, sneaky, lowdown trouble. Wally always was quick with his hands, beat up on me as soon as look at me. Just like my daddy. But I never minded that. I'd just let him have it right back, broke his jaw once, and most times we'd wind up in bed, sweating up a storm and laughing and hollering like crazy.

But then Angel Dora started growing her little titties and getting all womanly and flirty. My, she was pretty. Nothing at all like me. Naturally curly golden hair and big blue eyes with eyelashes a foot long. No bigger than a minute, not a great big clumsy hulk like her momma. Dainty, you know what I mean? Delicate. But not the teeniest chunk of good sense in her pretty little head. I sure do hope she's married somebody nice by now and settled down. For all I know, I could have some grandbabies by now. I told her to forget all about me, and I guess she did just that.

She always used to talk about getting out of that dinky little town and going off to New York or San Francisco or maybe even Hollywood, where she could have some fun and see something besides trailer parks and that puny little mall that didn't have anything worth craving for. Wouldn't have minded if she did, but I guess her daddy would have had something to say about it. Wouldn't have minded going off myself, but I never did see my way clear to do it.

Now I'll say this for Wally. He was a good provider. There was always food on the table, and plenty of it. Wally was a champ at the supper table. At the six-packs, too. And he liked his Wild Turkey something fierce. Me and the girls never lacked for anything we really needed.

He was a truck driver, you know. Had his own truck. Not the long-haul stuff, just around home and the towns nearby, sometimes as far as the state capital. Made a pretty good living at it, long as he stayed sober and didn't get into fights with the folks who hired him. Would have been better, maybe, if he had gone coast to coast. Then he wouldn't have been around so much, and I wouldn't have had so many kids, and maybe he wouldn't have done what he did to Angel Dora.

It's funny how they both kept it a secret from me for even

a minute. I didn't blame him so much for doing it. Or her. I told you already how Angel Dora was so cute and all, and how she started getting flirty. I mean with him. I could see that he would want to take her up on it. He didn't have much more sense than she did.

It made me recall how it was with my own daddy. Made me feel proud, it did. That he liked me better than my mother. Made me feel pretty for a change. I didn't think then about how it made my momma feel. Guess she must have known about it. Guess that's why she wouldn't let me come back home the first and last time I ever left Wally. That was before Angel Dora was born and I was sick as a dog and Wally whacked me something terrible 'cause I couldn't get up and cook his breakfast.

Angel Dora didn't need any reassurance on the pretty-face score. She was always primping herself in front of the mirror and begging for new clothes and lipsticks and what all. And whenever I said no, Wally, he'd say, "Ah, Eunice, get her what she wants. It ain't like we can't afford it, long as she don't run to mink coats and diamond doodads."

So that's the way it was with him and her. Didn't take no genius to figure out what those trips in the truck was all about. He said it was just to let her see something of the world and so he could have some company on the road. Some world she got to see!

I followed them one time in my old station wagon. Didn't get no further than a clearing in the woods on the other side of Punkie's Creek. You ever seen them bumper stickers? The ones that say "If the trailer's rockin' don't keep knockin'"? No, I don't guess you would, being from New York and all. Anyway, that truck took to rockin' like it was gonna fly into smithereens. I went on home and cooked supper. Stuffed pork chops and fresh peas from my garden, I believe it was that night. I remember shelling those peas with the tears dripping down on them.

No, indeed. That ain't why I killed him. I just regarded it as one form of birth control. The more he took Angel Dora on those trips, the less he bothered me. I just took her down to the clinic and got her some of those pills. Told her to keep it secret from him, otherwise he'd take 'em away from her and whale her good. Just like he did to me.

Boy, was she surprised! She thought I didn't know nothing about what they was doing. She said, "Ma, don't you care? Don't you mind?"

I told her, "Sure I care. Sure I mind. But how do you expect me to make him stop? Did you ever try to stop him from doing anything he damn well wanted to?"

She hung her pretty little head then, and said, "No, I never."

I had to hug her, she looked so sad and sorry. "You kinda like it, don't you?" I said. "Makes you feel special."

She bust out cryin' then, slobbering all over the front of my apron. "I won't do it no more, Ma!" she wailed. "I'll be good. I promise."

Then I had to pet her, and mop up all those tears. "It ain't your fault, honey," I told her, wondering all the time how either one of us could get him to leave off. And if he did leave off with her, wouldn't he just start up with June Ellen, who was next in age and maybe not as pretty as Angel Dora, but not a mess either?

Tell the police? Now how could I do that? Wasn't his brother, Elton, the only police we had in that town and what do you think he'd do if I told him a story like that? He'd tell Wally and Wally would come roaring home and break both my legs and wreck the house. Probably would have killed Angel Dora for telling me about it, even though she didn't and I found out for myself.

I did tell my mother about it, because I had to tell somebody. But she just stared at me as if I was clean out of my mind. Well, that's the way she looked at everybody after Daddy died and she turned peculiar. Not that she was crazy, you understand, just a little bit out of it. Pretended to be reading her Bible all the time, when everybody knew she couldn't read a word. I guess she had it memorized from listening to the preacher so much. She's gone, too, now. Died about a year or so ago. I don't think she ever really knew what happened to Wally, and that's a blessing. Would have really put her round the bend to think of one of hers in jail for murder. Even if she didn't like me and didn't even know who I was anymore.

Do I believe in angels? Course not. That's another thing didn't endear me any with the folks back home. I wouldn't go to any of their churches and wouldn't send my kids to their Sunday school. Some of them started saying I was a witch. Got nothing to do with how I named Angel Dora, if that's what you're thinking. She was named after one of Wally's cousins. All the girls were named after his family. He said if I had any boys I could name them after mine. Why do you ask that?

Oh, this little pendant thing. Well, one of the ladies here, she talks to angels and she makes these things out of candy bar wrappers and hairpins. She's in for forgery, signing away her dead mother's Social Security checks. She'll get out soon, but I dunno where she's gonna go. Worries me a bit. She puts a message inside each one she makes, a bit of advice from her angels. Gives them to her special friends. Far as I can tell, she gives them to everybody, but I'm the only one who's willing to wear it around my neck and don't make fun of her. Makes her happy and it don't bother me none. Want to know what my message was? "Don't get your bowels in an uproar." Now that's pretty angelic, don't you think?

Come to think of it, it's not such bad advice. About on a par with "Blessed are the meek." If I'd been a little meeker and didn't get so mad at Wally, I wouldn't be here today. But that never was my way. In my whole life, I never was able to cool down my temper. But I never got truly mad over stupid little things. Wally was really good at pulling off stupid big things that made my blood just boil until it sent the steam coming out my ears.

Aha! Yes! Why didn't I just leave him? Good question,

miss, and I ain't got a good answer for it. My lawyer asked me that and I didn't have a good answer for him either. I suppose I could have said it was because I loved him, but I'm not sure I did. I don't think I hated him either. To this day, I'm not sure how I felt about him, and I've thought about that a lot.

And it wasn't because I don't believe in divorce. I already told you I didn't go to church, and I don't go when they have the preacher come here. I got my own way of thinking about God and church and all, and it don't include most of what they tell you in church. I could have divorced him. I guess I should have. I guess I was just lazy.

I did think about it once or twice, but then I got to thinkin' about where would I go and what would I do. Had a job once, before I married Wally, cleaning rooms at a motel out on the highway. I was fifteen then, and Wally used to come in from time to time with one or another of his women. That's how I met him. He used to kid around with me and tell me I was the only woman he could trust. Didn't dawn on me then that what he meant was he could trust me because nobody would ever put temptation in my path.

Anyway, I sure didn't want to take up cleaning motel rooms again, and I never had any other kind of job. Married Wally when I was sixteen, and he didn't think too highly about me keeping that motel job. Said he'd take care of me. Didn't he ever!

Yeah, he was older than me by about ten years, and not bad-lookin' even if he did grease his hair down tryin' to look like Elvis. He used to try to make me jealous, tellin' me about how he could have any woman he wanted and if I didn't be nice he'd go off with one of his old girlfriends. Found out years later that he used to pay those women who went to the motel with him. I was really pretty stupid back then.

I was purely surprised out of my mind that Wally wanted to marry me. But I thought I might as well, since there wasn't anybody else gettin' in line. Found out later that he really had his eye on my daddy's farm.

Come to think of it, he didn't start beatin' up on me until my daddy told him that no way in hell would he ever turn the farm over to any Waddell, even one who was married to his daughter. Don't know why Wally wanted the farm. Maybe just because he didn't own any land of his own. That's a big thing with some folks. No way would Wally ever have known what to do with a farm. Guess he thought I would do all the work.

Guess one reason I married Wally was to get away from doing farmwork. It was a dairy farm my daddy had, and pigs and chickens too, and I had to tend to milking all those cows before I went to work at the motel. We had milking machines, but still it wasn't much fun. Cows are pretty stupid. I can't stand to drink milk to this day. The only part I liked was my vegetable garden. You can really see things bloom and grow and get ripe. That's a satisfaction.

Well, miss, it's nice of you to say that. But tell me, what do you suppose a murderer would seem like? Not like someone who likes to grow vegetables and knows about milking cows, I guess. You'd be wrong though. Besides me, there's about five or six others in here, and they're just ordinary people who just happened to be in the wrong place at the wrong time and got kind of upset about it.

Let me ask *you* a question now, miss. What does this place smell like to you?

Uh-huh. Not so wonderful, is it. It's funny how I can't even smell it anymore. But I can remember how it was when I first got here. Thought I'd never get used to it. Toilets and sweat and dirty socks and disinfectant. All I can smell right now is that perfume, whatever it is, that you're wearing.

Passion? Never heard of it, but it's a pretty funny name for a perfume. Had some lilac toilet water once, but Wally said it made me smell like a moldy old woman, so I threw it down the toilet.

Look, I don't think I want to talk about this anymore, and besides, that guard out there is about to come in here and tell us time's up. But before you go, would you do me a favor?

Would you look up Angel Dora and let me know how she is? You don't have to see her or talk to her, but I'm sure you could just find out where she is and if she's married and so forth. And the rest of them, too. I would like to know that.

Next week? Well, I suppose so. I ain't got any pressing engagements. If it's okay with the warden, it's okay with me. Give me a chance to think over this whole thing and decide if I want to do it or not. Sure would be a hoot. I don't suppose anybody back home would ever expect to see me on TV, except for the time I was arrested.

Well, here comes the guard. Guess it's time for me and you to go.

Okay, okay, I'm comin'. You have a good day now, miss, and I really mean that. You're the only person's been halfway decent to me since I can't remember when. Bye, now.

Guess what, miss. I got a letter from Angel Dora. Not a letter so much. One of them cards you send to folks in the hospital. "Get well soon," it said. Guess she couldn't find any for someone in state prison. "Hope you get out soon." Hallmark's sure missing a bet there.

Anyway, she said you'd been to see her, and you'd tell me all about it. Said she was trying to do like I told her and forget all about me, but it was hard. Hoped I was well and maybe she'd come and see me someday. Excuse me, miss, but why are you wearing them dark glasses? Ain't it gloomy enough in here for you?

Oh, my. Now that's a beaut of a shiner. How'd you get that? No, don't tell me. It ain't none of my business. But if it was your man, I hope you popped him right back.

Angel Dora did that? Go on! Whatever did you do to her to make her haul off and hit you?

Well, now, miss. That was pretty dumb, if you don't mind my saying so. I don't mind going on TV and spilling my guts. After all, my story was all over the newspapers and TV at the time it happened. I ain't got no secrets. But I never expected you would ask her to tell her side of the story. Might as well get the whole town on TV and have a free-for-all.

Did you and her get in a fistfight? She's littler than you, unless she's growed some, and not a bit brawny like me.

A frying pan? Hooeee! Now *that* I can see her doing. She was always throwing things whenever she would get in a temper. Was it full or empty?

Well, that's a blessing. Didn't ruin any of your pretty clothes with grease and all. Not to mention that it might have been hot. I bet it was that old cast-iron skillet of mine. I remember tossing that at Wally a time or two. I guess Angel Dora was watching and learning. Some lesson I taught her, don't you think?

Well, shiners do fade after a while, and you'll never know you had it.

But I gotta tell you, miss, I never meant for you to actually talk to Angel Dora. Didn't I say that? All I wanted was to know how she was doing and if she was married.

Not, huh? And no kids, I suppose. Oh well, she's still young. Maybe next year.

She's doing what? Good Lord-a-mercy! I can't hardly believe it. My pretty little Angel Dora, who hated school worse than poison, in college studying to be a teacher! If that don't beat all!

Well, of course, I'm proud of her. What do you think? I wonder why she didn't write that to me in her card. Come to think of it, she did get all the words spelled right for a change and she wrote it all real nice and neat. I been studying and reading a lot in here, and there's so much I never knew. Wish I'd have had the chance to learn things when I was young.

And now I understand why she threw that frying pan at you. You were pretty lucky to get out of there alive. She's trying to do something nice for herself and then you come along and look like you want to spoil it all for her.

Guess it means I can't go on TV and tell the whole truth about what happened. But maybe I never would have any-

way. I thought it over a lot since you were here before. See,
I was feeling kinda mean towards Angel Dora and just about
everybody else when we talked before. So I was ripe to spill
everything.

But now that she's getting herself an education, it wouldn't
be fair for me to bring up all that old stuff on TV where her
teachers and all would see it. I'm gonna write her a letter
and tell her so.

But I'm gonna tell you what really happened, just so you
understand next time you go messing around in people's
lives. You just can't ever know what you're gonna get yourself into. And you might not like what happens to you. You
were real lucky it was just a frying pan. And if you ever tell
another soul, why, I'll just say you made it all up out of spite
on account of I wouldn't play along.

The day that it happened, I remember it real well, I had
gone out to the mall to get some new underpants for the
twins. Billy Sue and Betty Jo. Theirs was getting kinda
raggedy. They was about five then, the youngest of the lot,
and they got to wear a lot of hand-me-downs. It was sum-
mertime, and I left Angel Dora in charge of the whole gang.
I didn't want to take any of them with me or else it would
take half the day, and I had a lot of other things to do.

Wally was down at his trucking office or somewhere,
'cause he didn't have any hauling work that day. Said he was
gonna give the truck a lube job and maybe change the tires.
He really took good care of that truck. It was his pride and
joy. But I knew he'd probably wind up at The Roost after-
wards with some of his cronies. So I wasn't expecting him
back until suppertime.

Anyway, so I'm gone about an hour and when I got back
I found the truck in the driveway and four of them playing
around in it, honking the horn and pretending to drive it. But
no sign of Angel Dora.

I shooed them out of the truck before Wally came out and
saw them and had a conniption. Then I went on in the back
door, thinking I would just have time to get supper started

and give Angel Dora hell for letting them little ones play in the truck. I just never imagined what I would find in the kitchen.

When I saw what was there, I closed the back door and locked it so the little ones wouldn't come barging in. Then I yelled out for Angel Dora, "You better get in here, girl, and tell me what happened!"

She came creeping in from the pantry, where I kept all the stuff I'd put up from my garden. Shelves and shelves of Mason jars full of vegetables and fruit. And wasn't she a sight!

"Are you gonna tell me or do I have to guess?" I asked her. She was shaking all over so bad she couldn't speak. So I guessed. "You did this, didn't you?"

She whimpered a little and nodded her head, which wasn't so pretty what with the blood all matted in her hair and smeared on her face and clothes.

I took her in my arms and held her strong, so she would stop shaking. And while I was doing that, I took stock of the situation.

There was Wally on the floor, as dead as he'd ever be. Blood all over the place, and him lying in a great pool of it. There was my machete, which I remembered hanging on its nail on the back porch. It was lying on the floor beside him, all streaked and smeared with blood. So all I needed to know was why.

"Let's go up to the bathroom, honey, and get you cleaned up," I said to Angel Dora. "You look a fright."

She came along, just as biddable as a lamb. I filled up the bathtub, undressed her myself, and bathed her just as if she was a tiny baby. The water was nice and hot, and she stopped shaking after a bit. First thing she said was, "I'm sorry, Momma."

"I know you are, darling," I said. "Now, don't you worry about a thing. Momma's gonna take care of everything." Even though I didn't know how I was gonna do that.

I could hear the kids outside, back in the truck and honking the horn like crazy. Best they should stay there until I got this thing figured out.

I got Angel Dora dressed in clean pajamas and tucked her into bed. I said, "I'll bring you some tea in a minute. You just rest now."

She grabbed my hand and pulled me down on the bed. "He wanted me to do it with him in your bed," she said, all whispery and slow. "I wouldn't never do that and I told him so. He got real mad and said he didn't have to put up with no lip from me and I better do what he said or he'd cut off my nose. He was waving that machete at me and as soon as he set it down, I grabbed it and . . . and . . ."

She pulled the covers over her head and I could hear her crying underneath them. I sat there for a couple minutes, thinking about how it was all my fault for not trying to stop him from messing around with Angel Dora.

Then I took her dirty clothes down to the old woodstove from the farm that I kept for old time's sake and to keep the kitchen nice and warm in the winter. Had to kind of skitter around Wally to do it. And that's when I got the idea.

Somebody was going to have to take the blame for this, and it wasn't gonna be Angel Dora. She just did what she had to do. Once I got the fire going in the stove and the clothes near burnt to cinders, I picked up the machete and dealt him a couple more whacks. Made sure I got plenty of blood on my hands and clothes and in my hair, just like Angel Dora.

Then I picked up the phone and called the police station. When Elton answered, I said, "Guess what! Your brother's dead. You better get on out here."

So, that's the true story, miss. That's how Wallace Otis Waddell met his end and I'll be spending the rest of my days in this dump. What do you think now, miss? Still want me to be on your TV show? Without Angel Dora and not mentioning any of what I just told you? I didn't think so.

Be real careful going out, honey. Don't get anywhere near that warden. You're just his type.

MORPHING THE MILLENNIUM

JUDITH KELMAN

COSMO DANZA CHOMPED the heel off his foot-long hot dog. He chewed with the rhythmic pooch and pucker of a sea bass. When he swallowed, his porcine features went slack with bliss. A low moan, like phone sex, escaped him.

"Mmmm—mmmm! I gotta tell you, Len, I don't know what Manny puts in these dogs, but I couldn't make it through the day without a couple or three."

Lenny Cambio tucked his revulsion behind a studied smile. He knew precisely what went into hot dogs: entrails, carcinogenic preservatives, incidental vermin and their droppings, and globules of artery-clogging fat. Lenny knew what got into people, too. *Fear.*

If not for the fear, he'd be sailing the Caribbean right now, enjoying the spoils of his well-earned success. But for blind, mindless panic, he'd be lounging on a deck chair, basking his Dustin Hoffman features in the sun. He'd be feasting on oysters and caviar, slaking his thirst with Dom Pérignon. Living the good life.

Instead, he was forced to squander his time in Manny Dibble's dive at the shabby outskirts of Stamford, Connecticut. He was sick of this town, this dump, this bleak, interminable cold weather. Most of all, he was sick of the blowhard glutton across the table.

Lenny's hands balled in furious fists. This was not the

151

way things were meant to be. Lenny's Morphosphere had been destined to be the toy of the century. Bigger than Pogs and Power Rangers, in more fevered demand than Cabbage Patch Kids, a classic of Barbie-esque proportions.

Then, destiny tripped.

Six months ago, an eight-year-old Cleveland girl named Pammy Pashkiss snuck into her big brother's room and swiped the Morphosphere he'd purchased with his paper-delivery money (Deluxe Arachnid model, $24.95—carrying case, storage box, and optional accessory pack not included).

Pammy tucked the toy under her Care Bears sweatshirt and skulked out of the house. In the driveway, she bounced the bright plastic ball for several minutes without incident. Then, the sphere rolled away from her and caught the spray from a neighbor's lawn sprinkler. On contact, the plastic orb morphed—as it was designed to do—into a strikingly life-like scorpion.

This dazzling ability to morph had made Cambio's invention the hit of Play-Expo '99 in Chicago last May. There, the Morphosphere had garnered an unprecedented trio of gold medals for originality, play value, and appeal. Huge press coverage had ensued. Lenny's company, Morphman, Inc., had been deluged with orders. The product had been promised a lead slot in the Toys "R" Us Christmas catalog. Prime window space at FAO Schwartz. A ten-minute segment on *Oprah*'s top-rated annual show on child-spoiling hints.

Then along came Pammy Pashkiss.

Confronted with the scorpion, the child shrieked with the force of an air raid siren. Unfortunately, this was the last sound to pass Pammy's lips. She was shocked mute, her blue eyes and rosebud mouth stretched in circles of perpetual surprise.

Medication proved ineffectual. So did a variety of therapies, including a visit by the child's idol, Vladimir Brozshky.

Brozshky and other chess greats banded together to express their horror at the tragic loss. For Pammy Pashkiss was a chess prodigy. At age three, she had plunked herself down at her big brother's chessboard. She'd refused to move until she had learned the rudiments of the game. By four, she had been winning master's level tournaments. At five, she had graced the cover of *Checkmate* magazine. The child had been hailed as the greatest child chess player since the dog-faced Ludwig Orloff. Plus, she was seriously cute. Pammy had been expected to do even more to boost the fickle popularity of the game than Orloff's nose job had done.

But after her encounter with the scorpion, the little girl devolved into a silent, sulking recluse. She spent her days glued to the Home Shopping Network. Experts on post-traumatic stress syndrome warned that Pammy might never return to normal, much less to her former genius.

The incident aroused the passions of the plaything watchdog group AMASS (Angry Mothers Against Scary Stuff). They held rallies, staged hunger strikes, lobbied Congress.

Soon, the Consumer Product Safety Commission placed the Morphosphere under investigation. Child-development experts glutted the airwaves with warnings about the toy. Pediatricians clamored for a nationwide recall.

Orders dried up. Morphman, Inc., was overwhelmed with complaints, returns, and threats of lawsuits. Lenny was stuck holding the bag, not to mention a two-million-three-hundred-forty-seven-thousand-eight-hundred-and-sixty-two-dollar invoice from Cyberplastics, Inc., supplier of the raw materials.

Cosmo Danza swiped his mustard mustache with the back of a hairy hand. He called, "Hey, Manny. Another Double Dibble Dog with the works. You, Len? Got room?"

Lenny's gaze dipped to the wadded hot dog bits stuffed in the napkin on his lap. He would never eat such pustulant rubbish. As a man of science, he knew the truth of the saying "You are what you eat." Cosmo Danza was, very definitely a hot dog.

Lenny patted his taut abs. "No more for me, Cosmo. Watching the old waistline."

Danza sighed. "Afraid I'm watching mine grow. Barely have time to breathe these days, much less exercise. Took me a year of sweat and diet to drop the extra thirty pounds of pork, and here they are, creeping back on me like something out of *The Blob*. You can't imagine what a guy has to do to keep going under circumstances like these. It's a bitch."

"How many accounts left to go?"

"After this, only one, thank the Lord. Started the year with fourteen, all big, hysterical emergencies. Long as I live, I'll never understand why so many companies waited until it came down to the wire like this. Experts have been warning about the Millennium Time Bomb for years."

"Maybe those corporate chiefs are village idiots like me when it comes to computer stuff, Cosmo. You've explained that Time Bomb business to me a bunch of times, and I have to admit, I still don't exactly get it."

"Hell, you're smart enough, Lenny. You must have some kind of mental block."

"I'm a blockhead all right. Hate to be a pest, but would you mind running it by me one more time?"

Bamsie Sue Dibble, the owner's big-haired blond daughter, ferried Cosmo's order from the grill. She wore a skirt the size of an Ace bandage and a fuchsia tank top. The hot dog lolled in the shade of her enormous boobs. "Here you go, Mr. Danza," Bamsie chirped. "One Double Dibble Dog. Fries are on the house."

Lenny's eyeballs bobbled to the beat of Bamsie's ass as she sashayed back toward the grill. If not for the fear, he'd have a juicy young thing like Bamsie Sue along on his cruise. She could fetch and carry and could soothe his fevered whatever. Give new meaning to the term *deck hand*.

Lenny grabbed Danza's plate. "Let me fix that up for you, Cosmo."

"Sure, great. No one dresses a dog like you, Len."

At the fixins bar, Lenny heaped the foot-long with mustard, relish, ketchup, mayonnaise, salt, sugar, Sweet'n Low, and sauerkraut. Whatever he slopped on to mask the taste would be fine. Danza was about as discriminating as a garbage disposal.

Cosmo crammed half the dog in his maw. Spewing sauerkraut scraps, he said, "You wanted me to explain the Millennium Time Bomb thing again?"

"I'd appreciate it, Cosmo. Maybe this time it'll sink in."

"No problem, kid. Here's the deal."

Lenny arranged his face so it appeared to be uninhabited by intelligent life. In truth, he knew as much about the Millennium Time Bomb as anyone on the planet. He'd studied the problem and all its glorious implications for months. That computer glitch was his ticket to salvation.

Cosmo licked the mustard drips from his porky chin. "It's like this. Back when computers were hatched in the fifties, dates were expressed in two digits to save space. 'Nineteen fifty' was 'five-oh,' for example.

"Because of that, old-time software isn't equipped to handle the transition to the year 2000. When the clocks move from ninety-nine to double zero, the computers would think time was moving in reverse. They'd go whacko. Crash city." Danza belched, spreading a garlicky haze. "You with me so far, Lenny?"

"It's pretty complicated."

"Nah, not really. What happened is, new programs were built around those old ones, which are called legacy software." Danza clicked his Bic and doodled a diagram on his grease-stained napkin. An old program, marked with an x, nestled in the center of a crazy quilt of modern applications. Separating out the old codes would be like trying to remove a single molecule of Dibble Dog from the mammoth blob of adipose tissue that Danza had become.

Pointing at the diagram, Cosmo explained, "Tiny pieces of the hundreds of thousands of lines of code in a company's files could be a problem, You gotta go in, find the glitches, and fix them all."

"Kind of like that genetic stuff, you mean?"

"You talking DNA?"

"Right, that."

Cosmo sucked down a fistful of curly fries. "It's sort of the same, only different. With DNA, when you screw up the code, you get some kind of disease. When it comes to the Millennium Time Bomb, everything looks hunky-dory until the clocks strike midnight on December thirty-one. Then, any company that's been dragging its heels is—to use the technical term—fucked. They can't get their bills out, pay-roll, anything based on the old-dated codes. Could take months to straighten out the mess. Meanwhile, if a business is the least bit shaky, it could go belly up."

Lenny frowned. "How do you prevent that? Are you say-ing you read every line of code yourself?"

"Hell, no. That'd take years. What I do is use special tools to pick up the date-sensitive bits in the company's software. It's a trip to get everything analyzed, but once I do and run the tests, the problem's solved." He scowled at his Timex. "Speaking of which, I'd better run back to Cyberplastics. Another day or two and I'll be ready to purge all those nasty bugs out of their system."

"What then? They throw a party? Blow you to a fancy dinner?"

"Yeah, right. I'm the invisible man, kiddo. I fax a report to the boss that the job's been done, send my bill, and that's that."

"A fat bill, I hope."

Cosmo sniffed. "Would you believe ten thousand eight hundred thirty-eight dollars and sixty-seven cents, including my equipment costs? By the hour, that's about a dollar and a half. But it's all I could squeeze out of those tightwad bean counters. Truth is, they don't give a damn about me, Lenny. All that matters to them is the fix." He patted his briefcase.

"You've got the solution right there?"

"You can bet the family jewels on it, kiddo. Never let this baby out of my sight. I even sleep with her, which tells you way more than you need to know about my love life."

Rising, Lenny tossed two singles on the table for Bamsie Sue. "See you tomorrow?"

Cosmo stood, raining crumbs from his pea green polyesters. "Sure will. Any day I don't show up for my hot dog fix, you can figure I'm dead."

Trailing Danza out, Lenny smirked. Dead, he thought. Exactly.

Seventeen minutes later, Lenny swerved into his prime spot adjoining the entrance to Morphman, Inc. In its heyday, the company lot was jammed. Three shifts worked seven days a week to meet production quotas. Lenny provided on-site sports facilities, self-sanitizing restrooms, and nutrient-intensive cafeteria fare to keep the plant and its worker bees buzzing at peak.

Now, a sorry smattering of cars was strewn across the lot. The untimely demise of the Morphosphere had forced Lenny to cut his massive staff to the bone.

Facilities, too. Lenny's heart shlumped at the sight of the place. Morphman, Inc., looked dim and dejected. Soiled snow mounds dotted the brown-patched lawn. The building was streaked with rust stains. Most of the windows were dark.

Lenny's secretary was hunched over the executive-suite reception desk, painting her toenails a bilious brown. The moment Morphman, Inc., fell in its lethal tailspin, Arliss Marden had abandoned her Katherine Gibbs professionalism for a smart mouth and sullen attitude. Her dour face was scored with frown lines. She glanced up at him through contemptuous, bag-rimmed eyes.

"I was just about to leave you a note. Soon as these piggies dry, I'm out of here. I'll give you a couple of hours tomorrow morning, but you won't see me Wednesday or Thursday. I've got stuff to do."

"Listen here, Ms. Marden. I don't pay you to take all this time off."

She cracked her gum. "Actually, you don't pay me at all."

"Rest assured, your salary with interest will be forthcoming shortly."

"Oh yeah? Try paying the fucking rent with forthcoming shortly. Try laying a stack of forthcoming shortlies on the fucking grocer."

Lenny shrugged off the insubordination. Lately, he'd struggled with feelings of hopelessness and depression, but today he felt his old ebullient self. Carefree, confident, on top of the world. The solution to his problems was in place.

The pellets were trickling down Cosmo Danza's esophagus. The glutton's fate was being sealed by the inexorable forces of gravity and peristalsis.

"That's fine, Ms. Marden," Lenny said. "Take all the time you wish. Retire early and often. You have my blessing and Uncle Sam's to pursue a more pleasing course of endeavor."

Arliss rolled her puffy eyes. "What the fuck's the matter with you?"

"How thoughtful of you to inquire. Actually, I'm fine. I'll be in conference for a bit. Hold my calls."

Lenny strode into his office and double-locked the door. Stooping, he worked the combination on the safe. He slid out his latest invention and bore it reverently toward the desk. Sweeping away the mountain of dunning notices, he set the prototype down.

Once this top secret device was launched, he would have all the boats and bubbly and bimbos he desired. Lenny's stock and the company's would soar once again. He would take his few remaining loyal staff members along for the ride. Impertinent shrews like Arliss Marden could ponder their perfidy on the unemployment line.

Lenny set the timer on his watch for ten minutes. Peering into a folding mirror, he positioned a strip of clear, plastic mesh on his head behind the hairline and pressed it firmly in place. He ran a brush over the mesh, extracting enough hair to cover the plastic. After applying another strip at his neck-line, he flipped on the heat lamp.

The mesh constricted, raising and tightening the flesh on his face. In seconds, twenty years melted from his middle-aged visage. Every line, sag, and bag vanished. He had long been taken for Dustin Hoffman's double. Now, he could pass for the actor's teenaged kid.

Lenny called his miraculous new invention About Face. The revolutionary nonsurgical facelift was bound to gener-ate incredible fervor in the marketplace.

The intercom razzed. "Phone for you," Arliss snarled.

"I asked you to hold my calls, Ms. Marden."

"Hold them yourself. My nails are wet."

Arliss clicked off before he could ask who was on the line. "Len Cambio speaking."

"It's Jack Baxter, Cambio. And it's four o'clock. Where's that payment you promised two hours ago?"

"Must be there by now, Jack. Have you checked today's receipts?"

"Only twenty, thirty times."

Cyberplastic's head bookkeeper had a voice like bad brakes. Lenny kept his own tone firm and commanding. "That can't be. I instructed my banker to wire the funds first thing this morning. Spoke to him myself, so there'd be no screwups." Lenny flushed hot with the lie. The mesh drew tighter, narrowing his eyes and angling them into single quotation marks.

"This whole thing has been a major screwup," Baxter mewled. "And the one getting screwed up is me. I stuck my neck out for you. You promised to deliver the entire out-standing balance by today."

"Let me call the bank and straighten it out, Jack. I'll get right back to you."

"Please. I'm drowning here."

Lenny killed five minutes studying his uplifted image in the mirror. As his blood pressure dropped, the eyes resumed their normal shape and position. The pallor eased as the circulation to his forehead was restored. His involuntary smile disappeared.

The mesh was a *teeny* bit hyperactive to heat. He'd have to modify the formula, maybe add a neutralizing agent. No big thing.

Cyberplastic's switchboard patched him through to the billing department. Jack Baxter seized the phone on the first ring. "What, Cambio? Tell me you've found the funds."

"Seems we've got a mystery on our hands," Lenny said. "My man swears he put the transfer through. He's tracing it. Should have an answer for us in a few days. Maybe a week."

Baxter groaned. "I can't wait a week. If management spots this hole in the ledger, it'll be my scalp."

"Speak to you soon as I know something, Jack. Keep the faith."

"You can't do this to me, Cambio. Christmas this year is hard enough on my four kids, now that all that's left of their mother is the medical bills. If I get canned, Santa will have to leave them IOUs."

"Not to worry, Jack. I'm on the case."

"You promised me, Cambio. You swore."

Hanging up, Lenny scowled. Baxter had some nerve whining about his dead wife and motherless kids and medical debts and flagging career.

All that was nothing compared to Lenny's problems. He was up to elevated ears in past due bills and government investigations. Righteous buttinskys kept telling him how to run his company. All his hard work on the Morphosphere had gone down the drain. His brilliant invention was trashed because of one sniveling little sneak.

In truth, Pammy Pashkiss had brought the horror on herself. She'd trespassed in her brother's room and stolen his toy. Instead of all the bad press, Lenny should have been praised for teaching the little bitch a lesson.

Well, damn Pammy Pashkiss. Damn Jack Baxter and his demanding brats. Damn them all!

Lenny's cheeks flamed. The skin drew hideously tight

across his face. Spikes of pain stabbed deep within his shrink-wrapped skull. The agony grew with such ferocity that Lenny feared he'd lose his mind.

In desperation he drew a glassful of frigid water from the cooler and slopped it over his head. He sighed his relief as the plastic eased its frenzied grip.

The alarm sounded, signaling the end of his daily test run. Lenny removed the mesh and returned it to the safe. Maybe he needed to use less PF386 and more XR244 to reduce the product's heat sensitivity. A minor adjustment.

Lenny breezed out through reception. "I'll be in the field for the rest of the day, Ms. Marden."

Arliss blew on her fingernails. "Ask me if I care."

Lenny brushed off the sarcasm. He'd taken all the care that was necessary with his schedule for the remainder of the afternoon. He would be seen in highly public places by hordes of unimpeachable witnesses. Though he was confident that he would have no need for an alibi, a bit of extra insurance never hurt.

By now, the pellets were entering Danza's distended stomach, swirling amid the semi-processed Dibble Dogs and greasy spuds.

Lenny visited the children's ward at St. Joseph's Hospital, where he'd arranged to distribute rejects from Morphman's product-development lab. These were toys deemed too flimsy or dangerous for sale. No reason they shouldn't be parlayed into a tax deduction, Lenny figured. What better place for the tykes to be, should an injury occur, than a hospital?

Next, he stopped at Westhill High School, where he was scheduled as a featured speaker for Career Day. His remarks were pithy and compelling, if he did say so himself. In conclusion, he said, "You want to know the secret to success in business? It's the same advice my look-alike, Dustin Hoffman, received in *The Graduate:* plastics."

Danza's stomach acids were slowly eroding the pellets' plastic casing.

At the Turn of River Volunteer Fire Department, Lenny met with the chief and pledged a generous contribution. He repeated the noble gesture at the Easter Seals Rehabilitation Center, the Association for Retarded Citizens, the Lower Fairfield County Child Guidance Clinic, the Rape Crisis Center, several nursing homes, and Our Lady of Perpetual Sorrow RC Church.

Lenny believed in charity, especially the kind that began at home. Altruism was the perfect antidote for his Pashkiss-soiled image. He would strong-arm his employees to make good on the pledges with a contribution to Morphman, Inc.'s, Community Awareness Fund when the time came.

At seven sharp, Lenny parked in front of his townhouse condo in the section of town known as Springdale. He wrestled a fruitcake from the collection of useless gifts he kept in the linen closet and rang his next-door neighbor's bell.

"Tidings of comfort and joy, Mrs. Ginolfi," said Lenny to the frumpy matron who stood holding the door.

"How nice, Mr. Cambio," she gushed. "I'm really embarrassed I have nothing for you. Normally, I make fruit-cakes—exactly like this one, in fact—but my arthritis has been acting up lately."

"Don't give it another thought, Mrs. G. Having a lovely, charming neighbor like you is all the gift a person could want."

"How sweet. Listen, I was just about to give Vito his coffee and dessert. Won't you join us?"

"Wish I could. Unfortunately, I have an enormous pile of work to plow through before the holidays."

He pointed to the illuminated window clearly visible from the Ginolfi's den. "I'll be right there at my desk, probably all night. You or the mister happen to be up, feel free to call or stop by. It'd be a nice break for me."

The pellet shells would take a minimum of eight hours to dissolve. The action could be delayed by up to two hours if the victim consumed large quantities of fatty foods, especially dairy products.

Mrs. Ginolfi smiled. "That's real neighborly of you, Mr. Cambio. Don't take this the wrong way, but Vito and I had the feeling you weren't the friendly type."

"Oh, I am. I just hate to intrude."

"Not at all. It's a pleasure. Merry Christmas to you. And thanks for the fruitcake."

True to his word, Lenny was up and churning all night. He doodled pictures of Cosmo Danza's digestive system. He dotted the stomach with dissolving pellets. Wavy lines represented the lethal dose of insulin seeping out of the pellets and coursing through the fat man's bloodstream. By morning, the big slob would be past tense. Dead of seemingly natural causes.

The following day dawned crisp and clear. Lenny waggled his fingers at Mrs. Ginolfi as he skipped toward his car. Joy to the world. Ho, ho, ho.

Squelching his excitement, Lenny kept to his standard routine. He jogged, toned, and stretched in the company gym. He read the *Plastic Fabricators Daily Gazette* at his desk. He reviewed his correspondence and dictated his replies to a distracted, gum-cracking Arliss Marden.

"Did you get that, Ms. Marden?"

"Yeah."

"Could you read it back to me, please?"

"I could."

"*Would* you?"

"What for? You write the same boring thing so many times, I've got it memorized. 'Dear Mr. Blah de blah. We at Morphman Inc. are blah blah blah de blah.' Now, if you'll get out of my face, it's time for *The Young and the Restless.*"

Lenny peered at his own watch and smiled. "So it is."

Driving toward the hot dog joint, Lenny savored an image of Cosmo Danza decomposing in his bed. The fat lard lived alone in a small house near the railroad station. No family. No cleaning help. No social life. His closest friend and confidant was a laptop computer. The body was likely to go undiscovered until the stench of gaseous effusions from the rotting organs permeated the neighborhood.

Lovely.

Bamsie Sue greeted Lenny at the door. "Table for two as usual, Mr. Cambio?"

"Mr. Danza's not in yet? He always gets here first."

"Haven't seen him."

Lenny shrugged. "Maybe he's too busy with that Millennium Time Bomb thing. One more week until the turn of the century. Hard to believe."

"I am, like, seriously excited," Bamsie Sue confided.

"You certainly have a way with words, my dear," said Lenny.

Fifteen minutes later, Bamsie Sue shimmied back to Lenny's table. "Maybe you should order, Mr. Cambio. You must be starving."

"Maybe I should."

For the next hour, Lenny stared toward the entrance. His heart squirmed at every slam of a car door in the adjoining lot. His pulse raced each time approaching footsteps thwacked the walk.

The lunchtime crowd was starting to thin when a bulky silhouette played across the frosted-glass window beside Lenny's table. The door squealed open with excruciating slowness. Lenny's throat closed.

An eternity later, the door gaped to reveal Manny Dibble in a padded Santa suit. Lenny went liquid with relief. The owner made the rounds, glad-handing customers and distributing coupons for his turn-of-the-millennium special offer.

"Merry Christmas, Len Cambio," Manny chortled behind the beard. "Have you been a good little boy and eaten lots and lots of hot dogs this year?"

"Yes, Santa."

"For that, here's a buy-one, get-one-free coupon for you. It's good for any Dibble Double or Triple Dog you buy before the March first expiration date. Offer may not be used in conjunction with any other offer. Void where prohibited."

Lenny beamed. "I couldn't be more delighted, Santa. Truly."

He floated back to his office on a cloud of contentment. Everything was proceeding exactly as he'd planned. Better than planned, in fact. Arliss Marden was gone. Lenny could finish his necessary work without the risk of unexpected intrusions.

Lenny composed a note to Charles Biggars Booth, CEO of Cyberplastics, assuring him that the company's software was now protected against the Millennium Time Bomb. Lenny had practiced Danza's razor-wire signature so many times that it flowed out of the pen almost as naturally as his own.

He set his fax machine to suppress Morphman's identifying information. Then, he faxed the note to Cyberplastics, checking the delivery confirmation twice. Next, he mocked up an invoice for services rendered in the amount of $10,838.67. This he faxed to his dear friend in the billing department, Jack Baxter.

Lenny whistled "Deck the Halls." 'Twas certainly the season for him to be merry. At the stroke of midnight on December 31, Cyberplastics' computers would crash. The company would be unable to generate a payroll or bills. By the time Cyberplastics straightened out the mess, About Face would be flying out of the stores. The couple of million Lenny owed would seem like petty cash.

Lenny sank in his chair and propped his feet on the desk. Done, he thought, smiling. *Finito.*

Millennium fever gripped the nation. Most companies closed for the week linking Christmas to the turn of the century. There were parades, fireworks, orgies of cloying nostalgia.

In the spirit of the event, Lenny staged a potluck supper for Morphman, Inc., employees. Staff members were assigned to bring the refreshments, music, decorations, and stocking stuffers. Lenny provided the space and the pleasure of his company.

Dressed in black, Arliss Marden resembled a dyspeptic prune. "What? No bonuses this year, Mr. Generosity? Guess you think we should be able to get by on those fat salaries you've been handing out."

"You can count on just recompense as soon as the company's finances are sorted out, Ms. Marden," said Lenny.

"Oh yeah? Well, you can count on these." Arliss hefted her middle fingers and stuck out her tongue.

Lenny remained unflappable. Nothing could burst his bubble of serenity. At the stroke of midnight on December 31, he would be a liberated man. January 1, 2000, would bring a fresh start and boundless opportunity.

Early on January 2, Lenny rolled through the virgin snow into his designated spot at Morphman, Inc. The lot was deserted at this hour, as Lenny had hoped. He wanted some solitary time to tinker with his new product.

He retrieved his prototype from the safe and headed for the lab. After coating the mesh with a neutralizing agent, he applied it to his scalp. Waiting out the trial time, he returned to his office to review his voice mail from the long holiday hiatus.

Of the twenty-odd messages, two were from long-distance carriers hoping to woo him with special discounts. The rest were hysterical rantings by Jack Baxter from Cyberplastics, exhorting Lenny to pay his debt. In several messages Baxter appealed to Lenny's alleged sense of decency. In others, the man threatened civil, criminal, physical, and even posthumous sanctions. He implied that Lenny was a person of dubious moral character and questionable lineage. "Cough up, you sonofabitch bastard," Baxter hissed on the final call.

Lenny's temper flared. The mesh on his scalp squeezed like a yarmulke made of boa constrictor skin. He clawed off the plastic, ripping out several clumps of hair in the process.

Lenny calmed himself with slow, measured breaths. Jack Baxter didn't matter. Not anymore.

The only important thing right now was About Face. Getting the product to market would solve Lenny's financial problems for good. But first, an adjustment in the basic formula was clearly in order.

Lenny returned the prototype to the safe and made notes for further study. *"Add high density alloy?"* he wrote. *"Up the ratio of XR244? Diminish mesh density? Test the efficacy of a smart-fluid buffer?"*

Satisfied that one of those solutions would work, he went to the company gym for his daily workout. There, on the stationary bike, he mused about his overdue yacht trip. Two weeks should suffice this time. Next spring, after About Face was established, he could sail for a month or more to some exotic destination. Fiji, perhaps, or the Greek isles. Lenny's mind filled with scores of Polynesian beauties built like Bamsie Sue Dibble. He conjured warm caressing breezes, a sea of fine bubbly, and the soporific sway of the tides.

Lenny was so lost in reverie he failed to hear the slamming doors or the crunch of footsteps. The barked demands did not penetrate. Then, suddenly, cold steel jabbed between his ribs.

"Hands up and spread 'em."

Lenny was startled to find himself surrounded by cops. "There must be some mistake," he sputtered.

"Yup, and it's yours, scumbag. Now, haul ass off that sissy-cycle."

Lenny clambered off the bike. "May I ask what this is about, officer?"

"I'd say it's about twenty to life. You have the right to remain silent . . ."

Lenny did. He sank deeper and deeper into a mute, trancelike state. At his arraignment that night, the words, charges, circumstances swarmed beyond his reach. Judge Morfogen, who'd been forced to spend the entire long holiday hiatus with his nagging wife, spoiled children, and over-bearing in-laws, denied bail.

Lenny was transferred from city jail to a state mental hospital for psychiatric evaluation. After a month of unsuccessful testing, his shrink gave up.

Lenny perched mutely on his back ward bed. Days, he watched the Home Shopping Network. Nights, he was tormented by a recurrent nightmare in which he was sailing the Caribbean when a ferocious school of giant hot dogs attacked his yacht.

A month later, at the urging of a particularly aggressive pharmaceutical salesman, the psychiatrist tried Lenny on a new antipsychotic drug. Slowly, his mind began to clear. Over the next few weeks, Lenny morphed back into his old, animated self. He soared with fresh optimism. This was a temporary glitch, he assured himself. Everything was going to be fine.

The psychiatrist declared Lenny fit to be tried. His case should have been scheduled for a preliminary hearing within days, but a mammoth computer foul-up had caused interminable delays. The city of Stamford had contracted with Cosmo Danza to protect its judiciary system against the Millennium Time Bomb. Sadly, Mr. Danza had been unable to complete the assignment.

In early May, a hearing was finally set for *The State of Connecticut* v. *Leonard Cambio.* Given the state of Lenny's finances, no decent attorney would take the case. His court-appointed counsel, Lizbeth Sagamore, was a bird-boned young woman with the presence of a sigh.

Still, Lenny was confident that he'd be exonerated. With Cosmo Danza dead, there were no witnesses. The pellets were designed to dissolve without any telltale residue. Lenny had purchased the insulin for cash in small lots with a variety of fake prescriptions at large, impersonal drugstores that were out of town. The charges would surely be dismissed for lack of evidence.

Lenny strode into court with an air of confidence. Then, glancing at the gallery, his jaw dropped.

The bailiff bellowed, "The court calls docket number 39628, *The State of Connecticut* versus *Leonard Cambio*. The Honorable John Polcer presiding."

Polcer, a shriveled little man in his eighties, peered over his granny glasses. "Is the prosecution ready?"

"Ready, Your Honor," intoned the venerable DA, Thomas Colworthy Harrigan.

"Ready for the defense, Ms. Sagamore?"

"Ready, Your Honor," Lenny's lawyer breathed.

"Call your first witness, Mr. Harrigan."

The gallery fell silent as a court clerk pushed the wheelchair up the aisle. With a labored grunt, the injured man rose and trudged into the witness box.

"Do you promise to tell the truth, the whole truth . . ."

"I do," the man said.

"State your name."

"Cosmo Danza."

DA Harrigan led his star witness through the preliminaries. "In your own words, Mr. Danza, please tell us what happened on the afternoon of December twenty-first."

Lenny sat slack-jawed as Cosmo told of leaving Manny Dibble's Dog House. On the way to Cyberplastics, he'd pulled to the side of the road. There, he'd intended to purge his system of the Double Dibble Dogs and curly fries he'd downed at lunch. "Believe me, I'm not proud," said Cosmo, shaking his head.

"Go on, please, Mr. Danza," prompted the DA.

As Cosmo exited the car, a young thug on a Harley attempted to pass. The bike skidded on an oil slick and plowed into Cosmo.

Fortunately, a volunteer firefighter happened by. He performed CPR until an ambulance arrived and rushed Danza to the hospital.

An emergency procedure was performed to unkink Cosmo's intestines and stem internal bleeding of unknown origin. Inside his stomach, the surgeon found dozens of small white pellets.

"They called in the FBI," Cosmo bleated. "Those guys interrogated me in the ICU. They accused me of being a drug courier. My health, my business, my good name were all nearly destroyed because of *him*."

Cosmo leveled a pudgy, accusatory finger at Lenny's head. "I thought you were my friend, Len Cambio. I thought you dressed those Dibble Dogs for me out of love."

"Please note that the witness indicates the defendant, Leonard Cambio," said DA Harrigan.

Next on the stand was Bamsie Sue Dibble, who testified that she'd seen Lenny sneak a vial of pellets from his pocket at the fixins bar. "I saw him poke some of these little white thingies into Mr. Danza's Dibble Dog. I figured Mr. Cambio was adding vitamins or something, though you'd think a smart guy like him would know that hot dogs are a nearly perfect food."

Jack Baxter told of Lenny's failure with the Morphosphere and his enormous debt to Cyberplastics. "The man was desperate. Everyone could see that. Plus, he had these really shifty eyes."

A switchboard operator from Cyberplastics testified that she'd received two faxes signed by Cosmo Danza which registered on the company's caller ID system as originating from Morphman, Inc.

Lenny's neighbor, Mrs. Ginolfi, swore under oath that Lenny's behavior on the night of December 21 had been completely out of character. "Plus, he gave me back my own fruitcake," she said with an indignant harumph.

Throughout the proceedings, Lenny's birdlike court-appointed attorney sat shaking her head. As Mrs. Ginolfi waddled back to her seat, Lizbeth Sagamore whispered in Lenny's ear. "I'm afraid that bit about the fruitcake was the fat lady singing."

But Lenny refused to concede defeat. He still had his secret weapon. After emerging from his catatonia, he'd taken business matters in hand. Over the phone, he'd instructed Arliss Marden to retrieve the About Face prototype from the safe and deliver it to Morphman's chief chemist in the lab. In a series of calls, Lenny coached the chemist through alterations that reduced the heat sensitivity of the mesh to acceptable levels. Final tests on the new prototype would be completed by the end of the week. Then, they could move to production.

By the time his case came to trial, Lenny would have the means to engage the finest criminal defense team in the country. Rich, famous men did not languish in prison. They made book deals, signed autographs, took respite from the strains of their celebrity on luxury sails.

DA Harrigan stood. "The state calls Arliss Marden."

Lenny snickered. That obstreperous old hag couldn't possibly have anything meaningful to say.

Lenny waited for the brown-nailed witch to appear, but someone he did not recognize strutted to the witness box in her place. She was wide-eyed and smooth-skinned with a firm jaw and a pert, uptilted nose.

"State your name, please," said the clerk.

"Arliss Marden."

"What?" Lenny snorted.

The DA went on. "Is it true that you've served for five years as executive secretary to Leonard Cambio at Morphman, Inc., Ms. Marden?"

"I did."

Lenny rose like a wave. "What the hell are you trying to pull? That's not Arliss Marden."

"Order!" barked the judge, smacking his gavel.

"Come on, Your Honor, this is ridiculous. Arliss Marden is sixty-two years old. She's got a face like a shar-pei's. That woman couldn't be a day over thirty."

"Order, I said," Judge Polcer howled. "Ms. Sagamore, control your client or I'll have him ejected from the courtroom." The judge frowned at the witness. "Did the court hear correctly, Ms. Marden? You're sixty-two years old?"

"And a half," cooed Arliss. "May I explain, Your Honor?"

"Please do."

"I left Morphman, Inc., several months ago to found a company called Fountain of Youth, Inc. We've developed a nonsurgical facelift technique that will revolutionize the cosmetics industry." She pulled back her hair to reveal the unscarred skin behind her ears. "As you can see, I've never had a lick of plastic surgery. With a simple five-minute application of Fountain of Youth every morning, I take a good thirty years off this old face of mine."

"You're sixty-two?" the judge blithered. "And a half?"

Arliss Marden raised her right hand and planted her left on the Bible. "As God is my witness. This miraculous product can do the same for you, Your Honor. For a mere forty-nine ninety-five, plus tax, you too can enjoy the benefits of eternal youth."

"But how?" the judge exclaimed. "It's amazing!"

Arliss flapped a brown-nailed hand. "Oh, it was nothing really. Nothing at all. I developed Fountain of Youth in my spare time, tinkering around in my basement. One of those bolt-from-the-blue things, you'd have to say."

She flushed from the lie. But the skin did not pucker or pull.

Lenny raged. "That's *my* bolt from the blue. Thief! Liar! You can't steal my invention!"

"Silence!" Judge Polcer bellowed. "Guards, remove the defendant."

As the uniforms drew near, Lenny felt the fog rolling in again. His mind bristled with shock. A brick of fear, thick and heavy as a dozen Double Dibble Dogs, dropped in his gut.

Behind him, the gallery erupted with excitement. "I need that—now!" someone called. "I'll give you a hundred dollars for yours!"

"Make it a thousand!" shouted another spectator.

"Two!" came from the rear.

Flashbulbs popped. Reporters raced to call their editors

about the astounding new product. Soon, news of Fountain of Youth would be all over the wires.

Lenny drifted from the courtroom. He was numb to the furor raging around him. All he wanted to do was settle in somewhere dim and quiet and watch the Home Shopping Network.

Nothing scary ever happened there.

ANOTHER DAY, ANOTHER DOLLAR

WARREN MURPHY

STEPHANIE CROWDER WAS told her brother was dead by the foreman who took her off the assembly line at the auto factory just outside Philadelphia. He told her he did not have the details but that the body had been found near Pittsburgh, and that someone in the personnel manager's office had the details.

"Okay. Look, let me finish my shift," Stephanie said.

"It's considered unsafe to let someone back on the line after a traumatic experience," said the foreman.

"I'm okay," said Stephanie.

She was installing doors in the new subcompacts and she had her rhythm for the shift and it would soon be over. There was a lot of noise, but there was always lots of noise on an assembly line. She could hum to herself. She could sing. She could even feel the rhythm of the line, and the shift was almost over anyway.

"You're supposed to be the next of kin. The only next of kin," said the foreman.

"Sure. I raised Nate. I'm sister, mother. He's the only person I've got. Can I get back to the line?"

"Did you hear me? Your brother is dead. There are some people up in the personnel manager's office who want to speak to you."

Stephanie Crowder shook her head.

"You didn't hear me?"

"He's not dead," said Stephanie. "He's not dead. Why are you saying that? Why are you saying those things? Because I'm a woman?"

She was crying, even though she had vowed, back when she began work on the line, that she would not cry in front of the men. She had come to the line fifteen years before, when women did not work the line. She had come out of the clean white office with the soft rugs and the gentle hum of the electric typewriters, where the loudest noise was a soft laugh from an executive, and if there was a spot on a desk, one called maintenance to remove it.

She had come down to this hellish din, fortified with warnings that women did not belong there. She had heard that she was too beautiful to be working down in the lines. There was always a lascivious wink with that, and she would ask:

"If I were white, would you say that?"

Stephanie Crowder was a beautiful woman with strong dark features and a sense of a majesty about her face. At first, almost everyone on the line had made a sexual advance, some even suggesting that she could make a fortune as a hooker, and even reaching into their pockets to prove it.

But Stephanie Crowder showed that she had what it took to do a day's work. She never complained and she never let anyone down.

Of course, for a while there she wouldn't lend anyone a dollar if he needed it for a blood transfusion. But they found out later it wasn't that she was cheap. It was just that she needed every penny for something. And when that had ended, more than a few years before, she became such a soft touch that her coworkers had to protect her.

She never dogged her work. She never buckled to either management or the union. She was, as everyone said, a standup guy. And soon, they called her "Steve."

For her part, Stephanie Crowder did not know what the fuss was all about. She had simply come to the line determined to show everyone there that she was as good as anyone else. In that, everyone agreed, she had failed. She was better than anyone else.

And Stephanie's first rule had been that she would not cry on the line, and now she was doing it.

"Why do you say things like that? Why do you say them?"

"Hey, Steve, I ain't making this shit up."

"Liar," she yelled. "Liar."

Two riveters seeing Steve Crowder yelling at the foreman knew something had to be wrong and it had to be the foreman. Steve Crowder wasn't a complainer, and that moron of a foreman had her crying and yelling. When the riveters quit, the other workers walked off the line too, because they thought there was a major grievance going on, and when they saw Steve Crowder crying and yelling, they were *sure* there was a major grievance going on.

The line stopped. Unfinished cars hung in mid-air. Riveting guns lay silent. Welding torches flickered out in a last dip of a blue-yellow flame as if the day were done.

"No," she cried. "No. No. No."

"Her brother died," the foreman explained sheepishly.

"Nate. God, no. Not Nate. Not my baby brother."

It took a while to get the line started up again. There were many women there now, unlike when Steve Crowder had come down there from the front office. There had been man jobs and woman jobs, just as generations ago there had been black jobs and white jobs. The auto industry led everything in America—from advancement to decline and then back to advancement.

And in this plant, they were all talking about Stephanie Crowder's brother. He had been killed in Pittsburgh along with his wife, and because he was black and his wife was white, some of them thought some racist did it. Whatever it was, he didn't deserve death, because if you knew Steve Crowder and you knew she had raised the boy, you knew he had to be a straight arrow.

Then one of Stephanie's close friends let everyone know why she had come down to the line in the first place. It had been that same baby brother, Nathaniel.

She had been a top secretary in the front office at twenty-one, some said the best typist, even among old-timers who had really learned well. Even way back then they were talking of sending her to school and making her an executive, or if not that, at least executive secretary to one of the vice presidents.

Then one day Stephanie Crowder came into her boss's office and said she wanted to work on the line. Her boss and the personnel manager and everyone else told her that was foolish, that she had a great future in the office.

"I need the money now," she had told them.

"You can get a loan."

"I need more money for a long time. And I don't want to owe anybody, thank you."

What she needed it for was her younger brother. Her parents had died and she was left to raise him.

"So that's why she wouldn't lend anybody money a long time ago?" asked one of the workers.

"Sure. She put him in a private school and then college and then graduate school. When she stopped paying for all that, she had money to spare," said the friend.

Stephanie Crowder did not hear her coworkers talking about her. She had followed someone to the personnel manager's office.

They were saying Nate was dead. They were wrong. They had to be wrong because Nate who was living very happily in Columbus, Ohio, was going on a vacation with Beatrice and the baby. He was an engineer now. He was doing very well. He knew how to save. She had taught him that. She had taught him the things he would need, all the things Dad would have taught if Dad had lived.

When Dad died, Nate was fourteen and beginning to hang around with a bad gang. There was dope. There were guns. And every time there was another shooting or drug incident, the schools would hold another sensitivity-training session for the white teachers to instruct them in what were supposed to be black values.

Well, the Crowders were black and they had values and those values weren't drugs and they weren't guns. Their main value was hard work and more hard work in a world that was not too kind to black people. It was saving. It was doing without. It was doing with less. It was living on secondhand everything because Dad refused to buy hot merchandise.

"Stealin' is stealin', Stephanie. Even if you don't see who was robbed. When you buy hot goods, child, you're stealin' from yourself."

There was pride in everything they owned because it was honestly come by. They didn't believe in big shiny cars. They didn't put all their money on their backs.

Dad and Mother were married in church and they didn't know each other physically until the night the reverend pronounced them man and wife.

They had a savings account. They had two children and they did not think philandering was cause for mirth and winking. In brief, they had very traditional black values and in their lifetimes, they lived by them.

Shortly after they died in an auto accident, Nate came home laughing about a "sensitivity outreach conference" where somebody had been stupid enough to pay him money to tell whites from the suburbs how their values were outmoded. Nate was always sharp and could talk a blue streak. He was fourteen. He had a pocketful of money. He talked jive. He was learning black English in school, busting verbs, slopping filth into his language, and laughing at it.

"Nate, Grandma talked that way because she didn't know better. But she wanted her children to know better. They didn't have schools for us when Grandma was young. But they do for you."

"You a jiveass nigger, turkey," said Nate. The first thing Stephanie did was to slap her younger brother silly. The next thing she did was enroll him at a private school outside Philadelphia. It was strict. It did not teach black English. In fact, it did not teach one course that was called relevant.

"That's what I want," she said. She didn't care what it cost. Nate was registered before she realized her secretary's salary wouldn't cover the tuition. It was then that she told the front office that she wanted an assembly-line job. She needed the money and she needed it right away. She did not tell them why. It was none of their business.

Later she would tell friends. Her values, her very black values, would not allow others to know of her troubles unless they were friends. She also did not want any favors because she was a woman. That was a black value too.

All she wanted was a job on the line.

She got it and when she first heard the din of the assembly line, she felt her head would break open in pain, but she told herself:

"Stephanie, don't you cry. Don't you dare cry here."

So she cried at night, when Nate couldn't hear her, and she cried for two years until, mercifully, her hearing started to go. And she didn't cry once on the line for fifteen years until the man came down to tell her Nate was dead.

Which couldn't be. Nate was such a fine young man. Nate couldn't be dead.

They had made a mistake. Lots of whites made mistakes when it came to identifying blacks. Maybe a black man had stolen Nate's wallet and was killed near Pittsburgh. Nate didn't want to worry her and he merely bought himself a new wallet. And the man who stole it, like many thieves, had gotten himself killed. Thieves were trash. They were killed all the time. And the people who found that thief's body just assumed that the black man was Nate.

That's what she was going to tell them in the personnel office.

They took her to a harshly lit cubicle behind frosted glass. Two men were there. They were Pittsburgh detectives. They told her that Nate and Beatrice were found strangled in some open land near the Pittsburgh airport.

"No, no. Nate's going skiing with his family," said Stephanie. She took off her grease-laden cap and shook out her wiry hair. She did not sit down, because she knew her pants would leave a stain on the furniture. "He must have lost his wallet," she said.

"Miss Crowder, we didn't identify him by his picture. We identified the body by fingerprints. Mr. Crowder was in a very sensitive technological job and his fingerprints were on file. So were his wife's."

"Nate," screamed Stephanie, feeling her legs go weak, not wanting to mess the chair up with her pants, not able to stand up. She leaned against the desk. "Nate. My baby brother. Nate."

"I'm sorry, ma'am," said one of the detectives.

Stephanie Crowder cried in the personnel office amid typewriters she had once been able to use better than anyone, in a very clean place that she was no longer used to working in. She did not know how long she cried, but when she finally looked up, there was a difference. The pain was still there, still to be felt, still to be suffered on so many nameless nights and mornings when little things would remind her of that fine young man now dead, and his beautiful wife, and their beautiful baby who would never have a chance to share her parents' love.

There was no more time for tears. There was a child to be looked after, a child to be raised right. Catrice was a black girl and she would need extra-special care because this was a world in which black girls were not safe from many things. There would be more time for crying perhaps when Catrice was grown up and strong, strong as her daddy had been.

"I will be seeing Catrice now. Where is she?"

"Who?"

"Catrice. Their baby. They went skiing with their baby."

"Was there a baby?" one detective asked the other.

"I don't know of any baby."

"Where is the baby? Where is the baby?" Stephanie Crowder was yelling again. The real horror was only beginning.

Because Stephanie Crowder did not blame all her troubles on whites did not mean she trusted them either. She knew too well how some whites thought that a black life was not quite a human life. She knew too well how a black child might not be as important in this world as a white one.

But what horrified her as she went from one office to another in Pittsburgh, and then to children's homes and juvenile courts and social services, was that the world was not safe for white children either.

When she gave her sketchy description of the missing Catrice, along with a half-dozen grainy snapshots her brother had sent her, a detective with compassion told her that the best thing she could do for herself was to forget the child.

"I'm not going to forget her. Do you know how dangerous it is out there for a little black girl? How easy it is for her to wind up with pervs? Or to be on dope? Nobody's going to care if she can even read or write. She's black and I've got to get her back."

"Lady," said the detective, "I'm not just talking about black children. Every year, maybe twenty-five thousand, maybe fifty thousand children disappear and are never seen again. That's like what we lost in Vietnam. And most of the kids are white. Do yourself a favor. Bury your niece in your heart."

"Sir, I am a Crowder. I do not give up."

"Then you're going to waste a life."

"I don't consider trying to save my kin a waste of my life. Failing to try would be a waste of my life. Good day, sir," said Stephanie Crowder. She walked out of the police station into the thick air of Pittsburgh, numb to the world and to the traffic. She did not know where to begin. It was a huge country.

She took a flight home because this one airline was even

cheaper than the buses. It charged for the water. It probably charged to use the toilets, she told herself, so she didn't drink and she didn't relieve herself, and when she got back to her walkup flat in a dismal development in Philadelphia, she wrote down what she was up against and what she had going for her.

On the top of her list was that she would not give up. Somewhere in the middle was the fact that she had good looks. Somewhere else was the fact that she was a bit more intelligent than the average person. And then she threw it all away and wrote down one word.

"Crowder."

It was a slave name, taken from the whites who had owned her ancestors, but at no time had she ever believed that the whites who owned the name did it more honor than the blacks. In fact, if she were to be realistic about the whole thing, she had never met a white Crowder that she didn't feel a little bit sharper than, although of course she couldn't be sure. Daddy had told her that too: "Don't judge, Stephanie. Not until you know."

She was a Crowder and that was what she had going for her. She started on the list of things she had going against her. It began with the difficulties of identification, the size of America, the possibility that Catrice might not even be in the country. It included among other things that she was going to need a lot of money to support her rescue mission.

That problem was solved when she returned to the plant to ask for a leave of absence. The people in the plant had raised $19,625.83 for her.

"We didn't know what else to do. We all just wanted to help. We felt so damned helpless. So take a vacation, Steve. Do something good for yourself for a change."

"I'll do something good for myself."

The next day she started her leave of absence. She bought herself new clothes that cost a thousand dollars, even though she bargained for them in one of the low-priced outlets. She bought things that accentuated her fine full bosom, the sleek curve of her waist, with shoes that showed legs that were still stunning.

"Stephanie," she asked herself. "Are you going to use your body? Are you really going to use it?" And she answered herself. Absolutely. She was going to use her body because she didn't have an army.

It was not hard to pick up a cop in a Philadelphia bar. But what Stephanie wanted was a homicide detective. She found one, a man she thought was a little bit too sweet to be a policeman. He couldn't believe his good luck. Stephanie, in her new clothes and makeup highlighting her elegant features, turned heads in bars. The detective was also surprised at how interested she was in his work. She told him her name was Florence.

"Tell me," she said. "If a couple is murdered, how would you go about finding their killers?"

His name was Big Mo, he was middle-aged, smoked awful cigars, and said, "What do you mean?"

"Two people traveling are killed, found dead. How would you go about finding who killed them?"

"Traveling is bad. That's a bad one. Say they're found in their living room."

"I'd prefer traveling."

"You want to learn or you want to teach?"

Stephanie went to Big Mo's dirty apartment and listened to him describe examining the death scene, looking to see if there were any signs of robbery, and if there weren't, finding the last people who had seen the victims, talking to their friends. Especially talking to their friends.

"Why their friends?"

"Because ninety-five percent of all homicides are done by people who knew each other."

"So if there's a murder and you want to find the murderer, you talk to the friends."

"Unless, of course, they're traveling."

"Why does traveling make it different?"

"Because that means they probably don't know the people who killed them and if that's the case you're probably not going to collar the killers."

"Why not?"

"Because just about the only homicides we ever nail are the family ones. You know, boyfriend kills girlfriend, wife kills husband, like that."

"What about detective work? What about looking for clues?"

"We look. Of course we look."

"What for?"

"Clues."

"I know that, dammit. What kind?"

"Who their friends are."

Big Mo had a hand on her leg. She had already decided that she was going to let him proceed further. But she wanted more information first.

"Suppose they're strangled?"

"Ain't too many stranglings. I had one once't a year or so ago, some woman near the airport. I think maybe her husband did it 'cause he left her to go be a mountain man or something, but we never could find him to pin it on him. A strangling is something you remember. We get a lot of guns but mostly knives. If you really want to stop the big killing weapon in the country, end the kitchen knife. Outlaw the kitchen knife," said Big Mo, then thought of something that gave him a chuckle, something for a bumper sticker:

"If kitchens are outlawed, only outlaws will eat."

"So you had a strangling near the airport?"

"Yeah."

"That's a coincidence. I heard of another one like that near Pittsburgh," Stephanie said.

"And there was one up in Allentown six months ago. So what? Come on. We didn't come up here to talk business."

"There might be a gang doing all these killings," said Stephanie. She pushed away his hand.

"Nahhh, it's people see somebody does something and so they do it too."

"How do you know?"

"'Cause that's the way it always is," Big Mo said. "What do you want from me anyway?"

"I want to know who, what, when, where, and why."

"What are you, a reporter?"

"I just want to know."

She got no further answers that night, and Big Mo did not get lucky either. She went to police headquarters the next day to ask about the Philadelphia airport strangling, but was told it was none of her business. What was she, a reporter?

But the police did not know they were dealing with a Crowder. If Stephanie Crowder was to find her niece, she had to have information, and just plain citizens did not get information. They got public relations.

She flew back to Pittsburgh on the same cheap airline she had used the last time. In a suburb, she found a newspaper fighting a lawsuit claiming it discriminated against minorities. She went in and, using the name of Beverly, applied for a job as a cub reporter, pointing out that with a single hiring, the paper could fill two minority slots, a woman and a black. The interviewer didn't even ask if she could type.

She could type, but she couldn't write. Still, with her looks there were a half-dozen male reporters willing to show her. The one she accepted help from, though, was a gin-smelling overweight garbage can of a man who told her that her copy stank and that she shouldn't expect to learn how to write in a week or so, if ever. He resented the fact that she had gotten the job because of her sex and her color. He didn't hide that.

But this man knew how to write a story, and he showed her. Her copy came back from him with more red pencil than there was typing. She knew then he was right. She wasn't going to learn how to write anytime soon.

"You don't have to learn how to write," he said. "Just keep on being a woman and being black. That may get you a Pulitzer Prize."

"I don't want a Pulitzer Prize."

"Then why'd you take the damned job?"

"Because I've got questions and I can't get answers unless I'm a reporter."

"What kind of questions?"

"It's private, but I'm trying to save somebody's life, somebody close to me."

"You type good, you think good. You ask good questions. Maybe I can get you by. But I've got to know what you're looking for."

"If I tell you, you'll turn it into a story and I don't want a story yet. I want somebody alive. I've got to be a reporter for that."

The reporter's name was Barney. He let her buy him a few beers. Then he let her buy him a few Scotches. They worked out a system where she gathered the facts—did the legwork, as he called it—and he wrote the story. She turned out to be a stunning legman.

A week later, the newspaper guild made her a member, and Stephanie immediately went to the city editor with a proposition.

When he heard the word "proposition," he said, "Any time," and winked.

It was a joke, of course, but Stephanie Crowder had not come up to the city desk to joke.

"I want to do a story on unsolved murders," she said.

"That's the police beat. You're on neighborhood news."

"I mean all over the country."

"What would we be doing a story about all over the country?" he said. "We're a dink paper in a dink town." The city editor was not a thirty-year employee on this small daily because he had much in the way of imagination or talent or skill. He became city editor the way most small dailies got their city editors, from the ranks of reporters who grew old without making major mistakes. His main job was to keep the paper safe. In a few more years, when he became even more cautious and less imaginative, he would be made managing editor. And if time and stomach problems did not take his life, sometime after that he might be made editor in chief, so he could speak at luncheons and dinners on the courage of the press.

"Are you against this story because some of the victims might be blacks?" Stephanie asked.

The city editor perceived a charge of racism looming over the horizon, threatening to obliterate his inevitable promotion to managing editor.

"How long would you want to work on this story?"

"A couple of months."

"Too long. You know how expensive it is to have a reporter cover a story. We can't have you go running around the country on one feature. It doesn't make sense. It's not racism. It's common sense. I happen to be very sensitive to racial issues."

"What if I take a leave of absence and you don't have to pay me?"

"Can't do that."

"Why not?"

"The guild. The union. They won't like it."

Stephanie had been around the newspaper long enough to know the reporters' union was not as strong as the United Auto Workers. On this newspaper, it was almost a social club.

"What if I get an okay from the union?"

"Well . . . I don't know."

But there was no okay from the reporters' union. The union saw this leave time as a device by management to get reporters to work for free. It saw a threat to the spirit of organized labor. It saw all kinds of dangers, but mainly it was composed of other reporters, who were afraid she might be on to a better story than any of them were doing.

Stephanie's friend, the sloppy drunk, had the answer.

"Just take off and do it," said Barney.

"Won't they fire me?"

"No. That would mean they have to do something. Somebody would have to make a decision. No reporter has ever gone off on a story by himself without pay before. If they don't pay you, you're not costing them anything. If they don't fire you, they can't be accused of racism."

"What about the union?"

"They'll be happy to see you leave town for whatever reason. You've already made them very nervous by suggesting such things."

"Thanks, Barney," she said and gave him a big kiss. But the stench of gin was so strong she had to back away immediately.

Stephanie Crowder, the descendant of Crowders and of people whose African names had been torched from memories with whips and guns, was on the attack.

She could now ask who, what, when, where, and why. And what she found out right away was that not everybody else asked those questions.

Nate and Beatrice had been strangled in a field near the Pittsburgh airport, probably with wire, soon after getting off their Westworld flight. There were no signs of a baby or a stroller anywhere near the bodies. The money had apparently been stolen from Nate's wallet but not from Beatrice's purse. And some witness, whose name the police forgot to get, thought she remembered seeing the young couple talking to a young white couple who were carrying knapsacks and who dressed like hippies.

She went to Allentown and found out from the police that the woman killed near that airport had been robbed of exactly $48.65. She had been strangled. Her jewelry had not been touched. She had been traveling with her baby and the baby was missing.

A reporter now, with a valid up-to-date press card issued to a fake name, Stephanie Crowder went to Philadelphia and talked to airport officials and to the police and found out that the woman who had been murdered near that airport almost a year before had been traveling with a baby, who was not found. She was strangled too, and the killer took her watch but not her diamond wedding ring or her money.

A witness recalled seeing the woman talking to two young people. "I remember them because they looked like Sonny and Cher in the TV reruns,—you know, like dorky clothes and all that."

Stephanie Crowder rented a motel room, lay on the bed, and put her good no-nonsense mind to work trying to figure out these mysteries.

First of all, they weren't really robberies. Robbers wouldn't have left so much behind with the bodies. Whoever it was just took enough to make it look like a robbery.

Obviously, the real thing of value that had been taken was a baby, and she was very upset that none of the police had ever thought of trying to link up these separate incidents into a pattern of crime.

The murders were all by strangling and they were all committed against people who had flown Westworld American Air.

She had a hunch. She went to a travel agency and got all the brochures she could find on Westworld American Air, which billed itself as "the country's lowest-cost airline."

Back in her room, she found out that Westworld had its headquarters in Columbus, Ohio, and that it flew basically shuttle flights among a handful of eastern cities. There were Pittsburgh and Allentown and Philadelphia and four more cities, and after tireless phoning of those other four cities— "I'm a reporter and I need to know"—she found out that all of them had had people strangled and babies missing in the last eighteen months.

She closed the brochures and sat at the small writing table in her dingy room and rubbed her eyes, trying to contain her excitement.

Catrice was alive. Nobody committed murder to kidnap babies if they were just going to kill them. She was going to get her back. And then she was going to raise Catrice as she had raised Catrice's father. There would be horrors to overcome, but the Crowders were used to that. She would get the child back. She would go on.

She flew Westworld to Columbus, Ohio, and at four P.M. was hanging around in the hallways outside the Westworld offices. A group of young executive types came out, and she followed them to a nearby cocktail lounge where singles met. She listened to them talk and then selected the highest-ranking one who was married, and on the next day, she bought him a drink. His name was Keith. She told him her name was Clarissa.

Men always liked to talk about their work and Keith was no exception, and Stephanie Crowder had always been a very good listener. So it was that a few days later, Stephanie had the passenger lists for the seven flights which had ended with someone being killed and some baby being kidnapped.

She told Keith that she had to go away for a few days and went back to her hotel room to study the passenger lists. She had not really expected that she would find some couple whose names would turn up on all seven flights, and she didn't, so she wrote down all the names and addresses of people apparently traveling as husband and wife. There were forty-one couples on the seven flights. She started to weep when she saw the names of Nate and Beatrice on one of the passenger manifests, but she angrily brushed the tears away.

The next day she rented a car and bought a map of Columbus and began driving all around the city to the forty-one addresses.

Seven of the addresses did not exist.

She needed a cop again and she found one, a paper-thin, elegantly dressed black detective, whom she followed to an Alcoholics Anonymous meeting. His name was Zach—she told him her name was Jasmine—and his hands shook nervously. She bought him coffee and told him she was a reporter working on a big story and the case would be his if he would just give her a little help.

He tried to find out what the story was, but Stephanie was not about to tell it to someone who had a drinking problem, even if he was recovering. She would have to know him a lot longer before she decided whether he could be trusted.

Besides, she meant to keep her promise. If there turned out to be a story here, she would give it to Zach, but only later. She told him exactly that, and Zach, with the hopeful fatalism that sustains the recovering alcoholic, simply nodded and took her list of names to headquarters, where he ran them through the department computers.

"We didn't have any of these seven couples in the computer," he said. Stephanie was so depressed she almost didn't hear him say, "But . . ."

"But what?"

"So I ran them through a different listing, and what do you know?" Zach was grinning. "Two of those names were used before as aliases by this couple of badasses."

"Who are they?"

"I pulled their sheets. Jack and Donna Kean. Theft, robbery, prostitution, con games. They're druggies. Man, they're young but they've been busy."

He showed her the long computer printout of Jack and Donna Kean's crimes. Looking at it, Stephanie Crowder said, "Why aren't they in jail if they're so bad?"

Zach took the paper back. "I looked that up too. They got a good lawyer, a guy named Fred Winslow."

"You know him?" she asked.

"Just by reputation. He's a rich guy out in the suburbs. He doesn't do much criminal law."

"Except for these two," Stephanie said.

"That's right."

"Odd, isn't it?"

"If you say it is."

When Stephanie went to the picturesque Ohio village where Fred Winslow lived and practiced law, she found out from page one of the local paper that he was being honored that night for "his trailblazing work in helping childless couples adopt unwanted children. He has enriched the lives of so many," the chairman of the testimonial dinner was quoted as saying.

While Winslow was delivering his speech at the local country club, Stephanie broke into his office, located his adoption files, and in one of them, found a photograph she recognized as her niece, little Catrice. She also found petty-cash receipts for air fares aboard Westworld American Air, on those seven days when people had been murdered and babies were stolen.

Catrice, listed as "abandoned, parents unknown," had been adopted by a family in Tenafly, New Jersey. They had paid the lawyer fifty thousand dollars in fees. Stephanie took the file folder with her and spent the whole night driving to Tenafly, a pretty, upscale town just across the Hudson River from Manhattan.

In the morning, she found the house where Catrice had been taken. She parked her car around the corner and walked by the house. It was Saturday morning, and she saw her little niece on a blanket on the manicured front lawn, being doted on by a young black couple. A plaque on the front lawn read:

FAMILY PHYSICIANS
DR. GERALD BATCHELOR
DR. ANNETTE BATCHELOR

Stephanie Crowder paused outside the house and looked over the white picket fence at the two doctors playing with their adopted daughter, who was smiling and cooing. When they looked up, Stephanie smiled and said, "Your daughter is beautiful."

"Thank you," the woman said.

"A gift from God," Stephanie said.

"We know."

And because she knew she was making them nervous by standing there, Stephanie Crowder choked back her tears, smiled, and walked away. Catrice was all right and she *would be* all right. She didn't need Aunt Stephanie to protect her from drugs and crime and poverty. Not now, anyway, and there would be time when she was all grown up to let her know that she had the blood of the Crowders in her veins and what that meant.

She walked to her car and started on the long drive back to Columbus, Ohio.

The next night, in what the local newspaper called "a tragic accident that has shattered the community," noted adoption attorney Fred Winslow was killed when his new Mercedes-Benz was forced off the road, apparently by a drunk driver who fled the scene.

A week later, Zach, the detective, received in the mail a badly written report documenting the murderous activities of Jack and Donna Kean, the baby stealers. The unsigned note that came with the report insisted that if the facts led to an arrest, Zach must be sure to personally call a small newspaper on the outskirts of Pittsburgh and let a reporter named Barney be the first to break the story.

The following Monday, Stephanie Crowder was back on the line in the auto plant outside Philadelphia. All day long, coworkers came up to ask if she was all right, and she gave them all the same answer: "I'm fine now."

Then the foreman asked her the same thing, and she said again, "I'm fine. Now let's let it drop. Did we come here to make cars or make conversation?"

Later in the day, Stephanie cut her hand on a piece of sheet metal. At the plant infirmary, the doctor closed up the wound with three stitches. Stephanie Crowder declined anesthetic and did not cry, even when the stitches were going in.

When the doctor commented on this, Stephanie Crowder said, "I'm a Crowder. We don't cry a lot. We just do what we've got to do. Now hurry up. I've got to get back to the line."

A Shooting
Over in Jersey

Justin Scott

November 15, 1910

Mr. Dyer sent me over to Jersey to investigate some pushcarts that was shooting a cliffhanger with an Edison-patented camera, on which they had forgotten to pay royalties to Mr. Edison.

Acquainted as I was with a number of those boys ready to take a long chance, and figuring they'd be keeping costs even lower by taking pictures with hijacked film stock, I telephoned a fellow at Eastman to arrange a suitable reward in case I happened to stumble across a quantity of their product in the wrong hands.

I stuffed a Navy Colt in my overcoat. A sap, or a hunk of lead pipe, used to suffice for investigations, but we'd suffered an incident while acquiring a studio recently, when the players reloaded their cowboy guns with live ammunition, and Mr. Edison had not been pleased that the police had taken note of the disturbance that ensued.

It was a bright morning, good for taking pictures. But a cold wind cutting down the Hudson River threatened short, dark winter days, and the players heading to work on the Weehawken ferry were shivering in their skimpy costumes. I bumped into an Indian-feathered, red-dyed player of my acquaintance who inquired whether I was still taking pictures for Mr. Pathé.

I'm not ashamed of being a detective—everybody's got to make a livin' somehow—but I saw no point in blabbin' that when he'd seen me cranking a camera, I had been engaged to conduct a patent-infringement investigation, undercover. So I told the feathered fellow I was looking for work, and offered him a breakfast snort from my flask. He had a couple more on the trolley up to Fort Lee, and turned loquacious.

Don't tell no one, he told me, but he'd heard that François Drake was taking pictures in a secret studio he'd hid in the woods up the Palisades. Since Mr. Edison's Motion Picture Patents Company—which licensed movies in order to protect the public from inferior product and collect royalties for his movie inventions—paid a generous bounty for exposing independent studios, I figured I'd have a look soon as I got done with the penny-ante pushcarts.

I found them shooting a one-reeler on a trolley siding they was making believe was the Union Pacific Railroad. They were using a Bianchi, a lousy camera that made jumpy pictures. But I couldn't help but notice that the fellow operating the Bianchi was cranking a little faster than he would of been if the camera were loaded with film. Which might explain why the players in Mexican-train-robber hats were aiming their faces at an ice truck parked nearby.

After I reported to Mr. Dyer by telephone that the boys hiding Mr. Edison's patented camera inside the ice truck had stopped shooting when the truck caught fire and someone heisted their Eastman film stock, I rented a Ford automobile from a filling station and went looking along the Jersey cliffs for François Drake.

François—Felix Dubinski to childhood acquaintances who remembered his Jersey City youth robbing blind newsies—was the most ornerily independent of the so-called Independents. He'd started out working for Mr. Edison as a manager—the fellow who directs the players in regards to the parts they're to take and the positions they're to be in during the scene. But for some time now, he had been sneaking around, manufacturing his own moving pictures with no license from the Motion Picture Patents Company, totally disregarding the legal rights that Mr. Edison's Legal Department had dragged so many Independents through the courts to win.

I couldn't find him.

You can't hide a moving picture studio all that easy, even in New Jersey. You've got scenery and costumes, offices, laboratories to process the film, machine shops to keep the cameras running, dynamos for the lights, props, dressing rooms, and usually a herd of horses. Then you've got your shooting stage. It's big as a barn, and since it has transparent walls and roof to admit every spark of daylight you can get your hands on, the entire thing is made all of glass. Glass walls, glass roof. Hard to hide as the Crystal Palace.

Still I couldn't find the darned thing. By dark I was beginning to think that player'd been pulling my leg. I stayed the night at Rambo's, a moving picture folks' hotel outside Fort Lee, the front of which you've seen in plenty of Wild West shootouts, and had my supper with an actress of my acquaintance whom I hadn't seen since we stood on the breadline for *A Corner In Wheat,* in which moving picture I was an extra while engaged to investigate undercover. I told her I'd just got back from trying my luck in California and she said why not try François Drake. She'd heard he was shooting "somewhere" in Jersey.

So had the fellow I sat next to next morning at breakfast. Right away, I left that place for another look. It was past noon when I happened to glance down the long driveway of a river mansion atop the Palisades. Just then the sun broke through the chilly overcast and reflected like a thousand arc lights on a building made of glass.

I was through the gate in less time than it takes to tell. But at the end of the drive all I saw was a big old greenhouse with a fancy roof shaped like a Russian church. It was the

kind of hothouse where some rich old geezer grew orchids.
Darn, I thought. False alarm.

But then a couple of gladiators came round the corner—
one with a net and pitchfork, the other carrying a sword.
They were deep in conversation with an Arab leading a
camel, and they didn't notice me until I asked, "Is this where
Mr. Drake's taking pictures?"

"Not for long if we don't get paid," said the fellow with
the camel.

"That don't sound so good," I said. "I was hoping to get
work."

"The son of a bitch has got one hour to pay up or they'll
be plenty of jobs."

"If someone don't shoot him first," said the player with
the net. As they were primed to continue in that vein for
some time, I slipped into the greenhouse. They were using it
for a shooting stage, all right. Instead of orchids, there was
a bunch of flimsy painted sets (each marked with the duck
that was the Golden Drake Motion Picture Manufacturing
Company trademark, so some even bigger crook couldn't
sell those movies as his by changing the title cards), arc
lights hanging from the rafters, banks of Cooper-Hewitts on
rollers, and one of Mr. Edison's patented cameras.

They weren't shooting moving pictures at the moment,
but they should have been because there was quite a show
under way. Four people—two men and two women—were
running around in circles, gesturing wildly and yelling at
each other.

I recognized François Drake in a white shirt with a silk
scarf at his throat where a necktie should have been; and
Gilda Riley, a redhead with a temper to match, who had quit
the Edison Players when Mr. Edison refused to pay her more
money than the others in the company. (Mr. Edison didn't
hold with that "star" stuff, Mr. Dyer told me, because he believed that moving picture audiences paid to see an Edison-
manufactured product projected with a genuine Edison

Vitascope Projecting Machine. Not some player who thought she was Sarah Bernhardt.)

From the red-faced yelling I deduced that the bulky fellow in tweed owned the estate, and that the good-looking blonde with whiskey eyes was his wife.

Felix saw me barging in the glass door, and he went white. Up until he saw me he had looked like he was almost enjoying the donnybrook. But now he groaned, "Christ on a crutch, it's Joe McCoy."

I said, "Hello, Felix." No longer under cover. We was acquainted from way back, and I had finally caught him red-handed.

"The name is François," he retorted automatically.

"Mr. Edison's going to be mighty unhappy with you, Felix."

"Who the hell are you?" asked the guy in tweed. "Say, what are you doing here? This is private property."

"So's that Edison camera."

He charged, a big guy who'd probably boxed in college, until he got close enough to think it over. I had once worked, for my health, in the retail coal business, which had built up my shoulders. He turned on François, instead. "You know him?"

"Gumshoe Joe McCoy. Joe McCoy meet Mr. Harpur, the owner of this fine shooting stage and a very astute investor. Mr. Harpur, this is Joe McCoy. One of Edison's bulls."

"Edison? The Trust? He's a Trust thug?"

I set him straight. "I am engaged by Mr. Dyer to conduct investigations for the Legal Department."

Harpur didn't seem to appreciate the distinction. "Edison, that damned monopolist and his blood-sucking greedy Trust! Well, let me tell you something." He waved his manicured finger in my face. "When Teddy Roosevelt gets back in office, he'll bust the Edison monopoly wide open."

I never debate politics or religion with strangers. But let me just say, privately, that "trust-bustin'," monopoly-smashing, Rough-Riding TR, who had been a fine President of the

United States in many respects, didn't invent the incandescent light bulb, or the phonograph, or the stock ticker, or moving pictures.

François said to me, "Maybe we can work something out."

"Maybe," I said. "Wha'd you have in mind?"

The ladies were still breathing hard, and the tweedy Mr. Harpur looked mad enough to kill, too, but also worried that Mr. Edison would shut down his investment, which, if I knew Felix, had run into a lot more cash than he had been originally led to expect would be the case.

Felix opened both arms to them like a saloon keeper greeting drunks on payday. "Would you excuse me while I treat with Mr. McCoy?"

He didn't wait for objections, but looped an arm through mine and hustled me toward the door. Outside, he said, "Great timing, Gumshoe. You should be in vaudeville."

"Which is where you're going to be when Mr. Edison shuts you down for infringing on his patents."

"Edison didn't invent this stuff."

"Oh yeah? How come he holds the patents?"

Felix sighed, like the fact that I'd had only two years of parochial school because of very poor health during my early days made me some kind of idiot, while three years of yeshiva before they threw him out made him a genius. "Okay, okay, what's it going to cost me for you to look the other way?"

"You can't even pay your players."

"I'm two hours from finishing." He cast an anxious look at the sky, where the best light of the day was going to waste. "Give me a break, Joe."

"How many feet you shot?"

"Eight hundred."

Nearly a full reel.

"I'm calling it *Saved From Caesar*—a real moneymaker. I see no reason why I shouldn't share the profits with an old pal."

"Yeah, what's it about?"

"Romans kidnap the guy with the camel's girlfriend. He gets her back."

"Sounds uplifting, Felix."

"The people who pay to see my moving pictures, you think they know who Julius Caesar was? They know he was a Roman. They don't want to know no more."

Even if his players walked out like they were threatening, Felix would have eight hundred feet of Golden Drake claptrap into three thousand nickelodeons before Mr. Edison's Legal Department could stop him. The nickelodeons paid for product that was "fresh." They didn't care if it was any good so long as it was new. But I was worried about something a lot more important than one lousy movie.

"Where'd you get your film stock?"

"Here and there. You know."

"Felix, if you want a break, you better deal square."

"Okay, okay. I bought it from Eastman."

"You're lying. They made a deal: Eastman sells only to the Patents Company."

"I'm not lying. I bought it fair and square."

"From Europe?" Stolen stock came back in from Europe. Boys like Felix met the boat at the dock.

"No. Fair and square from Eastman. They got a guy sells it under the table. Ask around, you'll see."

I'd heard the rumors, and they were bad news for Mr. Edison.

"Whadaya say, Joe?"

Mr. Dyer says that when we're playing poker I got a face like a cinderblock. I waited. And sure enough, after looking around to make sure no one was listening, Felix spoke first.

"I got bigger things going than this movie. You're looking at a man who can do you some mighty big favors very soon."

I looked through him.

He said, "I'm going to California, Joe. I'm going to set up a new studio to manufacture feature films. You know what feature films are? . . . They're long films. Three, four, five reels. People'll pay more than a nickel to see 'em."

I continued to look through him.

"You come too. I could use a smart guy like you watching my back."

Until, I thought, I turned *my* back. "Where you getting the money to move to California?"

"*Saved From Caesar.* That's why I gotta finish it. You in?"

I shook my head. No one of my acquaintance would sit still for four reels. Felix gave another sigh. This one would have gotten mercy from the Devil. "I gotta finish this reel. I'll give you fifty bucks to leave."

"Make it a hundred."

He bargained awhile. We settled for a hundred.

"I'll get the money."

He ran into the greenhouse. I walked back to my car, thinking what the hell difference would one more nickelodeon reel make. Some of the players had gathered nearby on the lawn, the gladiators, the camel jockey, some Roman senators, and a half dozen Vestal Virgins smoking cigarettes.

One hundred dollars was a hell of a lot of money considering most moving picture folk were lucky to see five bucks a day. If those unpaid players sniffed it out they'd mob Felix like crows on a dead squirrel. Wondering why if he had the cash to pay me off, he didn't just pay his players and get the thing done before the Legal Department could get an injunction, I went back into the greenhouse, to conclude our transaction in private.

"Felix? Where are you?"

I heard a gunshot.

A sharp, loud snap, nearby. Felix came in the back door, and hurried toward me. He was stumbling like a drunk. When he tripped over the arc light cable and fell flat on his face, the back of his white shirt looked like his properties boys had hosed him with blood.

People came running in through every door in the greenhouse. Harpur, his blond wife, a bunch of players, and Gilda Riley, who let loose a scream that poor deaf-as-a-post Mr. Edison must have heard all the way down in West Orange.

An envelope had fallen from Felix's hand. I palmed it before anyone saw, and rolled him over to press my ear to his chest in case his heart was beating. But he was a bloody mess in front now, too, and I saw that even if by some miracle it was still beating, it wouldn't be for long enough to make a difference.

"Somebody get the cops," I said, loudly, because when the cops asked, "What was Joe McCoy doin' in here all alone with the body?" I wanted them to hear, "Joe McCoy said, 'Somebody get the cops.'"

"Okay, folks, let's leave the body by itself until the cops get here." Good old public-spirited Joe McCoy. Wouldn't hurt a fly. I herded them out and watched faces as they gathered whispering on the lawn.

Far below, down on the river, a tugboat was steaming away. I walked to the edge of the cliff where I could see the bank. There were stairs. Harpur had his own dock.

"The cops" arrived in the person of a white-haired hick constable, who looked old enough to have cut his teeth fighting Indians. He puttered around Felix's body like it was something that needed watering in his garden, and questioned Gilda and the other players, and Harpur and his wife. Then he shuffled over and asked what I was doing there. I explained how I was engaged to do investigating work for Mr. Edison's Legal Department, and told him, straight out, almost everything I knew. When he locked me with a pair of ball-bearing eyes, I remembered the Indians had lost.

"Where was it you said you was, Mr. McCoy, when this moving-picture feller was shot?"

"I was here in the greenhouse."

"Alone?"

"Alone. Till he staggered in, already shot, and died there, where's he's lying."

"Which door?"

I indicated the door that led to the old furnace room where Felix had set up his shops.

"So you saw him die?"

"You could say that."

"Who else saw him die?"

"Anybody standing outside. It's made of glass."

He turned and stared at the glass as if seeing it for the first time. "They say they couldn't see through the reflections. — Would you please hand me that sidearm you got hid in your coat pocket?"

"I didn't kill him."

"Butt first."

I was quickly gaining the impression that before he'd polished off the Indians, he had taken on the Confederacy. Without appearing to move much he had slid his black coat aside and his wrinkled old hand was resting rock steady about a quarter inch from a holstered revolver.

I surrendered my automatic.

He hefted it.

"Guess you didn't use this on him, or you'd a blown him clear to Trenton." He sniffed the barrel anyway. "How come you carrying a weapon—oh, yes, you tole me you was a detective for Mr. Edison."

"You can check with Mr. Dyer of the Legal Department."

"Well, Mr. Detective, what do you think of all this?"

"I think someone didn't like him."

"Why would that be?"

"He was a crook, a cheat, and a liar."

"Well, you don't kill a man for being a crook."

"I agree."

"But someone on this earth don't agree, Mr. McCoy. Until we find him I'd appreciate you did not leave the state of New Jersey."

"Or her."

"Beg pardon?"

"Both those ladies seemed madder than hell at him."

The old cop looked down at Felix, then over at Gilda Riley and Mrs. Harpur. "I heard that too, but no lady I know could have done a thing like this."

Perhaps we had been acquainted with different ladies, but before I could venture that opinion, he explained, "The man was shot once. In my experience, you rile a lady mad enough to shoot, they'll keep firing till they run out of bullets."

I asked whether he had any objections if I reported to Mr. Dyer at the Edison Laboratory down in West Orange.

He thought about it longer than I liked. I pointed out he had my name, my address, and my Navy Colt, as well as the name of my employer, "Mr. Thomas Alva Edison, himself," which was a slight exaggeration, as I'd never met him, but I felt I needed all the help I could get.

"According to folks I talked to, your employer had it in for these film fellers who ain't part of his Patents Company."

"He sics his lawyers on 'em, hot and heavy," I explained, with emphasis on "lawyers."

He thought it over, shaking his head, and I began to envision a night in the hoosegow. I said, "I don't know if it means anything, but I saw a tugboat pulling away from the dock shortly after he was shot."

The old-timer pulled out a pocket watch. "I'm gonna take a chance on you, Mr. McCoy. Wait for me at Rambo's Hotel tomorrow morning. And don't make me come lookin' for you."

A Palisades mortician's wagon trundled in for the corpse. The constable left with it, and finally I got a good gander at Felix's camera. I looked specifically for a jury-rigged sprocket hole cutter in case the camera had been modified to use unperforated stock. After that I left that place and drove as fast as I could to West Orange.

The Edison Laboratory housed a chemical plant, machine shops, laboratories, and offices in a three-story brick building. Mr. Dyer had his Legal Department on the top floor, and there was a closet off it with a desk and a telephone I could use when I was in the neighborhood. The old dragon who was his secretary took one look at my poker face and said, "I'll tell him there's trouble."

Mr. Dyer was a big, dark-haired fellow with a ready smile and icebox eyes. He liked his cigar and whiskey—a real man's man. He listened without interrupting while I told him what had happened, minus the old cop's suspicions regarding me. The lawyer got right to what was important.

"Where'd Drake get his film stock?"

"Said he bought it under the table from Eastman."

"Do you believe it?"

"I checked his camera. It was Eastman film, all right. The sprocket holes were perforated at the factory."

"I was afraid of that. Eastman's a back-stabbing son of— Joe, you've heard all that talk about monopoly?"

"I don't understand it all," I said, delivering the answer he paid to hear, "but the way I see it, if it weren't for Mr. Edison, the streets would still be dark and dangerous as coal mines."

"Good man! Come on, we better tell him what's happened."

I was surprised. Letting a detective talk directly with the Boss indicated that the infringement situation had got real bad. Ordinarily I'd have been real excited to make Mr. Edison's acquaintance, but I had a morning appointment with the Palisades constable and a bad feeling I was going to end up his prime suspect in Felix Dubinski's murder. So I hoped it would be a quick meeting, so I could find out who the hell had killed him before the constable jumped to the wrong conclusion.

Mr. Dyer led me downstairs, past the supply room where a couple of fellows were signing out a hunk of elephant skin, past the time clock that Mr. Dyer said Mr. Edison punched every day just like the rest of them, and into a noisy machine shop that couldn't have been louder if they were dismantling locomotives.

Mr. Dyer was so agitated he marched me right into a private elevator marked "This Elevator Reserved For Use of Mr. Edison." From a gallery, we looked down at Mr. Edison's two-story office, which was a sort of book-lined library. He had a marble statue of a naked little boy sitting on a heap of busted oil lamps. The boy had angel wings, and was waving an electric light bulb.

"He's not here. Let's try the recording room."

That was a special soundproofed room they used for recording phonograph cylinders. Mr. Dyer pushed in and there was Mr. Thomas Alva Edison himself, with his teeth locked firmly on an upright piano like he was gnawing the lid for supper.

A fellow was banging the keys louder than Saturday night in a whorehouse, and Mr. Edison, Mr. Dyer explained, was trying to hear the music through his teeth. I could see gnaw marks all over the thing. Mr. Dyer went up, clapped both hands around the great man's head, and yelled in his ear, "Excuse me, Mr. Edison, we have a problem."

"What's that?" cried Edison and I realized I was in for a very long meeting.

It took quite a while to convey that Mr. Dyer was worried about the Independents buying film stock from Eastman, rather than the Easter Bunny, but I saw right off why he'd brought me along, and it wasn't good. Dyer was worried about the patents. Edison didn't seem all that interested. He kept talking about improving the cameras so they'd take color pictures and making them small enough for folks to use at home, but he talked about movies and nickelodeons as if they were a thing of the past.

"Movies are turning low class," he said, "since the Jews and Catholics took 'em over."

I looked at Mr. Dyer, who knew perfectly well I was a Catholic. He could have at least said that the Catholics weren't the same as the Jews. But as usual the Protestants stood together and he nodded agreement with Mr. Edison. I began to get a funny feeling I'd backed the wrong horse.

Worse, Dyer didn't shout a word about Felix's murder, which kind of told me I'd be defending myself on my own tomorrow morning without the might of Edison behind me. Mr. Edison did give me a cigar. But by the time I got out of that place it was dark and Mr. Dyer said he had things to do and he would talk to me one of these days real soon.

I climbed back in my hired car and drove all the way to the Palisades. The greenhouse was dark. The estate house had some lights on so I knocked on the door and shoved past the butler who told me Mr. Harpur wasn't home. I found him and his wife in the library, drinking cocktails. She was red-eyed and teary. He looked madder than hell when he saw me barge in with my overcoat collar up and my hat down low over my eyes.

"What the hell do you want?"

"You can start by telling me who killed Felix."

"Who the hell is Felix?"

"François. Who killed him?"

"Beats me. The important thing is the son of a bitch is dead."

"How can you say that?" Mrs. Harpur howled. She burst into tears. And when her husband growled, "Oh for Chrissake," she jumped up and ran from the room. He watched her go, his mouth working.

"What did Felix do to you?" I asked.

Harpur took a swig of his drink. "He said we'd make big five-reel feature films. Long ones with a story. He swore they were the big thing in the future. He promised I'd quadruple my investment. Instead, I quadrupled the money I poured into *Saved From Caesar* and he seduced my wife."

The only surprise there was why was he surprised.

"So you shot him?"

"I did not."

"Why not?"

"I went to punch him yesterday and my wife said she'd leave me if I hurt him."

That sounded like a fine solution all around, but Harpur

couldn't see it. He said, with another deep swallow, "I promised I wouldn't hurt him. She agreed to stay a little longer."

People in love, I thought, acted like they lived in a nickelodeon. "You mind if I talk to her?"

"Go right ahead. We've got no secrets anymore." He poured another drink. I went looking and ran into the butler, who said she had gone out. I had a feeling I knew where and sure enough I found her in the greenhouse, staring by the light of a candlestick at the dark mess Felix had left on the floor.

"Leave me alone."

"Did you shoot him?"

"Of course not—" She started crying again. After a while, when the moment seemed right, I patted her shoulder and she sobbed, "He made me feel beautiful."

I'd have thought the mirror would have done that. She was Gibson-girl gorgeous, especially by candlelight, but there's no figuring how folks see themselves.

"So why were you yelling at him this afternoon?"

"He lied to me."

"No!" I said and she told me the whole astonishing story, how "François" had promised she would star in his feature film. I could only blurt, sympathetically, that I had never heard of such a thing in all my years in the moving picture business.

"You idiot!" she yelled. "Don't patronize me."

I calmed her down and it turned out that Felix had outdone himself with Mrs. Harpur. He had not offered a movie career merely so she would sleep with him. Felix had slept with her to get an introduction to her husband the wealthy investor. "When you walked in I had just learned that he knew all along he was going to California. And taking that chippy with him."

"Gilda Riley."

"Tell me, what does a man see in a woman like that?"

I resolved to explain that someday, after I explained why

the sky was blue. Instead, I asked, "Did Gilda tell you Felix was going to California?"

"How did you know?"

"Is that why you shot him?"

"I didn't shoot him, you idiot. I loved him. And I don't know how to use a gun."

"Where did the tugboat come from?"

She looked at me, her eyes suddenly big in the candle flame. "How did you know—"

"I know, Mrs. Harpur," I answered, only a little less confused than she was, but hoping to spook her into giving me some information. "But I don't know all the people who were on it. Where'd the tug come from?"

"Sandy Hook. The harbor pilot who brought the film stock. You know."

Stolen stock coming back from Europe. "Of course. He brought film for Felix's picture."

"Not just Felix's. Everybody's."

"Everybody's?"

"Don't you—"

"Show me."

"I don't think I should."

"Felix is dead. What are you going to do with it?"

"I thought I would give it to my husband. Let him make his money back."

"Where is it?"

The metal canisters filled a former potting shed from floor to ceiling. Felix had bought thousands and thousands of feet of stolen Eastman film stock. He had practically cornered the market on it, using the money that Harpur had given him for *Saved From Caesar.*

"Are you saying somebody on the tug shot him?"

Mrs. Harpur shook her head. "I don't see why. They were happier with the money than poor Felix was with this."

"Who was he planning to sell to?"

"The Independents who couldn't buy from Eastman."

"But Eastman is selling it under the table."

Mrs. Harpur bowed her head. "Yes, that turned out to be a problem. But by then he had already promised to pay for this and when the pilot came yesterday, he had no choice."

"The Felix I knew would have stiffed him."

"He was armed."

"So Felix cornered a market on film that's less valuable every day and used your husband's money to pay for it— more money than he could ever pay back with the movie your husband thought he had invested in."

Mrs. Harpur nodded sadly. "All his dreams went bad."

"Then he got caught by you when Gilda told you he was taking her to California."

"That actress."

"You're sure you didn't kill him?"

"For God's sake, Mr. McCoy, would I be talking to you like this if I had?"

"What about your husband?"

"Jarvis knows perfectly well I would leave him if he misbehaved that way."

"And the man on the tug got paid. So who killed him?"

"Gilda Riley."

I left that place figuring that neither Mr. or Mrs. Harpur were lying. The stolen-Eastman-film tugboat-delivery story made perfect sense. Felix had arranged for the harbor pilot to snatch it off the ship miles before it docked. That left Gilda, who Mrs. Harpur had helpfully informed me was staying at Rambo's.

I got to the hotel about ten o'clock. There were some folks in the bar, but no Gilda. The night clerk owed me a big favor and accepted three dollars to give me her room number, but drew a line at her key, it being a respectable establishment. I knocked.

To my surprise, she let me right in. The men among her adoring public would have been disappointed. She was wearing a flannel nightgown that was about as revealing as sail canvas. She climbed back into the bed, indicated her dressing-table chair for me, and asked, "Do you have any-thing to drink?"

I passed her my flask. She poured some in a water glass, took a sip, and shuddered. Then she hugged herself tight. "What's up, Mr. McCoy? Are you really Edison's detective?"

"I'm engaged by the Legal Department to conduct investigations. Right now I'm trying to figure out who shot Felix."

"François."

"When I knew him he was Felix."

"What was he like then?" she asked eagerly.

"Smaller-time, just as crooked."

"Was he exciting?"

"I beg your pardon?"

"He was so exciting to know. You never knew what would happen next."

"Or not happen, next."

Gilda Riley threw back her pretty head and laughed. "He was such a liar. He said he would take me to California, but all the time he was screwing Mrs. Harpur."

"So you shot him."

"Of course not."

"What do you mean, 'Of course not'? He lied to you. He set you up with a promise and then ran off with another woman."

"If I shot every man who lied to me, Mr. McCoy, if that's your name, I'd have a worse reputation than Typhoid Mary."

I heard her. And I believed her. And in case I didn't, she cinched it by saying, "Look, if I had been holding a gun in my hand at the very second I found out about that society bitch and François had been standing right there in front of me, *maybe* I would have shot him."

I had run out of suspects.

I had a couple of drinks before they closed the bar, hoping to pick up some new leads. Everybody was talking about the shooting, but nobody knew a thing. I went to bed and lay there thinking, maybe the fellow with the camel? Had I seen him outside the greenhouse? Maybe a Vestal Virgin? It could have been any one of the unpaid players.

The morning newspaper revealed just how powerful Mr. Edison and Mr. Dyer could be on occasion. Not a word about the shooting, and I thought, Thanks for small favors. They'd kept me out of it at least in the papers.

A narrow shadow fell on the comics.

I looked up as the Palisades town constable settled into the chair across from me. The dining room had emptied out as folks rushed off to catch the light. The waitress poured him coffee. His eyes were flat as marble.

"Mr. McCoy. You're the only one I can think of who could have shot that movie fellow."

"Well think harder, because I didn't do it."

"Oh, I'm reasonably sure you didn't. But once I report what I saw to the county prosecutor, it's going to be out of my hands, and I'm afraid you're going to have a very difficult time proving your innocence. Which I'm sure you will, in the end, which could take a long time and it's unlikely the magistrate would grant you bail."

I sat there thinking, Am I hearing right? Am I hearing a request for a bribe?

"I didn't kill him," I said. "I told you the truth. Except for one detail."

"What was that?"

"Felix dropped this when he died. I palmed it. Here, it's yours."

"An envelope," he said. "What do you suppose it contains?"

"I haven't a clue."

He looked around. "Well, I'm going to open her up." He extracted an enormous knife from his boot and slit the envelope like he was scalping a captive. Out fell ten 10-dollar bills.

"I'll be damned. One hundred dollars. I wonder who he intended that for."

"I see something else in there," I said. I did, though I had no idea what it was.

He shook it out and held it to the light, set it down, donned spectacles, and read the fine print. "A railroad ticket. To Los Angeles." He stood up, sheathed his knife, pocketed the money, and reached for the ticket.

I can move pretty quick for a fellow my size. Maybe because I don't think about it. I took the ticket from under his hand.

"I could use a vacation. For my health."

The Phoebe Snow left from the Erie-Lackawanna Terminal at Hoboken. I connected with the Twentieth Century at Buffalo, and the Santa Fe train in Chicago. When it stopped, I'd run out of country, but I'd had a few days to think things over and I knew exactly where I was going and why I was in Los Angeles.

Still, it took me a week before I found him, on a temporary shooting stage he'd erected in Griffith Park, public land that didn't charge rent. His assistants were all women, motherly as a gang of lionesses. I waited until they were distracted by a city official complaining that the players firing blank cartridges had frightened off the deer and elk.

"Felix!"

"It's *Boris*," he answered with an accent he had dredged up from the old neighborhood. "Recently fled from St. Petersburg, where I enraged the Czar with my artistic license."

"Oh yeah? What happened to François?"

"Everything went to hell, Joe. François was finished. Broke. Investors angry. Women irritated. You and your Mr. Edison were the last straw."

"Who knows?"

"You, me."

"What about the old constable?"

"Just an actor."

"That man didn't handle a gun like an actor."

"Before he was an actor he was one of TR's Rough Riders. Before that he was an Indian fighter. I was hoping you'd use that ticket, Joe. You're going to be real happy you came out here."

I squinted around at the sun-blasted brush and the mountains baking in the distance. Late November—Thanksgiving and applejack season back in Jersey—and it looked hotter than the suburbs of Hell. I'd already pawned my overcoat. "Yeah? What's here for me?"

"Like I told you, I need a man to watch my back. You can't trust nobody in moving pictures. And a growing town like this could always use a good investigator."

"I don't know," I said. But then I noticed that the baking mountains had snow on top. I thought to myself, a growing town like this would attract all kinds of Felix Dubinskis. Mr. Edisons, too, for that matter. All kinds of boys ready to take a long chance.

Isn't it Romantic?

Peter Straub

N steered the rented Peugeot through the opening in the wall and parked beside the entrance of the auberge. Beyond the old stable doors to his left, a dark-haired girl in a bright blue dress hoisted a flour sack off the floor. She dropped it on the counter in front of her and ripped it open. When he got out of the car, the girl gave him a flat, indifferent glance before she dipped into the bag and smeared a handful of flour across a cutting board. Far up in the chill gray air, thick clouds slowly moved across the sky. To the south, smoky clouds snagged on trees and clung to the slopes of the mountains. N took his carry-on bag and the black laptop satchel from the trunk of the Peugeot, pushed down the lid, and looked through the kitchen doors. The girl in the blue dress raised a cleaver and slammed it down onto a plucked, headless chicken. N pulled out the handle of the carry-on and rolled it behind him to the glass enclosure of the entrance.

He moved through and passed beneath the arch into the narrow, unlighted lobby. A long table stacked with brochures stood against the far wall. On the other side, wide doors opened into a dining room with four lines of joined tables covered with red-checked tablecloths and set for dinner. A blackened hearth containing two metal grilles took up the back wall of the dining room. On the left side of the hearth, male voices filtered through a door topped with a glowing stained-glass panel.

N moved past the dining room to a counter and an untidy little office—a desk and table heaped with record books and loose papers, a worn armchair. Keys linked to numbered metal squares hung from numbered hooks. A clock beside a poster advertising Ossau-Iraty cheese said that the time was five-thirty, forty-five minutes later than he had been expected. *"Bonjour. Monsieur? Madame?"* No one answered. N went to the staircase to the left of the office. Four steps down, a corridor led past two doors with circular windows at eye level, like the doors into the kitchens of diners in his long-ago youth. Opposite were doors numbered 101, 102, 103. A wider section of staircase ascended to a landing and reversed to continue to the next floor. *"Bonjour."* His voice reverberated in the stairwell. He caught a brief, vivid trace of old sweat and unwashed flesh.

Leaving the carry-on at the counter, he carried the satchel to the dining room doors. Someone beyond barked out a phrase, others laughed. N walked down the final row of tables and approached the door with the stained-glass panel. He knocked twice, then pushed the door open.

Empty tables fanned out from a door onto the parking lot. A man in a rumpled tweed jacket and with the face of a dissolute academic, a sallow, hound-faced man in a lumpy blue running suit, and a plump, bald bartender glanced at him and then leaned forward to continue their conversation in lowered voices. N put his satchel on the bar and took a stool. The bartender eyed him and slowly came up the bar, eyebrows raised.

In French, N said, "Excuse me, sir, but there is no one at the desk."

The man extended his hand across the bar. He glanced back at his staring friends, then smiled briefly and mirthlessly at N. "Mr. Cash? We had been told to expect you earlier."

N shook his limp hand. "I had trouble driving down from Pau."

"Car trouble?"

"No, finding the road out of Oloron," N said. He had driven twice through the southern end of the old city, guessing at the exits to be taken out of the roundabouts, until a toothless ancient at a crosswalk had responded to his shout of "Montory?" by pointing toward the highway.

"Oloron is not helpful to people trying to find these little towns." The innkeeper looked over his shoulder and repeated the remark. His friends were nearing the stage of drunkenness where they would be able to drive more confidently than they could walk.

The hound-faced man in the running suit said, "In Oloron, if you ask, '*Where* is Montory?' they answer, '*What* is Montory?'"

"All right," said his friend. "What is it?"

The innkeeper turned back to N. "Are your bags in your car?"

N took his satchel off the bar. "It's in front of the counter."

The innkeeper ducked out and led N into the dining room. Like dogs, the other two trailed after them. "You speak French very well, Mr. Cash. I would say that it is not typically American to have an excellent French accent. You live in Paris, perhaps?"

"Thank you," N said. "I live in New York." This was technically true. In an average year, N spent more time in his Upper East Side apartment than he did in his lodge in Gstaad. During the past two years, which had not been average, he had lived primarily in hotel rooms in San Salvador, Managua, Houston, Prague, Bonn, Tel Aviv, and Singapore.

"But you have spent perhaps a week in Paris?"

"I was there a couple of days," N said.

Behind him, one of the men said, "Paris is under Japanese occupation. I hear they serve raw fish instead of cervelas at the Brasserie Lipp."

They came out into the lobby. N and the innkeeper went

to the counter, and the two other men pretended to be interested in the tourist brochures.

"How many nights do you spend with us? Two, was it, or three?"

"Probably two," said N, knowing that these details had already been arranged.

"Will you join us for dinner tonight?"

"I am sorry to say that I cannot."

Momentary displeasure surfaced in the innkeeper's face. He waved toward his dining room and declared, "Join us tomorrow for our roasted mutton, but you must reserve at least an hour in advance. Do you expect to be out in the evenings?"

"I do."

"We lock the doors at eleven. There is a bell, but as I have no desire to leave my bed to answer it, I prefer you to use the keypad at the entrance. Punch two-three-four-five to open the door. Easy, right? Two-three-four-five. Then go behind the counter and pick up your key. On going out again the next day, leave it on the counter again, and it will be replaced on the rack. What brings you to the Basque country, Mr. Cash?"

"A combination of business and pleasure."

"Your business is . . . ?"

"I write travel articles," N said. "This is a beautiful part of the world."

"You have been to the Basque country before?"

N blinked, nudged by a memory that refused to surface. "I'm not sure. In my kind of work, you visit too many places. I might have been here a long time ago."

"We opened in 1961, but we've expanded since then." He slapped the key and its metal plate down on the counter.

N put his cases on the bed, opened the shutters and leaned out of the window, as if looking for the memory which had escaped him. The road sloped past the auberge and continued uphill through the tiny center of the village. On the covered terrace of the cement-block building directly opposite, a woman in a sweater sat behind a cash register at a display case filled with what a sign called "regional delicacies." Beyond, green fields stretched out toward the wooded mountains. At almost exactly the point where someone would stop entering Montory and start leaving it, the red enclosure of the telephone booth he had been told to use stood against a gray stone wall.

The innkeeper's friends staggered into the parking lot and left in a mud-spattered old Renault. A delivery truck with the word "Comet" stenciled on a side panel pulled in and came to a halt in front of the old stable doors. A man in a blue work suit climbed out, opened the back of the truck, pulled down a burlap sack from a neat pile and set it down inside the kitchen. A blond woman in her fifties wearing a white apron emerged from the interior and tugged out the next sack. She wobbled backward beneath its weight, recovered, and carried it inside. The girl in the blue dress sauntered into view and leaned against the doorway a foot or two from where the delivery man was heaving his second sack onto the first. Brown dust puffed out from between the sacks. As the man straightened up, he gave her a look of straightforward appraisal. The dress was stretched tight across her breasts and hips, and her face had a coarse, vibrant prettiness entirely at odds with the bored contempt of her expression. She responded to his greeting with a few grudging words. The woman in the apron came out again and pointed to the sacks on the floor. The girl shrugged. The delivery man executed a mocking bow. The girl bent down, slid her forearms beneath the sacks, lifted them waist-high and carried them deeper into the kitchen.

Impressed, N turned around and took in yellowish-white walls, a double bed which would prove too short, an old television set, and a nightstand with a reading lamp and a rotary phone. Framed embroidery above the bed advised him that eating well would lead to a long life. He pulled the carry-on toward him and began to hang up his clothes, meticulously refolding the sheets of tissue with which he had protected his suits and jackets.

A short time later, he came out into the parking lot holding the computer bag. Visible through the opening to the kitchen, the girl in the blue dress and another woman in her twenties, with stiff fair hair fanning out above a puggish face, a watermelon belly, and enormous thighs bulging from her shorts, were cutting up greens on the chopping block with fast, short downstrokes of their knives. The girl lifted her head and gazed at him. He said *"Bonsoir."* Her smile put a youthful bounce in his stride.

The telephone booth stood at the intersection of the road passing through the village and another which dipped downhill and flattened out across the fields on its way deeper into the Pyrenees. N pushed tokens into the slot and dialed a number in Paris. When the number rang twice, he hung up. Several minutes later, the telephone trilled, and he picked up the receiver.

An American voice said, "So we had a little hang-up, did we?"

"Took me a while to find the place," he said.

"You needum Injun guide, findum trail heap fast." The contact frequently pretended to be an American Indian. "Get the package all right?"

"Yes," N said. "It's funny, but I have the feeling I was here before."

"You've been everywhere, old buddy. You're a grand old man. You're a star."

"In his last performance."

"Written in stone. Straight from Big Chief."

"If I get any trouble, I can cause a lot more."

"Come on," said the contact. N had a detailed but entirely speculative image of the man's flat, round face, smudgy glasses, and fuzzy hair. "You're our best guy. Don't you think they're grateful? Pretty soon, they're going to have to start using Japanese. *Russians.* Imagine how they feel about that."

"Why don't you do what you're supposed to do, so I can do what I'm supposed to do?"

N sat outside the *café tabac* on the Place du Marche in Mauléon with a nearly empty demitasse of espresso by his elbow and a first edition of Rudyard Kipling's *Kim* in near-mint condition before him, watching lights go on and off in a building on the other side of the arcaded square. He had used the shower attachment in his room's flimsy bathtub, had shaved at the flimsy sink, and had dressed in a light-weight wool suit and his raincoat. With his laptop case upright on the next chair, he resembled a traveling business-man. The two elderly waiters had retired inside the lighted café, where a few patrons huddled at the bar. During the hour and a half N had been sitting beneath the umbrellas, a provincial French couple had taken a table to devour steak and *pommes frites* while consulting their guidebooks, and a feral-looking boy with long, dirty-blond hair had downed three beers. During a brief rain shower, a lone Japanese man had trotted in, wiped down his cameras and his forehead, and finally managed to communicate his desire for a beef stew and a glass of wine. Alone again, N was beginning to wish that he had eaten more than his simple meal of cheese and bread, but it was too late to place another order. The subject, a retired politician named Daniel Hubert with a local antique business and a covert sideline in the arms trade, had darkened his shop at the hour N had been told he would do so. A light had gone on in the living room of his apartment on the next floor, and then, a few minutes later, in his bedroom suite on the floor above that. This was all ac-cording to pattern.

"According to the field team, he's about to move up into the big time," his contact had said. "They think it'll be either tonight or tomorrow night. What happens is, he closes up shop and goes upstairs to get ready. You'll see the lights go on as he goes toward his bedroom. If you see a light in the top floor, that's his office, he's making sure everything's in place and ready to go. Paleface tense. Paleface know him moving out of his league. He's got South Americans on one end, ragheads on the other. Once he gets off the phone, he'll go downstairs, leave through the door next to the shop, get in his car. Gray Mercedes four-door with fuck-you plates from being Heap Big Deal in government. He'll go to a restaurant way up in the mountains. He uses three different places, and we never know which one it's going to be. Pick your spot, nice clean job, get back to me later. Then put it to some mademoiselle—have yourself a ball."

"What about the others?"

"Hey, we love the ragheads, you kidding? They're customers. These guys travel with a million in cash, we worship the camel dung they walk on."

The lights at the top of the house stayed on. A light went on, then off, in the bedroom. With a tremendous roar, a motorcycle raced past. The wild-looking boy who had been at the café glanced at N before leaning sideways and disappearing through the arcade and around the corner. One of the weary waiters appeared beside him, and N placed a bill on the saucer. When he looked back at the building, the office and bedroom lights had been turned off, and the living room lights were on. Then they turned off. N stood up and walked to his car. In a sudden spill of the light from the entry, a trim, silver-haired man in a black blazer and gray slacks stepped out beneath the arcade and held the door for a completely unexpected party, a tall blond woman in jeans and a black leather jacket. She went through one of the arches and stood by the passenger side of a long Mercedes while M. Hubert locked the door. Frustrated and angry, N pulled out of his parking spot and waited at the bottom of the square until they had driven away.

They did this more than they ever admitted. One time in four, the field teams left something out. He had to cover for their mistakes and take the fall for any screwups. Now they were going two for two—the team in Singapore had failed to learn that his subject always used two bodyguards, one who traveled in a separate car. When he had raised this point afterward, they had said they were "working to improve data flow worldwide." The blond woman was a glitch in the data flow, all right. He traveled three cars behind the Mercedes as it went through a series of right-hand turns on the one-way streets, wishing that his employers permitted the use of cell phones, which they did not. Cell phones were "porous," they were "intersectable,"—they were even, in the most delightful of these locutions, "capacity risks." N wished that one day someone would explain the exact meaning of "capacity risk." In order to inform his contact of M. Hubert's playmate, he would have to drive back to the "location usage device," another charming example of bureaucratese, the pay telephone in Montory. You want to talk capacity risks, how about that?

The Mercedes rolled beneath a streetlamp at the edge of the town and wheeled left to double back. Wonderful—he was looking for a tail. Probably he had caught sight of the field team while they were busily mismanaging the data flow. N hung back as far as he dared, now and then anticipating the subject's next move and speeding ahead on an adjacent street. Finally, the Mercedes continued out of Mauléon and turned east on a three-lane highway.

N followed along, speculating about the woman. In spite of her clothes, she looked like a mistress, but would a man bring his mistress to such a meeting? It was barely possible that she represented the South Americans, possible but even less likely that she worked for the buyers. Maybe they were just a lovely couple going out for dinner. Far ahead, the Mercedes' taillights swung left off the highway and began winding into the mountains. They had already disappeared by the time he came to the road. N made the turn, went up to the first bend and turned off his lights. From then on, it was a matter of trying to stay out of the ditches as he crawled along in the dark, glimpsing the other car's taillights and losing them, seeing the beams of the headlights picking out trees on an upward curve far ahead of him. Some part of what he was doing finally brought back the lost memory.

From inside the telephone booth, he could see the red neon sign AUBERGE DE L'ETABLE burning above the walled parking lot.

"Tonto waiting," said the contact.

"I would have appreciated a few words about the girl-friend."

"White man speak with forked tongue."

N sighed. "I waited across from his building. Hubert seemed to be doing a lot of running up and down the stairs, which was explained when he came out with a stunning young lady in a motorcycle jacket. I have to tell you, I hate surprises."

"Tell me what happened."

"He dodged all over the place before he felt safe enough to leave Mauléon. I followed him to an auberge way up in the mountains, trying to work out how to handle things if the meeting was on. All of a sudden, there's this variable, and the only way I can let you know about it is to turn around and drive all the way back to this phone, excuse me, this lo-cation usage device."

"*That* would have been a really terrible idea," said his contact.

"I waited for them to go into the lot and leave their car, and then I pulled up beside a wall and climbed uphill to a spot where I could watch their table through the glasses. I was trying to figure out how many reports I'd have to file if I included the girl. Remember Singapore? Improvising is no fun anymore."

"Then what?"

"Then they had dinner. The two of them. Basque soup, roast chicken, salad, no dessert. A bottle of wine. Hubert was trying to jolly her up, but he wasn't getting anywhere. The place was about half full, mainly with local people. Guys in berets playing cards, two foursomes, one table of

Japanese guys in golf jackets. God knows how *they* found out about the place. When Hubert and friend drove out, I followed them back and waited until all the lights went out. In the midst of all this wild activity, I remembered something."

"Nice. I understand people your age tend to forget."

"Let me guess. You knew about the girl."

"Martine is your background resource."

"Since when do I need a backup?" Seconds ticked by in silence while he struggled with his fury. "Okay. Fine. I'll tell you what, that's dandy. But Martine does all the paperwork."

"Let me work on that one. In the meantime, try to remember that we've been mainstreaming for some time now. Matrine has been in field operations for about a year, and we decided to give her a shot at learning from the old master."

"Right," N said. "What does Hubert think she is?"

"An expert on raghead psychology. We positioned her so that when he needed someone to help him figure out what these people mean when they say things, there she was. Doctorate in Arab studies from the Sorbonne, two years doing community liaison for an oil company in the Middle East. Hubert was so happy with the way she looks, he put her up in his guest room."

"And Martine told him that his partners would have him followed."

"He never laid eyes on you. She's impressed as hell, kemo sabe. You're her hero."

"Martine should spend a couple of days with me after we're done," N said, almost angry enough to mean it. "Let me advance her education."

"You?" The contact laughed. "Forget it, not that it wouldn't be educational for both of you. If you could handle encryption programs, you wouldn't have to use LUDs."

It took N a moment to realize that the word was an acronym.

"I hope you realize how much I envy you," the contact said. "When you came down the trail, this business was a lot more individual. Guys like you made up the rules on the fly. I was hired because I had an MBA, and I'm grateful to help rationalize our industry, move it into the twenty-first century, but even now, when you have to dot every *i* and cross every *t,* fieldwork seems completely romantic to me. The years you've been out there, the things you did, you're like Wyatt Earp. Paleface, I was honored to be assigned your divisional region controller."

"My what?"

"Your contact person."

"One of us is in the wrong line of work," N said.

"It was a pleasure riding through the Old West with you."

"To hell with you, too," N said, but the line was already dead.

Thirty-odd years ago, an old-timer called Sullivan had begun to get a little loose. A long time before that, he had been in the OSS and then the CIA, and he still had that wide-shouldered linebacker look and he still wore a dark suit and a white shirt every day, but his gut drooped over his belt and the booze had softened his face. His real name wasn't Sullivan, and he was of Scandinavian, not Irish, descent, with thick, coarse, blond hair going gray, an almost lipless mouth, and blue eyes so pale they seemed bleached. N had spent a month in Oslo and another in Stockholm, and in both places he had seen a lot of Sullivans. What he had remembered during the drive into the mountains was what had brought him to the French Pyrenees all that time ago—Sullivan.

He had been in the trade for almost a year, and his first assignments had gone well. In a makeshift office in a San Fernando Valley strip mall, a nameless man with a taut face and an aggressive crew cut had informed him that he was getting a golden opportunity. He was to fly to Paris, transfer to Bordeaux, meet a legend named Sullivan, and drive to southwest France with him. What Sullivan could teach him in a week would take years to learn on his own. The job,

Sullivan's last, his swan song, was nothing the older man could not handle by himself. So why include N? Simple—Sullivan. He seemed to be losing his edge; he wasn't taking care of the loose ends as well as he once had. So while N absorbed the old master's lessons, he would also be his backstop, make sure everything went smoothly, and provide nightly reports. If Sullivan was going to blow it, he would be pulled out, last job or not. The only problem, said the man with the crew cut, was that Sullivan would undoubtedly hate his guts.

And to begin with, he had. Sullivan had barely spoken on the drive down from Bordeaux. The only remark he made as they came up into the mountains was that Basques were so crazy they thought they were the sole survivors of Atlantis. He had dropped N off at the hotel in Tardets where he had a room and a waiting car with the suggestion that he skip coming over for dinner that night. N had spoken of their instructions, of his own desire to be briefed. "Fine, I give up, you're a Boy Scout," Sullivan had snarled, and sped off to his own lodgings, which were, N remembered once more as the Peugeot rolled downhill from the telephone booth, the Auberge de L'Etable.

Though the inn had been roughly half its present size, the dining room was the same massive hall. Sullivan had insisted on a table near the lobby and well apart from the couples who sat near the haunch of mutton blackening over the open fire. Alternately glaring at him and avoiding his glance, Sullivan drank six *marcs* before dinner and in French far superior to the young N's complained about the absence of vodka. In Germany you could get vodka, in England you could get vodka, in Sweden and Denmark and Norway and even in miserable Iceland you could get vodka, but in France nobody outside of Paris even heard of the stuff. When their mutton came, he ordered two bottles of bordeaux and flirted with the waitress. The waitress had flirted back. Without any direct statements, they arranged an assignation. Sullivan was a world-class womanizer. Either the certainty that the waitress would be in his bed later that night or the alcohol loosened him up. He asked a few questions, endured the answers, told stories that made young N's jaw drop like a rube's. Amused, Sullivan recounted seductions behind enemy lines, hair-raising tales of OSS operations, impersonations of foreign dignitaries, bloodbaths in presidential palaces. He spoke six languages fluently, three others nearly as well, and played passable cello. "Truth is, I'm a pirate," he said, "and no matter how useful pirates might be, they're going out of style. I don't fill out forms or itemize my expenses or give a shit about reprimands. They let me get away with doing things my way because it almost always works better than theirs, but every now and again, I make our little buddies sweat through their custom-made shirts. Which brings us to you, right? My last job, and I get a backup? Give me a break—you're watching me. They told you to report back every single night."

"They also said you'd give me the best education in the world," N told him.

"Christ, kid, you must be pretty good if they want *me* to polish your rough edges." He swallowed wine and smiled across the table in what even the young N had sensed as a change of atmosphere. "Was there something else they wanted you to do?"

"Polishing my rough edges isn't enough?" asked the suddenly uncertain young N.

Sullivan had stared at him for a time, not at all drunkenly but in a cold, curious, measuring fashion. N had known only that this scrutiny made him feel wary and exposed. Then Sullivan relaxed and explained what he was going to do and how he planned to do it.

Everything had gone well—better then well, superbly. Sullivan had taken at least a half-dozen steps that would have unnerved the crew-cut man in the strip mall. But each one, N took pains to make clear during his reports, had saved time, increased effectiveness, helped bring about a satisfactory conclusion. On the final day, N had called Sullivan to see when he was to be picked up. "Change of plans," Sullivan had said. "You can drive yourself to the airport. I'm spending one more night with the descendants of the Atlanteans." He wanted a farewell romp with the waitress. "Then back to the civilian life. I own thirty acres outside Houston, think I'll put up a mansion in the shape of the Alamo but a hundred times bigger, get a state-of-the-art music room, fly in the best cellist I can get for weekly lessons, hire a great chef, rotate the ladies in and out. And I want to learn Chinese. Only great language I don't already know."

On a rare visit to headquarters some months later, N had greeted the man from the strip mall as he carried stacks of files out of a windowless office into a windowless corridor. The man was wearing a small, tight bow tie, and his crew cut had been cropped to stubble. It took him a couple of beats to place N. "Los Angeles." He pronounced it with a hard *g*. "Sure. That was good work. Typical Sullivan. Hairy, but great results. The guy never came back from France, you know."

"Don't tell me he married the waitress," N had said.

"Died there. Killed himself, in fact. Couldn't take the idea of retirement, that's what I think. A lot of these Billy the Kid–type guys, they fold their own hands when they get to the end of the road."

Over the years, N now and again had remarked to himself the elemental truth that observation was mostly interpretation. Nobody wanted to admit it, but it was true anyhow. If you denied interpretation—which consisted of no more than thinking about two things, what you had observed and why you had observed it—your denial was an interpretation, too. In the midst of feeling more and more like Sullivan, that is, resistant to absurd nomenclature and the ever-increasing paperwork necessitated by "mainstreaming," he had never considered that "mainstreaming" included placing women in positions formerly occupied entirely by men. So now he had a female backup: but the question was, what would the lady have done if M. Hubert had noticed that N was following him? Now there, that was a matter for interpretation.

A matter N had sometimes weighed over the years, at those rare times when it returned to him, was the question Sullivan had put to him before he relaxed. *Was there anything else they wanted you to do?*

In institutions, patterns had longer lives than employees.

The parking lot was three-quarters full. Hoping that he still might be able to get something to eat, N looked at the old stable doors as he took a spot against the side wall. They were closed, and the dining room windows were dark. He carried the satchel to the entrance and punched the numerical code into the keypad. The glass door clicked open. To the side of the empty lobby, the dining room was locked. His hunger would have to wait until morning. In the low light burning behind the counter, his key dangled from the rack amidst rows of empty hooks. He raised the panel, moved past the desk to get the key, and, with a small shock like the jab of a pin, realized that of the thousands of resource personnel, information managers, computer jocks, divisional region controllers, field operatives, and the rest, only he would remember Sullivan.

The switch beside the stairs turned on the lights for a carefully timed period that allowed him to reach the second floor and press another switch. A sour, acrid odor he had noticed as soon as he entered the staircase intensified on the second floor and worsened as he approached his room. It was like the smell of rot, of burning chemicals, of a dead animal festering on a pile of weeds. Rank and physical, the stench stung his eyes and burrowed into his nose. Almost gasping, N shoved the key into his lock and escaped into his room to discover that the stink pursued him there. He closed the door and knelt beside the bed to unzip his laptop satchel. Then he recognized the smell. It was a colossal case of body odor, the full-strength version of what he had noticed six hours earlier. "Unbelievable," he said aloud. In seconds he had opened the shutters and pushed up the window. Someone who had not bathed in months, someone who reeked like a diseased muskrat had come into his room while he had been scrambling around on a mountain. N began checking the room. He opened the drawers in the desk, examined the television set, and was moving toward the closet when he noticed a package wrapped in butcher paper on a bedside table. He bent over it, moved it gingerly from side to side, and finally picked it up. The unmistakable odors of roast lamb and garlic penetrated both the wrapper and the fading stench.

He tore open the wrapper. A handwritten note on lined paper had been folded over another, transparent wrapper containing a thick sandwich of coarse brown bread, sliced lamb, and roast peppers. In an old-fashioned girlish hand and colloquial French, the note read:

I'm hoping you don't mind that I made this for you. You were gone all evening and maybe you don't know how early everything closes in this region. So in case you come back hungry, please enjoy this sandwich with my compliments.

ALBERTINE

N fell back on the bed, laughing.

The loud bells in the tower of the Montory church, which had announced the hour throughout the night, repeated the pious uproar that had forced him out of bed. Ignoring both Mass and the Sabbath, the overweight young woman was scrubbing the tiled floor in the dining room. N nodded at her as he turned to go down into the lounge, and she struggled to her feet, peeled off a pair of transparent plastic gloves, and threw them splatting onto the wet floor to hurry after him.

Three Japanese men dressed for golf occupied the last of the tables laid with white paper cloths, china, and utensils. N wondered if the innkeeper's drunken friend might have been right about the Brasserie Lipp serving sushi instead of

Alsatian food, and then recognized them as the men he had
seen at the auberge in the mountains. They were redistribut-
ing their portion of the world's wealth on a boys-only tour
of France. What he was doing was not very different. He sat
at the table nearest the door, and the young woman waddled
in behind him. *Café au lait. Croissants et confiture. Jus de
l'orange.* Before she could leave, he added, "Please thank
Albertine for the sandwich she brought to my room. And tell
her, please, that I would like to thank her for her thoughtful-
ness myself."

The dread possibility that she herself was Albertine vanished before her knowing smile. She departed. The Japanese
men smoked in silence over the crumbs of their breakfast.
Sullivan, N thought for the seventh or eighth time, also had
been assigned a backup on his last job. Had he ever really
believed that the old pirate had killed himself? Well, yes, for
a time. In N's mid-twenties, Sullivan had seemed a roman-
tic survivor, unadaptable to civilian tedium. Could a man
with such a life behind him be content with weekly cello
lessons, a succession of good meals, and the comforts of
women? Now that he was past Sullivan's age and had prepared his own satisfactions—skiing in the Swiss Alps, season tickets to Knicks and Yankees games, collecting first
editions of Kipling and T. E. Lawrence, the comforts of
women—he was in no doubt of the answer.

Was there anything else they wanted you to do?

No, there had not been, for Sullivan would have seen the
evidence on his face as soon as he had produced his question. Someone else, an undisclosed backup of N's own, had
done the job for them. N sipped his coffee and smeared mar-
malade on his croissants. With the entire day before him, he
had more than enough time to work out the details of a plan
already forming in his head. N smiled at the Japanese gentlemen as they filed out of the breakfast room. He had time
enough even to arrange a bonus Sullivan himself would
have applauded.

Back in his room, he pulled a chair up to a corner of the

window where he could watch the parking lot and the road without being seen and sat down with his book in his lap. Rain pelted down onto the half-empty parking lot. Across the road, the innkeeper stood in the shelter of the terrace with his arms wrapped around his fat chest, talking to the woman in charge of the display case stocked with jars of honey, bottles of Jurançon wine, and *fromage de brèbis*. He looked glumly business-like. The three Japanese, who had evidently gone out for a rainy stroll, came walking down from the center of the village and turned into the lot. The sight of them seemed to deepen the innkeeper's gloom. Wordlessly, they climbed into a red Renault L'Espace and took off. An aged Frenchman emerged and made an elaborate business of folding his yellow raincoat onto the passenger seat of his *deux-chevaux* before driving off. Two cars went by without stopping. The cold rain slackened and stopped, leaving shining puddles on the asphalt below. N opened *Kim* at random and read a familiar paragraph.

He looked up to see a long, gray tour bus pulling up before the building on the other side of the road. The innkeeper dropped his arms, muttered something to the woman at the register, and put on his professional smile. White-haired men with sloping stomachs and women in varying stages of disrepair filed out of the bus and stared uncertainly around them. The giant bells set off another clanging tumult. The innkeeper jumped down from the terrace, shook a few hands and led the first of the tourists across the road. It was Sunday, and they had arrived for the Mutton Brunch. When they were heavy and dull with food and wine, they would be invited to purchase regional delicacies.

Over the next hour, the only car to pull into the lot was a Saab with German plates which disgorged two obese parents and three blond teenagers, eerily slim and androgynous. The teenagers bickered over a mound of knapsacks and duffel bags before sulking into the auberge. The muddy Renault turned in to park in front of the bar. Dressed in white shirts, red scarves, and berets, the innkeeper's two friends climbed out. The hound-faced man was holding a tambourine, and the other retrieved a wide-bodied guitar from the back seat. They carried their instruments into the bar.

N slipped his book into the satchel and ran a comb through his hair and straightened his tie before leaving the room. Downstairs, the fire in the dining room had burned low, and the sheep turning on the grill had been carved down to gristle and bone. The bus tourists companionably occupied the first three rows of tables. The German family sat alone in the last row. One of the children yawned and exposed the shiny metal ball of a tongue piercing. Like water buffaloes, the parents stared massively, unblinkingly out into the room, digesting rather than seeing. The two men in Basque dress entered from the bar and moved halfway down the aisle between the first two rows of tables. Without preamble, one of them struck an out-of-tune chord on his guitar. The other began to sing in a sweet, wavering tenor. The teenagers put their sleek heads on the table. Everyone else complacently attended to the music, which migrated toward a nostalgic sequence and resolved into "I Hear a Rhapsody," performed with French lyrics.

Outside, N could see no one at the kitchen counter. The air felt fresh and cool, and battalions of flinty clouds marched across the low sky. He moved nearer. *"Pardon? Allô?"* A rustle of female voices came from within, and he took another step forward. Decisive footsteps resounded on a wooden floor. Abruptly, the older woman appeared in the doorway. She gave him a dark, unreadable look and retreated. A muffled giggle vanished beneath applause from the dining room. Softer footsteps approached, and the girl in the bright blue dress swayed into view. She leaned a hip against the door frame, successfully maintaining an expression of indifferent boredom.

"I wish I had that swing in my back yard," he said.

"Quoi?"

In French, he said, "A stupid thing we used to say when I was a kid. Thank you for making that sandwich and bringing it to my room." Ten feet away in the brisk air, N caught rank, successive waves of the odor flowing from her and wondered how the other women tolerated it.

"Nadine said you thanked me."

"I wanted to do it in person. It is important, don't you agree, to do things in person?"

"I suppose important things should be done in person."

"You were thoughtful to notice that I was not here for dinner."

Her shrug shifted her body within the tight confines of the dress. "It is just good sense. Our guests should not go hungry. A big man like you has a large appetite."

"Can you imagine, I will be out late tonight, too?"

Her mouth curled into a smile. "Does that mean you'd like another sandwich?"

"I'd love one." For the sake of pleasures to come, he took two more steps into her stench and lowered his voice. "We could split it. And you could bring a bottle of wine. I'll have something to celebrate."

She glanced at his satchel. "You finished what you are writing?"

She had questioned her boss about him.

"I'll be finished by tonight."

"I never met a writer before. It must be an interesting way of life. Romantic."

"You have no idea," he said. "Let me tell you something. Last year I was writing a piece in Bora-Bora, and I talked to a young woman a bit like you, beautiful dark hair and eyes. Before she came to my room, she must have bathed in something special, because she smelled like moonlight and flowers. She looked like a queen."

"I can look more like a queen than anyone in Bora-Bora."

"I wouldn't be surprised."

She lowered her eyes and swayed back into the kitchen.

After parking in a side street off the Place de Marche, N strolled through shops, leafed through *Kim* and sipped *men-*

the à l'eau at cafés, watched pedestrians and traffic move
through the ancient town. In a shop called Basque Es-
padrilles he saw the Japanese from the auberge swapping
their golf caps for yellow and green berets, which made
them look like characters in a comic film. They paid no attention to his smile. Caucasians all looked alike. Passing the
extensive terrace of what seemed to be the best restaurant in
town, he observed elegant M. Daniel Hubert and adventur-
ous Martine in intense discussion over espresso. M. Hubert's black silk suit and black silk T-shirt handsomely set
off his silver hair, and Martine's loose white sweater, short
tan skirt, and oversized glasses made her look as if she had
come from delivering a lecture. Here the reason for his observation was no mystery, but how might it be interpreted?
N backed away from the terrace, entered the restaurant by its
front door, and came outside behind them. He drank mineral
water at a distant table and let their gestures, their moves
and countermoves, sink into him. After a sober consideration of his position in the food chain, M. Hubert was getting
cold feet. Smiling, intelligent, professorial, above all desir-
able Martine was keeping him in the game. What can we
conclude, knowing what we know? We can, we must conclude that the object of N's assigned task was not poor M.
Hubert himself, but the effect the task would have upon his
buyers. N pressed button A, alarmingly closing a particular
door. Another door opened. All parties profited, not counting the winkled buyers and not counting N, who no longer
counted. A series of mechanical operations guided money
down a specific chute into a specific pocket, that was all. It
was never anything else.

N trailed along as they walked back to M. Hubert's
building, and his wandering gaze sought the other, the hidden player, he whose existence was likely as unknown to
Martine as it had been to his own naive younger self. Hubert had settled down under Martine's reassurances.
Apparently pausing in admiration of some particularly im-
pressive window embrasures, N watched him unlock his

great carved door and knew that the little devil was going to go through with it. Would a lifetime's caution have defeated ambition had his "consultant" been unattractive? Almost certainly, N thought. Hubert had not come so far by ignoring his own warning signals. They knew what they were doing; Hubert would not permit himself to exhibit weakness before a woman he hoped to bed. But N's employers had their own essential vulnerability. They trusted their ability to predict behavior.

In the guise of a well-dressed tourist absorbed by sixteenth-century masonry, N drifted backward through the arches and found lurking within the *café-tabac* the proof of his evolving theory.

Standing or rather slumping at the back of the bar, the feral-looking boy with messy, shoulder-length blond hair was tracking him through the open door. His motorcycle canted into the shadow of a pillar. As one returning to himself after rapt concentration, N looked aimlessly into the square or across it. The boy snapped forward and gulped beer. With a cheering surge of the old pleasure, N thrust his hands into his jacket pockets and walked into the square, waited for cars to pass, and began to amble back the way he had come. The boy put down his beer and moved to the front of the *café*. N reached the bottom of the square and turned around with his head raised and his hands in his pockets. The boy struck an abstracted pose between the pillars.

If his job had been to instruct the boy in their craft, he would have told him: *Never close off an option until the last moment. Roll the bike, dummy, until I tell you what to do.* The kid thought making up your mind was something you did minute-by-minute, a typical hoodlum notion. N strolled away, and the boy decided to follow him on foot. A sort of cunning nervous bravado spoke in his slow step forward. All he needed was a target painted on his chest. Enjoying himself, N sauntered along through the streets, distributing appreciative touristy glances at buildings beautiful and mundane alike, and returned to the restaurant where Martine

had coaxed M. Hubert back into the game. He pretended to
scan the menu in its glass case. Two shops away, the boy
spun to face a rack of scenic postcards. His sagging, scruffy
leather jacket was too loose to betray his weapon, but it was
probably jammed into his belt, another thuggish affectation.
N strolled onto the terrace and took a table in the last row.

The boy sidled into view, caught sight of him, sidled away.
N opened his satchel, withdrew his novel, and nodded at a
waiter. The waiter executed a graceful dip and produced a
menu. The boy reappeared across the street and slouched into
a café to take a window seat. That wouldn't have been so
bad, if everything else had not been so awful. N spread the
wings of the menu and deliberately read all the listings. *Can't
you see? I'm telling you what to do. You have time to go
back for your motorcycle, in case you'll need it when I
leave.* The boy plopped his chin on his palm. N ordered
mushroom soup, lamb chops, a glass of red burgundy, a bottle of Badoit *gazeuse.* He opened his book. Plucky Kimball
O'Hara, known as Kim, presently in the Himalayas, was
soon to snatch secret papers from a couple of Russian spies.
The boy raked his hair with his fingers, stood up, sat down.
A bowl of mushroom soup swirled with cream sent up a de-
licious, earthy odor. The boy finally slouched off up the
sidewalk. N returned to Kim, the Russians, and the wonderful soup.

He had begun on the lamb chops when he heard the motorcycle approach the terrace, blot out all other sounds, and
cut out. N took a swallow of wine. Across the street and just
visible past the front of the restaurant, the boy was dis-
mounting. He shook out his hair and knelt beside his machine, an old Kawasaki with fat panniers hanging from the
saddle. After a sketchy pretense of fussing with the engine
for a couple of minutes, he wandered away. N cut open a
chop to expose sweet, tender meat precisely the right shade
of pink.

When he had paid for his lunch, he made certain the boy
was out of sight and ducked into the restaurant. The men's

room was a cubicle in a passageway alongside the kitchen. He locked the door, relieved himself, washed and dried his hands and face, and sat down on the lid of the toilet. Five minutes went by while he ignored the rattle of the handle and knocks on the door. He let another two minutes pass, and then opened the door. The frowning man outside thrust past him and closed the door with a thump. N turned away from the dining room and continued down the passage to a service door which let him out into a narrow brick alley. A vent pumped out heat above overflowing garbage bins. N moved toward the top of the alley, where a motorcycle revved and revved like a frustrated beast. The boy was supposed to carry out his instructions at night, either in the mountains or on the little roads back to Montory, but after having seen N, he was in a panic at losing him. The sound of the motorcycle descended into a low, sustained rumble and grew louder. N faded backward. Maybe the kid would want to see if the restaurant had a back door—that wouldn't be so stupid.

N ducked behind the garbage bins and peered over the refuse as the walls amplified the rumble. The boy stopped short with his front wheel turned into the alley. The bike sputtered, coughed, died. *"Merde."* The boy looked into the alley and repeated himself with a more drastic inflection. What he had figured out meant *merde* for breakfast, lunch, and dinner, as far as he was concerned. N waited to see what he would do next: plod to the nearest approved telephone to report failure or come down the alley in search of whatever scraps he might salvage from the ruin.

The kid pushed his bike into the alley and mooched along for a dozen feet. Muttering to himself, he propped the bike against a wall. N braced his legs and reached into the satchel. He closed his hand around the grip of the nine-millimeter pistol, fitted with his silencer of choice, and thumbed the safety up and the hammer down. The kid's footsteps slopped toward him from maybe twenty feet away. The boy was uttering soft, mindless obscenities. The sullen footsteps came to within something like ten feet from the far end of the garbage bins. N drew out the pistol, tightened the muscles in his legs, and jumped up, already raising his arm. The kid uttered a high-pitched squeal. His blunt face went white and rubbery with shock. N carried the gesture through until his arm extended straight before him. He pulled the trigger. A hole that looked too small to represent real damage appeared between the kid's eyebrows at the moment of the soft, flat explosion. The force of the bullet pushed the kid backward and then slammed him to the ground. The casing pinged off brick and struck concrete. A dark spray of liquid and other matter slid down the face of the wall.

N shoved the pistol back into the satchel and picked up the cartridge case. He bent over the body, yanked the wallet out of his jeans and patted for weapons, but found only the outline of a knife in a zippered pocket. He moved up to the Kawasaki, unhooked the panniers on their strap and carried them with him out of the alley into an afternoon which seemed sharp-edged and charged with silvery electricity.

A tide of black-haired priests with boys' faces washed toward him from five or six feet away, their soutanes swinging above their feet. One of them caught his mood and smiled at him with teeth brilliantly white. He grinned back at the priest and stepped aside. A red awning blazed like a sacred fire. Moving past, the boy priests filled the sidewalk, speaking machine-gun South American Spanish in Ecuadorean accents. Another noticed N and he, too, flashed a brilliant smile. It was the Lord's day. The priest's sculpted coif sliced through the glittering air. N nodded briskly, still grinning, and wheeled away.

By the time he got back to the Peugeot, his forehead was filmed with sweat. He unlocked the car, tossed the panniers inside, climbed in and placed the satchel next to his right leg. He wiped his forehead with his handkerchief and fished the boy's wallet from his jacket pocket. It was made of red leather stamped with the Cartier logo. Three hundred francs—about sixty dollars. A driver's license in the name of

Marc-Antoine Labouret, with an address in Bayonne. A prepaid telephone card. A membership card from a video rental store. The business card of a Bayonne lawyer. A folded sheet of notepaper filled with handwritten telephone numbers, none familiar. A credit card made out to François J. Pelletier. Another credit card made out to Remy Grosselin. Drivers' licenses in the names of François J. Pelletier and Remy Grosselin of Toulouse and Bordeaux, respectively, each displaying the image of a recently deceased young criminal. The forgeries were what N thought of as "friend of a friend" work, subtly misaligned and bearing faint, pale scars of erasure. He withdrew the money, put the wallet on the dash, and pulled the panniers toward him.

The first held only rammed-in jeans, shirts, underwear, socks, and a couple of sweaters, and everything was crushed and wrinkled, filthy, permeated with a sour, poverty-stricken smell. Disgusted, N opened the second pannier and saw glinting snaps and the dull shine of expensive leather. He extracted an alligator handbag. It was empty. The next bag, also empty, was a black Prada. He took four more women's handbags from the pannier, each slightly worn but serviceable, all empty. Fitting them back into the pannier, N could see the kid roaring alongside his victims, ripping the bags from their shoulders, gunning away. He had stripped the money and valuables, junked everything else, and saved the best to peddle to some other rodent.

Either N's employers were getting desperate, or he had misidentified a would-be mugger as his appointed assassin. The latter seemed a lot more like reality. Irritated, concerned, and amused all at once, he went over the past twenty-four hours. Apart from the boy, the only people he had seen more than once were Japanese tourists who went out for walks in the rain and bought garish berets. His contact had said something about Japanese labor, but that meant nothing. A siren blared behind him. Immediately, another screamed in from his left. He shoved the Cartier wallet into one of the panniers and wound back through the one-way streets.

A boom and clatter of bells louder than sirens celebrated the conclusion of another Mass. The traffic slowed to pedestrian speed as it moved past the restaurant, where uniformed policemen questioned the remaining diners on the terrace. Two others, smart in their tunics and Sam Browne belts, blocked the entrance of the alley. The traffic picked up again, and soon he was breezing down the wide, straight road toward Montory.

At Alos, an abrupt turn took him over an empty bridge. Halfway across, he halted, trotted around the front of the car, opened the passenger door and in one continuous motion reached inside, thrust his hip against the railing, and sent the panniers whirling out over the swift little Saison River.

The contact took twenty minutes to call him back.

"So we had a little hang-up, did we?" N asked, quoting his words back to him.

"I'm not in the usual place. It's Sunday afternoon, remember? They had to find me. What's going down? You weren't supposed to call in until tonight."

"I'm curious about something," N said. "In fact, I'm a pretty curious guy, all in all. Humor me. Where did they find you? A golf course? Is it like being a doctor, you carry a beeper?"

There was a short silence. "Whatever you're unhappy about, we can work it out." Another brief silence. "I know Martine came as a nasty surprise. Honestly, I don't blame you for being pissed. You need her like a hole in the head. Okay, here's the deal. No reports, no paperwork, not even the firearms statements. You just walk away and get that big, big check. She handles all the rest. Are you smiling? Do I see a twinkle in your eye?"

"You were at your health club, maybe?" N asked. "Did you have to leave a really tense racquetball match just for me?"

The contact sighed. "I'm at home. In the old wigwam. Actually, out in back, setting up a new rabbit hutch for my daughter. For her rabbit, I mean."

"You don't live in Paris."

"I happen to live in Fontainebleau."

"And you have a beeper."

"Doesn't everyone?"

"What's the rabbit's name?"

"Oh, dear," the contact said. "Is this how we're going to act? All right. The rabbit's name is Custer. Family joke."

"You mean you're a real Indian?" N asked, and laughed out loud in surprise. "An honest-to-God Red Man?" His former image of his contact as a geek in thick glasses metamorphosed into a figure with high cheekbones, bronze skin, and straight, shoulder-length black hair.

"Honest Injun," the contact said. "Though the term *Native American* is easier on the ears. You want to know my tribal affiliation? I'm a Lakota Sioux."

"I want to know your name." When the contact refused to speak, N said, "We both know you're not supposed to tell me, but look at it this way. You're at home. No one is monitoring this call. When I'm done here, no one is ever going to hear from me again. And I have to say, telling me your name would reinforce that bond of trust I find crucial to good fieldwork. As of now, the old bond is getting mighty frayed."

"Why is that?"

"Tell me your name first. Please, don't get tricky. I'll know if you're lying."

"What on earth is going on down there? All right. I'm putting my career in your hands. Are you ready? My name is Charles Many Horses. My birth certificate says Charles Horace Bunce, but my Indian name was Many Horses, and when you compete for government contracts, as we have been known to do, you have to meet certain standards. Many Horses sounds a lot more Native American than Bunce. Now can you please explain what the hell got you all riled up?"

"Is someone else down here keeping an eye on me? Besides Martine? Someone I'm not supposed to know about?"

"Oh, please," the contact said. "Where's that coming from? Ah, I get it—sounds like you spotted somebody, or thought you did anyhow. Is that what this all about? I guess paranoia comes with the territory. If you did see someone, he's not on our payroll. Describe him."

"Today in Mauléon, I noticed a kid I saw hanging around the café last night. Five-ten, hundred and fifty pounds, late twenties. Long blond hair, grubby, rides a Kawasaki bike. He was following me, Charles, there is no doubt at all about that. Where I went, he went, and if I weren't, you know, sort of reasonably adept at my job, I might never have noticed the guy. As it was, I had to run out of a restaurant by the back door to ditch him. Okay, call me paranoid, but this sort of thing tends to make me uncomfortable."

"He's not ours," the contact said quickly. "Beyond that, I don't know what to tell you. It's your call, champ."

"Okay, Charles," said N, hearing a murky ambiguity in the man's voice. "This is how it goes. If I see the kid again tonight, I have to deal with him."

"Sounds good to me," said the contact.

"One more thing, Charles. Have we, to your knowledge, taken on any Japanese field people? You mentioned this possibility yesterday. Was that an idle remark, or . . . no. There are no idle remarks. We hired some Japanese."

"Now that you mention it, a couple, yeah. It's impossible to find people like you anymore. At least in the States."

"Are these the Japanese gentlemen I'm seeing wherever I go, the past couple of days?"

"Let me ask you a question. Do you know how strong the yen is against Western currencies? It's a joke. If you fly first class on Air France, they give you sushi instead of escargots. Busy little Japanese tourists are running around all over Europe, the Pyrenees included."

"Sushi instead of snails." The knowledge that he had heard an almost identical remark not long before set off a mental alarm which subsided at the recollection of the drunken Basques.

"It's about money, what a shock. Walk right in, right? You want it, we got it. Just ask Tonto. What's our revenge against the palefaces? Casinos. That'll work."

"Like an MBA," N said. "You're too embarrassed to admit you went to Harvard, but you did."

"Now, just how . . ." The contact gave a wheezy chuckle. "You're something else, pardner. Heap proud, go-um Harvard, but people assume you're an asshole. Anyhow, lay off the Japs. You see the same ones over and over because that's where they are."

"Neat and tidy, peaceful and private. Just Hubert, Martine, and me."

"See how easy it gets when you dump your anxiety? Try not to mess up his car. Martine'll drive it back to town. The mule who's bringing her car down from Paris is going to drive the Mercedes to Moscow. We have a buyer lined up."

"Waste not, want not."

"Or, as my people say, Never shoot your horse until it stops breathing. I'm glad we had this talk."

Neat and tidy, peaceful and private. Lying on his bed, N called a private line in New York and asked his broker to liquidate his portfolio. The flustered broker required a lengthy explanation of how the funds could be transferred to a number of coded Swiss accounts without breaking the law, and then he wanted to hear the whole thing all over again. Yes, N said, he understood an audit was inevitable. No problem, that was fine. Then he placed a call to a twenty-four-hours-a-day-every-day number made available to select clients by his bankers in Geneva, and through multiple conferencing and the negotiation of a four-and-a-half-point charge established the deposit of the incoming funds and distribution of his present arrangements into new accounts dramatically inaccessible to outsiders, even by Swiss standards. On Monday, the same accommodating bankers would ship by

same-day express to an address in Marseilles the various
documents within a lockbox entrusted to their care. His
apartment was rented, so that was easy, but it was a shame
about the books. He stripped down to his shirt and underwear and fell asleep watching a Hong Kong thriller dubbed
into hilarious French in which the hero detective, a muscly
dervish, said things like, "Why does it ever fall to me to be
the exterminator of vermin?" He awakened to a discussion
of French farm prices between a professor of linguistic theory, a famous chef, and the winner of last year's Prix
Goncourt. He turned off the television and read ten pages of
Kim. Then he put the book in the satchel and meticulously
cleaned the pistol before inserting another hollow-point bullet into the clip and reloading. He cocked the pistol, put on
the safety, and nestled the gun in beside the novel. He showered and shaved and trimmed his nails. In a dark gray suit
and a thin black turtleneck, he sat down beside the window.

The lot was filling up. The German family came outside
into the gray afternoon and climbed into the Saab. After they
drove off, a muddy Renault putted down the road and turned
in to disgorge the innkeeper's friends. A few minutes later
the red L'Espace van pulled into the lot. The three Japanese
walked across the road in their colorful new berets to inspect
the food and drink in the display case. The blond woman offered slivers of cheese from the wheels, and the Japanese
nodded in solemn appreciation. The girl in the blue dress
wandered past the kitchen doors. The men across the street
bought two wedges of cheese and a bottle of wine. They
bowed to the vendor, and she bowed back. An eager-looking
black and white dog trotted into the lot and sniffed at stains.
When the Japanese came back to the auberge, the dog followed them inside.

N locked his door and came down into the lobby. Mouth
open and eyes alert, the dog looked up from in front of the
table and watched him put his key on the counter. N felt a
portion of his anticipation and on the way outside patted the
animal's slender skull. At the display counter he bought a

wedge of sheep's-milk cheese. Soon he was driving along the narrow road toward Tardets, the sharp turn over the river at Alos, and the long, straight highway to Mauléon.

Backed into a place near the bottom of the arcade, he took careful bites of moist cheese, unfolding the wrapper in increments to keep from dropping crumbs on his suit. Beneath the yellow umbrellas across the square, an old man read a newspaper. A young couple dangled toys before a baby in a stroller. Privileged by what Charles (Many Horses) Bunce called its "fuck-you" plates, M. Hubert's Mercedes stood at the curb in front of the antique shop. A pair of students trudged into the square and made for the café, where they slid out from beneath their mountainous backpacks and fell into the chairs next to the couple with the baby. The girl backpacker leaned forward and made a face at the baby, who goggled. That one would be a pretty ride, N thought. A lot of bouncing and yipping ending with a self-conscious show of abandonment. An elegant woman of perhaps N's own age walked past his car, proceeded beneath the arcade, and entered the antique store. He finished the last of the cheese, neatly refolded the wrapping paper and stuffed it into an exterior pocket of the case. In the slowly gathering darkness, lights went on here and there.

There were no Japanese golfers in Basque berets. The backpackers devoured *croque monsieurs* and trudged away, and the couple pushed the stroller toward home. An assortment of tourists and regulars filled half of the tables beneath the umbrellas. A man and a woman in doughty English clothing went into Hubert's shop and emerged twenty minutes later with the elegant woman in tow. The man consulted his watch and led his companions away beneath the arcades. A police car moved past them from the top of the square. The stolid man in the passenger seat turned dead eyes and a Spam-colored face upon N as the car went by. There was always this little charge of essential recognition before they moved on.

Obeying an impulse still forming itself into thought, N left his car and walked under the arches to the window of the antique store. It was about twenty minutes before closing time. M. Hubert was tapping at a desktop computer on an enormous desk at the far end of a handsome array of gleaming furniture. A green-shaded lamp shadowed a deep vertical wrinkle between his eyebrows. The ambitious Martine was nowhere in sight. N opened the door, and a bell tinkled above his head.

Hubert glanced at him and held up a hand, palm out. N began moving thoughtfully through the furniture. A long time ago, an assignment had involved a month's placement in the antiques department of a famous auction house, and along with other crash tutorials, part of his training had been lessons in fakery from a master of the craft named Elmo Maas. These lessons had proved more useful than he ever expected at the time. Admiring the marquetry on a Second Empire table, N noticed a subtle darkening in the wood at the top of one leg. He knelt to run the tips of his fingers up the inner side of the leg. His fingers met a minuscule but telltale shim which would be invisible to the eye. The table was a mongrel. N moved to a late-eighteenth-century desk marred only by an overly enthusiastic regilding, probably done in the thirties, of the vine-leaf pattern at the edges of the leather surface. The next piece he looked at was a straightforward fake. He even knew the name of the man who had made it.

Elmo Maas, an artist of the unscrupulous, had revered an antiques forger named Clement Tudor. If you could learn to recognize a Tudor, Maas had said, you would be able to spot any forgery, no matter how good. From a workshop in Camberwell, South London, Tudor had produced five or six pieces a year for nearly forty years, concentrating on the French seventeenth and eighteenth centuries and distributing what he made through dealers in France and the United States. His mastery had blessed both himself and his work: never identified except by disciples like Maas, his furniture had defied suspicion. Some of his work had wound up in museums, the rest in private collections. Using photographs and slides along with samples of his own work, Maas had educated his pupil in Tudor's almost invisible nuances: the treatment of a bevel, the angle and stroke of chisel and awl, a dozen other touches. And here they were, those touches, scattered more like the hints of fingerprints than fingerprints themselves over a Directory armoire.

M. Hubert padded up to N. "Exquisite, isn't it? I'm closing early today, but if you were interested in anything specific, perhaps I can . . . ?" At once deferential and condescending, his manner invited immediate departure. Underlying anxiety spoke in the tight wrinkles about his eyes. A lifetime of successful bluffing had shaped the ironic curve of his mouth. N wondered if this dealer in frauds actually intended to go through with the arms deal after all.

"I've been looking for a set of antique bookcases to hold my first editions," N said. "Something suitable for Molière, Racine, Diderot—you know the sort of thing I mean."

Avarice sparkled in Hubert's eyes. "Yours is a large collection?"

"Only a modest one. Approximately five hundred volumes."

Hubert's smile deepened the wrinkles around his eyes. "Not so very modest, perhaps. I don't have anything here that would satisfy you, but I believe I know where to find precisely the sort of thing you are looking for. As I stay open on Sundays I close on Mondays, but perhaps you could take my card and give me a call at this time tomorrow. May I have your name, please?"

"Roger Maris," N said, pronouncing it as though it were a French name.

"Excellent, Monsieur Maris, I think you will be very pleased with what I shall show you." He tweaked a card from a tray on the desk, gave it to N, and began leading him to the door. "You are here for several more days?"

"Until next weekend," N said. "Then I return to Paris."

Hubert opened the door, setting off the little bell again.

"Might I ask a few questions about some of the pieces?"

Hubert raised his eyebrows and tilted his head forward.

"Is your beautiful Second Empire table completely intact?"

"Of course! Nothing we have has been patched or repaired. Naturally, one makes an occasional error, but in this case . . . ?" He shrugged.

"And what is the provenance of the armoire I was looking at?"

"It came from a descendant of a noble family in Périgord who wanted to sell some of the contents of his château. Taxes, you know. One of his ancestors purchased it in 1799. A letter in my files has all the details. Now I fear I really must . . ." He gestured to the rear of the shop.

"Until tomorrow, then."

Hubert forced a smile and in visible haste closed the door.

Ninety minutes later the Mercedes passed beneath the street-lamp at the edge of town. Parked in the shadows beside a combination grocery store and café a short distance up the road, N watched the Mercedes again wheel sharply left and race back into Mauléon, as he had expected. Hubert was repeating the actions of his dry run. He started the Peugeot and drove out of the café's lot onto the highway, going deeper into the mountains to the east.

Barely wide enough for two cars, the winding road to the auberge clung to the side of the cliff, bordered on one side by a shallow ditch and the mountain's shoulder, on the other a grassy verge leading to empty space. Sometimes the road doubled back and ascended twenty or thirty feet above itself; more often, it fell off abruptly into the forested valley. At two narrow places in the road, N remembered, a car traveling up the mountain could pull over into a lay-by to let a descending car pass in safety. The first of these was roughly half the distance to the auberge, the second about a hundred feet beneath it. He drove as quickly as he dared, twisting and turning with the sudden curves of the road. A single car zipped past him, appearing and disappearing in a flare of headlights. He passed the first lay-by, continued on, noted the second, and drove the rest of the way up to the auberge.

The small number of cars in the wide parking lot were lined up near the entrance of the two-story ocher building. Two or three would belong to the staff. Canny little M. Hubert, like all con men instinctively self-protective, had chosen a night when the restaurant would be nearly empty. N parked at the far end of the lot and got out, the engine still running. His headlights shone on a white wooden fence and eight feet of meadow grass with nothing but sky beyond. Far away, mountains bulked against the horizon. He bent down and stepped through the bars of the fence and walked into the meadow grass. In the darkness, the gorge looked like an abyss. You could probably drop a hundred bodies down into that thing before anyone noticed. Humming, he jogged back to his car.

N turned into the lay-by and cut the lights and ignition. Far below, headlights swung around a curve and disappeared. He straightened his tie and patted his hair. A few minutes later, he got out of the car and stood in the middle of the road with the satchel under his arm, listening to the Mercedes as it worked its way uphill. Its headlights suddenly shot across the curve below, then lifted toward him. N stepped forward and raised his right arm. The headlights advanced, and he took another step into the dazzle. As two pale faces stared through the windshield, the circular hood ornament and toothy grille came to a reluctant halt a few feet short of his waist. N pointed to his car and raised his hands in a mime of helplessness. They were talking back and forth. He moved around to the side of the car. The window rolled down. M. Hubert's face was taut with anxiety and distrust. Recognition softened him, but not by much.

"Monsieur Maris? What is this?"

"Monseiur Hubert! I am absolutely delighted to see you!" N lowered his head to look in at Martine. She was wearing something skimpy and black and was scowling beautifully. Their eyes met, hers charged with furious concentration. Well, well. "Miss, I'm sorry to trouble the two of you, but I had car trouble on the way down from the auberge, and I am afraid that I need some help."

Martine tried to wither him with a glare. "Daniel, do you actually know this man?"

"This is the customer I told you about," Hubert told her.

"*He's* the customer?"

Hubert patted her knee and turned back to N. "I don't have time to help you now, but I'd be happy to call a garage from the auberge."

"I only need a tiny push," N said. "The garages are all closed, anyhow. As you can see, I'm already pointed downhill. I hate to ask, but I'd be very grateful."

"I don't like this, Daniel," Martine said.

"Relax," Hubert said. "It'll take five seconds. Besides, I have a matter to discuss with Monsieur Maris." He drove forward and stopped at the far end of the lay-by. N walked uphill behind him. Hubert got out, shaking his head and smiling. "This is a terrible place for car trouble." Martine had turned around to stare at N through the rear window.

"Finding you was good luck for me," N said.

Hubert came up to him and placed two fingers on his arm in a delicate gesture of reconciliation. Even before he inclined his head to whisper his confidence, N knew what he was going to say. "Your question about that marquetry table troubled me more and more this evening. After all, my reputation is at stake every time I put a piece on display. I examined it with great care, and I think you may have been right. There is a definite possibility that I was misled. I'll have to look into the matter further, but I thank you for bringing it to my attention." The two fingers tapped N's arm.

He straightened his posture and in a conversational tone said, "So you had dinner at my favorite auberge? Agreeable, isn't it?" Hubert took a brisk stride over the narrow road, then another, pleased to have concluded one bit of business and eager to get on to the next.

A step behind him, N drew the pistol from the case and shoved the barrel into the base of Hubert's skull. The dapper little fraud knew what was happening—he tried to dodge sideways. N rammed the muzzle into his pad of hair and pulled the trigger. With the sudden flash and a sound no louder than a cough came a sharp scent of gunpowder and burning flesh. Hubert jolted forward and flopped to the ground. N heard Martine screaming at him even before she got out of the Mercedes.

He pushed the gun into the satchel, clamped the satchel beneath his elbow, bent down to grasp Hubert's ankles, and began dragging him to the edge of the road. Martine stood up on the far side of the Mercedes, still screaming. When her voice sailed into outraged hysteria, he glanced up from his task and saw a nice little automatic, a sibling to the one in his bedside drawer at home, pointed at his chest. Martine was panting, but she held the gun steady, both arms extended across the top of the Mercedes. He stopped moving and looked at her with an unruffled, calm curiosity. "Put that thing down," he said. He dragged M. Hubert's body another six inches backward.

"Stop!" she screeched.

He stopped and looked back up at her. "Yes?"

Martine stood up, keeping her arms extended. "Don't do anything, just listen." She took a moment to work out what she would say. "We work for the same people. You don't know who I am, but you are using the name Cash. You weren't supposed to show up until the deal was set, so what's going on?" Her voice was steadier than he would have expected.

Hubert's ankles in his hands, N said, "First of all, I do know who you are, Martine. And it should be obvious that what's going on is a sudden revision of our plans for the evening. Our people found out your friend was planning to cheat his customers. Don't you think we ought to get him off the road before the customers turn up?"

She glanced downhill without moving the pistol. "They didn't tell me about any change."

"Maybe they couldn't. I'm sorry I startled you." N walked backward until he reached the edge of the road. He dropped Hubert's feet and moved forward to grab the collar of his jacket and pull the rest of his body onto the narrow verge. He set the satchel beside his feet.

She lowered the gun. "How do you know my name?"

"Our contact. What's he called now? Our divisional region controller. He said you'd be handling all the paperwork. Interesting guy. He's an Indian, did you know that? Lives in Fontainebleau. His daughter has a rabbit named Custer." N bent at the knees and planted his hands on either side of Hubert's waist. When he pulled up, the body folded in half and released a gassy moan.

"He's still alive," Martine said.

"No, he isn't." N looked over the edge of the narrow strip of grass and down into the same abyss he had seen from the edge of the parking lot. The road followed the top of the gorge as it rose to the plateau.

"It didn't look to me like he was planning to cheat anybody." She had not left the side of the Mercedes. "He was going to make a lot of money. So were we."

"Cheating is how this weasel made money." N hauled the folded corpse an inch nearer the edge, and Hubert's bowels emptied with a string of wet popping sounds and a strong smell of excrement. N swung his body over the edge and let go. Hubert instantly disappeared. Five or six seconds later came a soft sound of impact and a rattle of scree, and then nothing until an almost inaudible thud.

"He even cheated his customers," N said. "Half the stuff in that shop is no good." He brushed off his hands and looked down at his clothes for stains before tucking the satchel back under his left arm.

"I wish someone had told me this was going to happen."

She put the pistol in her handbag and came slowly around the trunk of the Mercedes. "I could always call for confirmation, couldn't I?"

"You'd better," N said. In English, he added, "If you know what's good for you."

She nodded and licked her lips. Her hair gleamed in the light from the Mercedes. The skimpy black thing was a shift, and her black sheer tights ended in low-heeled pumps. She had dressed for the Arabs, not the auberge. She flattened a hand on the top of her head and gave him a straight look. "All right, Monsieur Cash, what do I do now?"

"About what you were supposed to do before. I'll drive up to the restaurant, and you go back to town for your car. The mule who's driving it down from Paris takes this one to Russia. Call in as soon as you get to your, what is it?, your LUD."

"What about . . . ?" She waved in the direction of the auberge.

"I'll express our profound regrets and assure our friends that their needs will soon be answered."

"They said fieldwork was full of surprises." Martine smiled at him uncertainly before walking back to the Mercedes.

Through the side window N saw a flat black briefcase on the back seat. He got behind the wheel, put his satchel on his lap, and examined the controls. Depressing a button in the door made the driver's seat glide back to give him more room. "I almost hate to turn this beautiful car over to some Russian mobster." He fiddled with the button, tilting the seat forward and lowering it. "What do we call our armament-deprived friends, anyway? Tonto calls them ragheads, but even ragheads have names."

"Monsieur Temple and Monsieur Law. Daniel didn't know their real names. Shouldn't we be going?"

Finally, N located the emergency brake and eased it in. He depressed the brake pedal and moved the automatic shift from park to its lowest gear. "Get me the briefcase from the

back seat." The Mercedes swam forward as he released the
brake pedal. Martine glanced at him, then shifted around to
put one knee on her seat. She bent sideways and stretched
toward the briefcase. N dipped into the satchel, raised the tip
of the silencer to the wall of her chest and fired. He heard
the bullet splat against something like bone and then realized that it had passed through her body and struck a metal
armature within the leather upholstery. Martine slumped
into the gap between the seats. Before him, a long leg jerked
out, struck the dash and cracked the heel off a black pump.
The cartridge came pinging off the windshield and rico-
cheted straight to his ribs.

He shoved the pistol back home and tapped the accelerator. Martine slipped deeper into the well between the seats.
N thrust open his door and cranked the wheel to the left. Her
hip slid onto the handle of the gear shift. He touched the accelerator again. The Mercedes grumbled and hopped forward. Alarmingly near the edge, he jumped off the seat and
turned into the spin his body took when his feet met the
ground.

He was close enough to the sleek, recessed handle on the
back door to caress it. Inch by inch, the car stuttered toward
the side of the road. Martine uttered an indecipherable
dream-word. The Mercedes lurched to the precipice, nosed
over, tilted forward and down, advanced, hesitated, stopped.
The roof light illuminated Martine's half-conscious struggle
to pull herself back into her seat. The Mercedes trembled
forward, dipped its nose, and with exquisite reluctance slid
off the earth into the huge darkness. Somersaulting in mid-
air, it cast wheels of yellow light which extinguished when
it smashed into whatever was down there.

Visited by the blazing image of a long feminine leg un-
furling before his eyes like a lightning-bolt, N loped uphill.
That lineament running from the molded thigh to the tender
back of the knee, the leap of the calf muscle. The whole perfect thing, like a sculpture of the ideal leg, filling the space
in front of him. When would she have made her move? he

wondered. She had been too uncertain to act when she should have, and she could not have done it while he was driving, so it would have happened in the parking lot. She'd had that .25 caliber Beretta—a smart gun, in N's opinion. Martine's extended leg flashed before him again, and he suppressed a giddy, enchanted swell of elation.

Ghostly church bells pealed, and a black-haired young priest shone glimmering from the chiaroscuro of a rearing boulder.

He came up past the retaining wall into the mild haze of light from the windows of the auberge. His feet crunched on the pebbles of the parking lot. After a hundred-foot uphill run he was not even breathing hard, pretty good for a man of his age. He came to the far end of the lot, put his hands on the fence, and inhaled air of surpassing sweetness and purity. Distant ridges and peaks hung beneath fast-moving clouds. This was a gorgeous part of the world. It was unfortunate that he would have to leave it behind. But he was leaving almost everything behind. The books were the worst of it. Well, there were book dealers in Switzerland, too. And he still had *Kim*.

N moved down the fence toward the auberge. Big windows displayed the usual elderly men in berets playing cards, a local family dining with the grandparents, one young couple flirting, flames jittering and weaving over the hearth. A solid old woman carried a steaming platter to the family's table. The Japanese golfers had not returned, and all the other tables were empty. On her way back to the kitchen, the old woman sat down with the card players and laughed at a remark from an old boy missing most of his teeth. No one in the dining room would be leaving for at least an hour. N's stomach audibly complained of being so close to food without being fed, and he moved back into the relative darkness to wait for the second half of his night's work.

And then he stepped forward again, for headlights had come beaming upward from below the lot. N moved into the gauzy light and once again experienced the true old excite-

ment, that of opening himself to unpredictability, of standing at the intersection of infinite variables. A Peugeot identical to his in year, model, and color followed its own
headlights into the wide parking lot. N walked toward the
car, and the two men in the front seats took him in with
wary, expressionless faces. The Peugeot moved alongside
him, and the window cranked down. A lifeless, pockmarked
face regarded him with a cold, threatening neutrality. N
liked that—it told him everything he needed to know.

"Monsieur Temple? Monsieur Law?"

Without any actual change in expression, the driver's face
deepened, intensified into itself in a way that made the man
seem both more brutal and more human, almost pitiable. N
saw an entire history of rage, disappointment, and meager
satisfactions in his response. The driver hesitated, looked
into N's eyes, then slowly nodded.

"There's been a problem," N said. "Please, do not be
alarmed, but Monsieur Hubert cannot join you tonight. He
has been in a serious automobile accident."

The man in the passenger seat spoke a couple of sen-
tences in Arabic. His hands were curled around the grip of a
fat black attaché case. The driver answered in monosyllables
before turning back to N. "We have heard nothing of an accident." His French was stiff but correct, and his accent was
barbaric. "Who are you supposed to be?"

"Marc-Antoine Labouret. I work for Monsieur Hubert.
The accident happened late this afternoon. I think he spoke
to you before that?"

The man nodded, and another joyous flare of adrenaline
flooded into N's bloodstream.

"A tour bus went out of control near Montory and ran into
his Mercedes. Fortunately, he suffered no more than a broken leg and a severe concussion, but his companion, a
young woman, was killed. He goes in and out of conscious-
ness, and of course he is very distressed about his friend, but
when I left him at the hospital Monsieur Hubert emphasized
his regrets at this inconvenience." N drew in another liter of

transcendent air. "He insisted that I communicate in person his profound apologies and continuing respect. He also wishes you to know that after no more than a small delay, matters will go forward as arranged."

"Hubert never mentioned an assistant," the driver said. The other man said something in Arabic. "Monsieur Law and I wonder what is meant by this term, 'a small delay.'"

"A matter of days," N said. "I have the details in my computer."

Their laughter sounded like branches snapping, like an automobile landing on trees and rocks. "Our friend Hubert adores the computer," said the driver.

M. Law leaned forward to look at N. He had a thick mustache and a high, intelligent forehead, and his dark eyes were clear and penetrating. "What was the name of the dead woman?" His accent was much worse than the driver's.

"Martine is all I know," N said. "The bitch turned up out of nowhere."

M. Law's eyes creased in a smile. "We will continue our discussion inside."

"I wish I could join you, but I have to get back to the hospital." He waved the satchel at the far side of the lot. "Why don't we go over there? It'll take five minutes to show you what I have on the computer, and you could talk about it over dinner."

M. Temple glanced at M. Law. M. Law raised and lowered an index finger and settled back. The Peugeot ground over pebbles and pulled up at the fence. The taillights died, and the two men got out. M. Law was about six feet tall and lean, M. Temple a few inches shorter and thick in the chest and waist. Both men wore nice-looking dark suits and gleaming white shirts. Walking toward them, N watched them straighten their clothes. M. Temple carried a large weapon in a shoulder holster, M. Law something smaller in a holster clipped to his belt. They felt superior, even a bit contemptuous toward M. Labouret—the antique dealer's flunky, as wed to his computer as an infant to the breast. He came up beside M. Temple, smiled, and ducked through the fence. "Better if they don't see the screen," he told their scowling faces. "The people in the restaurant."

Already impatient with this folly, M. Law nodded at M. Temple. "Go on, do it." He added something in Arabic.

M. Temple grinned, yanked down the front of his suit jacket, bent down, clamped his right arm across his chest, and steadied himself with the other as he thrust his trunk through the three-foot gap. N moved sideways and held the satchel upright on the top of the fence. M. Temple swung one leg over the white board and hesitated, deciding between raising his right leg before or behind. Leaning left, he bent his right knee and swiveled. A tasseled loafer rapped against the board. N took another step along the fence, pulling the satchel to his chest as if protecting it. M. Temple skipped sideways and pulled his leg through. Embarrassed, he frowned and yanked again at his jacket.

N knelt down with the satchel before him. M. Law gripped the board and passed his head through the gap. When he stepped over the board, N eased out the pistol and fired upward into the center of his intelligent forehead. The bullet tore through the back of M. Law's skull and, guided by the laws of physics and sheer good luck, smacked into M. Temple's chest as blood and gray pulp spattered his shirt. M. Temple staggered back and hit the ground, groaning. N felt like a golfer scoring a hole in one during a farewell tournament. He bounced up and moved alongside M. Temple. Grimacing and blowing red froth from his lips, the Arab was still gamely trying to yank his gun from the shoulder holster. The bullet had passed through a lung, or maybe just roamed around inside it before stopping. N settled the muzzle of the silencer behind a fleshy ear, and M. Temple's right eye, large as a cow's, swiveled toward him.

Light spilled from the auberge's windows onto the row of cars and spread across the gravel. M. Law lay sprawled out on the board, his arms and legs dangling on either side. Blood dripped onto the grass beneath his head.

"A thing of beauty is a joy forever," N said. Whatever unpleasantness M. Temple offered in return was cut short by the fall of the nine-millimeter's hammer.

N grabbed M. Law's collar and belt and slid him off the board. Then he grasped his wrists and pulled him through the grass to the edge of the gorge and went back for M. Temple. He took their wallets from their hip pockets and removed the money, altogether about a thousand dollars in francs. He folded the bills into his jacket pocket and threw the wallets into the gorge. Taking care to avoid getting blood on his hands or clothes, N shoved M. Temple closer to the edge and rolled him over the precipice. The body dropped out of view almost instantly. He pushed M. Law after him, and this time thought he heard a faint sound of impact from far down in the darkness. Smiling, he walked back to the fence and ducked through it.

N opened the driver's door of the Arabs' Peugeot, took the keys from the ignition, and pushed the seat forward to lean in for the attaché case. From its weight, it might have been filled with books. He closed the door softly and tossed the keys over the fence. So buoyant he could not keep from breaking into quiet laughter, he moved across the gravel and walked down the hill to his car with the satchel beneath his left elbow, the case swinging from his right hand.

When he got behind the wheel, he shoved the case onto the passenger seat and turned on the roof light. For a couple of seconds he could do nothing but look at the smooth black leather, the stitching, the brass catches. His breath caught in his throat. N leaned toward the case and brought his hands to the catches and their sliding releases. He closed his eyes and thumbed the releases sideways. There came a substantial, almost resonant sound as the catches flew open. He pushed the top of the case a few inches up and opened his eyes upon banded rows of thousand-dollar bills lined edge to edge and stacked three deep. "One for the Gipper," he whispered. For a couple of seconds, he was content to breathe in and out, feeling all the muscles in his body relax

and breathe with him. Then he started the car and sailed
down the mountain.

When he turned into the walled lot, the bright windows
framed what appeared to be a celebration. Candles glowed
on the lively tables, and people dodged up and down the
aisles, turning this way and that in the buzz and hum of conversation floating toward him. This happy crowd seemed to
have claimed every parking spot not preempted by the
Comet truck, parked in front of the kitchen at an angle that
eliminated three spaces. N trolled past the dirty Renault be-
longing to the drunken Basques, the Japanese tourists' tall
red van, the Germans' Saab, and other vehicles familiar and
unfamiliar. There was a narrow space in front of the trellis
beside the entrance. He slid into the opening, gathered his
cases and, holding his breath and sucking in his waist, managed to squeeze out of the car. Beyond the kitchen doors, the
Comet man in the blue work suit occupied a chair with the
bored patience of a museum guard while the women bustled
back and forth with laden trays and stacks of dishes. N wondered what was so important that it was delivered after dark
on Sunday and then saw a bright flash of blue that was Albertine, facing a sink with her back to him. Only a few
inches from her hip, the innkeeper was leaning against the
sink, arms crossed over his chest and speaking from the side
of his mouth with an almost conspiratorial air. The intimacy
of their communication, her close attention to his words, informed N that they were father and daughter. What Daddy
doesn't know won't hurt him, he thought. The man's gaze
shifted outside and met N's eyes. N smiled at his host and
pushed the glass door open with his shoulder.

On his way to the counter he saw that his own elation had
imbued an ordinary Sunday dinner with the atmosphere of a
party. The Japanese men, the German family, French
tourists, and groups of local Basques ate and drank at their
separate tables. Albertine would not be free for hours. He
had enough time to arrange the flights, pack his things,
enjoy a long bath, even take a nap. As his adrenaline sub-

sided, he could feel his body demand rest. The hunger he had experienced earlier had disappeared, another sign that he should get some sleep. N took his key from the board and lugged the increasingly heavy attaché case up the stairs, turning on the lights as he went.

He locked his door and sat on the bed to open the case. Twenty-five bills in each packet, six rows across, three stacks high. Four hundred and fifty thousand dollars: no million, but a pretty decent golden handshake. He closed the case, slid it onto the closet shelf, and picked up the telephone. In twenty minutes he had secured for a fictitious gentleman named Kimball O'Hara a four A.M. charter from Pau to Toulouse and a five o'clock connecting flight to Marseilles. His employers' concern would not reach the stage of serious worry until he was on his way to Toulouse, and he would be on a plane to Italy before they had completely advanced into outright panic. The bodies could go undiscovered for days. N folded and packed his clothes into his carry-on bag and set it beside the door, leaving out what he would wear later that night. *Kim* went on the bedside table. He would push the satchel down a drain somewhere in Oloron.

Hot water pounded into the fiberglass tub while he shaved for the second time that day. The bath lulled him into drowsiness. He wrapped a towel around his waist and stretched out on the bed. Before he dropped into sleep, the last image in his mind was that of a rigid, magnificent female leg encased in sheer black tights.

Soft but insistent raps at the door awakened him. N looked at his watch: eleven-thirty, earlier than he had expected. "I'll be right there." He stood up, stretched, refastened the towel around his waist. A mist of sickeningly floral perfume enveloped him when he unlocked the door. Wearing a raincoat over her nightgown, Albertine slipped into the room. N kissed her neck and grazed at her avid mouth, smiling as she moved him toward the bed.

•　　•　　•

She closed the door behind her, and the three men in the corridor stepped forward in unison, like soldiers. The one on the right jerked open a refuse bag and extended it toward her. She shoved the bloody cleaver and the ruined nightgown into the depths of the bag. The man quizzed her with a look. "You can go in," she said, grateful he had not exercised his abominable French. All three of them bowed. Despite her promise to herself, she was unable to keep from bowing back. Humiliated, she straightened up again, feeling their eyes moving over her face, hands, feet, ankles, hair, and whatever they detected of her body through the raincoat. Albertine moved aside, and they filed through the door to begin their work.

Her father stood up from his desk behind the counter when she descended into the darkened lobby. Beneath the long table, Gaston, the black and white dog, stirred in his sleep. "Did it go well?" her father asked. He, too, inspected her for bloodstains.

"How do you think it went?" she said. "He was almost asleep. By the time he knew what was happening, his chest was wide open."

The lock on the front door responded to the keypad and clicked open. The two permanent Americans eyed her as they came through the arch. Gaston raised his head, sighed, and went back to sleep. She said, "Those idiots in the berets are up there now. How long have you been using Japanese?"

"Maybe six months." The one in the tweed jacket spoke in English because he knew English annoyed her, and annoyance was how he flirted. "Hey, we love those wild and crazy guys, they're our little samurai brothers."

"Don't let your stupid brothers miss the briefcase in the closet," she said. The ugly one in the running suit leered at her. "That man had good clothes. *You* could try wearing some nice clothes, for a change."

"His stuff goes straight into the fire," the ugly one said. "We don't even look at it. You know, we're talking about a

real character. Kind of a legend. I heard lots of amazing stories about him."

"Thank you, Albertine," said her father. He did not want
her to hear the amazing stories.

"You ought to thank me," she said. "The old rooster made
me take a bath. On top of that, I wasted my perfume because
he wanted me to smell like a girl in Bora-Bora."

Both of the Americans stared at the floor.

"What does it mean to say," she asked, and in her heavily
accented English said, "I wish I had that swing in my back
yard?"

The permanent Americans glanced at each other. The one
in the tweed jacket clapped his hands over his eyes. The
ugly one said, "Albertine, you're the ideal woman. Everybody worships you."

"Good, then I should get more money." She wheeled
around to go downstairs, and the ugly one sang out, "Izz-unt
it roman-tic?" Beneath his sweet, false, tremulous tenor
came the rumble of the disposal truck as it backed toward
the entrance.

DESPERATE DAN

WHITLEY STRIEBER

As Mr. Daniel Grace touched the pantry call bell with his toe, he was horrified to notice that its ringing mingled with that of the front door. Deepest instinct almost took over, but he pressed his fingers against the table edge and did not run. In a moment, his ancient waiter appeared. "Yes, sir," Eddie said softly.

Compelling himself to the quiet calm expected of a gentleman at his table, he indicated that Patricia's milk glass was to be refilled. At thirteen, she needed plenty. In the silence that filled the moment, he heard the familiar rhythm of Fielding's footsteps going down the front hall. He waited, his breath caught behind his mustaches. There was a loud, dull sound, the opening of the door. Now go away, be a wrong address, anything. He smiled weakly at his wife, whose eyes were regarding him with a glittering innocence that fair broke his heart. There were voices, yes—one Fielding's, soft and cultured. The other's . . . rough, a little nervous, full of bully authority.

Dan Grace drew breath at last, but it was with the hungry deliberation of a sailor overboard. Whatever happened, he determined that he would not fail in his dignity, not before his wife and children.

"Thank you, Daddy," his daughter said.

He blinked, returning in confusion to the ordered solace

of the dining room. "Eat as well as drink, my dear," he announced. "And Albert, that's meat you're at. Chew fifty
times for meat."

Albert chewed elaborately. Immediately Dan's awareness
returned to the drone of the voices in the front hall. The
brand-new double Derringer in his vest pocket weighed
against his breast. He touched his lips with his tongue.

To better bear the suspense, he surveyed his domestic sur-
roundings, so orderly, so appropriate. His daughter, although
tall, was graceful, her nose narrow like her mother's, her
brow broad and intelligent. Albert, with his wide eyes and
strong jaw, had already the appearance of a leader, and Mr.
Fallows, his tutor, claimed that a facility for mathematics
such as his was exceptional in one so young. He was a dili-
gent child, although perhaps a bit lacking in the sort of saucy
nonchalance that is so appealing in a boy.

"Mr. Grace," his wife said. She had become aware of the
disturbance in the hall—although it could hardly be so identified. But *anybody* calling at the dinner hour was a disturbance. There could be nothing regular about such a call.

"My dear," he responded, "pray, was your excursion satisfactory?" Best to simply ignore affairs without. Perhaps it
was indeed nothing.

"You shall see ribbon on her blue frock this very evening,"
Eleanora said.

"And a bonnet upon my mother's pretty head," Patricia
added.

Eleanora colored, ever so fetchingly. Of all the four
Hooper girls, Dan's wife was the only one who had inher-
ited her mother's delicate coloring, and the remarkable softness of feature—the rounded eye, the dignity in the carriage
and expression—that so infallibly indicated the breeding in
her ancient New England clan.

Quite suddenly, Fielding appeared, drawing aside the
wide doors that closed the dining room so quickly that they
rattled on their slides. "Sir," he said, "a gentleman to see
you."

Eleanora raised her eyebrows, her face frankly amazed. "Does he not know the hour, Fielding?"

"He knows the hour, madam."

Dan stood quickly, giving his family a smile he immediately suspected of being too bright. Sobering his features, he announced, "I'm sure it's nothing much." As he withdrew from the dining room, Fielding closed the doors. "Where is he, Jake?" Dan muttered to the old butler.

"Study. He's a bad'un, Mr. Daniel."

"I'm sure." He positioned himself, drawing down his waistcoat, preparing for Fielding to open the door.

"A copper," Fielding said.

So there it was. The deficiency had been discovered. But the damned thing of it was, it wasn't a deficiency at all. No indeed, it was *his* money and he was to have it back.

"Did he state his business?"

"No, sir. He said his business was with you, begging your pardon, sir."

That jackanapes Prior Downs had done this to save himself. No doubt the insolvency of the bank was to do with Prior's sinister meddling. No doubt his chicanery with Voorhis was also the cause of Dan's own sudden and complete destitution, which he had discovered but three days before.

He had considered the possibility that this moment would come. Flight, he had thought, or suicide, might be his only alternatives. "Is the fellow alone, Jake?"

"There's two coppers on the front door, sir." Fielding seemed quite unperturbed about it all. But then, he'd been serving gentlemen all his life.

"Right. And the back?"

"'Tother side of the carriage house, maybe. None in the mews anyway."

Dan heard his words like the clanking of chains. "Very well." His mind was seeking some escape, but he didn't see it. He wasn't a confidence trickster, accustomed to flight. His "crime" was an act of desperation, committed in a sick

dread, to steal what was his back from a man who was nothing more than a common thief himself. He'd never dreamed
that Prior would discover the game so quickly, or that the
police would actually come here. Who would suspect a part-
ner at the trust of vault looting?

Well, who indeed? To have caused this man to appear
here, Prior must have gone back after hours, opened the
safe, and counted the goldbacks. There were sixty thousand
of them missing, six hundred goldback centuries, the same
that were presently in Daniel Grace's gladstone in the upstairs hall, the same amount that he had lost in the Brooklyn
Pneumatic Railway shares that Prior had boosted on him
even as the devil sold himself into the boost.

Fielding rolled the doors open to reveal a man standing in
the middle of the room as if he were somehow foreclosed
from coming near the furniture. The man was small and
shabby, the cuffs of his trousers dragging the carpet, his
knees and elbows gleaming. A raffish derby bore down over
his eyes. Silently, he presented Dan with a dirty sheet of
paper. Dan knew that it was an arrest warrant; he did not
need to read it.

"You ought to be coming along, sir," the police officer
said, his rough diction slurring the carefully chosen words.
It was not every day that this man detained a nabob for the
Tombs. No doubt he'd be toasted in his copper-haunt
tonight, when he went for his supper of black sausage and
beer.

"Does Commissioner Voorhis know of this affair?" Dan
said.

The man nodded toward the paper. Dan glanced at it, and
saw that Voorhis himself had put his signature on it. "By
these presents, you are hereby directed to convey the body
of Mr. Daniel Lewis Hare Grace unto the place of detention
designated as the Central Gaol (Tombs), there to await the
assizes."

He would be in the Tombs for six weeks before the trial,
and he had no doubt of the outcome. They would send him

to prison for twenty years; he would not see daylight until well after the turn of the century, in the unimaginably distant year of 1906. He was going from his supper table to life in a hole, without so much as a by-your-leave.

Again he considered the notion of escape. But how to do it? Where to go? He couldn't think.

"Is the Black Mariah out there?" he asked, suddenly aware that such a thing would not do, not in lower Fifth Avenue.

"I have a hansom, sir," the policeman said. "You need to get your coat and hat, if you don't mind."

"I want to take leave of my wife and children. We were at our supper."

"Yes."

Dan slid the doors back. Fielding, who had been waiting there, stood aside as he passed back toward the dining room.

How the silver trays and flatware glittered beneath the chandelier, how fine was the mahogany of the table, how cheerful the big spray of hothouse roses in the centerpiece, how succulent the leg of lamb that still lay before his empty place. It rested upon a silver dish that had come with the Graces from England, in the year 1657. They had been cavaliers placed under ban by the Roundheads, escapees to the Virginia Colony. Unlike poor King Charles, they had kept their heads, had even prospered in Virginia. In 1788 Graces had also been living New Jersey, and had there joined the Committee of Protection for Trenton, fighting on the Tory side and against their relatives from the Virginia Colony, who were Continentals fiercely loyal to Washington.

Now here was Dan, who dimly remembered his great-grandfather, a narrow figure as pale as paper, who had kept an ancient spontoon and his epaulettes from the Continental Army.

Being a New York Democrat, Dan himself had bought off service in the Civil War. His economic and political sympathies had been with a continuation of the American Empire, but his emotional loyalties were with the Graces of Virginia and their wonderful history and genteel, cultivated ways.

"Mr. Grace," Eleanora said, drawing him out of his stunned reverie with the urgency of question in her tone.

"My dear. My children." He went in, heard the doors rolling closed behind him.

"And what was that about? Who is that ruffian in the hall?"

"Very well, my dear, all very well." He stepped to the far end of the room, slipping quickly into the back of the house. Mattie and Belle both looked up at him, both astonished. Mattie came quickly to her feet. "Sir?"

He crossed the pantry, then the kitchen with its sharp smell of wood smoke and sweeter scent of boiling pudding. There was also a scent of cigarette smoke, and he said absently, "None of that smoking, Belle."

"No, sir."

He went out into the mews, pulling the door closed behind him. There was fine rain falling, and a steady autumn wind rattling the dark limbs of the trees that lined the narrow carriageway. Immediately, the chill penetrated his evening clothes. He did not think that he had more than a few moments, and rushed across into his carriage house. "Monty," he called, "is anything in harness?"

"Lord, no, sir! Is there an emergency?"

"Give me your furnishings, then," he said, taking his coachman's thick wrap from its peg and donning his weathered old beaver.

"*My* furnishings, sir?"

He heard a cry without. He had to make haste, he dared not linger another moment. There was no chance to harness the carriage nor even saddle Flyer or Dobson. He threw open the stalls and backed Flyer out. She was the more docile of the two animals, though not the faster. Still, perhaps it wouldn't matter. A tired police horse dragging a hansom might not be able to keep up with a filly made frantic by live weight.

"Open the doors, Monty. Be quick."

Monty, who had served in Dan's father's house, complied without spoken question. But it just wouldn't do for a gentleman to ride an unsaddled horse, let alone in his evening clothes and his coachman's coat. And all the hurry! Monty had never seen a Grace hurry, not even when 4 Ann Street burned down in '77. So he obeyed with a sour expression. He was aware of his young master's unwelcome reputation for being ever so slightly "fast."

Dan nipped at the horse's flanks with his heels. "Let me bridle her, sir," Monty said.

Dan saw his son standing in the kitchen dooryard. "Father," he called.

"All is well," he cried.

"He has a revolver!"

And there was the policeman, a shadow in the yellow kerosene light cast through from the kitchen. Dan stared at the huge Colt as it came up, held in both of the man's hands. No word was said; the policeman braced the weapon and fired, disappearing at once in a great rush of powder smoke.

Perhaps Dan sensed the passage of the bullet, perhaps it was only the imagination of a man desperately relieved to be missed.

He kneed the horse, then when that got no response, kicked at her flanks. But she was a carriage horse, she did not really understand these signals. And then, coming out of the smoke, was his dear Albert. He marched right up to the horse. "Tally-ho," he cried, spanking her. There was spirit, my God. Young Albert was showing spirit!

Another slap and she shot forward, as behind them the pistol roared again. This detonation was followed by general cries of dismay. "Brigand," Dan shouted to Colonel Wilson, who had burst out of his own kitchen, his boiled shirt come right out from behind his braces. "Brigand in the mews!"

Dan rode on, as again the pistol roared. This time he most certainly did hear the passing bullet; he heard and felt it as a hot fist of wind pounding his ear. He came out into Eleventh

Street. The cobbles shone in the gas light, the rain came in fine sheets. It was an inhospitable night, the wind moaning out of the northeast, wet leaves mottling the sidewalk. Two street arabs huddled along, their newspapers wet, their day's hope gone. A beggar rattled his tin, some legless hero of the late war.

Automatically, Dan put his hand in his pocket, looking for a bit of copper or silver. But one did not carry change in the shallow silk pockets of dinner clothes, and the coachman's coat offered nothing.

He rode to the corner, then turned out into Broadway. There was a burst of laughter from the sidewalk, and he saw a man coming along, his form too dark to make out, his neck muffled by a fine silk scarf, his top hat slightly askew. Then there burst out of Twelfth Street the police hansom coming at the gallop. From within it there issued the high wail of a whistle. Ahead, Dan could see Henry Conroy, their beat cop, start, turn round, and begin running straight toward him.

Dan went into Broadway, turning uptown, instinctively drawn toward the familiar world of the Twenty-third Street hotels and theaters. He raced up the avenue, passing St. Thomas's Church, where his family had worshiped for three generations. There was little traffic, just a grinder and a hot corn man crying into the silence.

Behind him all was pandemonium. The hansom was coming so fast that he could hear its rumble even over the clatter of the filly's hooves. Again and again whistles sounded, as one beater after another took up the alert and began running toward Broadway.

It was appalling. He couldn't think what to do. And then he saw, coming up out of the gloom, a Broadway Stage headed downtown. In moments he would pass it. Could he jump off and somehow conceal himself by running along the far side? Oh, it was absurd to even consider. He was no athlete, to leap from a moving horse. But then he saw, ahead of him, three policemen coming out into Broadway. They aimed to pull him down, no doubt of it. Behind him, there was a cry, "Stop," which echoed off the dark buildings. Then, much closer: "Stop!" The man's voice was high; he was as excited by the chase as Dan would get on the Riverdale hunt, when the hounds screamed scent and the fox dashed in the hedgerows.

The stage was closer now, so close that he could see one or two figures within, huddling in the ghastly light of the interior. The driver sat atop the conveyance, his leather apron gleaming wet, his eyes peering out from beneath his sodden beaver. Then the windows were flashing past. Behind one he glimpsed a small face, a child, boy or girl, observing with amazement the sudden appearance of the ghostly figure upon the plunging horse.

The animal seemed to be going at a fantastic speed. He did not think that he had ever been this fast, not jumping, not even racing, and certainly not in the city streets. He dared not leap off, and in any case his chance was gone with the stage, which had disappeared into the lost world behind him.

In the event, he was going so fast that he simply shot right past the three coppers, all of whom blasted their whistles furiously. A blow to his knee, sharp, told him that one of them had got him with his billy.

The horse was a complete runaway and he knew well that he would not be able to stop it. The fate of an animal in this state was certain: it was going to dash itself to death and its rider into the bargain. He was clinging to its mane, pressing his knees into its sopping flanks, when it suddenly veered, thrusting itself away from the flaring lamps that stood before the Domestic Sewing Machine Building on Fourteenth Street. Once it bucked, twice, and then he was down. He was down with a terrific crack. His hat went rolling off toward the gutter, to be retrieved by an oysterman who was set up in front of the St. Denis Hotel, presently full of importance and bustle for the presence of Sarah Bernhardt, who was stopping there for the duration of *Flora Dora.*

And there he was, hurt and sprawled in the gutter, with the horse disappearing off up the avenue. Getting up, he discovered that he was whole, at least for the moment. Silently the oysterman handed over the hat. His crystalline glance demanded a bit of service, but Dan had nothing to give but what must have been a pretty dumpy smile.

Another man, a rough in a derby sporting a stogie, gave him a careful eye. He thought: he is a Broadway Squad sharp, thinking that I have stolen these clothes. For he was a peculiar sight: silk dinner clothes beneath the coarse wool of a coachman, and a twenty-dollar beaver hat with a livery band. That it was his own coachman's duds and his own family's livery colors the sharp could not know.

Brushing aside the temptation to duck into the St. Denis and see if he could book quick on the strength of his known face and name, he rushed along the avenue, collar up, hat down, avoiding the pools of lamplight like a proper desperado. On he went, hurrying along Fourteenth in search of a ferry looper, begging that one would come and save him. But the drivers were normally pretty cross for their nickels and he had not even that. How would he do it? In minutes, the coppers would be at him again.

Damn Porter, damn the Buckler Trust Company, damn Voorhis and the ruthless injustice of the city aldermen, to toss a gentleman into the Tombs where he would certainly acquire consumption or the whited sepulcher from breathing the noisome vapors. Not to mention Sing Sing, with its stocks and whipping post and a life in chains, and all because he had taken back what was his own, his patrimony and the wealth of the Graces.

Going along, unsure of how even to get fare, he suddenly saw a looper trundling along behind its steaming team. There were figures huddling in the open car, a family of immigrants, no doubt, just come up from the Brooklyn docks. He hungered to jump aboard. In any case, even if he made the Pennsy ferry, how would he pay for that, or for a chair in the train, or anything, even a sip of soup or a fifteen-cent oyster?

Soon the alarm would spread ahead, and he would find

the Sixth Avenue Squad after him as well. Then he saw, coming along, Mr. Samuel Wilson. He was a Yale man, Dan recalled, now in some manner of shipping or export trade. A tradesman, to be sure, but charming to good company, an excellent fellow.

"Oh, Wilson," he said.

The man kept coming. Was he drunk? How could Wilson possibly cut Dan Grace?

"Wilson, I say."

"Excuse me? Oh, my goodness, it's Danny! My God, man, what're you about?"

Dan thought quickly. He must not intimate the least trouble. Ahead, he heard the dreaded whistles starting in Sixth Avenue. The looper rumbled off. Dimly, he could see another one coming up from the North River direction. If he was not on that next looper, he was done. "Well, I'm in a bit of a treasure hunt," he said. "I'm to find a gold dollar hidden hereabouts, but my clues are rum."

Wilson blinked, then his expression became very pleasant. It would please him greatly to fall into society with a Grace. "Well, now, I think that I have one, Danny."

"Do you, sir? But I am supposed to find it." He withdrew the arrest warrant. "This is my map, you see." Wilson naturally made a move toward it, but Dan withdrew it back to the safety of the pocket. "I am . . . winded, shall we put it, eh? Not enough Moxie, I fear."

"Ah, then perhaps . . ." He withdrew a glorious golden dollar, and never had Dan seen this piddling sum as anything so fine. Escape!

"I have not the exchange of it."

"Oh, Danny, send it round, send it round."

Dan took the money. He could see the looper now, its lights swaying as it drew closer. The driver would give him the devil for cashing fat, but he didn't care and the devil take him back. They ought to be glad to get gold, the hellers. Halfway down the long block, a policeman's tall helmet was silhouetted against the glow from a distant lamp. Dan leaned toward Wilson. "Don't tell Voorhis," he said, winking.

"Voorhis! Never!" He laughed, excited and impressed by the name, as Dan had known he would be. "Voorhis, eh! That is rich, Danny! Rich!"

The looper arrived and Dan went out into the street. "Good-bye, Wilson," he called. "You shall see my man in the morning." Then he was on the conveyance, balancing against the lurching of the rain-slick duckboards. His pumps were no match for the muck, which was soon oozing up between his toes, making him squeeze them together. Outside, the copper was confronting Wilson, who was shaking his head vigorously. No, he would certainly be saying, he'd seen no brigand.

But the policeman seemed unconvinced by the slightly tipsy toff. He cast his gaze about, resting it finally on the looper. The operator, predictably sullen, took Dan's dollar, bit it, and turned it in the light of a smoky old lamp. "Thankee," he said at last, and drew from his pouch with maddening care ninety-five cents in pennies, nickels, and a silver half. Loaded with this handful of cash, Dan went to the darkest part of the car and, doffing his hat, sank down into an anonymity that was both wretched and glorious.

A moment later, the policeman came up onto the car. "There, pull it up," he said. The driver immediately braked the mules, which set up an angry hee-haw. At this hour they would be for their barn, as well they knew.

"Now, there's an alarum about in Fifth Avenue. Has anybody come up on this quick-like, like as you was crossing, say?"

"Just 'atun," the driver replied, face cast down, sullen with the copper.

"Well, 'atun is a swell and a friend of Voorhis hisself on some fancy affair," the copper announced, tipping his helmet in Dan's direction. "Good evenin' to you, mister!"

"And a fine good evening, my dear fellow," Dan said. Of course, the copper had only heard the alarm. He hadn't the least idea that the runner was of the Four Hundred. Such a thing was completely unthinkable. It would never occur to anybody, not without their being told.

So the policeman went down, moving off toward Fifth and the now-diminished sound of whistles. And they went rattling and rolling off, down to the end of Fourteenth and around to the Brooklyn piers, then along to the Battery, where the driver announced over the shriek of the leather brake and the caterwauling of the furious mules, "Pennsy Annex, Erie and Staten Island Ferries. Next stop Communipaw."

"Is the Annex running?" Dan cried, eager to take it if he could.

"Naw! It's off at sundown, that'un."

Then why call the damned thing, you fool? He'd have liked to cuff the dolt, but all he did was sink back down into his silence. He waited through the Communipaw to the Courtlandt Street. It ran to all hours, linking to the milk runs out of the Pennsy station on the Jersey side.

In the half-hour on the car, he had formed a mad plan. His intention was to await some prosperous fellow coming out of the Pennsy and waylay him with the Derringer. But how did one "waylay"? Surely there would be a certain skill, a roughness, if you will, of delivery, that would be de rigueur.

But he could not simply take. He must identify himself and give the man his card. A gentleman did not do robbery. In all his life, he had never seriously lied or raised his hand against another or been less than completely honorable in his dealings. His only desperate action had been forced out of him by the sheer extremity of the situation. Prior Downs had left him with nothing, not even enough to keep his house. Before the fortnight was done, they would have been turned out; it was that extreme. Not even his princely draw from the Knickerbocker could keep an establishment that carried rents and wages of a hundred and thirty a week, let alone pay the grocer and the butcher and all the others with palms extended.

He went down off the looper and moved quickly into the shadows. There was gas along the front of the ferry terminus, but otherwise the area was lit only by the fires of chestnut and sausage hawkers. He crossed the broad paving stones, moving toward the three arched entrances to the terminus. There was a distant rush of steam, then the deep booming of a ferry horn. Something was coming in. Well then, he would repair into the shadows and await his man.

The idea of starting a cigar occurred to him, but he dared not approach the vendor in the hall, and had left his cigar case on his bureau of drawers for good old Lex to refill. Damned bad business, that. A man could do with a cigar at so adverse a time.

A cluster of shrouded women came out of the terminus, nuns in their blinders and shrouds. They were followed by a lady, quite fine in a tall hat and gleaming oiled overdress, heading toward a carriage with her skirts pushed high, hoping to avoid collecting the wet cigar ends and chestnut hulls that thickly populated the gutter. Behind her came two men, but they were "shoddy," with their excessively high hats and buttoniers freshly stuck with dyed carnations.

Then there appeared what might have been a Jew, judging from the length of his whispy old beard. He was dressed, as they said, to the nines, but in the quiet manner of Gaylord and Manning rather than the flash of Kennedy's Emporium. So there was his man, obviously a financier or capitalist of some sort.

"Sir," he called, moving toward him with long strides. "Stand up, sir! Stand right up!"

The man turned, his eyes enormous behind a pince-nez. "Hallo?"

"I said, stand up!"

"Well, sir, I say not!" He continued, hurrying now toward the hansoms, which were not ten yards away. "Taxi," he called, "taxi!" Whereupon he leaped into the first in the rank, the one sign of discomposure the fact that he knocked his hat clean off as he dropped down into the seat. As it spun off, Dan heard the gruff voice say through the speaking hole, "Forty Union Square at the trot, please."

He sank against a lamppost. How could he manage this a second time? How could he possibly? It was all a horror, a terrific, dreadful horror. He found himself buying some chestnuts, breaking them and eating the juicy contents with gratitude. He was hungry, he had not finished his supper. He was wet and cold and his shoes were falling apart.

Two more people appeared, but both were women and it never even occurred to him that their purses might be accessible to the fingers of the thief. One may rob, but not women. It was not done, even by the roughest brigand.

No sooner had the ferry given its first blast than two of the horse patrol came galloping along. Fortunately, Dan Grace heard their approach before they could really see him, and he slid like some cutpurse behind a stack of lard barrels.

At the same moment, loopers came in from both directions, and the ferry gave its second blast. Hardly able now to choose, Dan rushed up to a man he did not know was coming or going. This time he showed the Derringer and said, "Deliver up your valuables," in the roughest tone he could manage.

The young man did it quickly enough. "Sir," he said in the careful accents of Dan's own class, "are you in want?"

"Sir, I am desperate," he said, taking out his card. "Please apply to my residence on the morrow, and you shall be compensated for your loss." He drew the folding money out of the fellow's purse, glanced at it. "How much is here?"

"Eighty-one dollars, sir. My whole profit from a month on the road."

"In the morning, call upon my man, Mr. Fielding. Present him with this card, and tell him that he is directed by the master to give you one hundred dollars."

The young man's eyes widened as he looked down at the card. "Mr. Grace!" he said in a high voice.

"The very same." With that he strode into the terminus. There was a strapping Negro with the *Journal,* which he

bought and tucked under his arm like the other rude travelers. With the coat buttoned, he blended into the common run
of men, as long as the fact that he was shod in burst leather
evening slippers went unnoticed.

He took a two-penny ticket and went in the crush of common people onto the boat. He found himself in a long,
dreary chamber lit by flickering kerosene lanterns. Above
him in the saloon, there was an orchestra and, he knew, hot
stoves and coffee and sandwiches. Down here was naught
but wind and spray and the stink of mules and men.

The ferry ground her gears, released a vast exhalation of
steam along with the last blast, then shuddered as her screw
churned and she slid out into the hurrying waters of the
North River. He went into the back of the crowd and stood
facing the great city that he was leaving. Before him there
unfolded the immensity of buildings familiar to him during
the day, but this time cloaked with darkness. It was nine o'-
clock of an October night, and steam rose against the gleam
of gaslights in thousands of windows. The city seemed vast
and vastly mysterious, a gaily lit machinery marked by car-
riages and stages moving, it appeared, lazily in the streets.
Their actual rumble and hustle was concealed by the rapidly
increasing distance. Hanging over all like a bridge for angels
stood the great Milky Way, and in the low east, a horned
moon blushing red.

His heart was aching in his breast as he turned away, leaving not only his place in the wide world, but also the intimacy of home and hearth. He longed to hear once again
Albert calling, "Father, Father," or feel his daughter leap
upon his knees, her face washed by joy. And Mrs. Grace—
how would she bear it, without the enfolding intimacy of his
embrace? And he, how he would pine for his Mrs. Grace.

Nevermore to see them or be happy with them again was
an appalling, incredible thought. Prior deserved to be
hanged. He moved off into the crowd, another sullen
shadow in the mass.

Another ferry loomed up in the ink of the river night and

then spun past, its stacks filling the sky with sparks. Somewhere boatmen cried, and he saw the pale outline of sails and a dim stern lantern. As they reached mid-river, he also reached the bows of the boat, and stationed himself in position to get off quickly. He did not think that the police could have come over any faster and be ahead of him, but there was always the damned wire ready to propel information across river or world as fast as an operator could speed his spark.

Quite suddenly, the ferry gave a blast and reversed her screws. The whole boat shuddered, and its steerage cargo moaned and swayed. Dan was frightened, too; every week, it seemed, one read of an accident in these waters, a blown boiler or a collision, and sometimes all were lost in the mutinous, unforgiving rip of the estuarial tide. But there was to be no collision, for the tremendous bulk of an Atlantic steamer blotted out the dim lights of the Jersey shore long before there was any danger. And he saw now a great ocean of portholes, every one lit, and behind them suggestions of glittering life, the flash of gaudy silk and the dark flicker of evening suits. And there, upon the fantail, the rising and falling glow of a solitary gentleman's cigar.

Then the ferry had turned, shifted, and went plunging through the muscular, phosphorescent wake of the departing leviathan.

Dan had embarked many a time upon a night departure, on the *Berengaria* or the *Flying Cloud,* and had danced with Mrs. Grace into the wee hours as the ship plowed the black Atlantic waters.

Now the ferry slip began to form as if out of a cloud, and he realized for the first time that a light fog was hanging on the Jersey shore. He watched until they were coming into a slip lip by torches. Then the gate went up and he walked off with the others into the Pennsy station proper.

He saw immediately that a Vestibule Limited was off at 12:15, going to Chicago via Baltimore and Washington. It was no high-ball express like the morning trains, but it did

the run in thirty hours, which was better than the forty af-
forded by a number train.

Also, the Vestibules were all sleepers, and he did not
fancy a night and a day in chair cars, chatting through the
miserable hours with commercial travelers. As he climbed
the long ramp into the station proper, he looked about for
policemen. Seeing none, he eyed first one loafer and then
another, wondering if any might be confidentials. But all
seemed indifferent to the passage of the crowd, aimed as it
was not for the trunk line railway, but for the horsecars, the
Jersey Rail line, and the Hackensack cable cars that departed
from the wings of the great terminus.

Fearing that a hand might at any moment drop down on
his shoulder, he approached the row of ticket windows. Behind this one stood a young man with gleaming, macassared
hair and a waxed mustache. A prime shoddy, this fellow.

"Good evening, sir," he said in an affable tone.

"Chicago, if you please."

"Limited or regular?"

"Regular."

"Yes, sir."

Dan handed over the twenty-six dollars, counting them
with the combination of studied unconcern and care that
identified his class to men such as the one behind the grate.
"Thank you, sir. I've got you behind the clubby." The "correct" car, where the very best travelers were stationed, gentlemen who would expect to socialize over the whist table
and drink the drinks the railway hoped to sell on the long
journey. Just ahead of "their" car would be the diner, meaning that they never had to pass across more than one
vestibule either to dine or to entertain themselves.

His ticket bought, he now had access to the first-class
rooms in the station, and proceeded into them quickly, feeling that they would offer some refuge from the police. Rail-
roads did not care to have them mingling in such places any
more than first-class hotels wanted them in their lobbies.
Just a cut above the criminal class, they were. He shuddered

to think of the man who had come into his house with his soiled warrant, who had been willing to fire his pistol at him. What normal policeman would dare to do that?

Had Prior, perhaps, bribed him? It might be that Prior would be embarrassed at a trial. It might even be that Prior would find it impossible to avoid the assizes himself, if Dan managed to produce the right papers. It might *even* be that Dan would be held innocent, but he did not think so. He thought that a jury would find him in the wrong for suborning the funds . . . and Prior, for being a plain fraudist.

He went into the restaurant. As soon as he saw the clean linen and the gleaming chandeliers, he felt all the tiredness and the hunger of a hunted man, and the whole room seemed to sway. He had to brace himself against the captain's stand.

"Sir?"

"Sorry." He gathered himself up, opening the coat and sweeping it off for all the world as if it was an opera cloak. Hands took it from behind him, then he turned and gave his hat also to the boy. He proceeded into the room, nodding good evening to the other gentlemen who sat here and there in the almost empty restaurant.

It was two hours yet until the train departed, so he ordered the full table meal, and sat eating a steady stream of courses, a robust oxtail soup, some rather less-than-fresh salads, a good bit of shad, a fine saddle of beef, and a rather raw wine, called in the bill of fare, simply, "vin de France."

He ate quietly, wishing that he dared telegraph Mrs. Grace, who must be wild with worry, and considering whether or not he was a coward. Was it ever right for a gentleman to flee? Should he not have stood upon honor and faced down the rough in the hall? But then, how could he possibly face down Voorhis and his lackeys, and what if Prior had brought the police commissioner into some scheme or other, compelling him to press Dan no matter the justice of the affair?

These were bad times for gentlemen, very bad times. Look at New-York, a palace of mammon, jammed with men gone lunatic for the dollar. Look at this newspaper, for example, a rude thing festooned with rotogravure and flash drawings. And what of the *Evening Post*. which could actually be read and considered? It was hardly making expenses, compared to the *Journal* and the *Press*.

It was mad times all over, with ancient names coming a cropper in an instant, and flash and shoddy everywhere taking the high ground, shouting their shabby propositions from the parapets of the nation. Had the Lost Cause prevailed, matters would have been healthier, certainly, with the states more like the small nations the Founders intended, instead of an aimless mass colonial to Washington, with its whims and its robbers and its roughs disguised as men of state. Instead, the gentlemen of the South had lost all their possessions, and spread out across the west of the nation armed only with their social graces. Many a card-sharper of this age began his career in the *salons* of Savannah and Richmond. These poor fellows traveled about with worn-down Faro boots in their carpet bags, wearing their old-fashioned frock coats, the silk of long ago fading with the years.

And he, also, a man of honor compelled to dishonor, was fading, too. He was clinging in a dark ocean to the last traces of his splendor, and soon, he felt, would see them wink out. He ate his saddle of beef with the heavy silver engraved with the symbol of the Pennsylvania Railroad, in the accustomed murmur of other gentlemen at their late suppers, beneath the starry light of the chandelier.

He thought that he might telegraph her just a few words. Three, he decided: "I am well." Yes, the telegrapher was open here all night. He could have it sent straight wire, for delivery with the dawn. But could the police not easily trace the telegraph? They would know, then, that he had gone on the night Vestibule, and would surely deduce his destination.

He finished the beef and found that he could not go for the cheese and sweet, and so stood up from his table. His evening clothes were still appropriate, although he now kept the coachman's things over his arm. He had no valise, no portmanteau. But who would know that? He would already have checked them into the sleeper, of course.

It was eleven-thirty now, and there was bustle in the station. Outside on the main line, the Vestibule Sleeper huffed and gasped as its steam came up. He went up to the telegraph office, wrote his note and passed it across the counter with a dollar. The clerk did not even glance up at him, such was the press of messages before him. His own was spiked, his fifteen cents change handed through, and the man went back to his key.

So, that was done. Now he could board. He walked out into the passageway, past the ladies' room, its curtains drawn at this hour, and down the stairway to the platform proper. Counting cars, he went toward the front of the train, knowing that his accommodation would be close to the engine where the smoke was highest.

The cars were dark green with gold trim, the Pennsy colors. The clubby was distinguished by the rich glow of its many green-shaded lamps. He mounted. "Good evening, sir," the porter said, taking his ticket and conducting him to his berth in the sleeper just behind. "You got bags comin', sir?"

"Presently," he said, handing over a nickel.

There was the slightest bow in acknowledgment, then the man took the wretched coat and topper. He would be all right in these duds in the clubby, but what was he to do on the morrow? Trains didn't carry tailors.

The train was clattering madly along at forty miles in the hour when he noticed a sudden alteration in its velocity. "What's that," he said over his hand, which was not too good. All night, the cards had been going pretty even, but now seemed to have turned against him.

"Can't think," murmured Edward Parkhurst, with whom he was playing a two-handed variant.

The slowing process continued. Now they were barely moving, and he soon heard points. But where would the

points be? They were on the main line, halfway between
New-York and Baltimore. No points crossed and there was
nothing coming up at this hour, so why would an express
have gone out on a siding? He did not care to inquire, not
and draw attention to his discomfiture.

Mr. Parkhurst looked up, then took out his watch. "Two
minutes, do you think, sir?"

"At least."

"Well, then, we shall be coming in late. I can't say it re-
flects well on the Pennsy."

"Steward," Dan called, "is there a problem?"

"Sir, there's a special coming up from New-York."

Slowly, Dan's mouth grew drier and drier. A special!
What might it mean? The president was not in New-York,
no heads of state were in the United States, there was nothing that would cause an express to stop for a special.

And what of its speed? To have caught them, the thing
must be cannonballing along at fifty or more. There was no
normal reason to cause a special to be laid down, but there
might be some abnormal one, such as a brigand on the run
and sixty thousand in goldbacks missing.

A lantern danced past below—a trainman gone to signal
down the line that they were sided out. "Well, this is something," Parkhurst said. "Five minutes. We shall be *very* late."

"What sort of a special?" Dan heard himself ask.

The steward came over. His teeth gleamed in an embarrassed smile. "Sir, I'm afraid that it is a police special."

Parkhurst said, "I've never heard of such a thing. What a
queer business!"

"There is a fortune stolen in New-York," another voice
said. The clubby was going from isolated clutches of card
players to a more general group, as the passengers tasted
their joined fates. "I heard of it in the street. They say there
could be a run on the Knick this morning."

Another man raised his voice. "Grace! You're in the
Knickerbocker. What's the truth of it?"

Dan was completely dumbfounded. How could he possibly be this commonly known? This total stranger knew him by face and by name. But then, he was rather prominent, he supposed. It was not something that he often thought upon. "No truth in it," he said.

A general silence fell. Obviously, not a man present believed him. They would run the bank in the morning, sure.

"No truth in it," Parkhurst agreed. "Mr. Grace would not be calmly playing cards with me if there were." He raised his eyebrows toward Dan. "Shall we continue, sir?"

"By all means." But his mind was now fevered with thoughts of escape. The special was coming! He would be dragged out of here like a common crook, he would suffer the agony of public humiliation. They had not hesitated to shoot at him, to *shoot*! Dear God in heaven, he was the victim of an empire of thieves. Worse, he would never be able to get instructions for the disposition of the money to Mrs. Grace, and she and the children would fall into want and penury. His boy would become a street arab, his daughter a damned chippie, one of those poor soiled lilies down at Scotch Annie's in Bleecker Street.

The cards slipped blindly past. Whist was a game of strategy and cunning, but he could not keep his mind on it. Mr. Parkhurst was winning easily.

Dan was in agony. What to do? Where to go? Now he heard the distant wail of a whistle. It would not be long before the special was here, not but a few minutes. He thought to step into the lavatory and shoot his brains through with the Derringer. But he could not kill himself, he had not the courage. That was, after all, the issue: where was his courage? A gentleman, his honor lost, did the proper thing. A gentleman found unworthy withdrew himself.

Dan could not imagine a world still rolling round the sun, still offering the sweetness and lies of life, without himself there at the table. But men die, they die like cattle—and he was no exception. It was just that he had not been expecting it. He had not been willing to face the consequences of taking the bag. And, after all, there must be consequences.

"Mr. Grace?"

"Sir?" He had not played. "Oh, I beg your pardon." He laid down a card, saw it trumped with alacrity. He gave Mr. Parkhurst what he hoped was a genial twinkle of a smile. "It's passing three," he said putting down his cards. "I think that I must turn in."

"But we're not finished, sir."

"I am, though. I must concede to Morpheus, I fear." He stood up, turned and made his way almost blindly toward the sleeper. When he went out on the forward vestibule he could hear the special clearly, a churning roar in the night. It sounded like the voice of a maddened bull out there, or some hungry monster in the dark. And then its headlight came up the line, bobbing, swaying, a cruel eye between the dim rows of the forest. The smokestack was gushing flame, and sparks poured down on the roadway from the fireboxes. He was transfixed by this apparition, a thing like a living demon, and he found himself as frozen to the spot as if he had been needing to be carried up the gallows.

Then there came the high shriek of brakes and the roar of releasing steam. The special was slowing down; it was stopping. There was no question now—it was just as they had said. It was for him.

He would never be able to warn Mrs. Grace. God only knew what she would do with the gladstone. She might never look in the poor thing at all. There was nothing up the line, not even a signal light. He knew this part of the track— an empty run through the barren wilderness of western New Jersey.

The special came to a stop on the main line just parallel to the sided express. It stood there belching steam, its boiler creaking from heat, its smokestack still roaring even as the fireman could be seen with his tamper, the furnace glowing and making yellow his sweating face and glittering eyes. Dan backed away from it, horrified by its silence, by the sense of awful incipience that it communicated. There was but a single car, black, its windows dim, which reminded him of the weeping Lincoln train that he had seen in his youth.

Without another thought, he stepped off the car, jumping the three feet down to the far edge of the road. Now the express was between him and the monster. He withdrew his pitiful little pistol, turned, and went blundering off into the dark forest.

In ten steps, he was plunged back from the nineteenth century into the world primeval. All around him were enormous trees, their trunks soaring upward into the unknown. Things rustled and scuffled and hissed; the forest floor sighed as if secret battles transpired in its loamy mire. He staggered about, his hands waving in helpless semaphore, seeking some direction, some sense to what was in truth the helpless wandering of a desperate man.

Branches tore at his clothes with the fury of skeletal fingers, ripping away the delicate silk like so much gossamer lace, leaving him abraded and contused and naked in his scraps. Still, though, he went on, moving steadily away from the light of the train, moving farther and farther, until he could no longer see anything or hear anything but the life of the forest itself.

He was half-naked now, his pumps mere bits of leather hung together by a few despairing buttons, his trousers all that still defined him as a man, let alone a gentle one. Brambles tore at his elaborate tonsure, ripping away parts of his muttonchops as he rushed along. Down a ravine he went, across a freezing stream, gasping now, falling, getting up again, crashing headlong into one tree and then another, staggering, pulling himself up and starting again—until he was suddenly in the clear.

He was in the clear, running, unable to understand quite what had happened, his arms windmilling . . . until something hard tripped him and made him fall heavily into what he knew at once were the cinders and ties of the line.

He came to his knees, agonized by his wounds, one eye shutting fast from the shock of striking the rail. And he saw lights, a glowing engine, and two or three lanterns. "Stop," a voice shouted, "Stop there!"

He had come full circle, around and around, and had ended up no more than fifty feet from where he had started. He groaned, he called on his God. They were coming down the line now, their lights swaying, their voices rising, "Stop, stop, who goes there!"

He saw them, hungry ghosts, sweeping toward him with their writs and their irons, and then also felt the pistol in his hand. He had dishonored his father's name, had shamed his family. The barrels tickled his gray temple. He adjusted his finger to be certain to pull both of the small triggers.

There was no sound, no flash of light, no drama at all except that he was aware of the steel of a rail suddenly stretching out before him, not even enough of his brain left to tell him that the shock of the detonation had caused him to topple on his side.

"He's shot! Shot himself!"

"I know it, George!"

Dan Grace heard nothing but the softness of memory receding, as around him the world sank into a strange sort of light, which seemed the glowing face of God to him, but was in the eyes of the living only a railwayman's dim old lantern.

"What the hell?" the one called George cried.

"He's all naked, his clothes—" They looked at each other, two old switchmen with greasy beards, their eyes shocked wide by the sudden appearance of death and question. Slowly they raised their eyes, peering into the enormous night.

Where could he have come from? Who on earth might he be? They were at a complete loss. There were no houses around here, not along this ancient and disused bit of track. He could not have gotten here from the main line, surely not. The main line was easily three miles away, eastward across a vast and trackless forest.